The Blood of Crows

CARO RAMSAY

PENGUIN BOOKS

PENGUIN BOOKS

Published by the Penguin Group

Penguin Books Ltd, 80 Strand, London WC2R ORL, England

Penguin Group (USA) Inc., 375 Hudson Street, New York, New York 10014, USA

Penguin Group (Canada), 90 Eglinton Avenue East, Suite 700, Toronto, Ontario, Canada M4P 2Y3
(a division of Pearson Penguin Canada Inc.)

Penguin Ireland, 25 St Stephen's Green, Dublin 2, Ireland (a division of Penguin Books Ltd)

Penguin Group (Australia), 250 Camberwell Road,
Camberwell, Victoria 3124, Australia (a division of Pearson Australia Group Pty Ltd)

Penguin Books India Pvt Ltd, 11 Community Centre,
Panchsheel Park, New Delhi – 110 017, India

Penguin Group (NZ), 67 Apollo Drive, Rosedale, Auckland 0632, New Zealand
(a division of Pearson New Zealand Ltd)

Penguin Books (South Africa) (Pty) Ltd, Block D, Rosebank Office Park, 181 Jan Smuts Avenue,
Parktown North, Gauteng 2193, South Africa

Penguin Books Ltd, Registered Offices: 80 Strand, London WC2R ORL, England

www.penguin.com

First published 2012

001

Copyright © Caro Ramsay, 2012
All rights reserved

The moral right of the author has been asserted

Set in 12.5/14.75 pt Garamond by Palimpsest Book Production Ltd, Falkirk, Stirlingshire
Printed in Great Britain by Clays Ltd, St Ives plc

PAPERBACK ISBN: 978-0-141-04436-1

OM PAPERBACK ISBN: 978-0-718-15557-5

www.greenpenguin.co.uk

ALWAYS LEARNING   **PEARSON**

To Alan

Four wee craws, sitting on a wa'.
One wee craw was greetin' fer its maw,
The second wee craw fell and broke its jaw,
The third wee craw couldn't flee awa'
The fourth wee craw wisnae there at a'.

Author's Note

The Blood of Crows is a work of fiction. Names, characters, places and incidents either are the product of the author's imagination or are used entirely fictitiously.

Prologue
31 January 1993

Pauline McGregor walked quickly towards the lift; the smell of petrol and exhaust fumes was making her feel nauseous. She was getting too old for this subterfuge. Not only too old, she was too pregnant – eight months now. It was nine weeks since she had been able to button her coat, and exactly seven weeks and three days since she had last worn her stilettos. Was she going to be a bad mother? Probably. But at least she would be a stylish one.

She hated the red pumps she had on; they made her ankles look fat and she could feel the cold of the concrete beneath her feet nibble through the soles. She pulled her scarf up round her neck. The forecast said it was going down to minus five tonight but the chill in the wind that funnelled through the first level of the multi-storey car park promised an even colder night was on its way.

She stopped at the lift doors and pressed the mangled button with a gloved finger, swaying from side to side as she waited, rocking the baby. The lift doors opened with a reluctant whine and she stepped forward, then back again, cupping her hand to her mouth as the stink of stale urine swept out to meet her. A discarded beanie hat lay in the corner, a syringe lying neatly on top of it. The mess that splattered the wall looked like a half-digested kebab.

One advantage of her flat shoes was that she could take the stairs. But at the door to the stairwell she heard voices higher up – hard, violent words answered by the sing-song anger of the drunk. She thought better of it and decided to walk up the narrow pavement that edged the spiralling exit at the centre of the car park. She shivered, and placed a protective hand over her stomach. It was dark and cold, and the sooner she was in her car and out of here the better.

She knew she was parked on the second storey, on the side that faced down on to Mitchell Lane. Sound travelled far on the cold evening air, and she could hear bursts of chit-chat from the pub on the street below, which echoed strangely off the bare walls, slightly disorientating her. Her gloves patted the way along the wall, the cashmere wool catching occasionally on the roughness of the concrete, and her breath billowed in front of her as she walked round a hairpin bend up to Level 2, her back and legs aching. She could hear fighting in the stairwell, then the slam of a door. A figure shot past the glass panel in the stairwell door, followed by another. Another slam and a nearby car alarm started to shriek, then fell silent. For the first time she hesitated, feeling a vague prickle of apprehension that she was being watched. All noise had ceased now, the silence in here somehow separate from the sounds of life going on down in the street. It was quiet. Too quiet.

She quickened her step, pulling the bone-handled knife from her handbag. She always carried it – it was part of her, a gift from her father. Then she heard a car door open on an upper floor, and she moved to the inside of the pavement, in case the car came past her. She wasn't so nimble on her feet these days.

She could see her own Merc waiting for her in the far corner. Looking carefully left and right, she stepped off the pavement to make her way towards it. All the spaces between her and her car were full.

She sensed him rather than heard him, and her grip on the knife tightened. He came out of the darkness between two cars. There was a few seconds' slow dance between them. Then his blade went low and into her ribs, like a hot knife through snow. Hers went high, into his face. Neither made a sound.

He raised his hand to stem the blood – a thick curtain of red, pouring down his cheek into his scarf – and walked off, making his unhurried way to the level above, leaving her to stagger against the bonnet of the car. She felt her knife slip from her fingers, felt the baby kick, then she sank to her knees on the ice-cold concrete. She punched the car on her left hard, and kicked the one to her right, relieved at the cacophony of alarms.

She curled up between the cars, her hand pressed to the wound. She watched the flow of her own blood spreading on the concrete. She raged silently at the betrayal. The baby kicked again, and she spread her fingers on her belly. *Be calm, be calm.* She was hidden from view, she realized; if anyone came past, they wouldn't be able to see her. Her fingers scrabbled against the wheel arch and she pushed her body a few inches, so her feet in their red shoes would be visible to anyone driving past. But would they see the red shoes, in the blood? She tried again, another few inches, then fell exhausted, out of breath.

But nothing was happening. There was no air coming into her lungs. She felt her chest collapsing to nothing.

The baby kicked, then kicked again, demanding oxygen.

She heard the shriek of a cold engine being gunned, the screech of tyres. A black car swung round the spiral, steering wide, then jerked left, aiming straight for her. She never felt the tyres go over her legs, crushing her ankles, ripping her shoes off. She only saw the raw ends of her own bones, so beautiful and pink.

A billow of exhaust hung in the air as one blood-red shoe bounced and rolled, and came to rest in a puddle of oil.

Sunday
27 June 2010

It was late on a hot summer night, Partick Central Station was sweltering, and DI Colin Anderson was bored – not tired, just bored. There was a pile of paperwork waiting for his attention but he couldn't concentrate on it. He really wanted a case he could get his teeth into – but all he had was the suspicious death of one William Stuart Biggart in a fire in the very early hours of the 21st of June, and that case had visited every other desk in Partick Central before landing on his. The forensic fire investigation unit were due to deliver a report first thing in the morning, after which he might have something of evidential value, but he knew his heart wasn't in it. The top brass would be better off putting their money towards LOCUST, the new organized crime initiative, rather than looking into the death of pond life such as Biggart, whose only evolution had been from a dealer in dodgy DVDs to a dealer in dodgy heroin.

He knew it was frustration. He should be a DCI by now – he had completed his required Competency Portfolio for promotion twice over; by right the next DCI post that came free would be his. But the current DCI Niven MacKellar was making it difficult for him to shine. The Biggart case was not going to be a career maker. He glanced over the room, noting the quiet chit-chat of phone calls, the odd conscientious cop typing at a computer, everyone catching up while they had a minute's peace, going through the door-to-door statements from the night of the fire. It was known to everyone that Biggart was dealing – and dealers, by definition, had connections. But nobody wanted to talk. Anderson couldn't blame them.

DS David Lambie was sweating just as much as Anderson, red hair clamped to his skull, his fair skin pink and angry along the hairline and the collar as if he'd caught the sun. He had been on the phone to every takeaway within 300 yards of Anniesland train station, which put them in close proximity to the scene of the fire at the Apollo flats. Lambie's voice showed he had little hope of getting any kind of lead at Suzy's Palace and was making notes in a suitably relaxed manner. Anderson looked closer; his sergeant was doodling. Then Lambie hung up the phone and gazed deep into the middle distance, rattling his biro noisily back and forth between his teeth.

Anderson coughed loudly to bring his sergeant back to earth, knowing that Lambie was thinking about his wedding to the lovely Jennifer again.

A phone rang. He looked round the office; none of the Partick boys seemed inclined to pick it up so he did, grateful for the diversion.

'A *what*?' he said, once the voice at the other end had paused for breath.

It was such a bad line that, even at eleven thirty on a Sunday night, when the room was quiet, he could hardly hear.

'Can you repeat that?' He caught Lambie's eye, made a dip of the head towards the door. 'Yes, we're about two minutes from it, we might get there first. No, we don't mind . . . yes, we're on our way.'

DS Lambie had already grabbed his jacket from the back of his chair. 'Where are we heading off to?' he asked as they rattled down the stairs.

'Down to the river. There's an incident just this side of Anderson Quay. Seems some drunken reveller aboard the *Waverley*'s reported somebody in the water.'

'If it's somebody in the river, shouldn't the marine police unit deal with it?' puffed Lambie, following Anderson out and across the car park. The air was still hot and heavy, the darkness of the summer night unconvincing.

'Disbanded, pretty much. It's just an anti-terrorism strategy now, a response to 9/11. If you fall in and are drowning, you only get an old guy in a rowing boat. But this guy is holding on to a ladder.'

'Why doesn't he climb up it, then?'

'Knackered? Pissed? Drugged? Anyway, those ladders are all covered in slime and weed. Bloody slippy . . . no matter what, it's a breach of the peace and a chance to get out the station.'

Four minutes later, Lambie pulled up on the Harbour Terrace. They both hopped out of the Focus, eyes scanning the river for any signs of activity. There were no lights, no patrol cars, nothing.

Anderson took his mobile from his pocket as he legged it over the outer barrier, and phoned Control.

'Are we in the right place?' he demanded. 'You said a squad car was on its way. But there's nothing here.'

With one ear he heard Lambie say, 'I'll get the torch, boss.' With the other, he listened to Control confirming the location.

'You should still be able to see the boat,' a woman said. 'Someone on board caught the image on their phone and called 999.'

Sure enough, several hundred yards away the old *Waverley* was slowly making her way up river.

Still on the phone, barking out landmarks to Control, Anderson climbed over the inner barrier and peered down into the water lapping at the concrete about twelve feet below. He heard Lambie slam the boot shut. He made his way cautiously along the edge, but there was nothing to see, just a concrete stanchion and the impatient slap of the river. Far in the distance, he could hear sirens.

He heard Lambie behind him at the barrier and reached for the torch, turning the powerful beam downwards, sweeping it back and forth along the slimy wall. He peered down at the iron ladder bolted to the concrete, and the crushed beer cans bobbing in the murky water. Then he stopped dead in his tracks. He had almost missed it, running the beam past it before his brain could register what he'd seen. In the dark swirl of the water, tucked right in against the wall, he could see what looked like a clump of seaweed, splaying out and flattening again with every wave.

Hair, his brain registered at last. Human hair.

'There's someone there. I'm going down,' he told Control, before thrusting the torch and phone at Lambie, and pulling his jacket off. 'For God's sake, keep the light steady.'

Ignoring the unspeakable stinking slime on the iron rungs, Anderson made his way down hand over hand, until his foot came level with the head. Down he went, his feet feeling for each rung, until he was in the water up to his shoulders. He hooked an elbow under the chin to lift the face clear.

'It's OK, I've got you, I've got you.' He could just hear a small mewling noise in response. 'She's alive,' he called up to Lambie. Then, 'Oh Christ, she's just a kid. And she's naked.' His voice was barely a whisper.

Above him the iron ladder shuddered and creaked. He heard Lambie call, 'I'm coming down, boss.' Lambie stopped as his feet reached the level of the girl's head. 'Can we get her up?' he asked.

Anderson tried to get a grip under the girl's arms, but couldn't. They seemed to be clasped tightly behind her. Then he realized she was not clinging on; she was tied on. 'I can't get her arms free. There's something tethering her.' He reached further down the ladder, swearing profusely as stinking water broke over his face every few seconds.

'Stay where you are, boss,' Lambie said, and launched himself off the ladder over Anderson's head. He surfaced a few seconds later. 'Shit!' he spat.

'Very probably,' Anderson grunted.

Lambie grasped the iron upright on the other side of the girl. He was still holding the waterproof torch. 'Can you see what's holding her?'

'No. Where the fuck is that squad car?' Anderson

13

looked up towards the wall. 'Is that wash from the boat, or is the tide on its way in?'

Lambie looked behind him, shaking the water from his face. 'It's coming in. We need to get her out. Now.' He took a deep breath and disappeared under the waves, pulling himself down by the rungs of the ladder. All Anderson could see was the light of the torch wavering up through the filthy water.

Anderson had noticed that, even in that short time, the level had risen and the river was now lapping at the girl's chin. 'You'll be fine. I've got you,' Anderson kept repeating, like a mantra. 'You'll be OK.' He hitched the girl's head as high as he could to keep her mouth out of the water, and tightened his hold on the ladder, preparing himself to take the full weight of her body if Lambie managed to untie her. The one thing they did not want was to drop her. He could feel Lambie's hands groping round his legs, trying to free the girl from whatever held her. He seemed to be having trouble.

'Come on, David,' Anderson muttered. 'We haven't got long.'

The girl was gasping now, in and out, whimpering fragments of words he couldn't understand. The beam of the torch ghosted from beneath the water, a rippling light shadowed on her face, and Anderson saw her face for the first time. He recognized with a shudder just how young she was. She had a little snub nose, and a gap in her front teeth. Her unfocused eyes, the largest hazel eyes he had ever seen, looked past him, her shock too deep for her even to realize he was there.

'Don't you give up on me now,' he told her fiercely.

He readjusted his arms, his fingers slipping on the slime coating the ladder. He threaded one arm across her chest, trying to lift her, giving her a little space, a little time.

Then her face rolled back, and she seemed to look at him. She whispered, '*Mamochka*.' Her eyes lost focus; a wave washed over her cheek but she didn't react.

Lambie's head appeared suddenly. 'Chains,' he spluttered, gasping for air. 'Some bugger's chained her. Hands and feet.'

'No!'

'Honest, Colin.' Lambie shook his head again, back-handing the surplus water from his face.

Suddenly a powerful torch beam illuminated the water, roving around until it settled on the ladder. 'You OK down there?'

'No, we bloody aren't!' Anderson shouted back. 'Bolt cutters! We need bolt cutters!'

'Er . . .' The head vanished for a moment, then reappeared. 'We haven't got any.'

'A snorkel? Plastic tubing? Anything like that?'

'We can send down some ropes.'

'No bloody good! She's chained on to the ladder!'

The head disappeared again. A few moments later, Anderson heard the crackle of police radios somewhere beyond the barriers.

'You OK, Lambie?'

'Fine, boss,' Lambie grunted. 'You?'

'Fine. We're all going to be fine. Everything's going to be fine,' Anderson said. He didn't know who he was trying to reassure – Lambie, the girl or himself. Close to his ear, the feeble whimpering had ceased, and the girl's weight felt inert in his arms. He twisted his head slightly to look at her again. Her eyes were still open. Another wave slopped across her face, but she didn't blink. Her gaze was vacant; she was staring out over the Clyde and way beyond.

Then the voice shouted again. 'We've radioed it in. Fire rescue's on its way.'

'Don't bother,' Anderson said bleakly. 'We won't be needing it.'

Monday
28 June 2010

DC Viktor Mulholland rubbed the sleep from his eyes. He'd eaten too late, and his stomach had been playing up. He had just been slipping off to sleep when Anderson phoned. The message was short. 'Get your arse down to the river.' For once Mulholland hadn't hesitated. Something told him his boss was seriously upset, and that wasn't like him. It must be bad.

And it was. He didn't want to think about what Anderson would be feeling now . . . the girl had died in his arms.

Logic was telling him that Anderson wanted this case, and Anderson had phoned him. Six months after being busted back to DC, he needed to get his stripes back. He needed it just as much as Anderson needed his promotion – and this case might just do it for them both. Poor wee lassie, but it was an ill wind.

Vik climbed over the inner rail and leaned out as far as he could over the outer rail, but even then it was difficult to see what exactly was going on in the water. He knew there were two boats circling the almost totally submerged body. He could hear the quiet instructions of Professor O'Hare, the pathologist, in the stern of the rowing boat as the old man at the oars kept the boat steady in the swell. Nearby, a rubber inflatable was tugging violently on its mooring ropes like an anxious horse, while a police cameraman on board struggled to keep the victim in the beam of the searchlight that was attached to the video camera.

Anderson and Lambie had gone back to Lambie's car to get out of their wet clothes, and to settle themselves. Both men had looked traumatized, merely nodding to Mulholland as they passed him.

Mulholland caught flashes of the scenario below as the beam of the light danced with the movement of the boat. The girl was gently lifted from the ladder and slid into the body bag beneath her. Then, accompanied by the babbling of the water, she started to rise.

Vik heard O'Hare ask the SOCO, 'Ten years old, would you say? Eleven?'

'Too young,' muttered Mulholland.

They were always too bloody young.

0.30 a.m.

Costello turned over and looked at the alarm clock for the third time. It was only half past midnight, yet she felt as if she had been in bed for hours, lying awake staring at the ceiling, sweating like a pig. Her body was tired, the kind of tired that goes along with being ill, the sort of deep-in-the-bones tiredness that made her think that she wouldn't be able to get up even if the place was on fire. Why couldn't the little voices in her head just shut up and let her get some sleep, a deep long decent sleep that would leave her refreshed instead of bloody knackered?

She thought about getting up and having a shower, or maybe a bath, but the sound of the water in the pipes would disturb her downstairs neighbours, and they had been good to her over the past few months. In fact, there was often – too often – a gentle tap on the door, a wee call through the letterbox: 'Are you all right?'

She began to prod at the side of her face, searching for the little incongruity, the little island of mesh that lay right under the skin. One day, she thought, she would search and it would not be there. Then none of it would have happened, and everybody could go back to the way they were.

She looked at the alarm clock again. Three minutes had passed since she last looked.

To hell with this. She got out of bed, padded off to the loo and washed her face in cold water, avoiding looking at herself in the mirror. She didn't recognize the old woman with the short mousy hair who looked back, the woman with the angry scar above her hairline. She went into the kitchen and put the kettle on to make a cup of tea, then went through to the front room and collapsed on the sofa. She stared at the balloon light shade overhead, focusing on a little tear in the white paper, covering one eye with her hand and then the other. The small crescent shape stayed in perfect focus with both eyes. It had been like that for a week now. But it wouldn't help; the machinery of the occupational health team and her psychological assessments moved as fast as an elephant on a Zimmer frame.

She liked the psychologist – a nice young woman. Unfortunately, Dr McBride had decided to make Winifred

Prudence Costello some kind of special study. Apart from just getting through life cursed with a name like that, there was everything else – the emotional and physical trauma of the last few months would have crushed the strongest person with grief. Dr McBride, with her nice smile, sensible footwear and thick tights, seemed determined to make an issue of everything and then to make sense of it all.

Costello was more of the opinion that if she didn't make an issue of it, she wouldn't have to make sense of it. Life didn't make sense; her years in the police service had taught her that. But no matter how hard she probed and got nowhere, Dr McBride refused to admit there was nothing there to probe at.

Costello felt no huge sense of loss, because there was no loss. What she'd never had, she didn't miss. She'd felt worse four years ago when she lost DCI Alan McAlpine, and had said as much to Dr McBride. That had been a Big Mistake.

'Hmmm. Did you consider him a father figure?'

'No, I considered him a boss.'

'Do you think you could be in denial?'

'No.'

'So, you are in denial?'

'No.'

And so it went on.

And on.

It was all a load of bollocks.

She got up and went to the window, opened the curtains and looked out. Seen from the huge picture window of her riverside flat, the Clyde was a shining meandering ribbon in the moonlight. She leaned her forehead against the cool pane. She would look a sight if anybody glanced up – a skinny wide-eyed woman with spiky hair, her face distorted by the glass. Below, in the distance, along the river into town, there was the familiar strobe of blue light. She could make out a cluster of cars but nothing definite.

It might just be in Partick's jurisdiction.

But even if it was, it was nothing to do with her any more.

0.45 a.m.

Lambie and Anderson had stripped their shirts off and were sitting in Lambie's car with the heating on full blast, Anderson with the tartan travelling rug from the back seat wrapped round him, while his sergeant had pulled on a T-shirt from his gym bag and wore a damp towel wrapped round his shoulders. DCI MacKellar's face appeared, and Lambie wound down the window.

'You two OK?'

'Not particularly,' said Anderson.

'You should both go home. We'll clear it all up in the morning.'

'If it's all the same, I'd rather stay here.'

'Not necessary,' said MacKellar. 'Not necessary at all.'

'I'd rather wait until she's away.' Anderson didn't look at MacKellar. They had said about ten words to each other in the three months Anderson had been at Partick Central.

'There's nothing for you to do. You have DC Mulholland at the coalface, so to speak, and O'Hare and two boats are down there. We'll look after her. So, go home. Now. Everything else can wait. And there will be health and safety issues arising from this – but I don't have to tell you two that.'

MacKellar walked back towards the mass of lights and vehicles at the edge of the quay.

'Health and safety issues!' Anderson's voice was incredulous. 'Fucking health and safety?'

'We went in the water without life vests on. That's a breach of protocol. We'll get a form to fill in.'

'In triplicate. In crayon.' Anderson pulled his blanket round him, letting a shiver run its way through him. 'I don't see what more we were expected to do.'

'I think we were expected to do less.'

'I tell you, David, the day I leave a wee girl chained in the river on a rising tide because of fucking health and safety regs is the day I –' Anderson's words were caught in a cough.

'The day you what? Emigrate?'

9.35 a.m.

Anderson slid his jacket from his shoulders and slumped into the nearest empty seat, feeling as though he had already worked a full day rather than being just about to start one. Today was supposed to have been a quick review of the forensic fire report and then a chat with O'Hare, half an hour to type it all up, then home. It was the first proper day of the school holidays, and Brenda had plans for a family outing to Largs, remortgage the house to buy ice creams, and have some of the quality family time that Brenda was always on about.

But last night had changed all that. He had simply put fifty quid on the mantelpiece and left Brenda sleeping.

He wouldn't forget last night for a long time. The girl had been so young. His daughter Claire was only a few years older. Some, he knew, would say that he shouldn't be doing the job at all if he ever got so desensitized that a ten-year-old could die in his arms and he could go home afterwards for a good night's sleep. He couldn't get that noise out of his head, that incessant quiet whimpering. And that one word she had said with complete clarity. He couldn't understand it, but it remained imprinted on his brain – *Motchka*? *Mamoska*? Something like that.

She didn't scream, didn't even try to keep her head up. Had she even known they were there, he and Lambie? How long had she been there? What sort of state had she been in when they chained her in place?

And who did it?

And why?

But they were not his questions to answer. He had waited for the case to be assigned by DCI MacKellar only to be rewarded by a single-line email asking him to provide a written report for DI Davis, who would now be heading up the investigation into the death of the girl. Anderson was to remain on the Biggart case. Anderson got that familiar feeling that his promotion was being ever so gently put on the back burner. The charitable side of his nature told him MacKellar would have his own staff –

staff he knew well, staff who were probably just as deserving of a DCI post as he was. The uncharitable side of his nature swore profusely.

Why bother with the Biggart case in the first place? The minute he was dead, another drug dealer would take his place.

The thought had just flitted across his mind when another email popped into his inbox, this time from a DI in B Division. It was a brief report, asking for any intelligence about an incident on Tuesday the 15th of June. The small country village of Balfron had been dragged into Glasgow's drugs war. Two dealers had been shot in the head, the third in the face, and the bodies lined up neatly against the wall. Red heroin with a street value of three grand had been left at the scene. There was a further note on the email explaining that red heroin was heroin mixed with chalk, typical of the supply coming from Afghanistan via the Baltic States. Anderson smirked at the village cop needing to explain that. In the city, red heroin was almost currency – called 'red' because of its Russian route as well as its slightly rusty colour. The DI had added for interest that Glasgow was emerging from a heroin drought and the latest estimated value of the drugs trade was over five million pounds annually.

So, there was another drugs war kicking off. What was the point of trying to stop it? Scum would always settle at its own level. But he thought he remembered a similar email naming three major dealers who had unaccountably sold up and left the city. Anderson pressed Print and watched the skinny, pock-ridden faces of 'Smoutie Waites', 'Hamster' and 'Speedo' slide out from the printer.

Anderson sighed; it all seemed pointless. At some point today he would be summoned to a meeting about the breach of health and safety protocol, and he would just have to button it and not argue. To get his promotion he needed a clean sheet.

He thought about going out to the machine for a coffee to wake himself up, but the coffee here was terrible – the asbestos at the old station posed the lesser health risk. Asbestos or not, he wished they were back at Partickhill with Costello to moan at. He wished she would text him on her way in, asking *Do you want anything?* He wouldn't even mind if she nicked all the chocolate Hobnobs and stuck them in her drawer.

Anderson smiled to himself.

'You look happy, DI Anderson. Are you sure you work here?' asked DC Wyngate, who had come equipped for the day with a tact bypass.

'Yes, unfortunately. Are there any Hobnobs in the tin?'

'It's the Partick biscuit tin and we are not allowed to touch.'

'So much for team spirit,' said Anderson.

Wyngate picked up the printouts from Anderson's desk. 'They look like three charmers. Known associates of Biggart?'

'No idea yet, but stick them up on the wall.'

Once Wyngate had made sure the A4 sheets were on the wall in perfect alignment, he sat down and flicked open his spiral-bound sheaf of papers. 'I heard about last night, sir. It sounds a bit grim.'

Anderson nodded. 'It was.'

Wyngate found the page he was looking for and passed

it to Anderson. 'It's the forensic fire investigator's report on the Biggart incident. Do you want to read it? It makes very interesting reading.'

'Paraphrase for me. Please.'

'Well, they mocked up Biggart's front room and the fire damage in some fancy computer program, just to confirm their suspicions.'

'Good for them.' Anderson looked at the floor plan of the fire scene in Apollo Court, as the building was named (in honour of its previous life as a cinema). Small crosses and odd symbols dotted the plan. He wondered how quickly he could get away to see O'Hare at the mortuary, then go home. It was too bloody hot in the office.

Wyngate placed a single sheet in front of him with a key for the symbols on it. 'Are you going to the funeral this afternoon?'

'Nearly. I'm going to the morgue. I have to look at Mr Biggart. So, this is where he died.' Anderson looked at the plans, the position of the body. 'Sorry, what funeral?' he asked as an afterthought.

'A retired constable, Tommy Carruthers, died last week.'

'Did he work here?'

'Presume so. Loads of the Partick boys are going.' Wyngate angled his head to make sure nobody was listening. 'He flung himself out his living-room window. Three floors up.' He looked up at his boss. 'Did you not hear about that?'

'Must have passed me by. But no, I'm not going. I've to meet O'Hare at the mortuary in an hour . . . to deal with this . . .' He tapped the report for emphasis. 'I think Mr Biggart is still in residence in a drawer there. And as far as

I'm concerned, he can stay there until the winter when he can be put out to feed the birds.'

'At least he'd be some use then,' Wyngate said cheerily. 'Fiona Morrison wants you to phone her if anything about this confuses you.'

'So, tell me what it's all about.'

The constable started pointing at the plan with the tip of his pen. 'Door there, window there, body in that corner. The usual scenario would be that Billy here is pissed, smoking, falls asleep in his chair, drops cigarette, is overcome by fumes and gets toasted. This is different. Biggart staggers a bit before the smoke gets him, in his bare feet, wearing a shell suit.' Wyngate held his pen up. 'So, Billy is found by the window, over here, and the source of the fire is to the right of the door, over here.' He tapped the diagonally opposite corner on the plan. 'The positioning is important. Petrol and rags were set alight here in the corner and the window above the body was open, which would draw the flames across the room. Which makes it arson – skilful arson.'

'And Biggart had soot in his airways,' offered Anderson, showing that he had been paying attention at the initial briefing. 'Which means he was alive when the fire took hold and he inhaled smoke. So that's either culp hom or murder.'

'Ms Morrison says the latter. And she can prove it in court. And there's more.'

Anderson sat up. 'OK, you have my full attention.'

'Consider, the initial source of the fire is in the inner corner of the room. Yet Biggart is way over the far side, under the window. It's as if he'd walked away from his escape route. Which raises the question, was he put there?'

'Tox report was almost clear.' Anderson pointed over his shoulder with his thumb, vaguely gesturing to his paper-laden desk. 'A small amount of alcohol, nothing to incapacitate him.'

'So, he could have walked out but didn't. Are we thinking he was incapacitated in some other way? You should ask O'Hare if there were signs of him being bound.'

'There's nothing obvious on the crime scene photographs,' said Anderson, flicking over to the photographs of the charred half-cooked mess, 'but his legs looked like burned sausages, nothing much to see.'

Wyngate continued. 'So, he's lying here, face up, unable to move for whatever reason. The fire started over there in the corner nearest the corridor, billowed quickly up to the ceiling – heat and smoke would cover the ceiling in seconds – drawn by the open window away from the exit door. But the dangerous thing for him, and the interesting thing for us, is that the radiated heat from the ceiling would start to ignite anything below, most flammable first. So, drawn by the air from the window, soot in the smoke in the ceiling gets hotter and hotter and reignites, causing a flashover which would come right down on him.'

Involuntarily, Anderson twitched.

'And judging from the charring and blistering on his torso, his chest in particular, his highly flammable shell suit simply melted on to him, like grilled cheese on toast. Incredibly painful. This means it was deliberate and extremely malicious. It indicates somebody who knows a lot about fires.'

'I almost feel sorry for him,' said Anderson.

'And they think Billy was breathing, maybe even conscious, as the fire rolled over above him. And he didn't do a thing about it. His clothes melting on to his skin, his skin blistering, his hair singeing. Ms Morrison says he might even have seen the fireball, before his retinas burned out. The reason why the fire investigation team have run this through their system again and again is . . . well, most arsonists would just splash some petrol about, fling in a match and leave. But not this guy. This set-up – the precise position of the accelerant – suggests he was keeping his exit clear for the longest possible period of time. It's not unusual for arsonists to hang around the scene and get some thrill from the drama of the firefighters and all that, but according to Ms Morrison this guy set this whole fire so that he could hang about in the room and watch Biggart being grilled to death.'

11.03 a.m.

Costello was bored out of her mind. She was sprawling on her sofa, still in her pyjamas, thinking about eating breakfast, thinking about having a shower, thinking about getting dressed, thinking about the commotion on the river in the early hours. And that was three things more than she had managed to think about yesterday. She had been on sick leave now for five months, two weeks and two days. The team had been in touch, of course. They had phoned now and again, but there was less to talk about – and more awkward silences. They'd invited her to DCI Quinn's leaving do, but she had declined. They just wanted to drink, and she couldn't. Nor could she drive, and she was still too wary of strangers and too wary of the dark to take a taxi.

She clicked the TV on to *Missing*, the occasional morning tear fest. The screen filled with Lorraine Kelly's concerned face, holding the picture of a six-year-old boy. Something sparked a glimmer in Costello's memory. She knew that face. Remembered the case. She picked up the remote control and turned the sound up.

Lorraine was now holding a book up to the camera. *Little Boy Lost*. 'Now, Simone,' she was saying, 'you can't deny that this is a very sensitive issue to write a book about.'

The camera homed in on the face of the author, investigative journalist Simone Sangster. 'Yes, I know, and that's what makes it so important. Somebody had to be brave enough to write the book. It was a very tragic case. It still is today. Alessandro was only six years old when he disappeared, along with the babysitter, a family friend, who was just seventeen himself. Nobody has ever been charged with any crime relating to their disappearance, and I can't help feeling that it's a stain on the reputation of the Strathclyde police force that this boy, Alessandro Marchetti, could be kidnapped and his body never found. I feel that the families are owed a reinvestigation of this case. They need to know what happened that night, and to see those responsible brought to justice.'

'It was the McGregors or the O'Donnells that did it, and yet nothing ever got pinned on the Glasgow mafia,' Costello mumbled, thinking. 'Aye, but it was the beginning of the end for the old regime. Bet you don't dare say that in your bloody book.'

'And do you really think that's likely to happen after all this time?' asked Lorraine, her brows furrowed in concern.

'I just hope that some good comes out of all my research, that the police reopen the case, and hopefully get to the bottom of what actually happened.'

Simone continued to witter on, explaining that her shocking theory that the family had been involved was just one of the many being explored, such as gangland activity, or the babysitter being complicit, which was why the legal action by the boy's parents had failed to prevent publication. All Simone wanted to do was selflessly bring it to the attention of the public once again.

'And make a few quid while you're at it,' Costello said to the TV as she pressed the mute button. For a while, Lorraine and the lovely Simone chatted on animatedly in silence. Then a still from a newspaper report appeared; Costello recognized Waterstone's in Glasgow. The day before, Simone had launched her book in the very city where the kidnap had taken place. Costello couldn't resist flicking the volume back on. The event hadn't lasted long. Maria Marchetti, the boy's mother, had pulled Simone off her chair at the signing. Lorraine suggested that the poor woman must be under great emotional strain. Simone nodded, graciously confirming that she would not press charges.

'Not up to you to press charges, you silly cow,' muttered Costello. 'It's up to the fiscal.'

'. . . but there have been at least three cases recently of people apparently coming back from the dead, having been held captive for many years. There have been two notorious cases in Austria, and one in the States.' Simone paused, then said, 'And there has never been a trace of Alessandro's body despite the searches made at the time. He would be nearly twenty now. The babysitter, Tito Piacini, would be in his early thirties.'

Lorraine leaned forward. 'Do you think *he* could still be alive? Surely if Tito was alive, he would come forward?'

Simone slid out from under the question. 'All I'm saying is that the family need closure.'

'No, they bloody don't,' Costello snorted, thinking about her own family. 'Believe me, hen, you don't want closure where your family's concerned. You want a gun.' She pressed the mute again and flung the remote at the TV. It missed and skidded into the skirting board.

She stretched out on the sofa, looking at the ceiling, feeling worthless.

11.10 a.m.

The car park, sandwiched in a narrow gap between the Apollo flats and the bottom of the railway embankment by Anniesland station, created the suggestion of a wind tunnel, but after days of still, balmy air even the slightest draught felt like a refreshing breeze. Anderson peeled the soaking shirt from his back; he had only been in the car for about ten minutes.

'Can I ask something, sir?' It was Wyngate, panting along damply in his wake. 'Why are we really here? I mean, here, at the flats?'

It was too easy to take the piss out of him, Anderson reminded himself. But sometimes the boy did himself no favours. As the recently retired DS John Littlewood once said, if it looked gormless and acted gormless, chances were it *was* gormless. Ambition simply wasn't a word in Wyngate's vocabulary, yet he was endlessly willing, and a good detective on a computer – unimaginative, almost humourless, but possessed of a dogged nerdiness that made him an invaluable part of the team. And once in a blue moon he came up with a stroke of pure genius.

'Well, we can't leave it,' Anderson told him, as they headed towards the huge art deco panelled glass doors, still very much reminiscent of the building's former incarnation as a cinema. 'We have to have another look in light of what Fiona said this morning. We compare evidence, review the case notes –'

'Now that the smoke has settled,' said Wyngate, sounding as though he was still genuinely confused. He stood back a step, looking up at the sky, watching the weather. That was the difference between him and the rest of the team. Vik Mulholland would have been looking up and down the street, gauging the situation. Costello would have had her face pressed against the glass, hand cupped to block the light, a good investigative technique bordering on sheer nosiness. He wondered how she was doing.

Anderson took a bunch of labelled keys from his pocket and tried the Yale in the lock. It slid open, and they were in the red-carpeted lobby – another reminder of the building's days as a cinema. A grand fan-shaped staircase swept up to a half-landing where it split to go left and right to the flats upstairs. On the ground floor, a narrow corridor on each side of the main lobby led to the rear of the building, and each had three flats, two on the outer side of the corridor, and one on the inner side with a view out of the back of the building.

'Along here, I think,' Anderson said. A chill ran through him as he walked down the left-hand hallway. The atmosphere in the hall was almost frozen by the air con. He rattled through the keys to find the one to G2.

'The woman, Janet Appleby, who lives in that one on the right, has been relocated to a hotel for now,' said Wyngate, pointing to the furthest door marked G3. 'This one, G1, was empty. And that one there, G2, was Biggart's — well, the one he was found in.'

'As might be indicated by the scorch marks over the door and the soot stains on the ceiling. As well as the bloody awful smell of old smoke and damp. The crime scene tape's a bit of a giveaway too.'

'Right,' agreed Wyngate, not noticing the sarcasm.

Anderson nudged open the door of Biggart's flat, having to shoulder it a little where the heat had warped the wood. Inside the door, the tiny entry hall, though it reeked of wet smoke and was filthy with ash, had been untouched by the fire itself. A small wrought-iron trestle table stood against the wall, with a neat stack of rental DVDs, packaged and obviously waiting to be returned, and a mobile phone. Anderson realized that Morrison might have been right — somebody standing here could watch the carnage in front of him. The heat and the flames would be pulled away from him by the open window, and all he had to do was retreat by stepping back into the hall where the flames had never penetrated. Anderson would never have thought of it himself. But then that wasn't his job.

'Tell you what, Wyngate, you have a good look and a sniff around here. And open all the windows, try to get a bit of a blast through here. Just remember to close them all properly when we leave. Look for evidence to support our theory. Or evidence to crush it.'

'Where are you going, sir?' the constable asked, scratching his ear.

'I'll be in the empty flat next door. Scream if you need me.' Wyngate looked scared at the thought of being left alone. But Anderson asked it of Costello, Lambie and Mulholland, and Wyngate had to learn.

Anderson left his reluctant constable thinking about taking the step over the threshold, and retreated to look down the corridor. He glanced at the name beside the door of G3, thinking it might be worth having a word with J. Appleby. He walked to the end of the corridor where a fire door opened on to the path that would take him back round to where his car was parked. To his right, in a rectangle sheltered by the flats at the rear of the building, was a small formal garden. He pushed the bar; the door opened easily and swung back and forth without a squeak, which meant it was either well maintained or in constant use. Or both. His fingers touched a keyhole. A fire door for emergencies, which could be opened with a key from the outside. He fingered the lock, springing the mechanism with his thumb. It would be a lot easier to bring shopping in from the car park via this door than to carry it all the way round to the front and then back through the building. He left the door open, as the air needed to clear, and walked back down the hallway to the first flat, G1, nearest the busy street. The spare key fitted.

Not much to see – the flat was obviously unlived-in. It was barely furnished, with a sofa, a coffee table, a dining table at the window, all covered with a faint layer of silky soot. Anderson's shirt was picking up the oily little particles; Brenda would go mad. He threw a casual glance into the bare, functional kitchen, and another glance into the first bedroom. The bed, a single, was still in its polythene cover. The insurance guys were going to love this. But the bathroom had soap and toilet roll. A towel had been discarded and dumped in the bath, and another was flung over the designer radiator. He went into the main bedroom. The bed was a bare mattress on a base, but used – definitely used. There were unsavoury stains on it. The frieze of Black Watch tartan wallpaper that ran the length of the room had been torn slightly over the bed. He looked into the en suite shower room. There had been water in the basin, and the soot had left a ring, as though someone had washed dirty hands.

Anderson gave one last look around the bedroom, aware of a puzzling little niggle. There was something he was missing. Then he saw it. Up on the ceiling there were soot stains everywhere, but also spots – dark, precise spots. He ran his eyes over the emulsioned plaster. Regular spots, in a line above the end of the bed. Then he saw another parallel row of six holes, obviously used to fix something. A plasma TV? In a flat that was apparently empty?

It was still troubling him as he locked the front door behind him and went back to the other flat, where Wyngate was standing holding his drawing of the floor plan.

'You can see it, you know.' Wyngate pointed out the pattern of deep burning in the right-hand corner, the arrow effect spreading diagonally across the ceiling to the far corner, the massive charring and burning in the area where Biggart might have been trussed like a pig and left to die.

'Easy to read once we know what we're looking for, eh?'

'And here, to the left of the door where we're standing, it's untouched by flame, so I'd say we're looking at an arsonist with a good sense of self-preservation. As Fiona Morrison said, he left his way out clear.'

'I suppose that kind of goes with having a successful career as an arsonist,' said Anderson, feeling a grudging admiration for the bravery of any man, or woman, who could tie up a drug dealer, set a fire, and stand watching as flames and smoke mushroomed over their head, then calmly close the door behind them and walk away. Was that what had happened?

He turned to Wyngate. 'Right, close the windows and lock up. And just before we go, you got any evidence bags in your car? Get those used towels from the flat next door.'

'But G1's not a crime scene, sir. It was only closed off due to the smoke damage.'

DI Anderson smiled indulgently at his young colleague. 'Let's prove it's not a crime scene first, eh?'

11.15 a.m.

'Have you got your black tie?'

'Yes, dear.'

'And is it clean?'

'Yes, dear.'

Rosie laid her head down on the pillows, which were already soaking wet with sweat. It was oppressively hot. She hoped she didn't smell. She had been bed bound for over eight years now, since the time her eating had got seriously out of control and her legs refused to bear her huge weight. The folds of fat that weighed her down were a haven for bacteria and in this weather she needed a blanket wash at least three times a day. She looked around; Wullie had boiled the kettle and left a basin of hot water within reach on the bedside table, a clean sponge floating in it. She had a flask of fresh water, a small box of Thornton's Continental, a cold Four Seasons pizza and some newspapers to catch up on. Being an ex-cop, she was interested to know what B Division was doing about the three drug dealers who had been shot in the car park of the Balfron Arms. But she would bet her last champagne truffle that they were doing nothing. Talking about it, but doing nothing.

Wullie was going to Tom Carruthers' funeral. He'd keep his ear to the ground and catch up on any news. Quiet, unobtrusive Wullie was wallpaper with ears.

At that moment Wullie emerged from the living room, whipping the long tail of his black tie under the knot.

'Wullie, have some respect. Roll down your sleeves.'

'Too bloody hot. I'll stick my jacket on once I get on the main road. I'll keep off the path, keep my shoes clean. Don't want to let the side down.'

'Well, look smart while you pay your respects . . .' Rosie kept talking while she smoothed down the sheet that covered her huge bulk. 'Can you just pull my tray away before you go? I'm tired. I'd like a nap.'

Wullie disconnected the laptop and wheeled the trolley table back against the wall. He picked up some DVDs, checked their titles and slipped them into their red cardboard sleeves. 'Are you done with these?'

'Yes, you can stick them in at the post office on the way past.'

'Aye, I'll do that. Will you be OK? I'll just go to the purvey for a sandwich and a quick hello, and then I'll get the bus back.'

'Just watch you remember to eat, and keep an eye on your blood sugars . . . and bring me back something nice. A surprise. Brad Pitt covered in chocolate.'

'You need psychiatric help, love. Or a box of Quality Street as usual.' He leaned over to kiss her, watching that his feet didn't touch the apron of fat that was her belly; it sprawled across the bed and on to the carpet in a huge gelatinous lump. She had weighed twenty-eight stone the last time she was on her feet; God alone knew what she must weigh now. 'Bye, love, see you later.'

1.00 p.m.

The mortuary was the coolest place Anderson had been in all week, and he felt himself relax. Jo, the pathologist's assistant, offered Wyngate something to smear under his nose, then offered it to Anderson. Anderson shook his head.

'Any further with Biggart?' asked O'Hare, reading his thoughts.

'Just can't figure out who he would let so close, for the

length of time it took to set the fire. Why didn't he walk out? He was a big guy, Biggart.'

'Yes, I know. I'm about to do his PM, remember?'

'Any ideas?'

O'Hare said, 'Maybe. It was somebody he knew, somebody he trusted – and he wouldn't have trusted many. I've seen the victims of these drug dealers, shot in the eye, in the back of the knees, or just through the head. Off the record, I don't think you've managed to nail him for any murders, have you?'

'No, but I don't doubt he was responsible. Though it was never him who took the fall, was it? Anyway, Fiona Morrison raised the possibility that Biggart might have been restrained to some degree. Can we address that?' Anderson said brusquely. 'I mean, he didn't get up and get out. He just lay there and burned. Why?'

'First things first. Here's your man.' O'Hare walked to the further examination table, where the white cover concealed an obviously large man. He pulled it back. The body of William Stuart Biggart had been burned to a crisp.

Wyngate turned green.

'You can go up to the viewing gallery if you want,' O'Hare said kindly, offering Wyngate an easy way to back out if he needed it. 'In fact, Health and Safety prefer it that way.'

'No, I'm fine,' said Wyngate, taking a deep breath and then regretting it.

'Well, there were no *visible* bindings,' O'Hare began carefully. 'He had on a shell suit which you can still see fused to his skin in places. On first examination it looks – though I'll have to confirm it – as though he had some sort of tattoos on his arms. His blood was clean, no drugs, so there's no obvious reason why he didn't get up and go, unless he was slipped something we don't know about. A new drug that we wouldn't know to test for,' he corrected himself.

'Like what?' asked Anderson.

'I'll come to that later.' O'Hare smiled slightly. 'But I'll take epithelial samples at his wrists and his ankles, see if there's any trace of a binding that has been burned off. In either case, you have a dangerous arsonist to catch.'

'So, this is how it ends. Forty-eight-year-old Billy Biggart, "The Bastard" to his friends and worse to those who weren't.' Anderson looked at the blackened fingertips, marvelling at O'Hare's confidence in finding traces of anything in the charred and splintered bone.

'And killed less than a week after the Balfron boys were shot in the head. The drug war is keeping the mortuary busy. Do we have a new king rising?'

'Or a vigilante? Somebody set on revenge? Biggart was a big-time dealer, red heroin was left at the scene at Balfron . . . it has the ring of revenge about it.'

'And the victims all neatly lined up. The scene was staged for effect, I would have said.'

'Of course, you were there.' Anderson rubbed his face. 'The person who did this must be *connected*, as they say. Biggart has – had – a lot of connections, and very few of them will be happy to speak to us.'

'That's their lookout. They might be running scared now.'

The pathologist glanced over at Wyngate, who was trying not to look ill – and failing.

'He'll do. We don't let him out much,' muttered Anderson, ignoring the vibration of his mobile phone. His mind drifted to the bed in the other flat, and the strange holes in the ceiling, and he turned to look at the small figure lying under a white plastic sheet on the slab behind him, illuminated by low bright lights suspended over her.

O'Hare followed the line of his gaze. 'Do you want to talk about her? Jo, I think DC Wyngate would be relieved to be taken for a coffee. Wouldn't you, Wyngate?'

O'Hare very pointedly waited until they were alone before he said, 'I want to tell you a few things, for your ears only.'

'Fire away.'

'Your young friend had a few stories to tell. Very young, pubescent but only just. Evidence of sexual abuse.' O'Hare turned away to sign something, and Anderson felt that familiar kick to his stomach; but it was O'Hare who said it, putting the clipboard down on the side table. 'I'm sure she would have been a delight to gentlemen of certain tastes. She's unidentified as yet. We didn't expect to get any trace evidence from her, since immersing a body in water is a really good way to do forensic cleansing, but surprisingly she might have held on to something for us.'

'And it is –'

'At the lab. The samples have been picked up by Matilda McQueen. She's the new forensic scientist. Looks about twelve and the height of nothing, but she's very good and she's been assigned to this case'

'Case?' Anderson caught O'Hare's eye, sensing an unspoken message, but O'Hare only pursed his lips as if he knew something he wasn't saying.

'So, on this table we have a victim, and on that table we have a drug dealer and pedlar of dodgy DVDs. Do you think she was used for that? Kiddie porn?' pushed Anderson.

'It's not a huge leap career wise,' O'Hare agreed gently. 'Maybe you can get on to it now and prove it.'

'Bit difficult if it's not my case.'

1.10 p.m.

It was almost time for lunch by the time Costello crawled out of the shower and got dressed in an old black trouser suit, sticking a pin in the loose waistband. She was still in two minds about going to the funeral but took some comfort that there would be few people there she knew. Or so she hoped. She'd stand at the back and pay her last respects to a nice old copper who had shown her the ropes as a rookie. She remembered how 'Top Cat' Carruthers had gently elbowed her away at the scene of her first fatality. She had been holding the head of a dying woman, keeping her hair from her eyes, encouraging her to keep breathing no matter what. She recalled the way she had held the woman. She had felt the victim's baby kick, a weird sensation. He'd told her to get out the way and find something bloody useful to do. So she had stood and stopped traffic entering the car park for three hours in the freezing cold.

She draped the towel over the cold metal radiator. The central heating had been off for a fortnight now, but it was still hot in the flat – an uncomfortable, airless, stuffy heat. Her riverside flat, laughingly called a penthouse by an estate agent high on aftershave and low on vocabulary, had a huge feature window overlooking the Clyde that turned her front room into an oven. Not a common occurrence in Glasgow, she had to admit, but she felt like a butterfly under a magnifying glass. Her carpet was streaked with track marks where she had dragged the sofa round following the passage of the sun yesterday, trying to watch crap daytime TV without the glare clouding the screen.

Tired from the effort of dressing, she slumped now on to the sofa, not caring if her wet hair left a damp patch. After the 'accident' they had had to shave her scalp, and her hair had grown back in a strange light mousy brown that she had not seen for years. Now, when bored, she would sit at the mirror, pulling her hair this way and that, checking the still-visible scar. Then her fingers would feel the bone of her cheek, where the mesh was. Putting it in had been a late decision by the surgeon once the swelling had gone, and the web of tiny hairline fractures began to appear on X-ray. Cosmetic, he said, not really necessary, but her cheekbone would heal flat unless they slipped some mesh in to give the new bone growth a frame. Now, every time she looked at it, she noticed it. Sometimes, she dreamed the mesh was growing right through her skin, turning her face into a mask of blood. Waking, she would probe it obsessively. 'Just leave it alone,' the doctor told her, 'and it'll be fine.'

'Do you feel your face is actually your own face?' Dr McBride had asked her.

What was she supposed to say?

She had stopped taking her antidepressant now – she

didn't need it, although the doctor said she did with everything she'd been through. *Blah, blah, blah.* At least now she could sleep – and sleep was a very welcome thing because being awake meant she had time to think, and thinking took her head to a dark place she did not want to visit, no matter how much Dr McBride wanted to take her by the hand and lead her there. The fact that there was nothing there, just a huge dark nothing, was the scariest thing of all. And the only thing that would take that away was work. She needed to get back. The funeral was a big test for her; she had to get out and socialize. She had to get signed off and back to work. The new Chief Constable had a view that cops were either fit to work or they were not. And if not, they were off the force. All she needed was a chance to prove herself.

Last night she had seen the activity on the river, but had been too far away to make anything out. The early Scottish news had reported: *News just coming in of the body of an unidentified female found in the Clyde. The police are treating the death as suspicious . . .*

Her old colleagues were all working out of Partick Central at the moment, as the small station at Partickhill was still closed while they removed the asbestos. It might never reopen. In fact, she didn't think they would ever work together again, and felt a twinge of loss at the thought. She even missed Vik Mulholland being an irritating opinionated bullshitter.

God, she must be ill.

And Anderson was busy, watching his back now as well as his career. He was still only a DI; the bastards hadn't even promoted him yet. She knew Brenda wanted to take him to Australia, and couldn't bear to think of life without him. It would be like losing a brother.

She heard the letter box rattle; a noisier flutter of pages and paper than usual meant the neighbours had stuck the newspaper through the door. They thought it helped her stay in touch. She slid off the sofa and wandered into the hall. The *Daily Record* was lying tattered and fanned on the carpet. She went to the kitchen and boiled the kettle, paper under her arm, then back to the sofa to read the headline.

Skelpie bloody Fairbairn was back walking the streets.

She felt sick, sicker than sick.

Fuck! She picked up her mobile and phoned the Partick-hill number from sheer habit; it was redirected. Partick Central answered. She asked for Colin Anderson and was told he was busy. She rang off and dialled his mobile, but it went straight to voicemail. She didn't bother to leave a message, but snapped her phone shut and tapped it against her chin, thinking, trying to calm herself. She stood up and smoothed down her suit. All she had to do was walk out the door, take it one step at a time. Stay busy.

Then the phone rang, making her jump. She didn't recognize the number.

'DS Costello?' asked a female voice. 'This is the Assistant Chief Constable of Crime Howlett's secretary. He'd like you to come in for a meeting. When would suit you?'

1.20 p.m.

'Not your case?' O'Hare folded the sheet neatly at her collarbone. 'But you *were* there.'

'She died in my arms. And I didn't even notice it happening.' The words caught in Anderson's throat. The girl lay between them, her face grey but perfect, unblemished, framed by dark hair, dry and tidily combed. Her lips hung slightly open, showing the little gap in her front teeth. 'How old was she?' he asked, the words difficult to form in his cotton-dry mouth.

O'Hare leaned on the side of the slab, arms outstretched, looking at her. 'Ten or so. She's slightly malnourished. And look at her skin – when was the last time you think she saw the sun?' He moved away from the central table. 'OK, so if this is not your case, this is off the record.'

Anderson nodded.

O'Hare fired the question at him. 'When you and Lambie were on the ladder, how was she?'

'Cold, terrified, naked. Seeing death coming straight at her with every wave. How would you expect her to be?'

'I would expect her to be hysterical with fear, but did she scream? Did she cry?'

'She was too busy just breathing.'

O'Hare nodded, as if this was useful information. 'Did she react at all? Did she look at you?'

Anderson thought for a minute and then shook his head. 'No, she was just making this little sound, like a tired baby. I thought she looked at me but there was no focus, no reaction. Then she muttered something, then . . . just stopped.'

'Nobody reported any screams along the embankment. And she didn't cry out when the boat passed – I know the people on the boat heard nothing. Her image was only picked up by a high-spec phone,' said O'Hare.

Anderson shook his head. 'But she hadn't the energy. She was blue with cold. She was . . . numb in every way.'

'It was more than that, Colin. Something flagged up in her blood sample, so I asked them to do a full screen, given her age. At first I thought it was Rohypnol.'

'The date rape drug?'

'Close to it, but not exactly. Rohypnol leaves no traces, no metabolites, after a period of anything from one hour to eight hours max. The stuff I found works even faster, but she stopped metabolizing it when she died. Which means she was put there very shortly before you got to her, possibly less than thirty minutes earlier. We don't know exactly what this stuff is. At the moment we're calling it R2. I've told the tox lab, so you can speak to them. But you might be dealing with a fast-acting compliance drug, which leaves no trace. We've only seen it since the turn of the year, but now that we know it's out there we can test for it. I requested a full tox analysis. However, Matilda McQueen had that thought before me and requested a further list of samples when I do my full PM – liver, brain, spleen, the lot.' O'Hare shrugged a little. 'Usually that's my choice, but a request is a request. She's being very thorough – and she was perfectly right.'

'Or she had a good idea beforehand about what she was going to find. She knew the results of a PM you hadn't yet done. I know she's good, but that's bloody marvellous. The logical conclusion is that she has seen it before.'

O'Hare raised his eyebrow but didn't answer the non-question. 'Well, R2 very probably contributed to the girl's death in this case. There was river water in her mouth, but no froth in her airway, and no diatoms in her blood, so

'I'm pretty sure she didn't drown in the normal sense of the word. I'd say it was reflex respiratory arrest – true dry-drowning, if you like. So there was nothing you could have done to save her.'

'And that's supposed to make me feel better?'

O'Hare shrugged. 'What might make you feel better is that possibly somebody gave Biggart the same stuff. But there's no trace because he lived long enough to metabolize it. Not easy to control a big man like that otherwise.'

'Made it easier to watch him burn. Worth thinking about.'

'And marvellous Matilda requested samples on that as well. So, somebody thinks there is a connection.'

'She's working under the orders of somebody other than a cop, isn't she? Somebody at national level?'

'Probably. No doubt we'll be told. Don't let it trouble you,' said O'Hare smoothly. 'You were the last person to see our little water sprite alive and therefore you're a valuable witness, so I should show you these.' He handed Anderson two sheets of paper that looked freshly faxed and one that was printed. 'Three gas chromatography results.'

O'Hare took the papers and moved over to a side bench.

'Three photographs.'

The third one was the perfect face of the girl in the Clyde. Her eyes were closed, and she looked at peace. The other two were of girls of a similar age, both lying on slabs as if asleep, eyes closed. The two men looked at them in silence.

Anderson traced his finger over their faces, noting the similar features. 'So, was this new drug, R2, found in those other two girls?' he asked eventually.

'No, but that doesn't mean it wasn't used on them. If enough time had elapsed between ingestion and death, they would have cleared it totally. But your girl died too soon and left us a clue.'

'So, why do you group them all together?'

'Because somebody else has, which suggests somebody somewhere has requested an R2 screen on any body we find that fits this profile.'

'And do we know who they are, those other two?'

O'Hare shook his head. 'Both were dumped in remote country areas, one in Tain, one in Argyll. One had multiple fractures post mortem as if she'd been dropped from a height. They were both left where there were sheep, ergo shepherds with sheepdogs that can sniff out a dead body half a mile away. Might as well have put a beacon on the deposition site.'

'So, who's interested? Exactly?' queried Anderson. 'This goes beyond Strathclyde's jurisdiction. Somebody on the National Crime Squad?'

'No idea,' O'Hare shrugged again. 'But both girls died within the past six months. I've just an interim report here but I'll request the full PM results from the Northern Constabulary . . .' He paused. 'Interesting that they're all three still unidentified, never listed as missing. I know society has gone a bit awry but most mothers in this country have some concerns as to their daughters' whereabouts. Three young girls, all abused, all dumped in a small country with a very big coastline.'

'It fits with the child porn theory. Or trafficking?' asked Anderson.

'Both are big business in this part of the world at the

moment. Might be why it's being kept hush-hush. And another thing – the similar features? Look at the high flat cheekbones, the big eyes. You said she muttered something – do you recall what it was?'

'*Moshka? Moochka?*' Anderson shook his head. 'Russian, do you think?' He pulled his mobile from his pocket, scrolled to a number, and pressed Call.

Mulholland answered almost immediately.

1.35 p.m.

Vik Mulholland closed his phone and tapped it against his perfect teeth. He suspected that the call from Anderson had something to do with the girl in the river, otherwise why would he be asking? *Mamochka* was a word a kid would use. But was Anderson getting the case? No matter, if there was a Russian connection anywhere, they surely must include him. He was bilingual in English and Russian. His Russian mother had always insisted it would come in useful one day, and maybe that day had come. But who should he back – MacKellar or Anderson?

There had been talk that a new taskforce was being set up under the grand acronym LOCUST – Local Organized Crime Unit Strategic Taskforce. The rumour was it was going to be at Paisley – the drugs capital of Scotland, Mulholland's old stamping ground. He wanted to get his stripes back, so he needed to get his rank reinstated. Maybe this was his chance to get on that taskforce. Mulholland pocketed the phone and went back to his work. The desk he and Anderson shared was rapidly filling with more paperwork on the life and history of William Stuart Biggart. That would keep him busy for a long time.

Mulholland reached for a file and had a flick through it. Every so often he tagged an insertion, anything to do with Biggart's association with the Apollo building. Across the room DS Lambie was munching on a chocolate muffin, forgetting he was supposed to be on a diet so he'd look good in a kilt at his wedding.

Mulholland handed a few pictures over to him. 'Fiona's photographs,' he explained. 'The fire investigator,' he added to Lambie's bemused face.

'This would be a bloody sight easier if we had a bigger board to put all these up on. How are we supposed to see anything, passing pictures back and forth like this?'

'Stick it on the wall. Not our fault if the board isn't big enough, just move Smoutie and Co down a bit. Fiona has a theory . . .' Vik went on to read out her theory about the flashover, word for word. 'So, the arsonist who set the fire might have stood and watched. I don't think O'Hare is going to contradict anything Fiona says, you know.'

'Might confirm some bindings, though. Biggart was a strange beast sexually; the rumour was he would do any-thing to anything. So, if he was into a bit of bondage, maybe that's how they were able to control him. The minute the Prof notices anything to confirm that theory he'll be on the blower.'

Vik looked from one photograph to the next. 'So, have we got any pictures of the part of the room that wasn't burned? The bit by the door?'

'There's a wee hallway just inside the front door . . .' Lambie muttered, as he pawed through the brown envelopes. 'Here. Don't think they found anything, though.'

Mulholland looked through them, then looked again. 'Who lived here?' he asked, pointing on the plan to the flat opposite Biggart's, the one that looked on to the little garden at the back. 'J. Appleby?'

'That's right. And the one we found Biggart in and the one next to it are listed as –' Lambie flicked through a file '– second accommodation, council tax paid by a rental company, Red Eagle Properties. Who never answer their phone.'

Mulholland muttered absentmindedly, 'So, Biggart didn't actually live here?'

'Not technically. He lives – lived – with his loving wife in the Mearns. One of those gated developments. Marriage for appearance's sake only. Like I said, he was a man of strange sexual proclivities – the stranger the better.'

'Do you know them? The family, I mean, not the sexual proclivities?'

'Melinda Biggart is scary, a bit like one of those dogs that let you in a house then growl when you try to leave. In Paisley we had our run-ins with Mr Biggart. Always well protected, never got his own hands dirty. Devious but not bright. Always a bit of a mystery how he got so far.'

'But ripe for somebody taking their revenge. It has that kind of feel about it, doesn't it, burning?' Mulholland began looking through the crime scene shots in his turn. 'And how would you describe a good night in, David? If you weren't hell-bent on committing matrimony?' Mulholland put the photograph of Biggart's front room flat on the desk and tapped it with his finger. 'Here we have a melted TV with a screen only a tad smaller than the cinema that used to be there, squashed beer cans, two big sofas, one burned, one half-burned. A stack of DVDs by the door. A . . . what's that?'

'I think that's the remains of a gaming console, and the remains of some games as well.'

'And next door, a huge bed. Bet that wasn't used for sleeping. And fuck all in the kitchen apart from beer. It's a bad boys' paradise, isn't it? A place to play out all kinds of sexual fetishes. Men, women, boys, girls, young, old, anything in between – as you say, Biggart was rumoured to have a wide range of sexual tastes, only a few of them legal.'

'I think we should chat to the neighbour, J. Appleby, about any other comings and goings. Order the CCTV footage for two hours before the fire started and an hour after it was put out. Get footage from Anniesland train station as well. The embankment is adjacent to the Apollo flats. You never know where it might lead us.'

Mulholland lowered his voice. 'But surely it's already been checked.'

'It would appear not. Not checked, not requested.'

'Why not?'

'I don't think the initial investigation got that far. Don't think they tried that hard.'

'And why should we?'

'Because while it's nice to think some kindly avenging angel killed Biggart to rid the world of a piece of scum, it's more likely that anyone who ever knocks off an evil bastard will be a bigger, more evil bastard. I don't find that a comforting thought. Do you?' Lambie went back to his chocolate muffin.

Half an hour later, his stomach rumbling for lack of lunch, Mulholland had a sheet full of scribbles. Five of the six flats on the ground floor of the converted cinema were owned by Red Eagle Properties of 266 West Sauchiehall Street, Glasgow – registered at Companies House as being owned by PSM Ltd. The sixth was owned by Ms Janet Appleby.

While there was nothing odd in one company owning a range of flats in a new development to rent out, the odd thing was that none of them had actually been rented out. Reduced council tax was being paid on them, but gas and electricity were being used. The only genuine inhabitant on the ground floor was Janet Appleby, who had been temporarily relocated to the incongruously named Highland Glen Hotel, up a lane near the Botanic Gardens. Vik looked at his watch. He phoned the hotel reception and was put through to the room. A sleepy voice answered. He apologized for disturbing her, and said who he was.

Silence on the other end of the phone. Then, 'Sorry, I was asleep. What is it you want? Is it about the fire?' She sounded young.

'I'd appreciate five minutes of your time.' He heard her yawn, imagined her lying under hotel sheets, the curtains closed tight against the rage of the sun outside. 'Just five minutes,' he said again.

She explained sleepily that she was long-haul cabin crew, she had just woken up, her body clock was all over the place. What time was it? What day was it? What country was it? 'Look, I'm almost too tired to think. And I'm about to fly out again tomorrow.'

'Can I ask you a few questions now?'

'Phone me back in half an hour, once I've had a coffee. Then you might get a sensible answer.'

The funeral mass of Thomas Eoin Carruthers had gone well and the mourners had retired to a private room of a small pub just off Maryhill Road for a cold refreshment and a warm sandwich. There was a sense of relief in the air – it was over, and now old pals could catch up, say what a nice service it was while taking care not to mention the deceased at all.

Costello was leaning on the wall, studying the grime on the window, when she saw DCI Niven MacKellar look around for somebody in particular to talk to, a plateful of sandwiches in one hand, a small cup of coffee in the other. 'Well, well, well, DS Costello, how are you?'

Costello studied his face, looking for any subtext, but decided she was just being paranoid. He was genuinely asking after her health. 'I'm keeping much better.' Then she added. 'Thank you, Niven. I thought I saw you at the chapel.'

'I presume you worked with Tommy at some point?' MacKellar nodded in response to his own question. 'I wouldn't have said he was the type.'

'Type?'

'Suicidal type.'

'I don't suppose you ever really know anybody.' It came out more philosophical than she had meant, and MacKellar gave her a look.

He leaned forward to whisper in her ear. 'Are they allowed to have a mass if Tommy committed suicide?'

'Doesn't really matter these days. Suicide is still a sin but it's been recategorized as a sin that you were too ill to realize you were committing, so you can still be given a mass.'

MacKellar regarded a triangular cheese sandwich, stuffing it into his mouth sideways. 'Same as divorce? Doesn't count if you weren't married in church?' He turned his back slightly to the grieving crowd, so his mouth was very close to Costello's ear. 'Why do I keep hearing rumours that it might not have been suicide? Is that just talk? The fiscal was convinced but . . .'

'But?'

MacKellar took a step back, and looked his colleague up and down. She looked businesslike but distant. He had worked alongside DS Costello before. She was one of the scruffy but committed-to-the-cause brigade, not the designer-suited-and-booted career type. But there was that hungry look in her eyes. Ready to get yourself back to work, thought MacKellar. 'I suppose folk have difficulty in accepting it, especially as he was a cop,' he said. 'But the fiscal was satisfied, and that's good enough for me.'

A pause hung in the air between them. At the far end of the room, a woman in her early sixties, her black handbag hanging on her arm, was making her way to the top table.

'Poor woman,' said Costello as the woman in question had a chair pulled out for her, and another cup of tea was poured. 'Happily married for nearly forty years, then he jumps out a window and she had no idea that he was going to do it? I find that hard to believe.'

'But you said it yourself – you never know what goes on in anybody else's head, do you?' MacKellar rammed a salmon paste sandwich into his mouth this time. 'Though

I think my wife always knows exactly what goes on in my head,' he said, trying for levity.

'If you stare at all women's tits the way you're staring at that waitress's, I've no doubt she does.' Costello turned round, her eyes passing over the mourners.

'Good God, that's ex-DCI Moffat back from Oz!'

'Where?'

'The one who looks as though he's interrogating the priest.'

As if he had heard, the tall, tanned grey-haired man looked up and raised his cup, signalling a hello across the crowded room. MacKellar nodded back.

Costello felt herself react. Eric Moffat . . . not a name, or a face, she would forget. It provoked a strong memory of cold and car exhaust fumes. Of course, Moffat had been Tommy's boss, they had worked together for years. It was Moffat who had told her to leave the dying woman alone, leave her lying on the concrete floor of a cold multi-storey – a bad place to die.

She turned away from the unpleasant memories to see a small woman in a bobble hat slip a salt cellar into her handbag. An elderly priest politely but firmly retrieved it and placed it back on the table.

'The family klepto,' muttered MacKellar with some amusement, as they watched the priest guide the old woman away and Moffat carefully sidestepped into the crowd at the buffet.

'He must know her, he's avoiding her.' Costello raised her glass, indicating Moffat then the bobble-hatted woman.

'Everybody's avoiding her; that's Rene, the demented sister-in-law. I remember Tommy telling me a few stories about her. God, she must be in her eighties now. Well, well, well. DCI Moffat – he's a blast from the past. I suppose he and Tommy had a long working career together. Talking of ex-DCIs, have you heard from Rebecca?'

'DCI Quinn? No.'

'She's on holiday in Bali, lucky sod.'

Costello didn't know what she was supposed to reply so simply commented that the weather was probably better here. Then she asked pointedly, 'Any sign of Colin Anderson being made up to DCI yet?'

'I wouldn't hold my breath, Costello. It's unfortunate, but this Fairbairn business is going to hit him hard.' MacKellar was talking like a spy at a secret assignation – quietly, out of the corner of his mouth. He was glancing across the room, saying silent hellos to various men who he obviously did not want to speak to. 'I mean, his track record with McAlpine was exemplary but this Fairbairn enquiry will prove that one "filing error" –' he made quote marks with his forefingers '– stopped the jury hearing support for his alibi.'

'Not much of an alibi,' retorted Costello. 'And neither Anderson nor McAlpine would have withheld evidence.'

'I know you are a loyal cop, Costello, but if there is a hint that McAlpine withheld it, Anderson will be tainted by association. If Anderson did it himself, then he deserves all he gets.'

Costello glared at him.

'I'm sorry, he's a good cop and if truth be told I feel a bit sorry for him. But he's my inspector and he will not be promoted until all this is over and done with. I have two other DIs who don't have an enquiry hanging over them.

So, if a DCI post comes up, it's not going Anderson's way. Not until it's all over and he's cleared.'

'Eighteen months to wait for the appeal? No wonder Brenda wants him to emigrate. He's one of the best cops I've ever worked with and that's what they do to him.' She saw MacKellar watch the buxom waitress go past. 'And he doesn't chase skirt like the rest of you.'

'You don't believe the rumours are true, then – about him and Helena McAlpine?'

'They are not. What about the bright-eyed boy DS Mulholland? Is he still a DC?'

'Oh yes, get back soon enough and you'll still be his boss.' MacKellar took a sip of coffee. 'Can you keep a secret, Costello?'

'I've nobody to tell it to.'

'There's a rumour that ACC Howlett has been asked by Special Branch to form a taskforce. Two hundred strong, plus.'

'Anti-terrorism?'

MacKellar shook his head. 'Operation LOCUST. Organized crime. With Biggart gone there's a vacuum, and we should be moving on it now. But what's happening? I've been hauled in for performance assessments. Do you know anything about it?'

'How would I hear? But have they decided who they want to head up this taskforce? It'd be the chance of a lifetime, for the right person.'

'I think a few names have been mentioned.'

'Is one of them standing right beside me?'

'Indeed. I think Anderson was being considered, but not now with the Fairbairn fiasco.'

'And he has no experience in organized crime. His wife wants them to emigrate. And that taskforce could run for years, so it'll be a long game. I don't think you have anything to worry about, Niven. If it was up to me, I'd put you in charge.'

'Cheers, Costello.'

'You'd do less damage there,' she said sweetly, thinking about her own meeting with ACC Howlett.

Oh yes, she could keep a secret.

7.30 p.m.

Anderson was sitting in his garden, showered, fed and sipping a beer. He let the cool evening breeze play on his face, enjoying the sun. He had been on the go for twenty-four hours, and it had been a busy day. He was glad of the time to reflect, think things through and address the niggle in his mind that he was missing something important. Everything Professor O'Hare had said depressed him, and by the time he got back to the station and the desk that wasn't really his, it was littered with pages from the daily papers. The press had gone to town on the Cameron 'Skelpie' Fairbairn story. Some bright spark had circled Anderson's own name on page 5. He was aware of eyes watching him, waiting for a reaction. He gave the story a cursory glance, noting with some pleasure that from the look of the photograph, Skelpie had had a tough time inside. His face was lined, the jowls sagged a little. He looked like a man approaching fifty rather than under forty. Anderson folded the paper and put it in the bin. He didn't have to read it, he knew it all already. He had wondered then if Costello had seen it and that was why she had tried to call.

By the time it was four o'clock he was pissed off and tired, in a foul mood and ready to take on DCI Mac-Kellar, only to find he was still at Tommy Carruthers' funeral. When MacKellar did return, he was in a solicitous mood.

The meeting in his office was almost pleasant. MacKellar assured him he had considered Anderson's objection about the reassignment of the 'River Girl' case. The DCI's argument was cohesive, and it was convincing – Anderson knew he had to think about the bigger picture. Now, looking back, MacKellar was probably right; not only did the Biggart case deserve just as much investigation as any other, it had to be *seen* to be that way. It was a massive PR exercise. This was a police force that treated all crime the same, no matter the identity of the victim. 'With the Fairbairn case in the papers . . .' MacKellar didn't need to finish the sentence. The Strathclyde force was going to have to appear whiter than white.

Anderson felt the evening sun warm his tense shoulders as he recalled the strange turn the conversation had then taken. MacKellar had asked him about LOCUST. As if a jobbing detective like Anderson would know about such high-level initiatives. Or was MacKellar letting Anderson know that he, being a lowly DI, was out of the loop?

Office politics.

But the cold water of the Clyde, the burned-out stench of Biggart's flat and the release of Cameron Fairbairn seemed a million miles away as Anderson sipped his beer, feeling a little more at peace. All day he had been in the car, at a mortuary or in an office, and this was the only fresh air and peace and quiet he was going to get. Well, it was reasonably quiet. Lorna next door had tried to have a chat over the garden fence, her conversation quickly turning to house prices and did he really think it was a good time to sell? He presumed Brenda had been canvassing some opinions without telling him. As long as that was all she was doing. Then Terry Lomax over the back decided to mow his lawn with his old-fashioned mechanical lawn mower, which purred on the push and growled on the pull.

Anderson now had a glass of cold beer in his hand, a warm dog at his feet and a belly full of spagaroni Bolognese that he and the kids had cooked up together, only realizing halfway through that they'd run out of the right kind of pasta.

He had enjoyed making a mess in the kitchen with the kids, being a dad, having some family time. He knew Brenda had been going out somewhere but had forgotten where, and for the moment he didn't care. He closed his eyes and rested his head on the back of the chair, practically asleep.

Five million pounds. The black dots on the ceiling of the empty flat. The face of the River Girl. MacKellar's words: 'But why don't you leave all your paperwork on the River Girl with me, plus any notes you made while talking to the Prof?' He had then added, 'Even if what he said was off the record.'

Anderson's silent response was, 'Over my dead body.'

The hall of St Boswell's Care Home stank of Brussels sprouts and pine air freshener. It was going on for midnight, and the home was quiet except for a radio playing gangsta rap somewhere down the corridor and the irregular cacophony of snoring from the bedrooms.

A lone figure sat at the bay window, hunched in his wheelchair, a rug over his bony shoulders to ward off any chill in the night air. Auld Archie O'Donnell always sat there. He had sat there for most of the last year, only moving for his breakfast, his dinner and his tea. He would be put to bed, then he would get up again, grab his Zimmer, get himself into his wheelchair and be off back to the window, back to his waiting, his watching. Put him in the day room, he'd be back at the window. They'd tried to talk to him, but he told them in no uncertain terms to go forth and multiply. And Archie was a man used to being obeyed.

This evening, he wore his rug over his dark blue cardigan and a short-sleeved cotton shirt. He had on clean flannel trousers and his good leather shoes. He always put his shoes on, even though they'd tried to take them off him and put on the slippers supplied by the home. Shoes caused problems for the cleaners. Sometimes it was easier if they all wore the same slippers. It was certainly easier if they all wore the same clothes. In fact, it would be easier if they were all dead. But Auld Archie was having none of it. At best he ignored them, at worst he swore at them. He hadn't actually hit any of the staff – at least, not anything they could prove was intentional.

But tonight he had asked four times if Richie the care

worker was coming on duty, and had been told four times that Richie hadn't turned up for work yesterday or today. Young people today had no sense of responsibility, they said. The senior care worker scribbled on his notes that Archie was showing signs of Alzheimer's.

Archie wheeled himself back to the window, and watched and waited.

11.59 p.m.

Rosie MacFadyean stretched in her bed, as much as she could stretch with the bulk and folds of fat and flesh that padded her arms and legs. She hated this weather, and the sweat that ran from her, soaking the mattress. The sweat got into places she could not reach, places it was impossible for her to clean and difficult for Wullie to reach when he was cleaning her. She needed another sponge bath now. She could feel her sweat turning acrid, feel it eating away at her skin, causing festering hacks which would ooze pus and a crusty, flaking exudate. Wullie had spent the hour before he went out washing her, drying her, powdering her, lifting the folds and flaps of her flesh, propping them up with a pillow if necessary, as he cleaned and creamed and powdered the irritated skin beneath. But that had been hours ago.

What was he doing, leaving her alone like this? Leaving her to use the sponge to urinate? In this weather, the urine turned sour really quickly. Wullie had left the windows wide open for fresh air, but it was a way in for the flies that were now buzzing to get out.

67

She had finished with the newspaper and wished, not for the first time, that technology would find a way to get a mobile phone signal down the glen. The details in the paper were scant – three men in their early twenties, with 'known drug connections', had been shot dead in a hotel car park. The paper didn't name them, but Rosie could. Smoutie, Hamster and Speedo. Three stooges and no loss to man nor beast. She read on, smiling at the tabloid jargon: *Even seasoned police officers were shocked at the murders.*

Shocked! Rosie had snorted in derision.

Police officers nowadays were made of chocolate.

Not like they were in her day.

Tuesday
29 June 2010

4.32 a.m.

Colin Anderson pulled the sweat-sodden sheet from his shoulder. The wide-open window in the bedroom was letting in more heat than cool air. He turned over and fell into a confusing dream, in which he was burning and couldn't get out of bed because his feet were tied. He could see the door but he had no chance of reaching it with the sheet wrapped round his feet. Who do I know who would kill me like this, he wondered. Why don't I fight back?

But all was well. He could hear the gentle ring of the fire engine on its way. He was nearly safe. The gentle ring of the fire engine . . .

Then he felt a tap on his shoulder.

'Your phone,' Brenda said sleepily. She turned over, pulling the sheet with her.

Anderson reached for the bedside light switch, knocking the phone to the floor.

As he scrabbled on the carpet with sleepy fingers, swearing gently, the bedroom door swung open slightly, and Nesbitt wandered in, his wee Staffie face smiling, eager for a very late or very early walk. As he automatically answered with his name, Anderson looked out of the window. It was just getting light, a very early dawn, but definite daylight on the horizon.

71

'Colin? Vik here. Something you might be interested in – a teenager took a dive off a bridge over the expressway, not far from the river. We have an eyewitness, who says he was dropped.'

'Dropped . . . ?' Something was trying to climb to the front of Anderson's sleepy brain. 'Signs of sexual assault?'

'Yes.'

'I'm on my way.' Then before he hung up he asked, 'Were you called out on this?'

'Yes.'

'But not me?'

'No, I'm calling you out. I'm not qualified to deal with this; I'm only a bloody DC, remember?' Mulholland snapped. 'And I have to get my stripes back, and you're the best chance I have of getting a good case.'

'Cheers,' said Anderson with muted sarcasm. He turned and kissed Brenda's exposed shoulder. 'Something's come up. I've been summoned.'

'Let the dog out before you go,' she said, and went straight back to sleep.

5.03 a.m.

'What the fuck's been going on here?' asked Anderson, getting out of his car. 'There's about a quarter of a mile of the bloody expressway coned off.'

DS Lambie was talking on a radio and cut the call short, just saying, 'Do what you have to, I'll let the boss know.' Then he said mildly to Anderson, 'Well, the traffic boys want us off the road before rush hour. Just as well it happened at four in the morning, not in the middle of the day. But it wasn't a suicide. And he's not dead. Young lad, not more than sixteen, they reckon. And there's evidence of violent sexual assault among other things, which is why we called you out, or why they called us out.'

'Why not MacKellar?'

Lambie didn't answer.

'You mean they did, but he didn't want to get out of bed?'

'That's the DCI for you.' Lambie opened the door of an unmarked police car. 'It'll be quicker if I drive you up there. They're trying to figure out a way of getting him out the truck he fell into.' Anderson climbed in beside him. The entire support service of Strathclyde police seemed to be parked the length of the inside lane. Lambie slowed the car just below an overhead bridge. 'A van stopped up there. A white Transit, we think.'

'Isn't it always a white Transit?'

'Two men pulled the lad out from the van and got him up on the rail, and he went over. We have a forensic team on the bridge right now.'

'Christ! So, where's the boy?'

Less than a mile ahead, Anderson could see a quiet commotion of flashing blue lights, orange lights and headlights. The vehicles were all pulled in round an articulated lorry, like bees round a queen. Lambie indicated left and crawled along a narrow gap between the edge of the road and the cones where the sparse early morning traffic was being waved through by the traffic cops, every car slowing more than was necessary as the driver turned to look. As they neared, the HGV began to resemble Lemuel Gulliver, with ladders and ropes everywhere. Anderson could just see that a fire engine had pulled over in front of the lorry and reversed back right up to it. Even from here he could see a ladder being wound down over the back of the truck.

Whatever was going on, it all looked under control.

'OK, what happened exactly?' he asked.

'Well, the lad went straight through the fibreglass roof of the lorry and fell on to boxes of whisky stacked on palettes to within inches of the roof. So he didn't really fall that far. The damage had all been done before-hand.'

'Druggie? Dealer? Another one to add to the list of Biggart and the Balfron boys?' asked Anderson.

Lambie pulled the car in and got out, and Anderson followed suit. 'It doesn't seem so; no signs of popping or mainlining. But when he went through the roof he fell on to one of the metal crossbars, and they think it might have ruptured his liver, so they're trying to get him out without causing any more damage. The paramedics are keeping him alive while the fire service try to cut him free. They have a line in and he's stopped bleeding, so they've a wee bit of time to play with.'

'Can you ask them to run some blood off?' asked Anderson, thinking about R2, thinking about establishing a link.

'What, now?'

'Just do it.'

'Will do. The driver of the truck's probably still in that ambulance up there. He was in shock when I left to get

74

you. He has no idea what happened.' They both looked round as a loud metal clang rent the air, and a few voices shouted in warning.

'There's an "and" to all this, isn't there?'

'The paramedics say they reckon he's been tortured – beaten, burned, fingernails torn out, stains on his jeans show he's been bleeding from his back passage. And he's only in his teens.'

'Yes, I get you, Lambie. Let's just hope he survives to tell us about it. And who's in that?' He gestured towards another ambulance a hundred yards further on, parked beside a light-coloured Corsa.

'That's Mrs Dorothy Elm. She was driving two cars behind the lorry, in the inside lane. She saw the whole thing. The lorry driver heard nothing and was still driving. So she pulled out, got up level with him and forced him to pull over. She's a good witness, saw a lot.'

They watched as a spinal board was passed from hand to hand up the side of the truck with much shouting, but they were too far away to make out anything in particular.

'Dorothy is very definite that they didn't drop him,' Lambie said.

'They threw him?'

Lambie shook his head. 'They had him by the ankles, dangling him over the bridge, then he kicked himself free. She saw him jerk just before he fell.'

Anderson looked back at the bridge and nodded slowly. 'If he kicked himself free, that explains why he landed on top of the truck rather than in front of it.'

*

Due to the early call-out, Anderson was due some down time so he went home for breakfast on the pretence of thinking about the incident on the expressway, but he knew it was more about avoiding the eyes of his Partick colleagues. The late edition of the *Daily Record* lay on the kitchen table, neatly folded at one end, the other end having entered the shredder of Nesbitt's canines. Being a dog of some discernment, he had chewed off Skelpie Fairbairn's face.

He had tried not to read it but it was there in its technicolour glory. Fairbairn, the evil predatory paedophile, was back on the street. That was the point that most of them seemed to be missing.

Underneath photos of the three men shot at Balfron, a headline screamed *Gang Murder!* and the article leaned heavily on the threat of a full-scale gang war breaking out on the streets of Glasgow. The men had shaved heads, wary eyes, their faces carrying the scars of short lives lived swimming with sharks. The paper had printed their nicknames: the Hamster, Speedo and Smoutie. Anderson was tempted to rip out that bit as well and feed it to Nesbitt, who probably had a greater sense of self-preservation than all of them put together.

The 'Bridge Boy' had made the headline on Radio Clyde's nine o'clock news. Just the bare facts and an appeal for anyone who had seen a white Transit in the vicinity to come forward. It had been a disciplined operation; it had needed teamwork. It had a sense of organized crime about it, and he wondered what the Bridge Boy had done to deserve such a traumatic fate. Anderson glanced at his watch; he had time to call in to the hospital and see how the boy was doing before he was taken off that case as well. His phone had been quiet – no messages, no missed calls. No news was good news.

Brenda was still in bed. She had come back late from her friend's house and immediately gone online, contacting another old friend who had recently emigrated to Oz. They had been chit-chatting by email for a few weeks now, much friendlier since they were thousands of miles apart. Brenda wanted the family to go out to the Gold Coast for four weeks over the winter holidays, to get Australia 'at its glorious best'.

It'd be too bloody hot, he knew – hotter than here. God knows why she wanted to go. She always burned painfully in no time, having red hair and pale skin, and Anderson, being blond and fair-skinned, didn't fare much better.

All he did know was that she wanted to get away from Glasgow, wanted to get him away, and hoped moving might make it all better. He was still young enough to apply to emigrate, and he couldn't deny the kids would have a better life in the sun. Brenda's friend's brother was a cop out there, and he said there was a lot of security consulting work going. A guy like Anderson would find it a doddle. He wondered how her dreams would pan out if he was made the official scapegoat in the appeal and the subsequent enquiry. Brenda had visions of swapping their three-bedroomed semi for a six-bedroomed house in the suburbs of Brisbane and there was no fault in her plan, no reason not to go.

Except he didn't want to.

He liked his job, he liked sitting thinking about the next move on the case.

He needed to get the Bridge Boy's description into the evening papers and get some kind of appeal underway. Mulholland was the man for that. Hopefully that would bring them an ID. Like any big city, Glasgow swallowed its fair share of runaways and throwaways, easy prey for the sexual predators who hung about Buchanan Street coach station waiting for anyone who got off a bus and looked as if they had nowhere to go. But this boy was different; he'd been tortured. Torture wasn't Glasgow's way. A body dumped in a ditch with a bullet in the head, that was the usual.

He opened the paper again, revealing a full-page feature with a picture of Simone Sangster, author of *Little Boy Lost*, the rehashed story of six-year-old Alessandro Marchetti who was mysteriously abducted in 1996 and never found. Nobody would ever write the story of the babysitter, who didn't have the photogenic features or the rich parents of his young charge but had no doubt suffered the same fate. Alessandro would be a young man now, if he were still alive, Anderson reflected.

10.05 a.m.

Costello got up, as she wasn't sleeping anyway. The black suit was still lying across the back of a chair, along with the fine silk headscarf to wind round her head to hide the scar that nobody else could see but she knew was there.

She had no idea why she had been summoned to see ACC Howlett. Something to do with Skelpie Fairbairn, that was the only thing she could think of. But she didn't believe there was anything she could add to that situation. And there was no way she was going to implicate Alan McAlpine in anything. Or Colin Anderson.

The Partickhill team had been after Fairbairn for years. They knew he had a liking for young flesh. Very young flesh. He had a reputation for hanging around in parks watching young girls. Two had been assaulted, and had woken up having been molested, but unable to remember anything. Fairbairn was a tentative link between them, but there had been huge gaps in the chain of evidence. And both girls knew him, anyway – he was their bus driver. And, it transpired, he always walked through the park, so of course he'd be there. All the police had was uncorroborated evidence, circumstantial coincidence and rumour – but this time the ice cream man remembered Skelpie being with the wee girl . . . the wee girl who'd been so insistent that raspberry topping was what she wanted. DCI McAlpine knew that this time, they had him. And then a couple of statements from his friends appeared, saying he'd been back in the pub with them by the time the attack took place.

The statements threatened to become inconvenient; nothing precise, but the timeline was thrown out just enough for any half-decent defence counsel to cause a jury reasonable doubt. Those statements had somehow – even Costello couldn't be sure exactly how – never found their way into the fiscal's file that went to the defence; they'd just been put in some other file. And now Fairbairn was out on 'interim liberation pending appeal', which was how it had been quoted in the paper. Evidence had not been disclosed – witnesses had made statements to give him an alibi, but those two statements had got lost. The witnesses had not been called by the defence and therefore the jury had not heard any alternative explanation of events. So, under the disclosure rule, Fairbairn was out. He would have his conviction overturned on appeal and he would be a free man.

Costello knew she would be called to the enquiry. She didn't know ACC Howlett personally or professionally so there was no other reason she could think of why he would want to speak to her. Could there be a damage limitation exercise going on? Did that mean McAlpine was going to be the fall guy? Four years dead, he couldn't defend himself. But she was not going to say a word against the boss, or against any of them.

Memories of Partickhill made her think again – what if this meeting was nothing to do with Fairbairn? What if they simply wanted her to leave? Partickhill was closed indefinitely, and Colin Anderson's promotion seemed to be stalled. Was that what it was about – just getting rid of them all? They couldn't sack her, of course; there was no operational reason why they should, as she'd done nothing wrong. But now that the occupational health team was saying that she would be fit for work in the near future, the problem of DS Costello was clearly not going to go away. Howlett was going to sweet-talk her and try to persuade her it was in her best interests to go. She had dictated a full statement from her hospital bed at the time of the enquiry following the incident that put her there, and there was nothing in it – nothing at all – that justified her walking away from her job or being told to go. And she had given another brief statement a fortnight ago outlining her minimal involvement in the Fairbairn case.

She took a sip of her tea, but it was stone cold. Yes, she could see how she and Anderson could be an irritant to the Strathclyde force. Some politician in Holyrood would be baying for blood – anything else would seem like a cover-up to the media.

And Fairbairn's lawyer was very media savvy.

10.30 a.m.

'So, what can I tell you?' Dr Redman flicked a few sheets of A4 back and forth, with medically clean hands and short nails, before positioning himself directly in the path of the cool air from the fan. The side room in the hospital was small and windowless. 'The boy was a mess when he came into A&E. Not so much the fall but the good kicking he received beforehand. And odd injuries that might indicate torture. Fingernails either were pulled out or burned.' Redman got up and closed the door that had clicked open. 'I've asked Professor O'Hare to come over and have a look. He's been to a few war zones, he'll recognize the injuries of torture – or "insults", as he calls them. He's helped us out before on injuries stuff like this.'

Anderson leaned on the back of his chair. 'So, the poor boy was thoroughly beaten and tortured before he went over the barrier. How did he come to this?'

Redman raised an eyebrow and sighed. 'Good question, especially as he is a well-nourished young man, his remaining teeth are in good condition. All dirt was super-ficial, he had good long-term hygiene – no nits, no fleas, good bone density, no yeast infections. The beatings had gone on over a period of several days. And he hadn't eaten for a good while.'

'So, what do you think happened to him?'

'Well, kicked, as I said. Hit with a blunt instrument. One tibia with a spiral fracture; the bone was subject to severe torsional stress. Great strength would be needed for that, or something mechanical. Don't ask, I have no idea what. He has a lot of lacerations from being rammed against a fixed object; you can still see the pattern. A pro-longed interrogation session, I'd say.'

'Any indication why?'

'You need to find out who he is first. And the blood on him was not all his, the samples are at the lab. The way things have been going in this city recently, there's proba-bly a drug connection. He didn't have a habit, but he might have known something that someone wanted to know. Otherwise, he'd just have been shot like those other three.'

'Well, he didn't get into that state overnight. But nobody has reported him missing. Any clues as to his identity?'

The doctor sighed. 'No major scars. We have X-rays of his remaining teeth. He has good dental work. There's a torn piercing up here, on the cartilage of his left ear.' Red-man tapped his own ear.

'Age?'

'Seventeen, eighteen, somewhere around there. Older than the ambulance guys first thought.'

'Still young, though.'

'The strange thing is, he seems to have been engaged in

sexual activity with men, or a man, over a period of time. But he's not a run-of-the-mill rent boy. Maybe a high-class rent boy? To me the signs are consistent with consensual homosexual activity, then a more recent incident of rape. Thickening suggests a long-term consensual activity but the bleeding suggest a violent and –'

'Yeah, we can ask O'Hare about that.' Anderson was thinking about the boy – not a user, from a good home. It was a hard one to accept.

'You know, there's been a big increase in stabbings and shootings in the last few months. What are you guys *doing* out there?'

Anderson shrugged. 'Trying to get one step ahead.' He paused. 'Did you say the samples had already been sent to Forensics?'

'No, somebody came to collect them.'

'Any idea who?'

Redman looked at him blankly. 'Sorry, I thought you'd sent her. Definitely police special services. She carried ID. Small girl, brown hair.' He shrugged. 'Eager, young.'

'Wasn't Matilda McQueen, was it?'

Dr Redman flicked over a few sheets of paper on his clipboard. 'Indeed, M. McQueen picked up the samples at seven thirty this morning. Took them over to that lab at the uni, I presume.'

Anderson nodded, he was getting the pattern. 'Will he make it? Bridge Boy?'

'One of those cases where we do what we can – we support body systems, keep his airway clear, give him blood, sew up what we can and then stand back and wait. If it goes well, so will he. If not, we could lose him at any stage.'

'If he says anything –'

'We're keeping him unconscious most of the time – we can control the pain that way – but when he drifts back to reality he repeats a word, as if he wants to tell us something.' Redman looked at the form again. 'It could be "brawny", or "Trelawney" – something like that. Does that mean anything to you?'

'No, nothing.' Anderson scribbled the words down, hearing again the barely whispered '*Mamochka*'. Images of limbs being tied, ankles bound, jostled disturbingly in his mind.

Redman was fanning himself with a file. 'How bloody hot do you think it's going to get today?'

'Far too bloody hot. Thanks for your time, doc.' Anderson handed Redman a card. 'There's my mobile. Buzz me if anybody phones, or comes to visit, or shows any interest in him at all. Just remember, they might not be family; whoever did this wanted to know something. Even if he told them, they still might be bloody annoyed he survived.'

'Hang on, somebody did phone. They refused to say if they were family.' Redman reached across and pulled a Post-it note from the monitor screen. 'Yip, they hung up the minute they were asked who they were, which means we would have told them nothing.'

'Did anybody try 1471?'

'No, we're a hospital, we don't tend to do things like that. But the nurse made a note that it was at eight this morning. Somebody reading the early paper, hearing the breakfast news, maybe?'

'Was the caller male?'

'According to this note, yes.'

Anderson closed his notebook and left, casting a glance at the victim's room as he left. There was little recognizable as a human being, just tubes and sheets and machines and wires. Anderson glanced at the framework over the bed, the cables connected to it, crocodile clips holding them in place, and the holes on the wall that held the framework.

He had a flicker of recognition, something else to think about.

1.30 p.m.

By the time Skelpie Fairbairn crawled out of his bed, it was half past one. He belched loudly, scratching his fat belly, and wandered into the toilet. He peed and spent a couple of minutes looking at his face in the mirror, assessing himself. He'd put on weight while he was inside – no longer the Skinny Jim he'd been when he was first arrested. Tomorrow he needed to start getting in shape for his appeal and try to bear some resemblance to a responsible citizen. Good shave, haircut, take a bit of weight off, get some colour into his sallow skin, he could almost look trustworthy. He could look like an innocent guy who would buy a wee lassie an ice cream on a hot summer day.

He went into the hall, and picked up the mail. The white envelope from Scottish Power he flung aside, and the one from 3 Mobile, but he eagerly opened the two DVDs he'd been sent to keep him entertained. He checked his mobile. No flashing light, no message yet that he could move on. So, he still had to sit tight in this social security hellhole. One of these days there'd be a phone call, and they would say the codeword which meant he could move on. If they didn't say it, he wasn't to go. But Skelpie was confident he was going to be looked after, and it would all look legit.

He stamped on the cushion, making a comfy dent for his head, then flung himself bum first on to the brand-new sofa. He bounced slightly on landing, and heard the base of the sofa crack. Bit of cheap shite, so it was.

Eyes on the TV, his hand scrabbled over the floor, doing a blind search through the grime and grease and dirt caught up in the fibres of the skanky carpet. A half-eaten KitKat, one fag packet empty and crushed, another fag packet half full, a bottle of Teacher's. That would do for his breakfast. Before starting his feast, he picked up the remote, pressed Play and waited for the DVD to load. He scratched himself with yellow fingernails, and bits of skin flaked into his belly button. Content now, he tossed his lighter from the back of his hand to his palm, catching it and then flicking it on. The click of the flame was ech-oed by that of the DVD player. He reached down and picked up the tinfoil tray from last night's Chinky to use as an ashtray and balanced it on his thigh.

Then he felt around on the carpet for the dregs of a can of lager and tipped that into the makeshift ashtray, to be on the safe side. Falling asleep while pissed and smok-ing equalled toast. As Billy the Bastard had found out. Skelpie would be more careful.

He burped loudly and lifted his bum off the sofa to fart. It was good to be out after four years of being locked up twenty hours out of twenty-four. And God, was he out! He was free now, on a firm legal argument that he couldn't make head or tail of – though he knew the word 'disclosure' came up a lot. Something the bastards at the fiscal's office ought to have said, but didn't. Something the cops should have revealed, but didn't. He was letting Faulkner, his lawyer, do all the talking for him. The wee shite had been Biggart's lawyer, and Biggart had footed the bill up front. But then Biggart, God bless his burned-out socks, had owed Skelpie big time.

He wasn't that innocent – he'd done plenty and got away with it – but it gnawed at him that he'd actually been banged up for something he hadn't done. Though he knew who had.

The story he'd given the cops was, for once, the truth. He was just the local bus driver, and he'd got caught up in a nasty situation. He knew all the local kiddies by name, kept an eye on them as they got on and off his bus. Wee Lynda Osbourne, a six-year-old with blonde pigtails, often got the bus to school with her granny. Then one day he'd left Hugh and Lenny in the pub and had gone up to the Botanics for some fresh air and a wee bit of business, intending to go straight back to the pub. It had been a hot day, like today, and he'd queued at the ice cream van. There was a summer fair going on, and the gardens were packed with parents and children; it was hard to tell which adults and children belonged together. He was already in the queue when he saw wee Lynda join the end. She seemed to have two older boys with her, but they started chatting to some friends, ignoring the wee girl. He had waved, offered to buy her a cone to save her waiting. He was just being nice; it wasn't safe for kids to wait. She'd really wanted raspberry topping, but they'd run out, and she'd had a wee tantrum. So, the ice cream man gave her a double dollop of strawberry and everyone was happy.

But that encounter had got him banged up for kiddiefiddling. Fairbairn could remember the first time he met McAlpine in the dark stinking corridor at Partickhill Station; as soon as they laid eyes on each other there was a wee flicker, as one liar recognized another. Well, someone had terminated the wee bastard not long after. Good on him.

Now Skelpie would just have to be a bit more careful.

He didn't want to end up back inside.

But he had choices, and this time he had friends in very low places.

He flicked through the DVDs from the rental company – *Saw, Saw II, Saw III*. His all-time favourites. But first he was going to enjoy this really good bit from another film.

A man hangs in midair, huge metal hooks pulling the flesh of his back into sharp peaks as he winches himself up . . . to hover above the dead woman – the drowned dead woman – he is about to have sex with . . .

Skelpie paused the action, so the drowned woman stared up at him with dead eyes, her short dark hair bordering her face like an ebony frame. He fancied a bit of that, if the truth be known. Not the hooks-through-the-skin bit – he was used to giving pain, not receiving it – but the shagging drowned women. Not drowned too long ago – he wasn't a pervert – but a wee bit of recently drowned.

Skelpie picked up a smart red envelope in the shape of

a pillar box, sliding out another DVD, then he ejected the hanging man and the drowned bitch, got up and placed the new DVD into the slot before flopping down again. The camera wavered about a bit before ending up on the figure of a young girl; her company was a little present for him to celebrate his release from jail. He recognized the stupid tartan wallpaper above the bedhead. The camera pulled back, showing his upper forearm with its RFC tattoo and the delicate script of *No Surrender* underneath. That was bad; that should have been kept out of shot.

Unconsciously, Skelpie reached for his forearm, scratching the tattoo.

2.05 p.m.

Vik Mulholland had been busy while Anderson had been at the hospital and now his constable was coming towards him, notebook in hand, with a focused expression on his face that had been absent since his demotion. Anderson was glad to see it back.

'Colin? The tabloids have been on the phone asking for a comment on the Fairbairn affair.'

'They can piss off,' answered Anderson automatically.

'And I've typed up this statement from Janet Appleby, the girl who –'

'Yes, I know. Just read it out.'

Mulholland cleared his throat and sat on the side of Anderson's desk. 'Name Janet Marion Appleby. Born on the 14th of November 1985, in Glasgow, single, moved into the first available flat in Apollo Court two years ago. She has the impression that she was not supposed to buy it, she thought the estate agent had his own ideas for it, but she was a cash buyer so he couldn't really –'

Anderson whistled through his teeth. 'Stop right there. Where does her money come from for a flat like that?'

'Dead granny, it's legit, I've checked. She was in London when the fire happened, she didn't like Biggart. I quote: "Just the way he looked at me." He would make remarks about the fit of her uniform. She's BA cabin crew, long haul. If she knew he was about, she wouldn't go out into the corridor, she'd wait until he'd gone.'

'But no direct threats or intimidation?'

'Unfortunately no, but there have been a few offers to buy her out. She can't recall the name of the company but she thinks it'll be in the paperwork at her flat.'

'So, they didn't like her being there?'

'Sounds like it. But she just thought he was a perv. She's a bright girl. She had deduced he didn't live there. She was always taking deliveries for him, PillarBoxFlix DVDs mostly, that was a pattern she did notice. A few people used to come and go, but not like a drug drop, not in and out. They stayed for hours – quiet partying, she said.'

'Fits in with the findings in the flat, the big boys' playground.'

'Well, they were always men, and they never used the front door of the flats. But she would recognize some of the callers again – one she called the cute guy who had, and I quote, "big brown puppy-dog eyes" and another two who always came as a pair; one had a funny eye, with a white bit across the iris, as though he'd damaged it. And tattoos on his left wrist, a pattern she said looked like leaves or something intertwined. She'll come in and look at pictures if we get any.'

'A single girl, long-haul cabin crew with no home to go to? Bet she's not going to be around much to interview, is she?'

Mulholland shook his head with some regret.

ACC Howlett squared the two buff folders on his desk, and placed the envelope with the photograph of DS Costello next to her latest welfare report from HR and every appraisal that she had had on a murder squad. The same three words kept appearing: intuitive, independent, observant. He set his fountain pen carefully to the side. He took a deep breath, exhaling slowly. He was about to stake a lifetime's reputation on a long shot, but time was running out – for him, and for them all. He dabbed the sweat from his forehead and tugged up his uniform trousers, cursing the unaccustomed slackness of the waistband, then sat down and composed himself to look the part. He retrieved the personnel file from the opposite side of the desk and took a brief glance at the photograph. It bore only a slight resemblance to the figure he had just watched on the security camera, with its slightly unsteady walk, not unstable but uneasy, as if she needed to stretch her legs after a long journey. Slim, she wore a dark suit and neat shoes with a slight heel, and a silk scarf folded narrow and tied round her short brown hair. He knew what that was hiding.

He pressed the intercom and asked Eilidh, his PA, to

bring the woman in. He had kept her waiting ten minutes, long enough to test her nerve.

'Coffee? Tea?' Howlett asked after the official introductions had been made.

His visitor shook her head and sat down without being asked.

'Just a coffee for me, then,' he said to Eilidh, while considering the way the woman had sat down.

Heavily? With relief? No, as if she was tired. Her hands gripped the strap of her bag so tightly that her knuckles were blanched.

Again, he inwardly questioned his decision. 'I'd like to thank you for attending at such short notice.'

'Not as if I had a lot else on, is it?'

Ah, there it was, that vague insolence. He smiled at her. She smiled back briefly, looking at him intently – as if he was speaking a foreign language, and she was concentrating.

'How are you keeping, DS Costello? I think your team are missing you.'

'I'm sure they are. I'm keeping perfectly well, thank you. How are you?'

'Er . . . fine,' he lied, wondering if she had heard the rumours. Howlett smiled again, and reshuffled his papers. 'Something has come to light. Something we think you might be interested in.'

DS Costello did not respond by looking interested; in fact, she didn't respond at all. All he got was that same steady, slightly insolent stare.

'This job could be right up your street,' he persisted. 'A bit unusual, but it might just help with your rehabilitation, help you on your way back to work. But I do need your complete discretion, guaranteed. If you decide that you can't help us out, then I ask that anything said or seen in this room stays in this room.'

There was a nod, a slight rise of the bony shoulders. 'Of course.'

Howlett left the silence to itself as the door opened and Eilidh brought in a tray with hot coffee and water, and a plateful of chocolate biscuits. He watched as the grey eyes of the woman opposite him flickered at the noise of a car horn outside, then darted towards the fax machine as it beeped and whirred. She was wary, jumpy.

'So, to cut to the chase –'

'Good,' said DS Costello. A pale bony hand tugged the silk scarf a little further forward, but not before Howlett had seen the scar, still red and angry, in her hairline. She saw him look, and met his gaze with a bland expression.

Howlett lifted the coffee pot and poured himself a cupful, adding a little milk. He kept his eyes down, intent on not letting his hand shake.

'Are you familiar with Glen Fruin Academy?'

The grey eyes registered a little surprise. 'I know of it.'

'It's a delicate matter.'

'Yes?' she said. Her hand went up to the scar again, and he noticed the slight tremor. It almost made him warm to her.

'There might be some rather odd goings on up there and we want you to have a look round . . .'

'Can you be more specific?'

'I'd rather send you in with no preconceived ideas.'

'OK,' said Costello slowly. 'So, what crime has been committed?'

'Technically, none – as yet.'

'So, why is it a police matter? As opposed to a school matter, I mean.'

'That depends on what you find, doesn't it?' answered Howlett with a degree of charm. 'I know you will come up with something. I'm sure you can already guess what it is – young people, money not an issue, testing the boundaries and the pressures of life.'

'So, they have a drug problem up there?' she asked.

She noticed Howlett was careful not to answer. Something bigger than drug usage, then. Dealing?

'I want you to go and live in. It's nearly the end of term. In fact, they have an end of term garden party there on Sunday and we would like you to have everything cut and dried by then.'

'So, no pressure, then. Do I get any clues at all?'

Howlett smiled again, the charm still in place. 'Your cover is that you are a design expert. Don't worry, nobody will ask you anything technical, but you can watch the movements of people and photograph who you like. Nobody will think it odd, the school has been talking about expanding for ages. You can pretend to do a logistical study on the movement of pupils.'

Costello nodded. Drug dealing, it had to be. She could see their predicament, she bet they knew who was using but didn't know who was supplying. Always better to catch the organ grinders than the monkeys. With no official police involvement, any pupils with a problem could go off to a clinic to get clean with their record clear. Though why *she* was involved was beyond her, except for the fact that she was not officially operational yet.

Howlett was talking on, smoothly rolling his fountain pen between the palms of his hands. Costello had the feeling he had rehearsed the speech.

'The parents are the sort of people who would need very good evidence in place before the school could politely ask them to take their children away. Without that evidence they might take legal action, and we can't afford any mistakes. I think Strathclyde police have enough mistakes to deal with at the moment. The one thing we must avoid is the media getting a sniff of who is involved. At all costs the school's name must be kept out of it. And we don't want the local force involved at all, it's been cleared at the highest level. We know you will not let us down. But I want you to keep it as quiet as possible, and get back to me. And nobody but me.'

'So, I have four days?'

'Three. Plenty of time for a detective of your experience. You have tomorrow to prepare, maybe do some background reading. There are some books in that envelope. History of the place, et cetera. Mr Ellis, the Warden – the headmaster, if you like – and the security man, Pettigrew, will know who you are and why you are really there. With the naval base being at the other end of the glen, the rest of the staff are used to a bit of cloak-and-dagger stuff.'

Costello didn't comment.

'Just approach it as you would any covert operation. Watch everything but say nothing. You need to make your own way there for first thing Thursday morning. You'll have your own quarters. It's like a hotel, and the food is supposed to be excellent. Dress appropriately. Apart from that, you have free rein. Any questions?'

'Glen Fruin itself is a good half-hour by road from Glasgow, and no public transport goes anywhere up the single track that leads to the school itself. Whatever is going on must need some transport in and out.'

'In terms of technology and transport, the whole place is like something from the eighties,' Howlett told her. 'There's a new road that runs the length of the glen on the north side, and an old road, not much more than a track really, goes across the lower part of the valley. The whole place is really cut off, bad for TV reception, little mobile phone reception, Internet by cable only. But it's well thought of among the progressive parents of today, who are themselves children of the hippies of the sixties.'

The grey eyes regarded him steadily. 'You know what's going on, don't you?'

'I have my suspicions. Some evidence would be nice.'

Costello's hand went up to caress the arc of her cheek-bone. 'But apart from all that, I can do what I like?'

Howlett felt another twinge of doubt, but he said, 'Of course you can.'

2.20 p.m.

Half an hour in the sub-Saharan temperatures in the sta-tion was enough. Anderson was glad to get out into the fresh air, and then into his car which he had left parked in the shade.

'Why don't I drive, and you can fill me in on the way? My car has air conditioning and yours doesn't,' said Lambie.

'Yes, it does,' said Anderson. 'It's called opening the

window. Have you brought your printouts of the Biggart file with you?'

'It's all in here,' Lambie tapped the side of his head. 'I've been studying it all morning. Look, sir, I'm not going to tell you how to do your job, but do we know what we're doing? I mean, have we heard from upstairs or are you kind of acting DCI without portfolio, so to speak?'

'Without portfolio, without a desk, without a bloody clue. To be honest, Lambie, I'm just doing the best I can. With all this talk about LOCUST, I don't think anybody has their eye on the ball. But it worries me that we have a sadistic and forensically savvy fire-starter walking about with a grudge. And the one person who has not been interviewed at length is Mrs Melinda Biggart. That's the next logical step, and it's a box we will tick. I don't see my promotion being thrust upon me so I might just as well stay busy. What else can I do?'

'Exactly what you are doing – a DCI's job on a DI's wages.'

Heading south towards Newton Mearns, Lambie found himself having two simultaneous conversations – one about Biggart's history as a career criminal, and the other trying to navigate Anderson to Thorndene Park gated community in the Mearns, where Biggart had lived the good life among neighbours who would have spent their entire existence trying to avoid him.

'Did you see it? In his history, when you looked over it?'

'See what?' Anderson missed the subtlety of a mini-roundabout and drove the Jazz right over the top. 'Christ, this place is well hidden.'

'He has a funny history. I was wondering if he was just found out?'

Anderson thought for a minute. 'You'll have to fill me in. I didn't find him that fascinating. I thought he was just a pimp and a drug dealer who'd made it big.'

'I do believe the expression, in his own parlance, would be "he was a fart trying to be a shite, and failing". He used to be a small-time pimp, with a few girls on the street, and a small drug habit of his own to feed. He was beaten up a few times – twice by his own girls for short-changing them, and twice by his own wife.'

'The lovely Melinda.'

'Then, about eight years ago, everything changed. He seemed to go straight, with a legitimate business, ran a night club.'

'The Zoo.'

'An old pal of mine says it was investigated for having a brothel upstairs but I can't find any record of it. Then he moved to another, and his sexual tastes changed – for the younger. Everything he wanted, he seems to have been given.'

Anderson halted the Jazz at some temporary traffic lights. He'd got the drift. 'So, was somebody financing him? He was a small-time loser, so why would they? Why him? Did they get fed up backing him and decide he was surplus to requirements? He's been well protected over the years – and, whatever the reason, I'm not losing any sleep over it.'

2.25 p.m.

Rosie lay back on her pillow. The heat was sweltering, and the sweat was running in rivers down her face and body and soaking the mattress. She had no idea where Wullie had got to. He had set off for the funeral yesterday and hadn't come back. He had never done that before, so something must have happened. And she was panicking. Yet, she told herself, she had no need to panic. She had food, she had water, she had her sponge to do the toilet, and she had her notebooks and pencils to work – and as long as she could work, she was good. She had things to do. Things to work out.

But she wished Wullie would come back. He'd probably met old friends from the force at the funeral, gone out, got drunk and fallen asleep face down on somebody's couch. Or had he had a hypo and been admitted to hospital? She couldn't bear to think of him, at his age, falling over, people ignoring him, stepping over him and thinking he was drunk, that he was a nobody. Wullie wasn't a nobody. He was a great guy, the best.

She wished her laptop was within reach. The mobile phone was on the table, too far away, and that was no use anyway, there being no signal at the cottage. She just couldn't move to reach anything. Her body was a great anchor that kept her pinned to her bed. She had a jug of water and a lot of chocolate, which she was trying to ration while trying to think. The cottage was hidden high in the treeline on the north side of the glen, invisible to the horrible jumped-up brats at the school. It was equally hidden from the road that ran along the top of the glen, the only access being an overgrown path. In the winter, once the old oaks and elms had lost their leaves, you could just make it out if you knew where to look, sitting in a slight natural bowl high on the hill. But in the eight years they'd been here, nobody had ever found it by accident. And nobody was ever invited.

Rosie knew she had no way of letting anybody know she was here. So, she'd just have to wait for Wullie to come back, which he would – he always did, sooner or later. She reached for a new box of Quality Street and truffled about inside for the raspberry creams.

She lay and watched the clock move slowly round to half past. The warmest part of the day was over. She slipped the sponge in between her legs, working it between the heavy rolls of fat, and peed, tightening her pelvic floor to stop the flow, removing the sponge and wringing it out in the basin of water. Years of practice had perfected the technique. Back and forth, back and forth, until her bladder was emptied.

She was ignoring the dull tightness in her bowels.

2.55 p.m.

Costello climbed out of the taxi and adjusted her shoulder bag. The big envelope that Howlett had given her was just a couple of inches too big for it. She had torn it open the minute she had left his office, of course. It contained a plan of the school and grounds, a pamphlet written by some former pupils, and a copy of Simone Sangster's book, *Little Boy Lost*. Intrigued, she had flicked through it in the taxi, finding Glen Fruin was mentioned in the index with references that spanned about six pages. She closed the book, glad at the thought she wouldn't have to read the entire thing.

Partick Central reception was busy. Costello smelled

that familiar smell of floor cleaner, disinfectant and blocked toilets. The desk sergeant was dealing with a couple at the glass window and the discussion was moving from the persistent to the argumentative. The woman with the low voice was obviously from the 'if I repeat it enough, it will happen' school of thought. Pacing the floor with annoying squeaky shoes was a man in an oil-stained T-shirt who was looking daggers at the couple at the desk window, then at the desk sergeant, and then at his watch in quick succession. He flashed a look at Costello as she walked past him, then dismissed her as somebody of no value and continued his pacing. Costello bet that he was there to report a stolen vehicle.

The seating area was nearly full. A group of three young men sat together with a weary patience, and there was an older woman, dressed in a black coat far too warm for the day. She was gripping a plastic cup of water with trembling hands. Costello recognized her from the funeral; it was Mary Carruthers.

At that minute, there was a knock at the glass window. DCI MacKellar beckoned her over, pointing at Mary Carruthers while ignoring the man with the oil-stained hands.

'Whatever she wants, can you see to it? I really don't have time.'

'No,' said Costello sharply. 'I'm here to see Colin Anderson. Is he in?'

MacKellar pulled a face at her, turned round, then had a few words with the desk sergeant who looked at a computer screen. 'He's out. Just take her for a cup of tea. Just get her out of here.'

Costello sensed the anxiety of a man faced with a weeping OAP. 'I can't do that.'

'Look, she's greetin' all over the place,' MacKellar said out of the corner of his mouth.

Costello looked at him, saying nothing.

'DI Anderson will not be back till five or so.'

Costello held her ground.

'It'll be one I owe you.'

'You'll owe me big time.' Costello smiled at him. 'And I'll get that in writing when I return. She turned away, but not before she heard MacKellar swear and slam shut the glass partition.

At that precise moment the man with the oily hands lost the plot and started shouting, 'How long is this going to fuckin' take?' to the desk sergeant, who asked him to watch his language. He kicked the wall as two phones started ringing, muttering that the moon landings had taken less time.

The others in the queue told him to wait his turn, as a young man with tattooed bare arms got to his feet. The door at the far side of reception flew open, and two uniforms came out.

Costello judged it a good time to make herself scarce and slid into the seat next to Mrs Carruthers. 'It's Mary, isn't it?'

The red-rimmed eyes stared back at her, a flicker of recognition. 'You were at the funeral, weren't you, dear?' One clammy hand clasped Costello's. Her skin was smooth as silk. 'Did you know Tommy?' She screwed her face up as the altercation behind her became more aggressive and made it hard to hear.

'I think it's time to get out of here. I know a nice wee tea shop across the road, somewhere quiet?'

Mary looked confused. Costello noticed she had been holding a piece of paper in the palm of her hand all the time; it was wet with sweat, moulded and creased to the shape of the plastic cup. 'But I need to talk to somebody.' She tried to juggle the paper, her shopping bag and the cup, her hands still shaking.

Costello showed her her warrant card.

Mary's relief was obvious. 'Oh, thank God. She handed over the letter to Costello, who unpeeled it and gave it a quick read, flicking a glance at the photocopy underneath.

She whistled slowly. 'OK,' she said calmly. 'So, let's have a wee chat. But we'll go somewhere nicer.'

3.00 p.m.

Melinda Biggart – Mel to her friends and Melons to her close friends – buzzed them in when they rang at the front door and introduced themselves through the speakerphone. A voice sandpaper-thick with a forty-a-day habit breathed huskily for them to come round the back, then added how young the police were looking nowadays. Anderson didn't rise to the bait by looking for the camera; he just smiled at the speakerphone and made his way through an ornate wrought-iron gate and round to the back of the house. A small swimming pool came into view, with a large blonde sitting in the shallow end. Behind her were a phone and a slightly larger device. The remote entry, Anderson presumed.

'DI Anderson, DS Lambie,' she greeted them, her lips

barely breaking contact with the cigarette at her mouth. One taloned hand was holding a bright pink drink, and she swished the water around with her other arm. Two small triangles of bikini strained to restrain her surgically enhanced assets. 'You should come in and join me, it's lovely and cool in here.'

She smiled at Anderson as Lambie moved behind him, out of her line of fire, and he heard Lambie mutter, 'You're the one who's Acting DCI, sir.'

'Mrs Biggart, we're here about your husband.'

'Good. Has Niven MacKellar given up on me, then?'

'I'd like to ask you a few questions,' Anderson persisted. 'So, why don't you get out the pool, cover yourself up, and we'll have a little chat. We'll try not to trespass on your obvious grief.' Anderson made his way over to the table and chairs on the patio, sat down and glanced casually at the neighbouring houses, refusing to watch as she got out of the pool.

'Grief? Relief, mair like.' It was a different Melinda who walked, feet flapping in flip-flops, making wet question marks on the stones, then sat down, wrapped in a blue sarong, all graces gone.

'Where were you the night your husband died?' he asked.

'Here. I told DCI MacKellar the morning after.' Her eyes did not leave Anderson's for a single moment. 'Ah know ma man wis a bastard, but he didnae deserve that.'

'All the more reason why we should track down who did it. But he had a lot of enemies. You know about anybody who was noising him up recently?'

'There was a queue. But anybody – anybody normal – would just have shot him. Bang-bang, dead.'

'Instead of which . . . He didn't die a good death, Mrs Biggart.'

'He didnae live a good life either.'

'Looks kind of good from here,' said Lambie, looking around the huge back garden, the conservatory, the Porsche 911, and the eight-bedroomed house in a gated community at one of the smartest addresses in Glasgow. 'But you've no idea who might want to knock him from his perch?'

She shook her head. 'The thing is this – ma man didn't like women – or men, come to that – that had had too many.' She knocked back a mouthful of the pink drink. Anderson could smell rum. 'And by that I mean birthdays, not drinks. So, our marriage as such ended about three years after we were married. After that, I could please myself. And I did. Often.' Melinda lit another cigarette and blew the smoke out in a thin stream.

Anderson gazed past her to the pool. The bright diamonds of reflected light hurt his eyes. 'But did you have anybody special?' he asked softly.

She didn't answer immediately, but her eyes caught Anderson's, giving him a glimpse of the girl she had been once. Did he detect a fleeting wistful look? 'Aye, I had somebody special. Haven't seen him for a while.' She looked away. The next drink was a bit hurried. That conversation was over.

'So, again, where were you when Billy died?' asked Anderson.

'I was here. You can ask the gateman, James. Sorry, don't feel like saying much more. You know who my lawyer is.'

They said goodbye. Once they were safely out of the

house, Anderson drove the Jazz round the corner and parked immediately. 'Just let's wait till I get my breath back. God, what a cleavage.'

'You could feed the whole GDP of this country down there, in cash! Silicone, of course. If they look like the guns of the battleship *Potemkin* in firing position, they'll be silicone.'

'I'm not going to ask how you know that.' Anderson shook his head, trying to clear the image from his mind, slipped the car into gear and headed out towards the gate. The barrier rose as they approached, but Anderson pulled into the monoblocked space designated for those not yet allowed to escape. The gateman came out, wearing his commissionaire's cap in the presence of authority.

The DI got out of the car, thinking that the Jazz probably didn't quite cut the mustard in a place like this. Still, it showed the police were suffering cutbacks just like everybody else.

'James?'

'Yes, sir.' The security man didn't actually stand to attention but it was not far off.

Anderson heard Lambie get out of the car behind him. 'I'm sure you're aware, James, that some – well, one – of the residents here didn't come by their wealth via the most legal means possible.'

'Couldn't really say one way or the other, sir. Rumours and idle gossip.'

'But you get my general drift?'

'Oh yes, sir.'

'So, we're obviously investigating the death of Mr Biggart.'

'Mr Biggart, yes.' James's face filled with fear. 'Mr Biggart,' he repeated quietly.

'And I'm sure you want to stay well out of it. You have your job –'

'Yes, I do.' James's face relaxed with relief.

'So, off the record, James, how often did Billy come in and out with somebody else in the car? How often did he have visitors?'

James shook his head. 'Not often, sir, not often at all. He always drove his own car, sir, a Hummer, a dark grey Hummer.' He rattled off the registration number. The vehicle was six months old. 'Not one for bringing his work home, not him. Not even a lot of visitors . . .'

'And?'

James nodded, as if a thought had struck him. 'I mean, there weren't a lot of visitors when Mr Biggart was in.'

'Meaning his wife had more visitors when he was out?'

'Mrs Biggart had a few visitors . . . you know, women. A few women came and went . . .'

Anderson was aware of Lambie behind him, scuffing the ground with his toe. 'And what about men? Did Mrs Biggart entertain any male visitors when Mr Biggart was away? Anybody in particular?'

'Wouldn't want to put it like that, sir.'

'How would you like to put it, James? Not in writing down at the station, I'm sure?'

James answered immediately. 'Well, her usual callers – her flowers get delivered, her hairdresser, her personal trainer. A company sends cleaners – all male cleaners – laundry delivery. All men.'

'Anybody new? Very recent? Any man who might be visiting on a more . . . friendly basis?'

Anderson could see the cogs turning in James's mind. 'Well, there's that young one, sir, dark hair, very dark eyes, handsome – almost pretty, you might say.'

Very dark eyes. Anderson thought about Janet Appleby's statement. Could the same man be a visitor to both the Biggarts? 'And you'd recognize him again?'

'Oh yes, I could. He drives a BMW Z3.' James rattled off another reg.

Lambie got his notebook out and scribbled it down. 'You didn't catch a name?'

'No, but he was pleasant, polite, a well-spoken young man. Always stopped and had a word.'

'Did he ever mention why he was here?'

'No, don't think so.'

'One more thing, do you have a phone here?'

'Yes.' James gave them the number, and Lambie wrote it all down.

'Thanks, James, we'll try not to bother you again.'

Anderson pulled the Jazz to a halt at the traffic lights and let his fingertips drum on the steering wheel.

'Did we learn anything from any of that?' Lambie enquired.

Anderson quoted, '"I had somebody special. Haven't seen him for a while." Her exact words. There's something going on there. Either somebody decided to take out Mr and Mrs Biggart in a two-for-one offer, or maybe Mrs Biggart was a bit fed up being second best? Wouldn't be the first gangster's wife to sleep with A. N. Other and decide to take over the company.'

'And decide to hire a hit man? I might go for that. But nobody hires an arsonist for a hit man, they just do insurance work.'

Anderson said, 'True, they'd just shoot him and put him somewhere we wouldn't find him. Like a flyover support on the M74.'

'I'll just phone those reg numbers through, see what the DVLA say.' Lambie spoke on the phone for a few minutes, then announced to Anderson, 'That BMW reg belongs to a Vauxhall Corsa.'

'Do you think James got it wrong?'

'He didn't get the other number wrong, did he? Curiouser and curiouser,' said Anderson, pulling on to the main road. 'And who'd have enough savvy to get a Z3 with a false plate? Gangster's moll, I bet!'

4.45 p.m.

Back at the station and bagged down with two mugs of strong tea, Costello was starting to feel vaguely sick. And more than a little confused. She had walked into the reception, now a haven of peace. The desk sergeant had nodded at her and then gone back to his screen; a uniform cop gave her a passing glance as he left, then automatically held the door open for her and, equally automatically, she had taken it from him, said thanks and walked through into the station proper. No questions asked. She headed for the stairs, nobody gave her a second glance, up to the CID suite. She looked through the glass panel in the door to see Mulholland flicking through a file in his lazy way, peeling the skin from an orange as if his fingers were getting tired. Wyngate, she noticed with a sudden flurry of affection, was sitting over a keyboard, battering away and pulling faces at whatever was not going right on the screen. Some things never changed.

Behind her she heard the door of the major incident room click open. She quickly bent her head, as if reading the letter. A female plain clothes cop came out and held the door open for her. Head still head bent in concentration, Costello took the door, muttering thank you. She walked in as if she had a right to be there. Two of the cops sitting working said hello to her, she said hello back and strode over to the photocopier. She opened out the letter and the already photocopied bank statement, placed her hand flat on the paper, smoothing it out, then held the lid down as the flash moved slowly from left to right and back again. She looked around the wall, seeing the pictures of a girl's face. A dead girl's face. In profile, then face on, a case number underneath in black marker pen. Next to them was a strangely proportioned photograph from the river, taken from the middle of the river, looking at the north bank. A street plan with that section highlighted, the CCTV picture of a white Transit van with a cross through its number plate. The number plate arrowed, reassigned to a tractor.

Costello took out the letter and replaced it with the bank statement, not daring to look round and see if anybody was paying her any attention. She nonchalantly placed her hand on her hip and pressed the button for four copies, just to take up more time. Her eyes scanned around, taking in smaller papers, files, the address, phone number and a contact name for the Russian Consulate in Melville Street in Edinburgh. On a desk, stuck to a monitor, were the photographs of two other girls, the same age. Dead. In the photographs they were badly bruised and distorted, covered in leaves and dirt, as if they had been left somewhere, exposed. She pulled the statement from the photocopier and her phone from her pocket as she turned to leave. She was on the phone to Central Records before the door had closed behind her.

She was feeling more alive than she had felt in ages.

It was time she got back to work.

5.00 p.m.

Back at Partick Central, Mulholland was still sitting flicking through a file, pulling out photographs of any known associates of Billy the Bastard Biggart, and trying to get rid of the smell of orange peel from his fingers. Wyngate was sitting hunched over a computer keyboard, his eyes inches from the screen. Anderson came in and looked from Wyngate to Mulholland, eyebrows raised.

'Who knows what he's doing? He's quiet, which means he's happy.'

Anderson made himself comfortable, checking through the paperwork on his desk. He had also asked O'Hare to supply him with the photographs of the other two girls, the ones who had been found dead, dumped miles from anywhere but they didn't seem to have appeared on his desk yet.

Anderson was still wondering if the 'cute guy' that

Janet had noticed in the hallway of Biggart's flat and James's 'pretty' young man might be the same person – a young gay man who was attractive to men and woman, cultured, educated. 'Good teeth' he added, automatically thinking about the Bridge Boy. Coincidence? Yes, but looking at the bigger picture – the violence, the association with Biggart – it fitted. He just couldn't see exactly how. Maybe Biggart had been charmed. There were rumours that Biggart was susceptible to pretty young men, among other things. But who was this young man? Anderson needed the IT guys to produce an image of the Bridge Boy's face before somebody had stamped on it. He needed that image to be put in front of James and Janet. That photo had to go to all the petrol stations along the train route. It wasn't usual for people to fill a container of petrol, and good-looking people got noticed.

Anderson felt a warm breath on the back of his neck. 'You've been looking at Wyngate for a long time. Do you fancy him?'

It could only be one person.

'DS Costello, as I live and breathe. How the hell are you?' He got up and hugged her, noticing how bony her shoulders felt under her jacket. Then he stepped back to look at her. It was Costello all right, but not the same Costello. He couldn't stop his eyes flicking up to the silk scarf, knowing what it hid, and scanning the slight indentation on one cheekbone. She was regarding him with a challenging look.

Mulholland and Wyngate both started to get up to greet her. She stopped them with a stare, so they just said hello and went back to their work.

'So, what are you doing here?' Anderson asked quietly, stepping aside and giving her his seat. He noticed that she just nodded and sat down; there was no unsubtle scan of the files on his desk, no fiddling with his stapler in a slightly threatening way, no overt or even covert nosiness at all. No, this wasn't the old Costello at all.

She clasped her hands in front of her, and placed them in her lap, a gesture that suggested she was trying to behave herself. 'It's amazing how I can get access to anywhere I want now. I just walk up to a door and the next person who comes out lets me in, two sets of security doors no problem at all. I bet I got in quicker than you ever do.'

She seemed genuinely surprised, and he didn't want to tell her that she had a certain degree of notoriety. Her face was now well known to every police officer in Strathclyde. She had their sympathy too, but he was even less keen to tell her that.

'You look as though you've been somewhere important,' he said. 'Has somebody died? The suit, I thought the funeral was yesterday –'

'Yeah, I'll talk to you about that in a minute. But you'll never guess where I've been.'

Anderson was immediately on edge. 'Were you called into Pitt Street? Have you been summoned for the Fairbairn review? Have they started already?'

'Nothing like that.' She was totally dismissive. 'But it was ACC Howlett.'

'Oh.' Anderson leaned forward over the desk. 'You haven't been asked to leave, have you?'

'Not yet. I don't really know whether it's a promotion, a test, or a slap in the face.' Then her voice drifted off somewhere else. 'What are you doing? Did you get the case of the girl in the river?'

'No,' came the terse answer

'They are getting nowhere fast with it next door. They are on the trail of a white Transit with false plates. Three girls, rather than one?' Her voice raised in a question.

Both Mulholland and Wyngate looked up. 'Dorothy Elm said it was a white Transit. Shit! I'm sure all this is linked somehow, in some way.'

Then Mulholland said, 'And how do you know that? You're on sick leave.'

Costello directed her answer to Anderson. 'I was snooping around next door and they are on to the Russian Consulate, but it doesn't look like they are getting anywhere. Why not ask MacKellar to work the cases together? Then you'll know if there is a link.'

'Fat chance. I'm not supposed to know what's going on next door, am I?'

'Oh, if he gives you any hassle, refer him to me – he owes me a big favour,' she went on rather airily and Anderson was reminded of why she was so annoying. 'So, you working on Biggart, then?' She turned to look at the photo of the old Apollo building. 'Did he do the world a favour, get suitably pissed, and fall asleep with a fag and torch the duvet?'

Anderson didn't dare tell her it was none of her business any more, so he ignored the question. 'No matter what ACC Howlett said, I'm sure you're not supposed to be here, having this conversation or snooping around this investigation.' Then he found himself looking at the flat-voiced woman in her neat suit, but thinking about the old acid-tongued Costello, and decided he owed her a little more consideration. He said quietly, 'Biggart wasn't quite the typical burn-yourself-to-death job. Somebody else did it for him. I'm running it, under MacKellar's watchful eye.'

'Well, at the end of the day, he is your boss.'

'I would rather you were shocked that I am not running this investigation as DCI. Then it would all be one big enquiry.'

There was no response. Costello just kept looking at the photographs.

He tried another tack. 'So, what brings you round here? Not that we're not pleased to see you . . .'

'I was forced to come in and see you as your phone is always off these days.'

'Just when I was in the morgue, that's all. Then I was . . . elsewhere.'

She picked up his stapler and began to fiddle with it.

'Well, OK, you actually only phoned once, but I was a bit busy at the time,' he expanded. 'I was hardly ignoring you.'

But in the old days he would have returned her call ASAP, and both of them knew it.

'So, Biggart was toasted rather than toasting himself?' she said, her eyes skimming over his desk.

'Yes. And you are not a serving police officer here, DS Costello, and you know –'

But she wasn't paying any attention. 'I'm back in harness, sort of.' She clicked the stapler closed, as if testing a firing pin. 'Here you are, doing all this, and what do I get? I get to stop a bit of mischief among the over-privileged wankers at Glen Fruin Academy.'

'No?' said Anderson, drawing out the vowel in disbelief. 'Well, that's good. I mean, it's a high-profile job. Prime ministers' children, offspring of rock stars. Absolute discretion called for.' He tried to keep the sarcasm from his voice. If anybody was badly suited for that job . . .

'You mean, why the hell did they ask me?'

'Just accept that they've given you something to do, something to get you back in the saddle. Sounds like you've been trusted with something important. More than I can say about me.'

'Bullshit.' The stapler thumped down. 'It means they think I'm not fit for real work. It means they wouldn't trust me with anything like this.' She tapped the photocopies of Mary Carruthers' letter.

'And what's that,' muttered Anderson.

'The grieving widow had a chat with her solicitor this morning, seems Tommy Carruthers had money in the bank. Untouched. Twenty grand.'

'Really.'

'I've just spent over an hour with her telling me why she doesn't think he killed himself – quite simply, she says he had no reason to. And I believe her. And now this. The solicitor is on to it, Colin. It needs to be looked at.'

'Why, are you involved in this? In any way?'

He recoiled involuntarily as she lurched across the desk. 'A cop who nobody says a bad word against? A good Catholic? He flings himself out the window the minute his wife's back is turned. Looks like a good cop? Or a bent cop? Twenty grand. That must be enough to raise a few questions.'

'The fiscal was satisfied. I think I have enough to do.'

'And the solicitor will pursue it; better you get in first.'

'And what do you want me to do? Hold a séance and ask him if he jumped, or was he pushed?'

'No, just review the file and the fiscal's case notes. It was very quick, they couldn't have done a halfway decent job.'

'You really want me to piss everybody off? I'm not exactly Mr Popular round here.'

'So, you have nothing to lose really. Think of it as a small error by an overworked young fiscal. That's how I might have phrased it, me being the tactful one.' She gave him that look of total resolution.

'Look, I'll send Lambie out to have a word, before I agree to anything. When are you buggering off to Glen Fruin?' he asked, hoping it would be soon.

'I've to arrive there tomorrow night.'

He took the stapler off her. 'Would you like me to run you out there? I don't imagine it's an easy place to get to without a car.'

She smiled. 'Yeah, I'd like that. They said they'd send a car. But I'd rather go there with you. We could have a bit of a chinwag on the way and see what progress you have made with Carruthers. How long will it take? About forty minutes, something like that?'

'Straight run to Duck Bay, then forever on a single-track road,' he told her. 'It's right up the glen, halfway between Loch Lomond and Loch Long. But don't worry, I have all evening.'

'Good.' She turned and looked at him directly.

Anderson realized it was the first time he had noticed that familiar determination in her face.

'Did I read in the paper that Helena Farrell McAlpine, or

whatever she calls herself, is now engaged to that idiot with the ponytail? Gilfillan, her so-called business partner?'

'I believe so,' said Anderson guardedly, relishing the familiar feeling that he would gladly smack her in the face. Costello could annoy him in a way that even Brenda, after eighteen years of marriage, could never hope to aspire to.

He expected her to pursue the matter with the bait of some seemingly innocent throwaway line, but all she said was, 'Thanks for the offer of the lift. I'll phone you later. And don't bother to order the paperwork on Carruthers, I've already ordered the reports from the fiscal's office and complete case notes from Central. I did it in your name, should be downstairs with you ASAP.'

Anderson was aware of his fingers tightening to form a fist, but she was gone, sliding out of the door like a ghost late for a haunting.

5.05 p.m.

Skelpie Fairbairn had been out for exactly fourteen days, three hours and twelve minutes. He'd thought it was boring on the inside, but now, sitting on the wall, watching the cars go past, he was mega-bored. Being bored when there was nothing to do was one thing, but being bored when everybody around him was having fun, that really was being bored. He'd watched all his DVDs over and over, and there were no more where they'd come from. So he'd come out on to the street.

It was hot, but he daren't hang around in the park. He didn't want somebody reporting him for looking at the young girls running around. Folk were paranoid nowadays; someone might challenge him, they might even call the cops. He'd every right to walk through the park, his lawyer had said, all the rights of a free man. But he hadn't really. If they knew where to look for him, they could find him.

His lawyer was sure the appeal would be successful. Then it would be time to move on, time to disappear back to the people who thought the way he thought. But with Biggart gone, he had to endure the wait until somebody contacted him with the codeword. And he was confident that they would. He pulled the copy of the *Daily Record* from his pocket and flicked through it. The centre spread was a full-colour picture of Alessandro Marchetti as he had been then, in 1996. Next to it, in a slightly overlapping box, was an artificially aged photograph of the way he might look now as a young man of twenty. There was only one mention of the babysitter, Tito Piacini.

Fairbairn smiled and folded the paper, then stuck it back into his pocket. He pulled out his lighter and his pack of Marlboros, and flipped the lighter from the back of his hand, catching it and striking the flame simultaneously. That had taken practice to perfect. He crossed the road when the green man flashed, and began to walk.

He had no real idea where he was going, but he was on his way.

5.40 p.m.

Somehow Costello felt justified in spending money now that she was earning it again. She had got a taxi up to

Sauchiehall Street, pleased with her day so far; she felt she was getting back into her life. The first thing she wanted was sunglasses, good sunglasses. She didn't care how big and dark they were as long as they kept the sun away from her left eye, which was still very sensitive. She picked out a lightweight grey suit, and a few collarless white linen blouses, the sort of thing she imagined an architect's assistant would wear. Then, in M&S, she went a bit mad and started to fling in all kinds of underwear and jewellery; it was such a long time since she had been out, she felt like a kid in a candy store. Afterwards, she went to ground in a corner of the in-store café and looked over her loot.

What else might she need?

She had a notebook, a good pen, she'd bought smart pyjamas, and a pair of black fleecy trousers and a jumper for kicking around in. After finishing her tea, she bought a frock – she didn't possess one – and thought she might as well treat herself to some new black court shoes, just in case. Her credit card would be in intensive care but it needed a bit of a workout every now and again. She crossed the street as she came out of M&S, intending to go to the shoe shop on the corner, but she was irresistibly drawn to Waterstone's four-storey bookshop. She went to the back of the shop where she knew there was a Scottish history section. She had a quick mooch through Mountaineering and Hillwalking, but there was nothing about Glen Fruin. She surmised neither the naval base nor the school would encourage random hillwalkers and the security difficulties they might bring. She found History. The Scots were very fond of the romantic idea of their own history, the glens running red with the spilled blood of noble clansmen defending their beloved homeland against the marauding English. But the battle of Glen Fruin was much more typical – two clans having a square go because one had killed and eaten some sheep belonging to the other. The book had a small chapter on Glen Fruin Academy, with photographs of the grand house sitting halfway up the hill, looking out across the river that snaked its way along the glen.

Money, Costello thought. It took money to build a fine house like a castle with a spectacular view, and money to send your child to be educated there. She'd have to keep her gob – mouth, she corrected herself – firmly shut. She picked up a few more books, including one that had a full chapter on the naval base at the other end of the glen. Just looking at it sent shivers down her spine. With the beautiful mountains behind, the huge submarine basking in the loch looked like a James Bond film set, the evil lair of Dr Death. She wondered what that meant for the kids at the Academy. Then she realized it made perfect sense. The school being so isolated, and with massive security at the top end of the glen, helped reduce the risk of the billionaires' brats being kidnapped.

Near the till she saw a huge display of *Little Boy Lost*, piles of autographed copies, and the smug face of Simone Sangster smiling out at her. Costello accidentally knocked it flat on her way past.

*

Mrs Carruthers had been trying to keep her sister in her flat, but Rene, complete with turquoise eye shadow and bobble hat, was determined to go out. They were both behind the front door when Lambie rang the bell, setting off a metallic screech of 'For These Are My Mountains'.

'Oh, that's fine,' Mary said, relieved at Lambie's request for a quick word. She slipped her heavy black coat from her shoulders and placed it back on the coat stand in the hall, asking him if he was a friend of that nice wee lassie and having a good look at his warrant card.

Lambie suppressed a smirk at Costello being described as such and took his own assessment of Mary Carruthers. She still had the look of a widow on the day after the funeral. She was a big woman, grey-haired, dressed in a long-sleeved jumper with a green pinafore over the top. She smiled at Lambie nervously; she had bad teeth and a slight growth of grey hair sprouting from her chin. She indicated that he should go through into the living room while she escaped to the sanctuary of the kitchen. Rene, the smaller sister, was hovering; Lambie said hello. She smiled back with manic enthusiasm, and Lambie judged her to be a good ten years older than her sister. She was carrying a photo frame around with her, tucked under her arm, against the folds of her cardigan, as if it was a precious thing. She scuttled off, following her sister into the kitchen.

The living room was beige, the hall was beige, the whole flat was beige, unbelievably beige, and Lambie thanked God he was marrying a woman whose idea of interior decor ran no further than white emulsion.

Left alone, Lambie took his chance to have a look at the window. It was about six feet wide and four feet high. The old safety catch had been replaced with a brand-new one. He ran his fingers over the newly painted wood, feeling the gouges. Somebody had been in a hurry to remove the old catch. The sill was at the level of his hip, so it wouldn't have been exactly easy to climb out. But it would have been very easy just to upend somebody and turf them out. And it would have been quick. Nobody had seen anything, Carruthers had not cried out, and the sole eyewitness said they'd only looked up to see the open window after the body hit the ground. Lambie regarded the width, and imagined a man in his sixties trying to climb out of the window and then pausing to compose himself before the final jump. He'd have to place his hands on the frame, there would be handprints on the gloss paint. And no such fingerprints had been found.

Lambie had been to a few suicide scenes – and a few that had been considered suicide before being ruled as unfortunate accidents – but this didn't seem right at all.

He heard the doorbell, the tuneless chime again, followed by the soft shuffle of shoes on the thick carpet and Rene chattering about there being somebody at the door without going to open it. For something to do, he picked up a photograph that stood on a pile of red and blue notebooks – diaries, he supposed – on the sideboard. It looked like Mary and Thomas on their wedding day. More photos – Mary and Rene on the beach in Benidorm, a much-younger Tommy on the top of a mountain – were littered across the top of the piano.

The bride, forty years on, appeared carrying a tray laden with cups and scones. Her eyes darted from him to the door. 'Oh, I need to get that. Can you pull out the stool from under the piano? You can just close the top down.'

Lambie replaced the picture, and closed the top of the piano stool, but not before he had noticed the older, battered diaries piled in the wooden well of it. Somebody was having a clear-out.

'It'll be Father McCabe; mustn't keep him waiting. Do you think you can do anything about the money? Can you find out where it came from?'

Lambie knew he had seen enough to warrant a close look at the file, so he got to his feet. 'I'll have a wee look around for you, but don't you worry. I'll leave you and the Father to it.'

6.30 p.m.

The girl from IT had been good, better than good. She had enhanced a shot taken from the CCTV camera at the railway embankment next to the Apollo flats. The face that stared back at Anderson from the high-spec version could be both James's 'pretty' young man and Janet's 'cute guy'. With his slightly curly shoulder-length hair, his big brown eyes, he could easily be termed a hottie. 'Wyngate, get on the phone to the security guy on the gate at Thorndene Park. Email him that image of the boy's face, and ask him if he recognizes him, and if he has a name. Then tell him to delete it and say nothing to anybody. His number's in the file. Mulholland, do the same with Janet. Text it, email it, just get it to her no matter where she is on the face of the planet.'

Anderson placed that picture upright on his desk and looked at the scene photograph of the Bridge Boy, pinned on the evidence board. Behind all the swelling and blood it could have been anybody – Lord Lucan, even – but for that telltale tear in the cartilage of his ear where his earring had been. Dr Redman had called back from the hospital saying that, to his totally untutored eye, the ear in the photograph was a 'probable' match for the ear on the boy but he couldn't be pushed to a 'positive'. Anderson had asked if it was OK to put somebody on duty to protect the boy. Somebody had already tried to take him out once, and would probably try again. He asked if a photographer could go in now, and take a picture of the boy's face. Then they could superimpose it on the CCTV image and tinker with it to see if there was a match between the bone structure.

Redman had snorted.

'It's a technique used for juries,' Anderson explained. 'They don't like looking at the battered faces of little old ladies, so the photographers retard the image to before the assault, airbrush out the swelling, bleeding and broken teeth, then put them in again using nice clean graphics. It sanitizes the violence.'

'But to do that you do need some bones in the face unbroken.' And Redman had rung off, leaving Anderson staring at the phone.

Lambie came in, talking on his mobile about getting measured for a kilt. Anderson glared at him. Lambie caught the look and said a quick goodbye.

'Sorry, sir. Jennifer's worried that I'm putting on too much weight.'

'You are. How did you get on?'

'I'm feeling more uneasy about it. I want to look through the files for pictures of the window frame at the time.'

'Of course.'

'I didn't really have a chat with Mary and her sister, as the priest arrived just after I did and I made myself scarce.' He shrugged slightly. 'It looks like Tommy kept diaries going back years. So, if he was a man who recorded every innermost thought then that is the place to look. I'll chip away at getting a glance at them.'

Anderson handed Lambie the blown-up picture of the Bridge Boy. Lambie took it just as Wyngate, still on the phone, gave them a thumbs-up. The security man had recognized him right away.

'Get a full description if you can. Well spoken, he said. But any idea of height? Anything he said in conversation?'

Wyngate looked flustered, so Lambie took the phone from him. 'Hello, James? DS Lambie here. We met earlier . . .'

Anderson scribbled him a note to ask about a white Transit van, then left him to it. He walked over to the wall and moved Melinda Biggart's name from the bottom of the list to the top.

Anderson was wondering who to send round to interview Melinda, and wished Costello was back on the squad. Neither was a woman easily intimidated. Better to apply to the sheriff for a warrant and do a search of all the Biggarts' bank records, then question her about the boy. First thing was to find out who he was, where he came from, and how he was involved. Maybe Melinda was indeed thinking about taking over her husband's empire. Anderson wouldn't put it past the woman to hire a young lover to take out her husband.

So, if the boy had been set up to take out Biggart, had he left a trail of some kind? Had some Mr X, on a mission to find out who had killed Biggart, been surprised it was a young boy and ordered him tortured to find out who was behind it? Anderson went back to his desk and sat down and thought about the boy's injuries. Nobody could have stayed silent under such torture; even the strongest would have succumbed eventually. He himself wouldn't have lasted two minutes, and the boy on the bridge had lasted longer than that. Much, much longer. Maybe he had held out to the very end, after all.

He swung round in his chair and ran his hands through his hair. 'Have we got the CCTV from the bridge yet? I did ask . . .' His eyes scanned the room.

'Er, what do you think I've been working on for the last two hours?' asked Wyngate, trying not to sound aggrieved.

'Sorry, Wyngate. You got anything?'

Wyngate pressed Print. 'Best so far is this.'

Mulholland, who was nearest the printer, pulled out the sheet of A4 and looked closely at it before handing it to Anderson. The angle made it impossible to see much – the van door, and a male passenger in a white T-shirt and dark glasses, his forearm leaning on the window, the impression of a tight bracelet round his left wrist. There was no clear view of the driver.

'What time was this? Four in the morning? I know the nights are light but they don't need bloody sunglasses!

Trace it up and down the street, will you, Wyngate, see if you can see the plate?'

Wyngate rolled his eyes.

'Sorry, of course you've already checked that. Sorry,' Anderson said again.

'Janet said something about one of Biggart's visitors having a scarred eye – "a funny eye, with a white bit across the iris, as though he'd damaged it". That might explain the shades,' said Mulholland. 'And that he had a tattoo there, on his left wrist.'

Lambie hung up the phone, and it immediately rang again. 'Yes, James's description matches that picture, and he nearly pissed himself laughing when I asked about a white Transit van – ten a penny.' Then he said very politely into the phone, 'DS Lambie, how can I help you?' He pulled a face, and handed the phone to Anderson.

'Yes,' Anderson said. Then he looked at the clock and again said, 'Yes.' He smoothed down his tie, as though whoever was on the phone was important. 'Pitt Street? Yes, I can make Pitt Street if that suits you. Tomorrow at half eight then, sir.' He put the phone down. 'Bloody hell! That was ACC Howlett.'

'Bloody hell, indeed,' Lambie agreed. 'Does he want to see you about Fairbairn?'

Anderson shook his head nervously but said, 'I doubt it. Do you think lightning ever strikes twice?'

'Might be your promotion. What about this LOCUST thing? That's Howlett's initiative, isn't it?' said Lambie, allowing the upward inflection to ask a question.

'Hardly, judging by the way MacKellar is acting. Surely he'd be told first.'

'You'd think so.'

Anderson didn't even want to think about it. He could hardly dare to hope.

Instead, he reached for the original CCTV still. He sat back and examined the lower half of the picture. T-shirt, an expanse of flat stomach, low-slung jeans, and a set of keys clipped to the belt. The iPod was in the boy's front pocket, his left hand slightly covering it. The right hand had reached round to steady the rucksack.

'Wyngate? Can you get a close-up of those keys? Make that image a bit clearer? They might match the keys we have for the flats.' Wyngate's fingers ceased their rapid tapping over the keyboard, clicked on the mouse, dragged, then another click, and an image of the key ring almost filled the screen. A curtain of pixel activity descended the screen, as if cleaning it from top to bottom, leaving a crystal-clear image behind.

'Sometimes, Wyngate, I understand why you were put on this planet,' said Anderson, giving his constable a pat on the back. He leaned over Wyngate's shoulder, looking at the screen. 'Now what is that, there?' he asked carefully. 'Mulholland, come over here. Can you make out what that is, hanging from his belt? It looks like a knife, one of those pointy things martial arts people use, those things they throw about in kung fu.'

'The thing that looks like a can opener? It's a key ring for the BMW Z3, in the shape of a Z,' Mulholland said loftily.

'And so we have him: the cute guy, the Bridge Boy, the pretty one and the arsonist?' Anderson peered at the image. 'But who the hell is he?'

Anderson was sitting in the garden, having enjoyed a rare picnic of fajitas and salad with Brenda and the kids. He was now sipping a beer and looking at the sky, wondering when the weather would break and trying to gather his thoughts on what had been a long, hot and eventful day. DCI Niven MacKellar had some kind of hold over his career, and there was no trust between them – none at all. He wondered if the River Girl being Russian made MacKellar think she could be a stepping stone to a squad like LOCUST. Even in death that wee lassie was being used, and it left a bitter taste in his mouth. He was glad that his ruminations on the day were constantly interrupted by Nesbitt dropping a stinky half-chewed tennis ball into his lap, waiting for it to be thrown so he could scamper down the lawn on his three matching legs and the other one, skid past the ball and then return, good ear up, bad ear down, with his prize. Then he would drop the slaver-wet ball, ready for the game to start again. He was starting to wear out the lawn.

'Are you worried about it, this Fairbairn thing?' Brenda asked, turning over the page in the newspaper she was reading. Her voice was low so that Peter and Claire, each sitting on the grass with a Nintendo DS, didn't hear.

'Not worried as in I did something wrong and I'll get found out.'

'But you are worried about it, Colin? What could they do to you?'

'Well, nothing that the federation wouldn't fight, but it would be a question mark over my career. The end of any hopes of promotion, I suppose.' He rubbed the back of her hand, 'But no need to worry until we have something to worry about, eh?'

'How long will it be hanging over us?'

'More than a year.'

Brenda frowned. 'So, why do you think this Howlett wants to see you tomorrow?'

'I don't know.' He thought about it. 'But Costello came back to work today.'

'Did she? I thought she wasn't fit.'

'She's not. She's signed off to be operationally fit but she's been given an "observational role" I suppose you'd call it. She'll be good at that. She's very nosey. She was a bit reckless, though.'

'No change there, then.'

'Maybe I've just forgotten what she was like.'

Brenda licked her finger with the tip of her tongue and flicked another page over. 'Colin, you really didn't do anything to get that guy off the streets, did you? I mean, with the best of intentions.'

'No, I didn't,' he answered quietly.

'Did McAlpine? Could he have done something that will get pinned on you?'

Anderson was searching for an answer that sounded honest and was glad when his phone rang.

8.20 p.m.

Melinda Biggart was floating face down in the swimming pool, blonde hair undulating gently. As soon as the cloud of red around her dissipated, a movement in the water produced another release of stronger red. Her arms were tied behind her back, the red-taloned nails pointing upwards like a sea anemone, the fingers blue and wrinkled. Around the wrists was a white plastic tie, which cut deep into the flesh.

'I think we can drop the theory that she was hell-bent on taking over Biggart's empire,' Anderson said, not looking. 'I mean, she clearly didn't drown. Who found her?'

'The guy on the gate called it in,' O'Hare answered. 'He said you were here talking to him earlier. He just wanted to check she was OK before the end of his shift. He says he didn't see anything or let anybody through the gate, but provisionally I'd say whoever killed her was here within minutes of you two leaving. She was actually killed in the kitchen, but you don't want to go in there – it looks like a bloodbath.'

'OK, do you want to pull her to the side, get her out?' Six hours – it had been barely six hours since he and Lambie had visited her, but now the tranquil pool area with the mosaic tiles resembled a scene from a Hammer Horror film.

How had her killer gained access to the house? For the second time, Anderson cast his eyes around the neighbouring houses, the walled garden. If James on the gate had not let anybody through, that meant somebody had found another way in. The back of the house wasn't overlooked, so it would have been an easy kill. A SOCO was skimming the garden wall with a gloved hand, assessing whether it might yield any interesting samples. But Anderson knew he was unlikely to find anything. These people were good. Professional. Quick in, quick out, like the SAS. He shivered. Organized crime again: teamwork, quick, efficient, planned.

Melinda was being gently lifted in a cradle from the pool on to a plastic sheet. O'Hare turned her over carefully; as he did so, the body opened up like an accordion, the ribs spreading freely and the massive breasts lolling grotesquely. Melinda's eyes, black-ringed like a panda's, gazed unseeing at the sun, her make-up and lipstick smeared into an obscene mask. Her heart and lungs, drained of blood, were a soft grey-pink colour.

'Sweet suffering Christ!' Anderson was appalled. 'What's been done to her?'

O'Hare's face remained impassive as he probed the ribcage with a gloved finger. 'It's been skilfully done,' he said reflectively. 'Do you see how she was cut open with one very assured stroke? Then her killer, or killers, disarticulated the costochondral joints the length of the sternum, right up to the manubrium. Even the xyphoid process –'

'In words I can understand, Prof!' Anderson was trying to look anywhere but at the horror that had been Melinda Biggart.

'Sorry, Colin. Her ribs have been neatly snapped away from the breastbone. They did it carefully; none of the ribs has actually been broken. Contrary to what most people imagine, the ribs and the breastbone are not a single unit of bone. Everything's connected by cartilage. And it doesn't just involve skill. Human cartilage is tough stuff; this would have taken considerable strength as well as manual dexterity.'

'Would you say they'd done it before?'

'Undoubtedly. And often,' the pathologist said gravely. 'This would have taken plenty of practice to perfect.'

'And . . .' Anderson could hardly bring himself to ask the question, not wanting to hear the answer. 'Do you think she was . . . ?'

'Alive? Judging by the amount of blood in the kitchen, I fear so,' said O'Hare, deep in thought. 'But I doubt for very long.' He paused. 'Colin, leave it with me but it reminds me of something. I'll phone you, just leave it to me.'

'Thanks.' Anderson made his way carefully round the poolside, his hand covering his mouth, his feet slipping inside the shoe covers. He walked through the huge conservatory into the state-of-the-art kitchen. The black marble worktops and white floor were indeed thickly spattered with blood. He said hello to a uniformed constable who was watching the photographer.

'Handbag?' asked Anderson.

'Over there,' said a SOCO. 'I've got the phone already. But the place has already been searched, by somebody other than us. Purse is still here.'

'Any idea what's missing?'

'Nothing, as far as I can see. There's a safe upstairs, untouched.'

'Keep me posted.' Anderson pulled on gloves and opened the handbag. He took out the purse, and flicked through an astonishing quantity of gold credit cards. He looked swiftly through a diary with a few appointments scribbled in large handwriting, and finally fished out an electronic personal organizer. He looked at it vaguely, and the SOCO pointed, showing him how to switch it on. It requested a password.

'How long to crack a password on these things?' he asked.

'Five minutes. Try her name, his name, mother's maiden name, pet's name.'

Anderson typed in a few variations, the screen lighting up when he tapped in MELONS. It flashed on to a picture of a handsome young man, leaning on the bonnet of a BMW Z3. Anderson noticed a small stud earring halfway up his left ear.

'Hello, pretty boy,' he said.

9.30 p.m.

'Do you know why I wanted to see you?' asked DCI MacKellar, his heavy gold bracelet rattling as he sat down at his very tidy desk.

'I'm more concerned about the timing of it, sir. It's getting late, I've been run ragged in the last forty-eight hours,' Anderson said smoothly. 'I think my time could have been better spent at the scene.'

DCI MacKellar took no notice. 'Any progress with Biggart?'

Anderson was careful in his response. 'I've just got an email from O'Hare. We asked him to have a look at Biggart's skin. As well as an indistinct tattoo on the biceps, he found a thickening of the skin round his ankles and wrists, indicating mild restraint over a period of years. It's already been suggested that it's not difficult to tie somebody up if they are into bondage where there is a degree of trust.

135

The Bridge Boy showed signs of a consensual homosexual relationship, so maybe those two things are linked.'

'Bridge boy and Biggart?' MacKellar shrugged, unimpressed. 'There were loads of rumours that Biggart swung both ways. The Bridge Boy – you made any headway with him?'

'It's all in my report. We're close to getting an ID.' Anderson was aware that he was holding back, and couldn't quite identify the reason why. But he went with his instinct, sure that none of his boys would talk without telling him. 'We have a good likeness of him, and an appeal is going out tomorrow.'

'Good, good. Another thing . . .' MacKellar's voice was a little softer. 'I didn't realize how close you and McAlpine were when Fairbairn was first arrested.'

Anderson gave no response to the non-question.

'Strange that those statements in particular, the ones from Hugh McAdam and Lenny Wood, were overlooked on the file. They give him an alibi for the time Lynda Osbourne was assaulted.'

'Not really, sir. As I recall, it just altered the timeline a little.'

'But apparently none of you noticed that this evidence was not put in front of the fiscal. It won't be long until somebody establishes where it went and who should have noticed.'

'It's bloody easy with hindsight. Sir, you know how much paperwork a case like that generates,' Anderson answered. 'But the bottom line is that Fairbairn's a paedophile, end of.' He shrugged. 'Is that not what's important?'

'In the eyes of the law, he's an innocent man.'

'Are you not concerned there's a paedophile walking about out there, free, unmonitored? Not on any register?'

'No, that's not my concern.'

'Maybe it should be,' snapped Anderson.

'He's always claimed he was innocent.'

'Of course he would. Maybe he got his friends to alibi him.'

'And maybe your experience has altered your perception of the case. Mr Fairbairn was well liked by the passengers on the school run, don't forget.'

'Typical behaviour. They like to get children to trust them.'

'And he requested to be taken off his bus run immediately the allegations were made. And now he has a swanky new defence team who have gone straight down the non-disclosure route. It's not a question of new evidence, it's a point of law, and there is nothing we can do about it.'

Anderson remained silent.

'I've seen his statement,' MacKellar went on. 'Fairbairn states clearly that DCI McAlpine, the senior investigating officer, hated him and made no secret of it.'

Anderson noted that there must have been a meeting about Fairbairn somewhere up on Mount Olympus, but he just shook his head. 'That's not fair; we all hated him.'

'McAlpine was desperate to put him away.'

'We all were. Fairbairn's a kiddie-fiddler.'

MacKellar sighed with impatience. 'Not in the eyes of the law, DI Anderson. And the record makes McAlpine look like an overzealous officer suffering from bad judgement. Did McAlpine tamper with evidence? Did he "lose" that file?'

'DCI McAlpine wasn't that kind of cop,' answered Anderson with a bland smile. 'Mistakes happen.' He stood up. 'Can I go now, sir? It's just that it's late and I've had a bit of a busy day.'

9.50 p.m.

Rosie was getting panicky. Another day had passed; she knew that from the fading of the light that was filtering through from the kitchen. Soon she would be in darkness. Her water was nearly finished, and she was rationing it to a mouthful at a time. Her chocolate had been finished long ago. She didn't know how long she could survive.

She had no way of getting in touch with the outside world. Nobody else knew where Wullie lived. They might miss him in the village, might start asking questions, but what would they think? That he had gone for a few days' holiday? That he'd gone into hospital? The post office would just hold on to his mail as they always did. Cars would pass on the road half a mile to the north and have no idea there was a cottage lying deep in the woods. Her only hope was to try to get out of bed, to try to reach the mobile phone. She had no idea where she would get a signal; Wullie was always cursing about it. But she hadn't been out of her bed for years, and her bones had thinned down to spindles as her body mass increased. She hadn't seen a doctor in all that time, but she knew. The skin on her right side was starting to fester, the infection slowly eating its way into her skin. That was what would kill her.

Occasionally, during the day – the last days, she couldn't

really recall – she woke up hungry and thirsty and simply went back to sleep, as if her brain was searching for a quiet way out. And in those moments, when she thought she was lucid, she thought she could remember things, dreams and daydreams and nightmares all becoming one. She had thought she was eating toasted cheese and crisps and cheesecake, drinking Coke. She woke up hungry and thirsty. She had thought she could smell cigarette smoke but woke up to find the air foetid with her own stink. She had thought Wullie had come back, but she woke up alone.

She thought she had no water left, but the jug was full again; she could see the top of the water through the glass, clear fresh water. And she drank from it. Then it was empty and she knew she had been dreaming.

For the first time since her wedding day, Rosie Mac-Fadyean started to cry.

10.30 p.m.

It was a couple of months after Auld Archie arrived at St Boswell's Care Home that the whispers began to filter down, just a rumour at first that grew to fact, and was talked about with such certainty that Matron was forced to call a meeting to put the staff straight. Yes, Auld Archie was one of *the* O'Donnells, one of the biggest gang families in Glasgow. But it would be wrong, Matron emphasized, for them, as professionals, to adopt anything other than a professional attitude. He was to be treated no differently from any of the other residents. He was just a tragic old man now, with no friends, no family. He had seen two of his sons shot dead in front of him, and his only surviving son, Wee Archie, would still be in jail when Auld Archie died; he wasn't even allowed out to visit his father on compassionate grounds. There were no grandchildren to drop in for a visit.

He didn't get on with any of the staff, apart from that wee part-time boy on his gap year – and handsome and helpful though the boy was, he hadn't been round for a while and he hadn't even bothered to give in his notice; he'd just not turned up for work. Matron agreed that the young man had made Auld Archie's moods more stable, and that now he was a nightmare. But they were *professionals*, she repeated. So, they were to treat Auld Archie just like anybody else, no matter who he was. Or who he had been.

The staff listened, arms folded, chewing gum, desperate to get out and have a fag. Their attitude did not change at first, but as time went on information researched on the Internet started to filter down. Auld Archie's past life read like a Hollywood film script, full of prostitutes and shootings, arson and protection rackets. He had had a reputation for being fearless, and there were reports of him being shot twice. The next time Ella, his reluctant but designated care worker was giving him a shower, she had a closer look and saw the ugly scars among the folds of liver-spotted skin.

And then the staff's attitude changed again. They became scared. Agnes and Ella summed it up over a quiet mid-morning cup of tea. There they both were, wiping the backside of one of the most feared men in Glasgow.

But it wasn't who he had been that was scary, it was who he was now. 'The way he looks at you,' they whispered. 'Like a mad dog. Nothing behind those eyes.'

But Auld Archie was not as blind or deaf as he made out, nor was he as gaga. He had made it to their office and used the phone that morning to phone the hospital without them noticing. The wee cow at the other end wouldn't speak to him. He tried to stop the tremor in his hands. He was nervous these days – not bad nervous, but nervous like he used to get before he shot somebody in the head, and God knows he'd done that more than once. Auld Archie looked out at the darkening sky, and he knew the days were about to get darker, in every sense.

There would be blood spilled. The death of that no-good arsewipe Biggart was just the start.

Wednesday
30 June 2010

His third day on the case started badly for DI Colin Anderson with an angry phone call from the sergeant who had initially investigated the Carruthers case up at Maryhill. He was furious that somebody else was reviewing the work, and he was going to get his DCI to complain to Anderson's DCI. He sounded like a little boy in the playground, saying, 'My dad's bigger than your dad.' Anderson had affably wished him good luck with that one and put the phone down. He had a spare few minutes before his meeting with Howlett so he set the alarm on his mobile, just in case he got too engrossed, and picked up the Carruthers file from the tray. The fiscal's office had ruled his death a suicide because of the contents of this file. Coffee in hand, he began to read.

On the face of it, it was indeed a straightforward suicide. The post mortem report said death was due to 'multiple injuries consistent with a fall from a height', and the fact that the safety catch had been removed with a screwdriver tended to rule out an accident in the eyes of the fiscal. Mrs Carruthers had no explanation for that; her statement said they always used the tilt-and-turn when they cleaned the windows, which appeared to rule out an accident.

So, the safety catch had been removed, but by whom?

Anderson skimmed on, flicking the pages over. There was no mention of a screwdriver, no mention of the screws. Had somebody picked them up and pocketed them? The thought didn't make Anderson feel any easier.

He looked at the black and white pictures of the body of Thomas Carruthers, aged sixty-eight. The only emotion on his poor smashed face was surprise. If, in his last minute on the planet, he had seen his former life flashing before him, or the pearly gates opening up for him at the end of a brilliantly lit tunnel, it had surprised him. At least, something had. His feet, twisted at impossible angles, were covered by bloodied socks. A dark slipper, circled in red, lay right at the edge of the picture. The next photo was a close-up, in high resolution. Anderson could see the little craters in the concrete, and tiny fronds of moss holding on to tenuous life, all in sharp focus under the scrutiny of the camera. The internal scaffolding of Carruthers' face had collapsed under the impact into a weird asymmetry, and there was a lake of blood spreading under his eye, with little rivers forming in the runnels of the concrete. A mangle of broken glass and dark plastic that Anderson presumed had been his specs was compressed against the bruised flesh of his cheek.

Why did he still have on his slippers and glasses? Why didn't he take them off and leave them neatly, with a note? The way suicides are supposed to.

Anderson paused, looking down at the picture; the point of his finger drifted on to Carruthers' exposed hip, to the small linear pattern of bruising on his skin.

8.30 a.m

ACC Howlett's office looked as though it should smell of old leather and cigarette smoke. Instead it smelled faintly of TCP. Howlett himself was smaller than Anderson remembered – not just thinner, but as though the man himself had shrivelled.

'Quite a reputation you've carved out for yourself,' Howlett observed, then continued without waiting for a response, 'I was talking to a colleague of yours only yesterday.'

'DS Costello? Yes, I know.'

'You two are close? I understand you've worked together for the last five years or so with no hint of disruption between you.'

'I think we know each other's strengths and weaknesses,' answered Anderson ambiguously.

'So, if DS Costello was alerted to something, do you think she would come to you?'

'Unless she was expressly told not to, sir. In which case, she wouldn't.'

Howlett smiled a little. 'But I presume she has told you that we have her back in harness, so to speak.'

'And that was all she said. She can be far more discreet than she makes herself out to be.' Anderson crossed his legs, giving the impression of relaxing. He hadn't trusted

Howlett when he had first walked in, and he had no ink-ling that he was about to reappraise the man any time soon. 'She did tell me where, because she would have dif-ficulty getting there – she hasn't been able to drive since what happened in February – and I offered to run her out there tonight.'

'Good. So, if she came to you with vague suspicions of something, you would not be dismissive of her opinion?'

Anderson had no hesitation in answering. 'I would never dismiss DS Costello's opinion.' He thought he had a glimmer of where this conversation might be going.

'So, you know we're sending her to Glen Fruin Acad-emy. Did she tell you why?'

'No.'

'It's a great school with a great tradition.' Howlett nodded to a photograph of what looked like the school rowing team. 'I was there for a couple of years myself.'

'I think I had heard that,' said Anderson, realizing that he now had no idea at all where this conversation was going.

'Good, good,' said Howlett, as if Anderson had answered an important question for him. Then he changed tack completely. 'Did you make any progress on that girl in the river?'

'Not my case, sir.'

Howlett ignored him 'Do you have any reason to believe she's foreign?'

Anderson looked at the ACC's face, but it was unread-able. 'I think there might be a suggestion of that. O'Hare would know more than me. No doubt he'll furnish you with the paperwork in due course. Why don't you ask the man in charge? I think that's DCI MacKellar?'

'Because I am asking you. So, that's as far as you've got?'

'As I said, it's not my case, sir, and the Prof is not a man to be hurried.'

Howlett folded his arms, considering this, and frowned in concentrated thought. 'And you have established that Biggart was probably burned alive. Any idea by whom?'

'We have a sighting on CCTV. We're making an appeal this morning for a positive ID; the young gentleman is definitely key to all this. There's no misper that matches him so time to go public, I think.' Anderson couldn't resist flicking a look at the clock.

'I am insisting on a media blackout on most of this. So, just appeal for the ID of the young man in connection with an arson attack. That's all they need to know.'

'Don't worry, the team are committed to tracing him,' Anderson elaborated.

'Oh yes, the team that came with you.' Howlett rubbed his fingers gently together, as if he was slightly bored now. 'And what about Biggart himself?'

'Well, the murder of his wife last night puts a different —'

Howlett did not seem interested. 'But apart from that, the man himself?'

'They had a nice house and he seems to have lived there. But he also used a flat he paid no rent for — a perk of some kind, we think. The flat is one of several that also appear to be unrented — well, unoccupied, at any rate. It doesn't look like a typical love nest away from the wife and kids.'

'More like a hive of industry?' The question was very matter-of-fact.

'Might be. I've requested some samples from the towels in the flat next door.' Anderson took a breath and started to theorize. 'I have an idea that the ceiling was rigged for lights. I think that Biggart might have graduated from dealing in films to making them. O'Hare was mooting the possibility that that is what the River Girl had been used for.' Anderson watched Howlett for any response. There was none; he got the feeling he was not telling him anything new. 'That means there might be a supply of girls from somewhere.'

Howlett's eyes watched Anderson carefully from behind his gold-rimmed spectacles, scrutinizing him rather than listening to him. 'But you suspect there was some questionable sexual activity going on.' Howlett's statement didn't invite a response. Instead he leaned forward, fixing Anderson with his deceptively mild gaze. 'If you feel you are being constrained in any way in this case, come and see me. Directly, I mean.'

Anderson nodded, feeling a slight stab in his stomach. There was a lot going on here that he knew nothing about. Did Howlett think he knew a lot more than he did? Maybe there was some new test for a DCI – work out what the bloody job is before you get the chance to do it.

'Not a pleasant man, Mr Biggart. Whoever lit that match did the world a favour.' Howlett pulled a thick file from his drawer. Old, crumpled, dog-eared and stained with coffee rings, it must have been read many times. Anderson felt his heart sink further. 'No doubt you will be looking for somebody who hated his guts. Somebody who might have watched him blister and burn then quietly let himself out the door.'

'I didn't know you were so well informed, sir.'

'I am well informed about everything in this case, DCI Anderson,' said Howlett. 'And I *mean* DCI Anderson.'

'Oh – er – right, sir. Thank you.'

'I am well informed about you, about your team as you like to call it, and about your career so far and exactly where it is going. By that I mean upwards. You have a good track record.' Howlett stood up and sat on the edge of the desk, a very casual pose, but there was nothing casual about his words. 'If you are looking for somebody who hated Mr Biggart then you are looking at a fair few. This file will help you in your search. But I would rather you read it and then locked it in a drawer out of sight of the lower ranks, no matter how much you think you can trust them. A few years ago, a very few years ago, Biggart was just a small-time pimp who beat up anyone smaller than him. Then something changed. It looks as though somebody started backing him, giving him advice, funding him almost, no doubt while vastly overestimating his intelligence. If they'd realized they'd made a mistake, they would just have shot him. They wouldn't have bothered going to all that trouble. The manner of his death leaves some questions unanswered. The manner of his wife's death even more so, the "blood eagle" so beloved of the Russian mafia. With that degree of violence, the execution of the operation, almost military in its precision. Nobody saw anything. Nothing at all.'

'It had struck me, sir.'

'I guess you're starting at the bottom of the pile, investigating the person who lit the match. Find out who he is, but don't stop at the fire setter; you'll get further looking at Biggart. If you get anywhere at all, come to me, please.'

Anderson took the file, it was thick and very heavy. 'Are we looking for somebody in particular?'

For the first time Howlett looked uncomfortable. '*Kukolnyik*,' was all he said.

'And that is what?'

'More of a who. "The Puppeteer" is a literal translation. He – or she – who pulls the strings and has us dance to his tune. Most of that file is background. You will pick up the invisible thread of some puppet master in there, and that's who I would like you to find. I don't really want that being made common knowledge outside your team – just say you are working on the Biggart case.' Howlett went on. 'And if you need any more detailed information about Biggart, you should speak to Eric Moffat, who's here in Glasgow for a little while. He was fully operational in Biggart's youth, so speak to him and see what background he can give you that never made it into the official record. Listen well, but say little. And I want *you* to speak to Moffat, not Lambie or any of the others. I'm not sure if Moffat fully understands how the force has changed since he left . . .' Howlett leaned back in his seat, and took a breath as if he had a pain some-where. 'I've consulted Dr Mick Batten about this, you will find notes from him in the file. I intend to call him in, I know you two work well together. How are you getting on at Partick?'

'Fine. Be nice to be working with Mick again,' said Anderson, hoping Howlett would explain why a psychologist had been called in.

He didn't.

'From your record, I notice you feel comfortable working long hours with a small team. Not a practice that can easily be tolerated in today's police service.'

'No, sir, but it is effective. Yesterday I narrowly avoided a meeting that was purely about scheduling some more meetings.'

Howlett smiled thinly. 'Such is the role of the DCI.'

'I was a DI then.'

'Your approach – delicate work, the need-to-know principle – does have its uses. But I'm afraid it'll be a few months before the work at Partickhill is complete.'

'I've worked in much worse places than Partick Central.'

Howlett steepled his fingers. 'So, I take it you wouldn't be interested in setting up a little unit of your own, just across the road at the university? In the lecture hall the hospital uses? Just for this operation, if you'll pardon the pun?'

It was a command.

'Anything that's beneficial to the enquiry. And the precise objective of this operation is . . . ?'

'To break the Puppeteer, simple as that. I've released Lambie, Wyngate. And you will liaise with Matilda McQueen and only her for any forensic work you need done, I don't want any of this lying around a general lab. And Mulholland, of course – he'll be useful.'

'They're all useful, sir,' Anderson replied carefully.

'They don't all speak Russian, though, do they? The one stipulation is that I want tabs kept on each and every one of you, where you are every minute you are on duty. I want someone to be able just to look at the noticeboard and to know where you are and who you're with at any time.'

'OK, but for the sake of completeness, can you ask DCI MacKellar if he can reassign the case of the River Girl to me. And there's a white Transit and –'

'Indeed, consider it done. I wasn't fully aware that MacKellar had split the investigation. I'll sort it out straight away,' he lifted the phone, pausing halfway. 'And don't forget DS Costello in all this.'

'But she's at –'

'I know. I'm just telling you not to forget her. I'm afraid I don't have any female staff free, so you might want to keep in close contact with her and the security team at Glen Fruin Academy. It was the Warden of the Academy who called us in. They don't have a headmaster like any normal school; they have to have a Warden.'

'Sounds like a hostel. But Warden or no, I presume he wants it kept quiet?'

'It had better be kept quiet – he's my brother-in-law. I'll phone MacKellar now.'

It was a subtle dismissal so Anderson got up and left, letting his fingers run along the back of the leather chair. Howlett had mentioned the Russians twice. As fact.

He wondered what else Howlett knew.

Sitting in his car, parked on the steep hill at Pitt Street, Anderson thought about nipping into Costa in Sauchiehall Street and getting something to eat. Even the metropolitan bustle of the precinct, thronged with shoppers and sightseers, would be quieter than that bloody station at Partick, with the phone going every two minutes, and the strange habit they had of shouting across the room rather than just getting up and walking all of ten yards. The first thing he did was read the notes by Batten – the word 'profile' had gone out of favour – in which Batten had referred to the Puppeteer's 'characteristics'. He glanced through it, his heart chilling: intelligent, well read, patient, probably a businessman, flash with his money, very engaging, does charity work, probably has a legitimate reason to travel internationally, background in military, family or some kind of community tie, he will have a team working with him, people at his disposal. The word 'communication' had a question mark after it.

He turned the key in the ignition, so he could wind down the window, and rested his elbow on the door, letting the stifling car cool. The steering wheel was almost too hot to touch so he couldn't drive away yet, anyway. He slipped on his sunglasses, glad of the anonymity they afforded him.

Anonymity? Was that why the passenger in the van was wearing them? Did that suggest that he thought his face was traceable, recognizable? Anderson didn't want to insult Wyngate by asking him to enhance the tattoos on the man's arm and then do a search on them. He needed to trust his team and let them get on with it. He was a DCI now, time he started to behave like one.

He needed time to think about what Howlett had just offered him. He was considering going somewhere quiet to have a look through that file. The ACC was no fool; he had handed Anderson either the opportunity of his career on a plate, or something that everyone else considered untouchable.

He picked up his phone and dialled Wyngate. 'Gordon, I want you to pack up everything for the Biggart case, and the case of the girl in the river from next door.'

'Biggart, right. And Rusalka. Yes, we've already started.'

'Rusalka? You have a positive ID on her?'

'No,' said Wyngate sheepishly. 'Just a name Mulholland's given her. It's some opera he knows – sounded just like *The Little Mermaid* to me.'

Anderson sighed. 'Trust Vik to know about something poncy like that. Never mind, it'll do. Look, just pack all that stuff up in boxes.'

'Do you want me to do that now?'

'Why, have you got something more important to do?'

'Well, I've just had a strange call from HQ. I've to go to the Western and get the keys to the university lecture theatre from a janitor. And they want me to hang about at the theatre because some computers are being delivered. For us to use. I presumed you knew about it, sir, from the way it was said.'

Anderson put a smile into his voice. 'Yes, it's OK, just that the right hand doesn't know what the left hand is doing. You sort it out any way you can but by five p.m. tonight we will be working out of there rather than Partick Central.'

'Is that why the IT guys are getting a system up and running for us?'

'Probably. Phone me if you have any problems.' He rang off.

A small hand-picked team all to himself, nothing too formal, nothing too traceable. But why?

One explanation came to him as easily as an ice cream down the back of the throat. They had been a secure unit at Partickhill and all Howlett had done was to take the four or five officers he knew he could trust, the implication being that there was somebody in Partick who could not be trusted. A mole.

Clever. If Anderson didn't know what he was chasing, he wouldn't go looking for what he wanted to find. He would simply find it without prejudice.

10.40 a.m.

They were still packing up, their colleagues watching with a mix of pleasure at seeing the back of them and a touch of envy that they were moving somewhere with double the floor space for a tenth of the staff, when the door of the incident room opened and DCI MacKellar came in. With him was a tall tanned man with grey hair and gold-rimmed glasses, in a pristine white long-sleeved white shirt and expensive linen trousers, who looked around as if he owned the place. A few of the Partick team said hello, and two older members of the CID went up and shook hands warmly. The heartfelt double-handed handshake might have been

Masonic for all Anderson knew. He looked enquiringly at Lambie, but Lambie shrugged, 'No idea.' Mulholland scribbled something and slipped a scrap of paper to Anderson as he walked past: *If his name's Moffat then he's God.*

So, this was the man Howlett had told him to talk to.

Anderson went back to reading the list of injuries and identifying marks on the Bridge Boy when MacKellar tapped him on the arm.

'I think congratulations are in order. Well done.' The handshake was genuine. 'I was kind of hoping for it myself, you know. But, well done.'

'For what?' asked Anderson. 'All I have is a DCI position, nothing else.'

MacKellar dropped his voice as there was an outbreak of laughter at some in-joke by Moffat. 'You didn't get LOCUST?'

Anderson shook his head, then added mischievously, 'In fact, I think we are moving out to give you more room. Make what you will of that.'

'Great, ta. Nice one, Colin.' MacKellar punched him on the arm. 'Cheers.'

Anderson went back to his reading, ignoring the adoring throng around Moffat. The Bridge Boy was holding on, Dr Redman had reported, but only just; he might be in need of a liver transplant. Anderson made a mental note of points to look for on the missing persons register, though one flick-through had produced no likely matches. He couldn't help but watch Moffat from the corner of his eye, thinking about Batten's list. Moffat had obviously lived abroad for a while, Australia from the sound of it – somebody called him 'Crocodile Dundee' to a hoot of laughter – and was well enough respected to be allowed to walk around the station freely. Arrangements were being made to go out for a drink.

'Yeah, I'm over for a whole load of reasons, but wasn't expecting Tommy's funeral,' Moffat was explaining.

Anderson could not help listening. Lambie, who was loading files into a box with the slow deliberation of one whose concentration was elsewhere, was clearly listening as well.

'And who are these guys? I think I know you,' Moffat said to Anderson. 'By reputation, if nothing else.'

'Don't believe everything you hear. DCI Colin Anderson,' Anderson said, relishing the sound of his new title.

Lambie's head jerked up in surprise; he grinned but said nothing.

'DCI Anderson? I'm glad the grapevine was to be believed.' Moffat smiled. 'Congratulations. You're very well thought of by the top brass, I hear.'

'More than I ever get to hear,' said Anderson.

'And you worked with an old mentor of mine, I think – Alan McAlpine.'

'Yes, I did.' Anderson was confused for a minute. Moffat was older than McAlpine had been by a good few years.

'I was in the military before I joined the force,' explained Moffat, as if he had read Anderson's thoughts. 'He showed me the ropes. Hard bastard, but fair.' His blue eyes looked deep into Anderson's. 'If I can be of any assistance to you, *any* assistance,' he emphasized, 'in the next few days, just let me know. I'm not going back to Oz for another week.'

Anderson nodded to show that he understood; a subtle invite to an off-the-record conversation passed between the two of them without any of the others noticing. 'This is DC Mulholland, and DS Lambie.' He waved a hand at them in introduction. 'DC Wyngate is around somewhere. So, you moving on?'

Moffat looked down at the paper Anderson had just been reading. His old colleagues drifted away, waving and calling that they'd see him later. 'So, somebody did for Billy the Bastard. I'm glad I lived long enough to see that.' Then Moffat leaned over and asked under his breath, 'The lad with the ears – Wyngate – is he trying to track those tattoos?'

So, he had clocked the photograph pinned to the file – the last thing to go into the box so it would be the first out. Anderson nodded.

'Get him to do it quickly, then let me have a look-see; I might be able to help.'

'For ID?'

'I'll tell you once I see them.' Moffat looked closely at Anderson. 'I do remember you, you know.'

'You have the advantage of me, though I recognize you from somewhere.'

Moffat slapped Anderson on the back. 'Of course you do, boy, of course you do. I used to kick your arse when you were a probationer. God, that was years ago.'

'Eric? Eric Moffat? I don't recall. But then I got my arse kicked by loads of people in those days.'

'Well, rumours of my death were exaggerated, as you can see – I just retired to Australia, where it's only slightly cooler than hell.'

'Must have a chat with you about that. My wife wants us to go out there.'

'Nice place, can't say a word against it.' Moffat polished his glasses on the end of his tie before slipping them on again. 'Look, let's meet for a beer when there're fewer folk about.' He pulled a card out from his top pocket. 'There's my cell number, call me and we'll have a chat. Might save you a lot of legwork.'

Anderson looked at the card. Moffat lived in Brisbane, in Queensland. And he couldn't say a word against it. Oh God, Anderson prayed, please don't let him and Brenda ever meet.

2.00 p.m.

Anderson decided there was no point in him being there while they were connecting computers and dragging furniture around, so he left the boys to it – they knew what to do. He would go home and sit in his garden with a blank sheet of paper and try to make some connections.

A colour print of the mocked-up image of the Bridge Boy had arrived, and Anderson was impressed. It was a good image for the appeal, he'd called in a few favours, and Bridge Boy's face would be all over the morning editions. He was keeping a tight rein on anything going to the papers, but he needed help with this one. The boy's fingerprints were not on record. His dental records were proving useless – so many of his teeth had been pulled out. And DNA testing would only be of use if they had a comparison. Better to put his face out there, place a guard on his bed and see what came out of the woodwork. He decided to go home and plan his strategy for the case.

But getting out of the station proved to be difficult.

A rather harassed-looking Lambie met him on the stairs, and pulled him back through the security door. 'Look, can I speak to you about Carruthers? There's a few things that don't really add up. I've requested the CCTV film for the area round the flat. For the six hours before the . . . incident.'

Anderson looked out of the window, watching Wyngate manhandle a box into the boot of his car.

'I've talked to the solicitor. You know that Carruthers put twenty grand in a bank account his wife didn't know about, one single payment in November 1996. Well, it's a lot more than that now with interest. Untouched, totally. The bank records show it was a win on a horse, and they were shown all the paperwork at the time. Enough to satisfy them, seemingly,' Lambie continued in a low tone.

'Except – don't tell me – Tommy never bet on anything in his life. *Seemingly* may be about right.'

'Once the solicitor told Mrs Carruthers, she told Costello. She really had no idea about that money. She seems almost scared of it.'

'And Carruthers was a cop at that time.'

'A bent cop?'

Anderson shrugged. 'If that money is all they find, only bent once, from the look of it. But whatever he did to earn it – could it really have been something bad enough to drive him to suicide fourteen years later? Or maybe he was murdered for it. Keep on it, keep me posted. Tell me, what do you know of ex-DCI Eric Moffat?'

Lambie shrugged. 'Off the record?'

'Dish the dirt.'

'Masonic, bit too sectarian for my liking but give him his due, he almost brought down gangland Glasgow single-handed. He took both the O'Donnells and the McGregors on and wiped the floor with them. I never worked with him for long, though. He went Down Under, probably for his own good. Is he back because of that bloody book about the Marchetti boy? I think the author gives him a roasting.'

'Was he involved in that?'

'Is the Pope a Catholic? That's how he made his name.'

4.00 p.m.

Now, Anderson was back in his garden sipping a cup of hot strong coffee. Nesbitt was at his feet, chewing at his favourite tennis ball with loud growling noises, and Brenda was leaning against the garden fence, yattering to the neighbour about Australia, no doubt. She was standing with one hand on her hip, just where Carruthers' body had had marks, Anderson was reminded. He had noticed them in the post mortem photographs, particularly the one that clearly showed straight, linear scrapes among the chaos of injuries caused by the fall – the tipping point, the pivot. A jump wouldn't have caused that. He could get O'Hare to have a look at the pictures – well, pictures were all they had, as the body had been cremated.

And another thing: Moffat comes back on the scene and Carruthers is found dead at the bottom of a block of flats. This is just after the publication of a book about the kidnap of a boy, and Moffat was in charge of that. The kidnap that made Moffat's career – not because he solved it but because of the disruption it created in the criminal underworld.

Was it all connected somehow, and did Howlett know? There was nothing really, thought Anderson, running through it in his mind. Apart from the timing – and, as they say in the theatre, timing is everything. Lambie really needed to look at those diaries he'd spotted in Carruthers' flat.

Nesbitt sneezed loudly and Anderson went back to his blank piece of paper. He made three headings: 'Bridge Boy', 'Biggart', 'River Girl'. Then he scored them out. He wrote 'Rusalka' across the top, and the word 'Russian'. 'Biggart' with a red line through to show he was deceased. 'Melinda Biggart' with a similar line. He put a '+' between them, with 'pretty boy' in between. Anderson was sure he had torched Biggart, but he had not killed Melinda. Then he recalled Howlett saying that the 'blood eagle' as a method of killing was . . . what was the word he had used? . . . *beloved* of the Russian mafia.

He pulled out his phone and keyed in the words 'blood eagle' and read that it was a method of torture and execution mentioned in Norse sagas. He scrolled down, reading the method, which involved cutting the ribs of the victim by the spine, then breaking the ribs so they resembled blood-stained wings. He closed his eyes, forcing himself to think about Melinda. She had been cut down the front, a reverse blood eagle that had immediately brought the Russians to Howlett's mind. And Rusalka was, probably, a Russian.

He keyed in the word 'Rusalka', uncertain how to spell it. He was interested to know why Mulholland of all people had given the dead girl that name. Up flashed a Wikipedia article: . . . *an opera by Antonín Dvořák . . . first performed in Prague in 1901 . . . based on Slavic fairy tales . . .* Curious, he scrolled down to the synopsis. Rusalka was a water sprite, who fell in love with a human prince betrothed to a princess, and lost the power of speech. Wyngate was right; it was a darker, more elemental version of *The Little Mermaid*.

But without Walt Disney's happy ending.

9.45 p.m.

'Do you have some cover story for this?' Anderson flung Costello's small suitcase into the back seat of the Jazz, slammed the door, and got into the car. He reached across and picked up the book lying on top of her bag on her knee. *Little Boy Lost* by Simone Sangster. 'And why are you reading this shite?'

'It came with the job. I may as well as read it.'

Anderson was confused.

'This place was implicated as a getaway route.' She looked at him. 'Do you know anything?'

'Obviously not, but I don't think you'll learn much reading that crap. The Marchettis tried to get it banned, you know. Does it mention Eric Moffat anywhere?' He noticed Costello startle slightly.

'Yes, but I've not got that far.'

'But you do know him? What do you think?'

'He dumped me from a case. The only time in my career. So, no, I don't think much of him.' She adjusted her short hair. 'He's back for Carruthers' funeral, isn't he?'

Anderson pulled on to the dual carriageway, looking at the water of the Clyde, a deep sapphire blue in the late light, rhomboids of silver flashing across the top of subtle waves. He imagined them as pieces of the jigsaw, coming together and then being pulled apart. Moffat, Glen Fruin, the kidnap? He kept his voice level. 'Did you deserve to get put off the case?'

Costello seemed to consider her answer. 'I was a rookie. '93, was it? A woman had been stabbed in the NCP in Mitchell Lane. I was first on the scene, but he turned up and said I was useless. He wasn't wrong, but it was the way he said it while this poor woman was just lying there, pregnant, on oil-stained freezing concrete. She was covered in blood. I held her hand. Her nails were bitten right down to the quick. Moffat said I was being useless and sent me on my way.' She looked out of the window, her head against the glass. 'It wasn't nice.'

'And what happened.'

'Nothing. I was never asked to write it up. Nobody was ever charged. Not long afterwards, they had found the body of a man named Liam Flynn, decapitated with a machete, and I was told that Moffat had stopped looking for any more suspects. Some kind of street justice had been done. I was told to leave it at that.'

'Was she connected, then?'

'Only slightly. Pauline, part of the McGregor family but not an active one.'

Anderson's mind was racing ahead, looking at the facts, his brain trying to make the pieces of the jigsaw fit. 'So, how far have you got with the book?'

'It's mostly about Sangster's theory that the family had something to do with it. Don't you think it's strange to have a male babysitter? But then, the parents did know him well – he'd worked for them for some while in their restaurant. Piacini, he was called. And the normal baby-sitter had let them down at the last moment. It's a crap read but the bit about Glen Fruin is interesting.'

'And what happened here?'

'All it says is that a car similar to one seen somewhere near the Marchettis' flat was seen forty minutes later driving through Glen Fruin. But it's all maybes – there was no concrete evidence. It's a good conspiracy theory, though. That they were getting the kid out to the coast. That's one thing about this country, we have a great coastline for hiding things.'

That was the second time in so many days that Anderson had heard that sentiment. 'So, the first time Piacini is left in charge, he and the child both go missing? And stay missing? Dead or alive, they must be somewhere.'

'Must be dead, otherwise they would have resurfaced. But were they brought through here to get to the coast or be dumped somewhere? The glen was home to some torpedo testing centre during the war or something, it being long and narrow and tucked out of the way. It's not easy to kidnap a child and keep him secure somewhere. There's all sorts of underground, hidden-away things up here.' She sounded excited, like a child. 'There's a great underground tank there that they used to test the Dambusters' bouncing bomb, then it was used for hydro-ballistic research.'

'Like you'd know what that was.'

'Good deposition site for a couple of dead bodies. It's an overflow reservoir now.'

'I read in the *Herald* recently that a lot of the older tunnels and drains are being tested for recommissioning, something to do with anti-terrorism. But that's down at the un-posh end. You'll be up in the seriously posh bit. You do know that there's bugger all up there but the school? The nearest shop is six miles away.'

'There'll probably be a Harvey Nicks on site,' Costello grunted.

Though it was going on for ten o'clock, the light was only just starting to fade, and the midges were out in force. Anderson could smell Costello's citronella repellent spray. 'It'll be a nice drive. Glen Fruin is one of the most attractive glens in Scotland, you know.'

'So, not only are the kids a load of over-privileged little sods, they have a nice view as well.'

'I don't think that attitude is going to help, Costello. The term "button it" comes to mind. Just be careful. There're not a lot of places you can run to, and you can't drive.'

'I'm only going up to have a look around, not start a revolution.' Costello ignored him. 'But I'll need to use a landline; the mobile reception is patchy.'

'Well, you have my number if you need me, if you get stuck.' Anderson turned on to the expressway and headed west. 'What is it all about, anyway?'

'Important people send their children to Glen Fruin.

So I cannae tell you,' Costello said, bored and leaning her head against the window.

As they neared Glen Fruin, Anderson turned right, taking the low road through the glen. Within minutes the trees had closed over the road, creating a long dark tunnel that still held the balmy heat of the day trapped under the canopy of the leaves. He had the feeling it was an omen that Costello had no real idea what she was being sent to 'observe'.

'Sorry to nag,' he started again. 'But is there somebody you can trust up here?'

'Apart from the Warden, there's a security guy called Pettigrew. Colin? What the hell do you think I can't cope with? These kids can't even wipe their own arses without a nanny.'

'Be careful, and watch your back. Don't drink anything or eat anything that might have been tampered with. Just be on your guard.'

There was a slow head-turn from the passenger seat. 'Do you really think I can't look after myself?'

'Fine,' said Anderson, and he put his foot down.

10.25 p.m.

Rosie wondered how long it would take her to die. She knew you could die within hours without water, especially in this weather, and she'd had no water now for . . . how long was an hour, anyway? She had had to void her bowels again, and the air in the bedroom was wretched and foul.

Then she heard a bluebottle, a gentle hum that came

close and louder until it seemed to be buzzing in her ear. She couldn't lift a hand to wave it away, and it kept landing on the soiled sheets, trying to get through to eat at her skin. Then there were two of them. Then another, and another, until she couldn't fight them off any more. Now she really started to panic. She was going to die of thirst, and the flies were going to swarm over her and eat her as she rotted, stinking the whole house out. She closed her eyes, and thought about Wullie. She thought about death.

She heard a noise, and her eyes shot open. It was Wullie, coming back! She tried to call out to him, joy flooding her heart, and her voice caught in her throat. Wullie was back, he was back . . . Then reality caught up with her – the noise was scuffling, a thud. Even if he had forgotten his key, Wullie knew that there was a spare one under the stone – he was terrible with keys. Her eyes automatically darted to the laptop, to the disks.

She closed her eyes again. Wullie had not come back, and now they were coming for her. She screwed her eyes closed as somebody walked into the room. She could hear his quiet footfall, could hear him breathing, smell a waft of cigarette smoke. Somebody was watching her. Now she knew true fear, total terrifying fear. Only one of them – why had they sent only one? He still wasn't moving. He just stood there, watching her, smelling her, and she could feel his eyes crawling all over her exposed flesh. The bluebottles rose from the bed to buzz in circles round the ceiling.

She held her breath, and waited – for the blow, the bullet, the knife.

'What's that over there?' asked Anderson.

'Over where?'

'In those trees, what a racket!' He pulled the car to a halt. 'Down there, just at the treeline. It's like a scene from *The Birds*.' He leaned across to get a better look out of Costello's window.

'Can't see anything, but those crows are having a good investigation of whatever it is.'

'They are pulling at something. Oh God, that's horrible. Listen to them.'

The noise of them screeching and squawking filled the air.

'Probably just a dead sheep?' She could hear them crowing and cawing, she could hear the wind high in the trees, and she tried to quell the panic. *She could do this*. She closed her eyes tighter, in quiet desperation, when she heard the key click in the ignition and the engine die. 'Can we not get a move on, Colin? It's getting late, and it's dark.'

'Just a minute. I want to have a look.' Anderson unclipped his seat belt and got out of the car. He walked round the back of the car and paused on the grass verge, peering up into the woods.

Costello resisted the urge to lean over and press the lock on his door. Instead she watched him walk away, before taking a step down into a dip. He paused, bending forward, his hands on his knees, moving his head from one side to the other, his eyes fixed on something low down. Without standing up he reached into his back pocket for his phone, and pressed a single button. Then he started talking, straightening up and looking over his shoulder, giving somebody their location. Costello felt a cold hand round her heart. She was starting to feel trapped. But she forced herself to open the car door, intending just to get out and stand there.

Anderson heard the sound of the door opening, and turned and saw her. He held up his free hand. *Stay there.*

But, hypnotized by the shadows in the trees, she started walking.

'Costello, stay back!'

She walked on, her mind filling in the details her eyes saw: the blood, the eyes – no, no eyes – the flies, the green mottled skin of the face, the crows pecking at it, stripping it of its flesh . . .

'Costello, get back to the car!'

But her feet were rooted to the ground. In a tree beside her, a crow scrawked loudly. Anderson clapped his hands to make it fly away. But it only flapped its wings and hopped from one branch to another.

'Costello,' repeated Anderson. 'Go – back – to the car – *now!*'

Costello looked at the crow again. It cocked its head at her. Its grey beak was half open, and something once living was dangling from it.

'Right,' she said. 'I'll go back to the car.'

11.05 p.m.

A black car pulled up, and a man got out of it, slamming the door and jogging across the road, giving Costello, who was now sitting in the car, a quick glance as he passed. He jumped over the ditch, down to the lower ground, and went over to talk to Anderson. Costello wound down the window, trying to listen to the conversation, but they were talking too quietly for her to hear. The other man was small and fine boned, but had a degree of muscle definition that was evident through his white T-shirt. Something about him was not right; he was much older than he appeared to be at first. He had a tan, and dark hair that looked dyed. And his teeth looked as though they belonged to somebody else. He slapped Anderson on the upper arm, like an old friend saying goodbye after a late-night drinking session. Such camaraderie, so soon?

Costello felt a twinge of jealousy. Who was he, and why had he appeared? Had Anderson phoned him, and if he had then why didn't Costello know who he was? She thought about getting out of the car and going back across the ditch, then she looked up to see the crows still moving from branch to branch, edging closer until some signal was given by one of them and they all moved again before settling, watching, dark eyes fixed on the carrion below.

The small man was coming back up to the road. As Costello wound down the window, he opened the rear door and pulled out her case.

'Come on, you,' he said. 'You can't stay here. You've had a shock, and your boss will be here for ages once the accident investigation guys appear. I'll take you up to the school.'

'I haven't had a shock,' said Costello, not moving.

'Then why is your face the same colour as sour milk – and just as pleasant to look at, at the moment – if you don't mind me saying so?'

'I do mind.'

'You'll get used to it. I'm Jim Pettigrew, security consultant, or insultant if you prefer. Now, do you mind getting your arse out of there so that we can get out of here before the MPs come along? If not, we'll be here until the next World Cup while they go back three generations trying to find a Muslim or a Catholic in your background. Uh-oh, here they come. Time for us to get out the way. Move it.'

Costello got into the black car, a small Corsa. 'And who are they, the blackshirts over there?'

'The military police. Any incident along this road and they're automatically notified and come sniffing. Otherwise they don't really have that much to do up here, apart from bugger the sheep and make sure the nuclear submarines are parked properly.'

'And you're head of security at the school?' asked Costello.

Pettigrew pulled the car away, waving at the two MPs who were getting out of their car.

Costello laid her head back in the seat. Oh, she had been here before. Something in the way he spoke. 'You're ex-job, aren't you?'

'Indeedy,' he said. As he drove past the MPs he gave them a two-fingered salute below the level of the car window, whistling the theme from *The Great Escape* as the car sped away.

Auld Archie O'Donnell sat in the corner of the day room, his head hunched into his shoulders, chewing on his gums. He hated this bloody place. They'd taken him away from his favourite spot at the bay window to sit among this festering mass of dribbling window-lickers, and that was just the staff. He'd had dogs that were more intelligent than the morons in this place, and if he still had his gun he'd put the whole fucking lot of them out their misery. He chewed on his gums slightly more aggressively, enjoying the pain as soft flesh gave way to blood. He had been happy looking out across the garden and into the street where he could see the world go by. He was happy in his room, alone with his memories of the good days, able to have a shit without a fucking audience. Of course, it was easier for the staff to keep them all confined in the day room, tethered like animals, so they didn't make a mess of the place after the cleaner had been round, just in case there was a random inspection and some poor sod had dared to leave a crumb somewhere.

Being in the day room meant there was no bloody peace at all. The huge TV sat unwatched but blaring out so the staff could hear it all over the home. Soap after soap after chat show, and reality show after soap. TV for the brain dead. Once in a blue moon they left it on a channel where they actually spoke the Queen's English, and today had been such a day. He had heard the news; he'd had no choice. He had seen the appeal, the mocked-up face of the boy who had fallen from the bridge. It was expressionless, dead-eyed, but it was him. Auld Archie had then pulled a late copy of the *Scottish Sun* from a coffee table and stuffed it behind his cushion, pulling it out to read when the staff were on yet another coffee break and the other inhabitants of the day room were semi-comatose and drooling.

The boy was alive – critical, but alive. That's all he needed to know.

Then Archie had sat, drawn deep within himself, until Ella had come to move him as the night air became chilled, and he had snarled at the woman, mouth open as if ready to bite her, and the stupid wee cow had buggered off to file a report about his aggression.

So, now he was alone, his head pulled well down. Alone in his world. He would not let them see his tears.

Thursday
1 July 2010

Costello's arrival at the school shortly after midnight was something of an anticlimax. She had been expecting some dramatic approach to the grand house of the photographs. But there was no sight of the grand blond sandstone turret or the immaculate sweeping driveway. No line of four-by-fours parked on the expansive gravelled forecourt, no tennis courts or neat hedges. Instead, Pettigrew simply drove, whistling tunelessly, along a tiny single-track road lined by trees, a mass of potholes with grass growing down the middle.

'How on earth do you get any supplies in, with the road in this state?' she asked. 'I'd have thought a place like this would have a proper drive, with huge gates.'

'We keep it like this,' he replied. 'For security – you can't get in and out of here quickly. The remoteness of the school is a form of security in itself, though it's only half an hour's drive to Glasgow Airport. Well,' he corrected himself, 'half an hour until you get to this last bit. My house is well hidden at the top of this road, so I hear everybody go past – hence the rough road.'

Costello glanced around, seeing his point. She ignored the shiver of nerves that ran through her. 'So, who was he?'

'The dead guy?' Pettigrew shrugged. 'God knows. I wouldn't recognize my own bookie if he'd had his face pecked off like that. And what the hell was he doing out there, miles from anywhere? It looked like a dump site. They'll have left tyre marks, as they must have turned to go back down the glen. Nobody in their right mind would come up this road unless they knew it really well. All sensible folk take the high road.'

'How do the pupils get here? And out again?'

'I drive them mostly, pick them up at the train station in Balloch or go to the airport to get them. A few of the older ones have cars.'

'Really? They're allowed?'

'Oh yes, as long as they're taxed, insured, et cetera. If you're paying £25,000 a year for an education, it's no hardship to shell out on a wee motor. But they're not allowed to go off on their own. Makes my job bloody hard, though, trying to keep tabs on the wee buggers.'

Costello thought back to her conversation with Howlett, seeing a bigger pattern to his problems. These were not kids who could be contained. 'Is that really part of your remit?'

'Technically, not at all. Once they're off campus they can do what they like. They're eighteen, some of them, legal adults, so what can we do to stop them? But at the same time the school has a duty of care.'

'Supposedly.'

'This is your place, here.' He had brought her right to the door of an old stable block at the rear of the school.

She could now see the dark outline of the turret nearby, its crenellations etched against the sky, and she could smell the sweet scent of a lawn recently cut. There was no great history lesson; Pettigrew simply handed her a key.

'I think it's all been set up for you. If not, give us a buzz and I'll come over. Don't use your mobile, the signal's terrible unless you go higher up the hill. There's a landline phone in the room, and my number's on the handset.'

Costello looked out at the night, and the dim rolling hills that seemed to rise like tsunamis on both sides of the valley. It was an oppressive place. 'And where are you?' she asked, wary of being on her own, out here in the dark.

'Like I said, I'm at the top of the drive. But don't worry, you'll be fine.' He jumped into the car, and drove off, leaving her standing alone with her bags on the sandstone paving.

She slid the key into the lock and the old wooden door opened without a sound. Before she stepped inside she felt around for the light switch. Her fingers found an old-fashioned round switch, and she flicked it.

The interior of the room was like a Scandinavian hotel, all polished wooden floors, with a sofa, a TV, a big fire, a bathroom, and a wee kitchen at the back of the living room, then a set of wooden stairs up to a mezzanine where she presumed the bed would be.

She was so tired she just wanted to make a cup of tea and flop under the duvet. She closed the door behind her, and turned on the light in the bathroom – nice clean tiles, and a brand-new shower with huge cream fluffy towels. In the kitchen, somebody had left her a welcome pack of tea, coffee, bread and butter. Enough to make some tea and toast. That made her mind up – she was going to put the kettle on, then have a shower and wash the midges out of her hair so she could stop scratching.

She was trying not to think about the body, about the crows that had been feasting on its face, their black wings flapping and clapping over their banquet. And she was absolutely not going to think about the crow that had looked at her, and what it had had in its beak. She was determined to feel safe here. She turned back to the front door to lock it. There were four deadbolts on the inside.

9.00 a.m.

'My God, what is that smell?' Lambie wrinkled his nose.

Anderson answered without lifting his head from the newspaper. 'Vik's aftershave.'

Lambie slipped his lightweight jacket from his shoulders, and looked round for somewhere to hang it. Not seeing any coat stands or hangers, he hung it over the back of a student's hard chair, before selecting a padded chair to sit on. Wyngate was filling the huge whiteboard with photographs of Biggart's crime scene, and a side panel was dedicated to the death of Mrs Melinda Biggart. The smaller of the two lecture rooms had been turned into a handy little investigation room, the only downside being the lack of natural light, and no windows to open. The upside was the glorious silence and the well-tuned air conditioning. The fact that it was near the hospital café and their wonderful coffee was a bonus.

'Can you put up something about wee Rusalka?' Anderson asked. 'There's a few ideas of my own I was sketching out last night before I drove into a Hitchcock set. Not nice.' He handed Wyngate a single sheet. 'I'm sure Rusalka is connected to this. And I'm sure Biggart has been making films in that room – it's the only explanation I can think of for the strange holes in the ceiling. Even if there's no connection, I want whoever put her in the river nailed to a wall slowly. We are three full days into this and we are getting nowhere. Have you seen this, Lambie?' He tossed the newspaper over to his sergeant as Wyngate went to the door in response to a knock.

'Bridge Boy? They've done a good job. We'll get a whole load of stuff come in on that.' Lambie looked around the room. 'Are we supposed to be manning the phones?'

'No, the calls are going through to a helpdesk at Partick. They'll phone through with the possibles. Did I tell you Costello was going out to Glen Fruin Academy to take a wee look at a situation they have? On the drive out there last night we found a body.' Anderson was handed an envelope by Wyngate, blank apart from the words 'DCI Anderson' written on it in small neat writing. It was the first time he had seen it written down.

'Sheep?'

'Pardon?'

'The body, was it a sheep?'

'No, human. Like I said, it was a scene from a Hitch-cock film.'

'Really?'

'Hit and run, then eaten by birds. But why out on that road, and why wearing a suit?' Anderson shrugged. 'No ID, not a thing. But he did have money on him.'

'Did you look?'

'Wouldn't you? The security guy at the school was a plod up at Maryhill in the past, so we had a wee mosey around. Called in the locals, who called in O'Hare. A uniform from Balloch and I nipped up to the road. Tyre tracks everywhere. The lab is getting on to it now.'

'And we care because . . . ?' asked Lambie.

Anderson was busy tearing the envelope open, 'Because there's something bloody weird going on up at Glen Fruin and I'm not happy that Costello is there, isolated.' Anderson missed the look Lambie was giving him. 'O'Hare thought the body had been run over, then the vehicle reversed and ran over it again. So, he called in the road incident guys. That was when I bowed out and came home.'

'Nothing to do with us,' repeated Lambie, wondering what his boss was thinking.

'Howlett sent us here and sent her there. Think about it.' Anderson read the single sheet of paper. 'Well, listen to this. The body was kicked off the road a wee bit, and just left. And Matilda says it was a van, a Transit or some such from the tyre tracks. She'll get back to us later with something more exact.'

'Hundreds of Transits about, Colin,' Lambie said warningly. 'But you are right, it is some kind of recurring theme.'

'And the only one they managed to trace had false

plates.' Anderson pointed at the Bridge Boy on the white-board. 'That was *this* Transit van, and its front offside tyre has a cross-shaped insult on it. Distinctive and identifiable. Once she's analysed the tracks in Glen Fruin, we'll know for certain whether there's a connection.'

'It bothers me that the forensic services are putting us at the top of their priorities.'

'Why does that bother you, DS Lambie?'

'Because it feels like we are doing somebody's dirty work for them. Howlett's?'

Anderson ignored him. 'What about Carruthers? Anything?'

'Had a quick word with the priest. He said Carruthers was honest, devout, stable, didn't smoke, gave up all alcohol more than thirty years ago.' Lambie pulled a face. 'I kind of feel he's trying to tell me something, but the secrecy of the confessional and all that . . . even with Carruthers dead.' Lambie paused for a minute. 'There's nothing big in the story.'

'Apart from the fact the man died.'

'The doc is the same – evidence that something had been troubling him recently. His GP notes say he stopped drinking, just like that –' he snapped his fingers '– in early 1977. He's been on sleeping tablets on and off since.'

'So, what happened to him in 1977?'

'Indeed. I need to speak to Mary without Rene being there. But she lives on the same landing, and any time somebody goes to Mary's door, she's out there like a demented troll. I asked the good Father if he thought Carruthers had killed himself, and he said no, not under any circumstances. He was too good a Catholic for that.

He would have gone to the priest first. He always has in the past. But whatever was on his mind, it had been really troubling him over the last few weeks. Might have been the money?'

'Well, I think the safety catch on the window could have been removed by A. N. Other, and I think somebody could have tipped Tommy Carruthers up and out the window. There are marks on his hip that I think support that theory. I'll get the Prof to take a look at them. It wouldn't be that hard, to fling someone out a window – 'defenestrate', I suppose the word is. You'd just need to get them out the room, maybe making a cup of tea. Then you remove the catch, get them over to the window. That's not hard either – you just comment on the view of the Campsies, ask what this or that building is – then you just tip 'em up and out.'

'And having done that, how would they get out of the Carruthers' flat without being seen by the CCTV . . . ?' Lambie said suddenly.

'What would I do?' mused Anderson.

'Apart from throw yourself out the window?'

'I'd buy a newspaper, a can of Coke, take my iPod or a good book, go in, kill Carruthers, then leave the flat and go up in the lift. Get out, head for the emergency stairwell. You'd be well warned if anybody was coming.'

'But who are we talking about? I need to ask Mrs Carruthers if . . .' Lambie was interrupted by a noise like a wounded wolf howling across the tundra. There was a crash of furniture, more howling, and footsteps came pounding towards their door. Wyngate was nearest; he hurtled towards the door and met the woman face on, his momentum pushing her back into the other room.

Anderson and Lambie were both on their feet. The howling wasn't aggressive. It was painful, anguished.

'Let me see him, *let me see him!*'

Wyngate backed in through the door. Beyond him, Anderson could see a woman sobbing in the arms of a male uniform.

'You might want to deal with this, guv.'

'I doubt that,' Anderson said quietly. Beyond the swing doors, a few people were hanging around, drawn by the commotion. The distressed woman was in her fifties, with unnaturally dark auburn hair, and was wearing a badly fitting black summer dress. She looked as though she carried the pain of the world with her. Then Anderson noticed she was wearing blue fluffy slippers.

'I'll take her through,' he said firmly.

'I wouldn't advise it, sir,' said the uniform. 'She might be better having a seat in here.' Then he spoke directly to the woman, pulling her hands from his neck like a mother with a clinging child. 'Now, you sit over here and DCI Anderson will come and talk to you.' As she sat down, he said in a side whisper, 'I'll call the medics. Just don't let her see any of those photographs, sir.'

The woman jumped to her feet, mascara and tears running down her face. 'Let me see him!'

'OK, OK, but calm down, will you? Just calm down.' Anderson tried his best to get her to sit down again.

'Don't tell me to calm down!' she screamed in his face. 'Just tell me where he is!' She thrust a copy of the *Daily Record* at Anderson. 'Tell me where my boy is!'

Costello had some toast and tea for breakfast, sitting in the small kitchen with the front door open to let the sunshine slant across the wooden floor. After throwing up, she had ventured out for her first real sight of Glen Fruin. The banks of Munros on either side had looked lilac in the distance, their peaks still shrouded by morning mist. But now the sun had burned off the haze to reveal the glen in all its verdant glory, with the river winding its lazy way from east to west. She went out and sat on the front step, in her new pyjamas, a cup of tea held firmly in both hands, closed her eyes and held her face up to the sun. There was a complete absence of any sound of so-called civilization, only birdsong and the lowing of cattle further up the glen.

She felt the warmth relaxing her face, but she was aware too of tightness in her shoulders, tension in the back of her neck. That meant there was a nagging worry somewhere. She didn't think it was finding the body last night; she had merely been a witness to that. And it wasn't Pettigrew, who had been efficient and understanding, delivering her to her accommodation with a merciful lack of fuss. No, her problem was that she was back at work, and she didn't know if she could cope.

She showered, dressed in her suit and heels, and thought about what to carry, what she was supposed to be doing. Empty hands looked ridiculous, so she slipped her handbag over her shoulder and picked up the envelope Howlett had given her. With that under her arm she set off to explore.

On her way to the main house she walked along a small bricked path, coming across a snake of school-children who were walking in pairs, making their way down to the river. All were dressed in perfectly match-ing blue tartan uniform, and all had wellies on their feet. They chatted quietly to each other, nodding or saying a polite hello to Costello as they passed by. She watched them all go – in her school they would have legged it to the bike sheds as soon as the teacher's back was turned.

Smiling to herself, she went on her way. The main house was slightly lower than the stable block, and the badly tarmacked road wound round to the front of the house where it opened on to a vast forecourt covered in fine gravel so deep any normal car was in danger of being bogged down. Two statues stood either side of a flight of stone steps that led down to a formal garden with beautifully manicured lawns. One she recognized as the standard likeness of Robert the Bruce. The other she guessed, from the sandstone swathe of plaid and the huge claymore, would be Sir Humphrey Colquhoun, a man who'd seen a bit of bloodshed in his time, fruit-lessly defending Glen Fruin from the vengeful McGregors. His staring eyes seemed fixed on a diagonal line of sprinklers lying idle across the lawn. The smell of freshly mown grass still hung in the air. Two boys, even younger than those going to the river, were photograph-ing some flowers close up; one held the camera while the other made careful notes. She could imagine the future botanist filling his page with details, his tongue held between his teeth in concentration. Costello leaned on the balustrade to watch them for a few minutes, then she started to gaze at the view over towards the bank of green velvet on the south side of the glen. From somewhere behind her came a clattering of dishes from the distant school kitchen.

It was remarkably deserted out here; there must be lots of people around but every single one of them seemed to be hidden away in a classroom somewhere. She heard laughter, a female voice made a comment, and her ears caught the louder response. Costello couldn't see anybody, but the voice had come from below her, as if people were sitting against the wall. She walked along nonchalantly, her face turned towards the house, seemingly studying the intricate heraldic carving over the main entrance, with the Colquhouns' motto 'Si je puis' wound round the antlers of a stag. She trailed her fingertips along the balustrade, and hoped she looked perfectly normal, perfectly casual.

Just as she drew level with the main door of the school she heard the laughter again, and there was a flurry of movement below. A group of senior pupils were breaking up; some came up the stone steps towards her and another three girls set off across the lawn, their pace slow and measured as if they had all the time in the world. Even in school uniform, Costello thought, those three came from Planet Beautiful. She thought of giraffes in the Serengeti, models on the catwalk – these were women who existed to be looked at. They were almost a cliché – the leggy blonde, the brunette beauty, the milky-skinned redhead – like three perfect gemstones in a single setting, each showing the others to best advantage.

As they walked off, the tall blonde turned and raised a

hand in greeting to Costello, as if she had known she was there all along.

'I'm really sorry about this,' Dino Marchetti kept saying, sweating profusely and mopping his forehead with a damp handkerchief.

'Not totally your fault. The desk at Partick should never have told you we were here.'

'But it's that bloody book that's stirred it all up for her. We tried to take out a court injunction against it being published, you know.'

'And they refused. Yes, I did know,' Anderson said mildly. They were sitting in the sun outside the Western Infirmary. Dino needed a smoke.

'The lawyers said we'd do better to find something libellous and sue, but Maria's in a terrible state – well, as you've seen.'

'It would be nice to think that the book might help in some way, provoke a bit of a response from the public,' Anderson tried. 'It might move the case on. It's never officially been closed, you know. Sorry, I'm just trying to find something positive in all this.'

Dino shrugged. 'It's been fourteen years. I've tried to move on but every time a body is found she thinks it's him.' He took a deep draw on his cigarette. 'It's so hard for her. She's on a lot of medication.'

Anderson recognized that Dino needed to talk, and decided to let him.

'I really thought Maria was beginning to accept it, until those lassies were found, two in Austria and one in America. Somebody'd kept them locked up for years and years, but they all came back. So every time a lad in his teens or twenties turns up unidentified, she's convinced it must be him. That's bad enough, but then something like this appears in the newspaper.'

Anderson still kept quiet. Both Marchettis were slim, dark-haired and fine featured, like the boy. He could understand why the mother would feel that flare of hope.

'The worst thing is not knowing what happened, or why. Everyone thinks if you're Italian, you're in the Mafia, but we weren't like that. We just ran a restaurant and an Italian deli. If someone had asked for money, I could understand that, and we'd have paid it, whatever they wanted. If some crazy person had stolen him and killed him, even that, you could see a reason for it. And we would have a body, something to bury. But this . . .' Dino spread his hands and shrugged. 'Nothing. Not a word. No trace of our son. Who could be so cruel?' He mopped the back of his neck. 'Has anybody identified this other boy yet?'

'Not yet, unfortunately. '

'You know, she won't calm down until they do.'

'We're going to do a DNA test. That will tell us –'

'That he's not our son!' Dino glared almost accusingly at Anderson.

'I don't doubt for a minute that this boy is not Alessandro. I'm sorry. But I think your wife needs proof. And a DNA test will provide that.'

Dino sighed. 'You know we moved out the flat the day Alessandro was taken; we never went back.'

'What can you tell me about the babysitter?'

'Tito?' Dino did not appear surprised by the question. 'He was a good boy, we thought. No dad, ever, and his mum had died. Too fond of the drinking. And she was a little . . .' He tapped his temple, adding a slight twisting movement. So, the mother had been a screwball as well as a drunk. 'He started working in our kitchen at weekends when he was fourteen. Like I say, a good boy, played with little Alessandro in the shop. It was the first time he'd actually babysat him, just sitting in, watching TV. Maria and I were out at a charity dinner. We got home to find our son missing, Tito missing. There was blood every-where but none of it matched the samples they took from Maria and me. The blood was not from our son.' Dino crossed himself, and Anderson wondered how many times he had been through that story. 'Is there any chance you might reopen the case?'

'As I said, it was never closed. But I need a reason to reactivate it.'

Dino Marchetti placed a hand on Anderson's shoulder and gave it a firm squeeze. 'Please do it – if not for me, then for her. Just to let her sleep at night.'

'Can I ask you, and I have no reason for asking you, but were you happy with the way Eric Moffat conducted the investigation?'

Dino looked surprised. 'I have nothing to compare it to. At the time yes, I was happy.' The shrug of his shoulder was very Latin. 'But with this book, I don't know what to think.'

'Do you recall a cop called Carruthers from that time? I know it was a long time ago.'

'Oh, I remember them all, Mr Anderson. Every single one. But no, there was no Carruthers.'

11.00 a.m.

Costello turned at the sound of hurried feet on the gravel. A thickset woman with wire-wool hair was running towards her, arm outstretched as if getting ready to pass a baton. 'Hello, hello,' she trilled. 'I'm Rhona McMillan. I'm the Registrar here.'

Costello immediately wanted to smack her.

'And I bet I know who you are!' The woman pointed at her, excited as a kid in a chocolate factory. She hushed her voice. 'You're DS Costello. From the *police*!' she added with relish.

'That's right,' said Costello, slightly wrong-footed. She started to walk along by the balustrade, forcing Rhona to walk beside her. Three men in suits were coming out through the front door of the school, and Costello wanted a private conversation.

'And I for one am very glad you're here,' Rhona hurried on. 'I mean, of course it's all very hush-hush, but we all know. I just hope you can do something about it.'

'I'll do the best I can,' Costello replied sweetly, having no idea what the woman was blethering on about but feeling intrigued.

'Well, I hope you got some sleep last night after that terrible news.' Rhona looked over her shoulder nervously. 'I'm sure it's nothing to do with us.'

'Any reason why it might be?'

'Oh no, I'm just being silly. Anyway, have you had your breakfast?' Rhona glanced at her watch. 'Mr Ellis – he's the Warden – wants to see you at twelve. He knows far more about it all than I do.' She was one of those women who ask a question without expecting an answer. Probably nobody ever really listened to her.

'I've eaten, thank you. Can you tell me who they are – the three girls walking over the lawn?' Costello asked with her back towards them.

But Rhona stuck her head out, as unsubtle as an elephant. 'Oh, Saskia, Keren and Victoria. They're very beautiful, aren't they? Funny how they gravitate towards each other. They'll be leaving Glen Fruin this week for good.' Rhona sighed. 'It's always sad when they go.'

'Surely it's good to get out and take on the world,' Costello said. 'I was desperate to leave school.'

Rhona threw her a look as if to say, 'Well, you would be, wouldn't you?' But she said, 'Saskia is going on to study in Italy. She's actually Russian, well – half Russian, half Dutch. The Dutch being the Saskia, the Russian being the Morosova.' She looked skyward, thinking. 'Yes, that's the right way round. She's been here for four years now, perfecting her English, doing some more highers. Victoria is going back to the good old US of A and . . . oh, I'm not sure where Keren calls home. Dubai at the moment. She's Irish, one of the Cork O'Learys.'

That was obviously supposed to mean something. 'Quite a mixture,' was all Costello said.

Costello's eye was caught by Pettigrew, walking briskly

after a plump dark-haired girl, both moving quickly into the cover of the shrubbery. The girl was upset, crying. She threw her arm out, pushing Pettigrew away. He obviously decided not to follow, saying something too quiet for Costello to hear, but his body language was an apology in itself.

'What about her?' Costello interrupted, pointing.

'Oh, Elizabeth Hamilton. Poor girl, she really shouldn't be here. I don't know much about her. I think she lost both parents when she was very young, and her grandfather sent her here to be looked after as much as educated, as is the way with many boarding schools now. She boards, although he lives in Glasgow. She has nothing in common with the other girls, with their ponies and parties and frocks. She can't keep up academically, financially or socially with any degree of confidence. She just doesn't fit in. She rarely goes home, or to stay with any of the other girls here, and there's no pairing up at weekends. She just keeps to herself. No close friends, nobody wants her. Except she doesn't care, so it doesn't bother her.'

Costello felt a stab in her heart.

The girl turned and looked after Pettigrew, who was walking back up the garden, then disappeared into the rhododendrons.

'She'll be going down the path to the bridge. She often sits there – *smoking*.' Rhona made it sound as though the girl was guilty of ethnic cleansing. 'You can't help thinking that, no matter what her home situation is, she would be much better at an ordinary state school; she gains nothing from a school like this.'

'But if she's from Glasgow, why doesn't she go to a local school? Nothing to stop her. What age is she?'

'Seventeen.'

The girl became visible again, walking along a wooden path that led to a bridge, her ungainly short steps in stark contrast to the Three Graces' elegant glide. She disturbed a crow that cawed loudly, taking off and flying up towards the school. The girl didn't flinch, but watched it fly away, as if she envied the bird its freedom.

12.30 p.m.

The Marchettis' Mercedes pulled out of the car park, narrowly missing Mulholland's Audi as it cut the corner on the way in. Anderson thought it wise to hold the door open for him. Mulholland drove like that when he was in a mood, and the mood was confirmed as he slammed the door and approached his boss.

'I've got news for you. O'Hare has an ID on the body you found at Glen Fruin, and he wants to know why your mobile was turned off when he wanted to speak to you. And I would like to know when I become your answering service. So, I'm going for a coffee, DCI Anderson, before anybody else thinks I am your personal secretary.' And with that he was gone, striding across the car park, leaving a trail of aftershave hanging in the air.

Anderson rang the pathologist's number on his mobile,

as he followed Mulholland across the car park to sit on the low wall. If O'Hare looked out of the window he would see him.

The phone was answered and O'Hare asked him to hang on. 'No, don't leave it there,' he was saying, obviously trying to keep his exasperation under control. 'It has to go in the fridge. No, not that fridge, *that* fridge.'

Anderson could imagine some bemused young student wandering around with a body part.

'Colin, sorry to keep you waiting. Just thought you should know that your dead body is William Andrew MacFadyean.'

Anderson waited for the next bit; it meant nothing to him so far.

'He was run over twice, as we suspected, killed on the road then taken to one side, out of sight. You should have a word with –'

'Matilda McQueen. Yes, I will.'

'But what was he doing up there?' O'Hare went on. 'He had money on him, but no identification, no credit cards, nothing. And we have no address for him, just his DNA on file from when he was a cop – oh, yes, he's ex-job. Based at Shawlands, Southside, never got further than constable.'

'Ex-cop? Dead ex-cop?' murmured Anderson, thinking of Carruthers. Dead at sixty-eight. 'What age was he? And what year did he graduate?'

'I know I'm good but I'm not that good.'

*

After her very formal but totally uninformative meeting with Mr Ellis the Warden, Costello had spent a whole hour Rhona free. She had used the time walking once round the buildings that comprised the school – from the grandeur of the old house to the modern technology block and the games hall built into the side of the hill. It had been well done; new trees had been planted to screen the walls of the new buildings and, where possible, the old walls of the original gardens screened the paths and walkways.

It was very pretty.

She saw the Three Graces sitting on the wall above the formal garden. With their youth, beauty and assurance they were everything a man could wish for. Each was exquisite in her own way, but all three, together, would turn heads – women's as well as men's – wherever they went.

Costello wondered if she could get out her phone, take a covert photo and send it back to the boys at the lecture room – see if the girls were on some system somewhere. But it was not legal, she cursed silently. And anyway, there was no mobile phone signal.

Saskia moved off the wall, and the other two followed. Costello had a notion to take them down to the old station at Partickhill for an hour or so. Ten minutes in an interview room still rank with the stench of last night's vomiting drunks might just take the edge off their lovely lives.

She thought about following them but went up to look at the old house instead. Inside the main hall, as Costello walked up the huge stairway, feet almost bouncing on the thick red carpet, she realized she was feeling better. She smiled at a dusty portrait of some tartan-clad Jacobite that hung high above her head. If she could get some mobile reception, she would phone Anderson and find out the progress on the body in the wood.

She took in the view from an upstairs window . . . it would be very easy to get around unseen.

Costello returned to the garden and sat on the wall, watching the pupils come and go. The older they got, the more relaxed the dress code seemed to be from the blue-and-black tartan mix. But then, it was the second last day of term, and it was all winding down. She was deliberately eavesdropping on two boys looking forward to seeing their parents at the party on Sunday. One had a painting in the exhibition, and he would be guiding some parents round it. He was nervous and excited.

'Oh, hello!' It was Rhona again, popping out from behind a pillar as if she had been lying in wait. 'I know you can't tell me what Mr Ellis said, but I've found him! I thought you might want to come and see him, and do an assessment or something.'

Costello had already surmised that Rhona was off on a wrong track somewhere, but decided to go along with it, secretly enjoying the fact that there might be more than a few problem pupils kicking about the school. Rhona was adept at walking and talking, though not really saying much that made sense, just a constant stream of vagueness. They went back down to the main hall on the way to the front door. More dusty portraits of the family that had originally built the house hung on the walls, and a huge table stood in the middle of the hall, covered with brown envelopes and a neat stack of newspapers.

They went across the gravel at the front of the house, and down the steps to the lower garden, where a few pupils were lolling around on their mid-morning break.

'There he is,' said Rhona, pointing.

'OK,' said Costello. 'Let's keep walking. Don't make it obvious we're looking at anybody.' She followed Rhona along the creeper-hung wall below the balustrade. 'Who am I looking at exactly?'

But even as the words left her mouth, she knew. An extremely thin young man, about sixteen or seventeen years old, was standing in the hot glare of the sun, wearing a full-length leather coat, dark glasses and black jeans. His long black hair had obviously been dyed, and he was attempting to grow a beard. He was talking to himself, reciting something that Costello couldn't hear, probably a fluent repetition of something he'd learned. There was something about the boy that made the hairs on the back of her neck stand up. He didn't seem to be quite of this world.

'Does he do this often? Do you know what he's saying?' she asked.

'I never get close enough to hear any of it, but he is talking to himself!' Rhona looked quickly over her shoulder. 'As you've probably been told, it's this obsession with violence thing – he's totally obsessed. And not *normal* stuff . . .' She shook her head, unable to find the words.

'Hardcore?' offered Costello.

'His essays are much too explicit, disturbing. He collects images of death, violence, guns, knives, you name it.'

'Guns?' asked Costello.

'Especially guns,' said Rhona. 'Photographs, magazines, books. That's why you're here, isn't it, to find out if he's a danger?'

Only to himself thought Costello, wondering what the boy might be on. But all she said was, 'Mmm.'

'I really think Drew Elphinstone could turn this school into a new Columbine. All these tragedies start somewhere, you know.'

It seemed an absurd statement to make, in the grounds of a grand stately home, on such a lovely sunny day, yet Costello was in no doubt that Rhona McMillan believed every word she was saying.

2.30 p.m.

Skelpie Fairbairn sat in a corner at the ABode Hotel, thinking to himself that the beer was expensive, the food was bloody expensive, and the women were far too fucking expensive. Made-up, dressed up, and stuck up, they would smile at him, maybe even exchange a few words, and then they would back away. Nothing specific, just a vague indication that they didn't fancy him. To his left, two guys were eating a huge pile of onion rings at a posh hotel, and two burgers each. He'd tried giving them a wee smile, even tried to pass a comment when the food came: 'You're never going to get through that lot before closing time.' They'd smiled politely, acknowledging his little joke, then the closest one had slightly turned his back, striking up a quiet conversation with his pal, cutting Skelpie out swiftly and completely.

Things had not changed.

He got up, nodding goodbye to the onion-ring eaters. They didn't acknowledge it. He walked up on to Byres Road, thinking about going back to the flat in Dumbarton Road; he was keeping to the west side of the city, north of the river, away from his previous hunting ground. It was high time he moved on, as too many people knew where he was. He hoped, when the codeword came, he'd be moved up to the Highland Glen Hotel, where he could be really anonymous.

He did fully intend to turn right towards Dumbarton Road but something made him go north, up into the Great Western Road, towards the hotel, telling himself he was just checking it out, but he recognized that twitch in his subconscious, as if something feral had been woken in him. Something had registered, something on his radar. He slowed down, taking his time. After all, he was just a guy strolling along, enjoying the weather. He scanned the pavement like a cat sensing an injured bird. Then he saw her. She was standing on her own outside the big green-grocer's shop with its wares piled in baskets all over the pavement, highly polished fruit on one side, pristine clean vegetables on the other. A queue of customers snaked past buckets of flowers and decorative greenery, but she was leaning against a wall to one side – waiting for her mother? He guessed she'd be ten or eleven now. She was wearing jeans, and a white T-shirt with short sleeves rolled up to her shoulders, and sunglasses pushed up to pin back her short, light brown hair. Suddenly she looked up from the game she was playing on her mobile phone, as if aware of his scrutiny.

He would have known her anywhere. He whispered her name to himself.

He had served time for her. Lynda Osbourne.

But he kept walking, and found himself right up at the top of the road by the corner at the Botanics. He could see Kirklee Terrace from here, where Helena McAlpine, wife of the bastard cop, lived. He decided he could do with a walk; it would do him good.

3.00 p.m.

Lambie practised the conversation in his mind, working out each response that Mary might give. He took a deep breath and picked up the phone. She was so long in answering it, he nearly gave up.

'Mrs Carruthers, I'm sorry to bother you, I know this is a difficult time for you . . .'

The others could hear a chit-chat answer down the phone.

'Can I just ask you if your husband knew a William Andrew MacFadyean? . . . Oh yes. They met at the police college, did they? We know that they shared a fair bit of time working at Partick.' Lambie gave Anderson the thumbs up. 'No, don't you go upsetting yourself, Mrs Carruthers.' Lambie's tone changed, and he pulled the receiver closer to his ear. 'I'm afraid Mr MacFadyean has passed away, yes. I wasn't at Tommy's funeral but Wullie was, wasn't he?' He frowned as the voice at the other end chattered on. 'Mrs Carruthers, did Tommy keep a diary?' He was confident he knew the answer to that one. 'Really? Do you think I could have a look at them? . . . Yes, they might be useful . . . Yes, I appreciate that. And one other thing, did your husband ever go near Glen Fruin? . . . No? It means nothing to you? . . . OK, thank you, Mrs Carruthers.' He put down the phone. 'Well, well, well.'

'Have you just played a hunch that has come off?'

'I don't think she was totally surprised that Wullie Mac-Fadyean is dead. Carruthers and MacFadyean knew each other, and they were killed within fourteen days of each other. Carruthers was fretting about something.' He tapped his desk with the nib of his pen. 'But she is happy for me to look at the diaries. I think that might be very enlightening.'

3.20 p.m.

Anderson had spent the last hour going through the paperwork Howlett had given him. He was getting very uneasy about all this. He was telling himself that one murderer was just like another. The end result was the same. But the thought that they might be on the trail of anything international in general, and Russian in specific, made him feel very out his depth. He had no specialist training in or knowledge of any of this. He dropped his head down, letting his forehead lean on a pile of dirty brown files.

'Is it that bad, sir? I think you just need some sleep,' said Lambie.

'I think we are getting caught in the middle of something here. Let's have a review,' said Anderson as Mulholland appeared with a tray of hot coffee. 'For a start, we need a brief history of how Biggart got to be where he was. From the early 1900s – the good old days, some might call them – two families controlled the east and north of Glasgow. By the time we get to the 1980s, things are getting serious, big drugs are moving in, but the O'Donnells and the McGregors are still very much in charge. Over the years they seem to have done a good job of killing each other off. Often with a private joke about killing each other by shooting into various body orifices. They never, ever went for cutting people open up the middle of the ribcage. That is a trick of the Russian mafia. Are we agreed so far?'

Lambie and Mulholland both nodded.

'But,' said Anderson, 'by the end of 1996 all that had gone.'

'The time of the Marchetti kidnap? Which Moffat was in charge of.'

'And that's when the Russian mafia appear on the scene.' Anderson rubbed the tiredness from his eyes. 'That's the theme of all this. Companies being bought by companies who are owned by companies with Russian directors. At the bottom line, they buy taxi companies, sunbed salons and sandwich bars.'

'Money laundering, then,' said Lambie. 'And cutting people open sounds more like them. Eagles, double eagles.'

'You sound like a golfer,' muttered Mulholland.

Anderson ignored him; his heart was sinking. 'Do you also think that human trafficking sounds like them?'

'You'd be naive to think it doesn't. People are cheap currency nowadays. Kids even more so. You can buy a kid in the Ukraine for a few hundred, worth thousands over here,' said Mulholland. 'And where there is money to be made, organized crime follows.'

'But I always thought the Glasgow gangs were just a bunch of thugs that went about demanding money with menaces from little old ladies,' Lambie said, shrugging slightly.

'That would have got you a stab, if you'd hit a little old lady. They'd rob a post office or nick your car, but not the little old lady thing. Ice cream vans, scrap yards, selling stolen goods at the Barras, that was their sort of game.'

'Very moral of them,' muttered Anderson. 'Eric Moffat is mentioned in this file at an incident Costello attended as a proby, in the city centre. It's kind of passed into folklore but there was, according to this, a meeting between the McGregors and the O'Donnells – well, the women. They had each had nearly everybody important to them killed by the family of the other. Pauline McGregor had lost her husband and both brothers, and Mo O'Donnell, who was married to Auld Archie, had lost two sons and the third was in the Bar-L. They agreed that the two families would stop fighting between themselves, and keep each to their own territory. The theory was that they were thinking it was the only way to stay strong, to stop the Russians moving in.'

'Didn't work, though, did it?'

'Somebody must have really wanted it not to happen. Pauline was fatally stabbed in the car park coming away from that meeting. She was pregnant. No one ever stood trial for it but Archie – Wee Archie, I mean – was later convicted of chopping the head off one of his own people. Don't know if they ever got the guy who actually stabbed Pauline, though.'

'Why? If they were on opposite sides, why should it matter to the O'Donnells who killed Pauline?'

'Outwith the code? Punishment for acting without authority? Who knows? But after that there were a couple of years of peace. Either they'd listened to their women, or they'd simply run out of men. Everything was quiet for a while. We didn't know that at the time, of course. But with hindsight, that's when it all started to quieten down. Post 1996, post Alessandro Marchetti's disappearance, all hell broke loose, each family accusing the other of kidnapping the kid to make them look bad. In the end, both families fell apart.'

'I don't follow,' said Lambie, intrigued. 'Surely over the years somebody has come forward? Somebody must have said something.'

'It's the sheer silence, the lack of concrete evidence that suggests it was one of them. Only gang families like that can make people look the other way for such a long period of time. But nobody admits anything. Nobody . . . total silence. If somebody had a shred of solid evidence, it would be out by now.'

'So, nobody has ever really known who was behind the abduction of the boy? But whoever it was, they had the organizational skills to take a kid – that was a whole new ball game.'

'It was a cool hard snatch. In and out,' Anderson observed. 'There'd be problems keeping the child and the babysitter in a safe place, and you could argue that only an organized crime family had the means to do that. But then again, they'd certainly never done anything like it before, either lot. They were a bunch of thugs, yes, but they had brains. The bit that doesn't fit is that neither the boy nor the babysitter were returned. And, despite what Simone Sangster says, no ransom was ever asked for. Either family would have fulfilled their part of the bargain, if a bargain had been made. Because it was business. If they'd taken the money and not returned the child, there'd be no point in doing it again, would there?'

'So, what age is Archie O'Donnell now? Is he still alive?'

'He'd be an old man, if so.'

'I'd really like to know what they're up to now, in 2010. Those who are left.'

'Eric Moffat might know. He was at the sharp end of the police investigation into the families for five years – the years that saw their decline.'

'I think he was even shot at by Archie O'Donnell once,' said Lambie with some delight. 'But don't start him on that story, or you'll never get away.'

4.20 p.m.

Anderson was trying to resist the temptation to make the Marchetti case active. He could only justify it if there was a stronger link than Moffat being in charge. But, as much as he liked Dino and felt desperately sorry for Maria, he couldn't do it. As soon as the Bridge Boy's DNA came back, and the findings had been communicated to the Marchettis, that would be that.

The report on Melinda Biggart's finances had come in and been sent off to the fraud squad accountants. They'd had money, those two – it seemed crime did pay – but the initial consensus view was that Mrs Biggart was hiding nothing from her husband. Well, nothing financial, at any rate.

'Can I talk to you a minute?' said a familiar voice, and he looked up to see Helena McAlpine standing in front of his desk. She gave a little sideways glance around the lecture theatre. 'In private?'

Anderson stood up. 'Those were the days, when I had an office of my own. Or I could borrow my boss's.'

'Indeed, those were the days.' She said it cheerily enough, but did not move.

Anderson dearly wished she would. But there she was, still with that same smile, and that same scent of Penhaligon's Bluebell – mingled with the aroma of turps or brush cleaner, or whatever it was. And his heart sank. That was the thing about Helena McAlpine – the world around her seemed to change, but she herself stayed the same. Today she was wearing stonewashed jeans and a blue-and-white striped T-shirt. She had not tanned in the summer sun; her freckles had just joined up a little more.

'We could go out to the canteen,' he offered.

'I don't think so,' she replied. But still she did not move.

'You got your car?'

'It's across the road.'

'Good,' he said. 'Come on.'

4.30 p.m.

It was a hot afternoon with close airless weather. The wind was stuck elsewhere in the glen; Costello felt the sweat run down the back of her neck, and the skin of her face was moist. The midges were gathering in bundles, sensing that the temperature was ready to drop as the evening approached. Costello sat on the wall at the balustrade, her stomach full with salmon and boiled new potatoes followed by cheesecake. And tea in a cup with a saucer. Howlett had been right, the food here was lovely. She was pretending she was working, listening to the noises around her – gentle noises caught in the summer air. Some pupils were playing tennis, the hollow thump, thump of the ball hitting the dry grass. They scored badly. A fun game. Their friends lay on the low banks of grass that surrounded the courts.

More extracurricular art seemed to be going on on the upper lawn. Sketch books out, pencils and pastels scattered at their feet, young talented hands doing lazy sketches. It was idyllic, listening to the noises of people interacting, but not getting involved. She realized how lonely she had been in the flat. She had enjoyed casual chit-chat over lunch about the difficulty of moving kids from class to class, the problems of the old school –which Costello took to mean the original building – and the new school with its classrooms and technical block built into the side of the hill on the north-east side of the old house. Costello's flat was further to the south. She knew they were subtly complaining about the set-up to her, in her position as somebody who was going to report back on how to make it all better.

She watched the Three Graces strolling together. They went over to sit on the stone bench where several boys gathered at their feet in some kind of subtle migration of the beautiful people.

She had sat there for a while, enjoying the sights and sounds, when she saw the little plump girl Elizabeth walk across the lower path, well away from everybody else. She was not walking quickly but there was something about the way she moved that pricked Costello's interest. 'Furtive' was the word that floated into her mind. And the way she was dressed – the trousers, the long cardigan, the flat shoes. Dressed to be out, not to enjoy the summer afternoon. Costello had been told to watch for anything that sparked her interest, and . . . she had had her interest sparked.

She looked down, watching the figure walk to the bridge over the stream. Was there a subtle look behind to check that nobody was following her? There was a definite pulling of her hand from her trouser pocket, a flick of the wrist and a quickening of the stroll that was not be as relaxed as it seemed. Costello slid from her place and went slowly down the stone stairs, turning round to look at the house every now and again, impressed by its grandeur as a newcomer should be. But she was subtly watching the figure dressed in black.

Costello paused at the bridge, searching for the path where the girl had gone. The path followed the stream running down to the river. The path and the stream twisted in and out of the old forest to reappear further down the glen – which also meant they twisted in and out of sight, Costello realized. Elizabeth had gone into the older forest which, Costello presumed, was out of bounds – if anything *was* out of bounds in this place. But she felt like she was trailing a suspect, and she had always been good at that.

Keeping well back, she entered the subdued light of the old oak forest, staying close to the trunks of the massive trees. The air was cool in here, light dappled on the path, highlighting the clouds of buzzing and whirring insects. She walked on, catching glimpses of the girl in front of her each time the path straightened out for a few yards. She kept well behind, pausing only when the main path went to the left up the hill and towards the Forestry Commission land with its regiments of pine trees. Elizabeth had chosen a much smaller, less defined path that seemed to run down towards the river. Costello could hear the water – louder, gently rolling, as if there was a waterfall nearby. The small path had overhanging branches, which meant she had to protect her face, and she wondered how often people passed this way. But Elizabeth knew where was going, confidently climbing over a fence that had the top wire bent for easier access. There was a sign in faded paint, warning politely that they were now leaving school premises and giving a list of warnings about what might happen to them in the big bad world outside.

Costello followed her over the fence, still keeping her distance, then moved on and trailed her for a good five minutes. She kept looking at her watch in case she was losing her sense of direction in the middle of the trees, thinking back to Hansel and Gretel. There was the sound of a waterfall – not a big one but a gentle ongoing rumble of slow water. Here it may not rain for years and yet the river would still flow, the water draining down from springs high in the hills. She paused, instinct telling her that Elizabeth had stopped. The girl was crossing the river on some stepping stones, arms out for balance, heading for a slight clearing on the far side. Costello hid behind the trunk of a large tree, its bark rough to the skin of her hands and face as she leaned her face against it. She was soaked with sweat as she got her breath back and watched.

Then Elizabeth seemed to look around her, waiting or watching for something. Her dealer? Was this what Howlett had been talking about? The girl turned to look back in Costello's direction. She withdrew, her back to the tree and waited. Nothing. She looked out again; Elizabeth had moved along the path a few feet and was kicking something with her shoes – some dead pulled grass covering a small hole that had been dug in the ground. She muttered something as she kicked the grass away. It sounded like 'fucking maddie' or 'fucking saddoe'.

She seemed infuriated by this, and raised her voice, calling out with her face turned away from Costello so she only heard the end of the word . . . the 'ewe'.

Was she calling for Drew? The *fucking maddie*?

Elizabeth spun round, calling again. Then she screamed and stumbled back. Costello stepped out on to the path to see the girl rolling on the ground, holding her ankle. Elizabeth was in agony.

Costello ran towards her, nimbly jumping over the stepping stones, getting her toes wet. 'God, what happened to you?'

The girl looked up in surprise – mild surprise, she had expected somebody but not Costello. 'I fell down that fuckin' hole, didn't ah, went right over on ma ankle.'

Costello was now close enough to see the black-lined eyes and the pockmarked skin that was almost white with make-up. On the ground the girl looked like a bad clown. She knelt down to look; a spike of wood had gone through the girl's trouser leg and the sock and had broken the surface of her skin badly, in a dot-dot-dash-dash pattern. Even as Costello watched, it started to bleed.

'Where did you spring from?' asked Elizabeth, recovering her Glen Fruin accent.

'I was exploring that wee path. I thought you had gone up the other way – sorry if I frightened you.' She leaned over to help the girl up.

Did she imagine that Elizabeth looked into the forest, worried that whoever she was expecting might appear? Drew? Her dealer? Was she expecting to score? And just for herself?

Then Costello looked behind her to the two perfect holes cut into the earth, the second one filled with pieces of cut wood, sharpened to spikes and stuck into the earth to remain upright. 'Bloody hell! What on earth is that – a trap of some kind?'

'Bugger if I know, but I fell right into it.'

'But that first one was badly disguised – so you walked round it, almost forcing you to step right into this one.' She knelt down. 'This one was well disguised and –' Her attention was caught by a movement in the trees, somebody in black, darting from the cover of one tree to another. 'Did you see that?'

'Who?'

Who?

Elizabeth sounded scared, and just for a minute Costello realized how young she was. 'Nothing, just the shadows playing tricks on my eyes . . . Let's get you up, the damage seems to be only skin deep. Hop to that tree and see if you can stand on that ankle.'

As she gave Elizabeth some support, the young girl swore. Costello was aware of the constant rumble of the water; she was able to talk to her companion at close quarters but it would be hard to hear anybody creeping around. She looked back at the two small pits, each a perfect rectangle, and noticed the way they were lined up. She looked around her – at the trees and the dark, deep forest.

She registered the feeling that they were being watched, something dark moving in the trees alongside them.

Something to report.

'Come on, let's get back. Just lean on my arm.'

The girl did so, holding tighter than was necessary.

'So, why were you down here? It was a bit of a trek.'

'Why were you?' came the easy reply.

*

When he first got into the Beamer, balancing coffee in a tray, Anderson tried to press the switch to roll down the window.

'Well, you can do that if you want,' said Helena dryly, turning down an opera aria on the CD. 'Or we could put the air con on.'

He laughed. 'I've been demoted to a Jazz, remember?'

'I know. Bad days.'

Anderson took a sip of coffee, and felt himself relaxing as a cool refreshing draught came through the air-conditioning vent. 'So, what do you want?'

Her fingers curled round the steering wheel. 'Colin, I need to know the truth. About Alan. Was he bent?'

Anderson's head jerked round. 'Alan? Bent? No! He was a good copper; he was DCI at – what – thirty-eight? Alan never did a bent thing in his entire career! Or do you think Fairbairn was innocent? Because he wasn't, he was guilty. Some lawyer's making a play of the new disclosure law, that's all. And no, again, Alan was not bent.'

'And you would know.'

'Yes, I would,' he answered without hesitating. 'OK, I don't have proof, but I don't need any. Full stop.'

'Not a single doubt in your mind?'

'Not an iota. Alan was too much of an upfront in-your-face little shite to be taking any backhanders. He might go to bed with the bad guys but he'd tell everybody about it. Not orthodox, but not illegal.'

Helena bit her lip and nodded. 'It's just, with this

Fairbairn business, people have started talking. Denise said –'

'She would. She's another criminal lawyer, and a man-hater.'

'She happens to be my best friend.'

'If she was your best friend, she wouldn't be talking shite about your late husband.'

'I guess not,' Helena said quietly.

'The fact that she's Terry Gilfillan's sister might have something to do with it.'

Anderson watched her face. There was no reaction to Gilfillan's name, no hasty, 'Oh, I meant to tell you, we're getting married.' He wondered what it would be like to go out to dinner with Helena, properly. He lifted his coffee to his mouth, thinking about how to phrase an invitation, to make it sound casual . . .

'There's something else,' Helena said after a while.

'Yes?' He was grateful that she had interrupted. Better that than hear her say no.

'I think somebody is watching me. I'm not imagining it.'

'I'm sure you aren't.'

'I think it's Fairbairn. I've seen him three times now, on the grass up at the terrace, and in the street outside the gallery. But it was when I saw him yesterday, outside the gallery again, that I realized he wasn't just somebody out in the street having a fag; he was following me. He does this little trick, flipping the lighter before he lights up – I remember Alan trying to do it.' She spanned her fingers, palm down, jerked her hand palm up then closed her fingers. 'And it dawned on me who it was. It *is* him.'

'OK, I'll see what I can do.'

'Apart from the fact that Alan arrested him – you're sure there's nothing else?'

'If there was, I would tell you.'

'So, it might just be coincidence. Even if it isn't, I can look after myself.'

'And can I ask you – did Alan ever have a working relationship with either Archie O'Donnell or any of the McGregors?'

Helena ran her fingers through her hair, checking it in the rear-view mirror. Then she looked directly at Anderson, the significance of his question sinking in. She was offended. 'He wasn't on the take from them or anybody else. I'm surprised you have to ask that.'

'It's not what I meant. Top cops, organized crime. There's often a subtle relationship. That's all.' He realized his hand had slid on top of hers. He removed it.

'It's a long time ago, Colin. I know Alan thought William McGregor was as tricksy as a box of monkeys. He did meet Archie O'Donnell a few times. This is Glasgow and I'm not naive enough to think there wasn't a sectarian side to that.'

'O'Donnell would talk to a Catholic cop if he wanted to talk to a cop at all,' agreed Anderson.

'And I think there was a degree of mutual respect, if that's what you mean.'

Anderson nodded and sighed. It was bloody hot in the car. 'Talking of Terry . . .' He turned to Helena.

'Which we weren't.'

'You never told me you were engaged.' By some miracle his voice sounded quite normal, even congratulatory.

Helena levelled the rear-view mirror with her fingertip. 'I'm not sure that I am.'

Anderson couldn't help feeling as if a knife had been stuck in his stomach.

She smiled at him. 'I remember Terry asking me to marry him, but I do not remember giving him an answer. I certainly didn't say yes. Where does this come from?'

'I just heard a rumour.'

'And you were annoyed that I hadn't told you?' She smiled that rather mocking smile. 'That's rather touching.'

'But none of my business.'

'No, it's not really, is it?' She placed her hand on the back of his. 'But there's something that is. You were the next most senior investigating officer in Fairbairn's case, weren't you?'

'Yes.'

'And how long do you think it'll take Fairbairn to figure out that the girl who comes to the gallery to show me her pictures is your daughter?'

5.10 p.m.

'Elizabeth? Are you OK?' asked Costello as her companion slumped on to the wall at the far side of the school garden.

'Please don't call me that, I'm not the friggin' queen. It's Libby, and I'm going to stop for a fag before we go any further. I know you won't tell.'

Costello frowned slightly. 'And how do you know I won't tell?'

'Because you think they're a bunch of wankers. I can tell. Fag?' Libby Hamilton slumped to the ground and pulled her trousers up above her knee, laying plump white legs bare to the sun, exposing the angry red dash on her calf. 'It must be some kind of curse, to have such dark hair and not tan. Why is that?'

'Curse of the Celt, I think – or is it the Bretons? There's one lot that have dark hair and blue eyes and don't tan.' Costello sat down beside her, drawing her knees up and closing her eyes. The light of the sun made the veins dance in her eyelids. She could smell Libby's cigarette smoke wafting across her face. 'Are you OK?' she asked again.

'Of course.' There was an unconscious wipe of the thumb under her eyes, as if to remove any sign that she had been crying. 'Why are you here?'

'I'm casing the joint,' Costello said, half in jest.

'I don't think that's so far from the truth,' said Libby with a total lack of humour. 'You struck gold with a body on your first night.'

'Could have done without that. So, do you like it here?'

'As I have no experience of any other type of school, I can't really say.' There was the sound of a quiet kiss as Libby took the cigarette in her lips and drew hard. 'As prisons go, this is nice enough. Warm, great food, and the company is *endlessly* amusing. But none of it's real. Like you.' She flicked her cigarette ash with some anger.

'Like me?'

'You're real; you don't belong here. And the fact that you're real means that you are, by definition, fake. Like finding a sane person in a lunatic asylum – they must be there for a reason.' She let out a long plume of cigarette smoke. 'The staff view you with some suspicion, yet you're not a school inspector – if you were, you'd have had a fit the minute I lit up. And I've seen you bite your lip at a few things.'

'At people who don't need mortgages because they inherit?' Costello mused.

The rear wheels of an approaching car spun up some grit from the drive, which bounced across the lawn like hail. The gardener stood upright from his wheelbarrow and lifted out a rake. 'Bet his language is choice.' Libby moved along the stone wall a little and turned to look at Costello. 'Anyway, why are you prowling around like Miss Marple in the midnight garden? Looking for clues?'

'It seems a very lax kind of place. I thought it would be more regimented,' said Costello, standing up as the chill of the stone started to eat through her trousers.

'Yes, but it's a business,' Libby said baldly. 'They have to give us a certain degree of freedom or everyone would just tell Mummy and Daddy that they don't want to be here. And for all he'll huff and puff, the Gruppenführer knows that. It's not a good school in the sense that it turns out geniuses – academically it just scrapes through inspections, though they say it used to be good – but it does have its advantages.'

'Like what?'

'It's near the airport.' Libby smiled at her little joke. 'And the cheesecake is good.'

The minute David Lambie appeared on the landing where Mary Carruthers lived, Rene came beetling out from her door, practically helping him press the doorbell, repeating, 'Oh, you're back again already. Mary will be pleased . . .'

When Mary opened the door she didn't seem pleased to see her sister, but she dutifully replayed the same routine with the tray and the tea, saying nothing about the money. She watched as Rene took an empty cup off the tray and sat down with it. Mary took it back and placed it on the tray, shaking her head. 'She picks up everything and moves things around. Teapot in the fridge, my glasses in the bin.'

Lambie's eyes were fixed on the diaries, which had all been stacked neatly. There was a used envelope stuck between 1976 and 1978 – that meant there was one missing. Lambie wondered if that made it all the more important.

'Wullie MacFadyean?' Mary said, once Rene had settled down and Lambie could get a word in edgeways to ask her. 'Oh, I don't recall much about him. Quite a shock to see him at the funeral.' She was trying to hold back the tears, while Rene nibbled away at a scone like a demented rabbit, smiling eagerly at Lambie, who just smiled back.

'You know Wullie left his first wife,' Mary went on, 'and he got married again, to a girl who worked at the station – a high-up cop, well promoted, you know. I can't remember what she was called, but she had a strange job. I think there was a bit of an age difference. Tommy didn't approve of that kind of thing. Wullie was sent to Shawlands, and Tommy stayed at Partick. He liked it there.'

'Would you happen to have a photograph of Wullie, even an old one?' Lambie asked. Wullie's face hadn't been that much use for ID, not after the crows had finished with him.

'There was one of them all out on the hills. I saw it recently, but . . .' she shook her head, thinking.

Lambie didn't want to pressurize her but his big problem was that nobody seemed to know where Wullie lived. They were trawling all the MacFadyeans on the electoral roll and the council tax register, and hoping that somebody, at some point, would report him missing. The ex-cop had been dead for twenty-four hours now and it was as if nobody had noticed.

'You don't know if he was still married?'

'I wouldn't know, son. I think he was on his own yesterday. But I wasn't paying attention.'

Lambie found himself trying with difficulty to follow what Mary was saying. Rene kept butting in, asking him something about the old Co-op bakery and telling him she'd got the scones there that morning.

'Doubt it,' muttered Mary. 'It was knocked down forty years ago.'

But Rene was nibbling again, and saying, 'I said to Mary but she didn't understand. Well, she did, but she has a lot on her plate – you know, planting your man, it's not easy – so maybe she didn't. Or if she did, I don't think she found it –'

'Found what?'

'The photograph of the boys, the boys that all went hill-walking that time. You know the one? The one the man was asking for.'

Crystal clear. Lambie looked at Mary, who slowly shook her head.

'What do you mean, Rene? What man?' Mary stood up and went over to the far side of the room, her face deathly pale. Lambie watched her carefully as Rene kept talking.

'You see, the man was asking for it, and she – her there – said she didn't have it, and I know that she did have it because I've seen it. When that other girl –'

Mary shook her head, finally understanding. 'Sorry, Mr Lambie. She's thinking about the girl who wrote that book. She came round last year or the year before – you know, the way they do – wanting to speak to Tommy about the Marchetti kidnap case, but he had had nothing to do with it. But she kept on and on, as if he had. It upset him, mind you.' Then, briskly, 'But that's what Rene is thinking about. It's in the papers again, and it's reminding her, that's all.'

Lambie nodded. 'So, Rene, who was asking about the photograph?' he asked gently.

'That man at the funeral, the man who came up in the lift with me, with the gloves.' Rene dunted Lambie heavily in the ribs with her elbow. 'I mean, gloves! I think he was a bit simple, but who would have gloves on, on the warmest day of the year? That's what I said to him, and he laughed. He was nice looking, though. Just like that man on the telly. You know the one – Michael Aspel!'

'Do you know this man?' Lambie looked from one sister to the other.

'I've no idea who she's talking about.' Mary shrugged. 'I mean, there is an old picture somewhere. It's normally with the diaries but it's not there now.' She wiped a tear from her cheek, and sat down. 'Tommy, Eric Moffat, Wullie MacFadyean and – oh, who were those other two now? Graham . . . ? Graham Hunter and Jason Purcie. They all used to go hill-walking, camping, when they were younger.'

Lambie reassured her. 'I'm sure it wasn't that important,' he lied. Mary was an old woman, she was upset, so he let the silence lie.

She twisted her hanky in her fingers and went on. 'You know, when Tommy died, I was going through his things, and I checked all the diaries, to make sure they were in order. There's one missing. He wrote his diary every day until a couple of years ago. Now, his life's not complete . . .' The tears were threatening to start again.

He turned his attention to Rene, and asked her the most important question. 'And when did you meet the man in the lift, Rene? The man who was at the funeral? Was it the day of the funeral?'

'Oh no, it was the day Tommy died, the day I'd been to the hospital, with my knees.'

'And when did you get back?'

Rene lowered her voice melodramatically. 'Not until after – you know . . .' She nodded, so Lambie would understand.

'She didn't get back until the afternoon,' said Mary. 'One of the neighbours took her in. Told her, gave her a cup of tea.'

At that point, Mary composed herself and relaxed into the sofa, her face still pale. This was obviously news to her. Slowly she began to question her sister. There had been a man in the lift on the day of Tommy's suicide who had also been at the funeral. The man had asked her about a photograph of Tommy Carruthers out hill-walking with his friend Wullie MacFadyean.

'Can we rely on what she is saying?' asked Lambie out of the side of his mouth.

Mary nodded her head, still confused. 'She must be right. She wouldn't make that up.' She ran her fingers through her hair.

Lambie waited for her to think it through.

'She would have got the hospital bus back. It drops her at the rear of the building, so she'd have come in that door. There's a small lift back there, near the stairs, but people don't use it much. Everybody uses the lifts at the front.' She cupped her fingers over her mouth. 'Was there somebody here? A man who knew my husband?' She looked at Lambie, reddened eyes full of confusion.

Lambie stood up, and put a comforting hand on her shoulder. 'We'll find out if he was here, don't worry.'

A few uninterrupted hours with the CCTV footage and a strong coffee, and they might know exactly who 'he' was.

8.00 p.m.

Ex-DCI Eric Moffat was not totally happy to meet at the station; he asked Anderson to come up to the Lodge On The Loch, a hotel by the side of Loch Lomond. 'We can have a full and frank conversation, totally off the record, and well away from prying eyes and ears,' he said. 'Anything else, you can simply ascertain by calling up the old records on the computer.'

Anderson could imagine a cold beer in the early evening sun, by the lochside, with the sun glinting off the water, Ben Lomond in the distance. He was sure he could think of better ways of spending a Thursday evening if he tried – but, apart from dinner with Helena McAlpine, nothing jumped to mind. What he hoped to get was the situation surrounding Biggart, warts and all.

When he arrived, Moffat was already there and had commandeered a table outside. They ordered a couple of pints from a waitress, and sat in silence as the *Maid of the Loch* steamed past, full of holidaymakers. Moffat was looking hot, and the dry flakes of a previous sunburn were still apparent round his receding hairline. The tan was obviously coming at a price.

'If you don't mind me asking,' said Anderson, 'how the hell do you survive in Australia? Do you not just burn up all the time?'

Moffat shook his head, downing a gulp of beer. 'That's the thing about Australians – they know about the sun and they know how to deal with it. They're prepared. My grandchildren never go out without their factor thirty and a sun hat. Everywhere they go there's air con. It's a healthy life. My daughter, Carolyn, had really bad asthma as a kid, on steroids all the time. One of the reasons they went out. She's not had an attack all the time they've been there. Scotland is a splendid country, but God knows the weather is shite.' Moffat raised his beer glass to the ben, looming at the head of the loch.

Anderson let his eyes flit across the water. 'If the weather was like Australia, this place would look like a desert,' he said. 'So, your daughter went out before you did?'

'Yeah, I stayed to finish my time in the force. The minute I'd done my thirty, I was out there.' Moffat drained his beer. 'But I guess it's different for you, being a bit younger.'

'And the kids not yet at exam age. But we might be better going now, while they still have a couple of years to fit into the Australian system.'

'With us it was no contest. Carolyn was ill, so she went. Then my wife followed, just for the summer. Then that turned out to be permanent. The minute they landed in Brissie, Carolyn's lungs lost their sensitivity. The air's warm and dry, not this damp muck we breathe. She has a good job, rather than the life of an invalid she would have had here. But both my boys married Glasgow lassies and refused to follow us out. They're both on the force in Glasgow – Callum and Johnnie – doing well. You got your promotion yet, by the way?'

'Yes. But I'm not totally sure what I'm chief of.'

'I think Howlett's keeping you for something special. LOCUST, maybe?'

'I think he might have something on his mind.' Anderson recalled what Howlett had said about saying little and listening a lot.

'So, nobody's mentioned it by name. It's supposed to be a new initiative to clean up the streets of Glasgow. But if they weren't thinking of you for it, they wouldn't have asked me to meet you. I always reasoned that the one they sent to speak to me would be the one heading up the new team.' Moffat settled back, comfortable with his audience. 'So, for now, officially, you are working on the Biggart case. While shielding your back about the Fairbairn case, and trying to forget the fact that an abused minor died in your arms. Tough one.'

'It is when you put it like that.' Anderson was beginning to find Moffat's charm wearing thin. 'Does that mean anything to you?'

Moffat tipped his sunglasses with his forefinger, studying the photograph Anderson was sliding towards him. 'Is that the tattoo on the van driver?'

'The passenger – yes.'

'Do you know what it means?'

Anderson waited.

'It means trouble,' Moffat said quietly. 'It means he's done time in a Russian prison. If he has more tattoos on his upper arm, black wavy lines, then that means big trouble. The lines represent crows in flight. One crow means one kill. Three crows, and they're allowed to prove themselves with a blood eagle.' He didn't elaborate. 'These guys are not playing peek-a-boo, Colin.'

'A blood eagle?' A vision floated into Anderson's mind – taut arms, splayed ribs. Blood . . . 'What does that mean?' he asked evenly, drawing Moffat out.

'It's a rite of passage,' Moffat explained. 'It's like a promotion, a graduation.'

'Who for?'

'The Russian mafia, of course.' Moffat downed half his pint.

'So, the guy with the barbed-wire bracelet would be in our system?'

'No, he would be in the Russian prison system,' said Moffat impatiently. 'They view time served as a matter of pride, hence the visibility of the tattoos. Biggart had a tattoo on the biceps of his left arm, didn't he?' He was making a connection.

'Did he?' Anderson was surprised, then remembered that O'Hare had found traces of one, deep in the skin.

'You didn't know?'

'He was burned to a crisp.' He sipped his pint, eyes on the photograph, wondering who had blabbed. 'To tell you the truth, I'd much rather get after the bastard who did for the girl. ACC Howlett seems to think that you might be able to shine some light on it all.'

'I can give you some background. The thing is, nobody really knows how Biggart got where he did. He used to be so low on the O'Donnell family totem pole that they'd only use him to wipe their arses if there was no sandpaper left. He was not a clever man –' Moffat drained his glass '– but he was crafty, certainly crafty enough to always be one step ahead of us.'

'Background, you said?'

'Well, he used to run with the O'Donnell family, like I said. Wee Archie O'Donnell in particular. But once the Marchetti boy was taken, and they were all at each other's throats, we had the upper hand, and the rest is history. Wee Archie'd be in his forties now, maybe a bit older. He's doing life in the Bar-L for taking somebody's head off with a machete, so he's not likely to get out any time soon.' Moffat smiled. 'Those days produced a stream of intelligence for us. People found the nerve to step forward, and there was a secret information amnesty, if you like. We just picked them up and locked them up. The families were never hugely into drugs – that was a cultural thing – but there was an outbreak of the usual fighting for territory, and that caused the great heroin drought of 1999 to 2000. Prices were going through the roof. Biggart found a supply and moved into the vacuum. Quickly. So, one minute he was a two-bit pimp, and within a couple of years he was the bee's knees with an endless supply of red heroin.'

'So, somebody was backing him?'

'I don't doubt it. Didn't doubt it then, don't doubt it now. Presumably he'd proved his worth. Hence the tattoo. But, at the time, we had no idea what a monster he would turn out to be, did we?'

'How about Mrs Biggart? She had a close association with a much younger man, apparently. And it's possible he might have known her husband as well.'

Moffat grinned. 'Is that a euphemism? If he was a good-looking young man, Biggart may well have *known* him. Any idea who he was?' It was a direct question

Anderson said evasively, 'I think we'll know by tomorrow. What we don't know is why Melinda Biggart was killed.'

Moffat waved a cloud of midges from above his head. The heat was starting to wane. 'In that game, any association is a dangerous one. And there's another drug drought on now. Somebody is squeezing the supply again. Just look back over the last eight months. You've noticed a lot of dealers have been killed or packed up and moved on? A kind of ethnic cleansing of the unclean. Which means somebody is holding on to the supply, so that when the balance tips they'll be in the driving seat.'

'And a new king moves in?'

'Or queen,' said Moffat. 'The trouble is, the price drops with the flood. There's more activity, more chance the cops hear about it and intervene. It all gets messy.'

'Seems messy either way.'

'You want another?' He reached for Anderson's drained glass.

'Coke for me, please. I'm driving.'

Moffat got to his feet. 'All I'm saying is, Colin, always look behind what you see. You're still on the job, and I don't expect you to say anything, but if you know, definitely know, of any more dead girls out there, young girls, with any hint that they're foreign, then we're talking about human trafficking. Human flesh is good currency nowadays. People will invest a lot in that kind of business. A child can be bought in Nigeria for twenty dollars, and sold over here for thousands. And that means you're looking at organized crime. Russian, if we consider the evidence of the tattoo.'

'Yes, we've got that far. Is that what LOCUST is being set up for?'

'That's the rumour. But no matter what, Special Branch will come along and take it off you, so please don't think you owe the job too much. Because they won't think they owe you anything. If it suits them, they'll throw you to the lions.'

8.30 p.m.

Mick Batten got off the subway train at Hillhead, with a battered leather satchel slung over one shoulder, and an overstuffed rucksack over the other. He liked Glasgow – it reminded him of his Liverpool hometown – and he was starting to feel quite at home here, as if he was coming back to see family he actually liked. He and ACC Howlett had been emailing thoughts and documents backwards and forwards to each other for a couple of weeks now. Batten was a forensic psychologist, not a criminologist, but he could see the bigger picture perfectly well, and Howlett had been impressed – as people often are when somebody else comes along and not only does their job for them, but does it better. Criminal psychology was simple in a case like this. All he had to do was separate the wood from the trees, stand back and take a good look.

He walked down Byres Road, pausing to take his leather jacket off and stuff it in on top of his rucksack. He stopped for a pint of cold beer at the Blind Pig, a pub with an open frontage. Instinctively he held his hand over the satchel – anybody who stole that would be in for a few sleepless nights; when it came to violence Glaswegians made Scousers look like the cast of *Joseph and the Amazing Technicolor Dreamcoat*.

Batten had examined the pictures of the three dead girls – children, he reminded himself – that O'Hare had linked from the post mortem findings. The three live girls represented somebody's insurance; but the dead children would have netted him pure profit. And more. They could simply have been shot like dogs once they were too beaten and traumatized to be of any further use. Instead, their deaths had been cruel, protracted and deeply disturbing. As they were meant to be. The message would have come across loud and clear: *Mess with us, and this is what you get*.

And if somebody could waste human resources like that, it meant he had a supply coming from somewhere, and that meant human trafficking.

Batten sipped at his pint. Glasgow and Liverpool: both had a tradition of football, shipbuilding, alcohol and sectarianism. And gangland feuds. Every so often somebody got taken out and the hierarchy readjusted itself. And it was in that period of readjustment, while the lie of the land was changing, that things got dangerous. In the case of Glasgow the dynamic had always been more like shifting tectonic plates; the tension would build up for years and then there would be a massive rumble. Batten knew exactly who was ruling at the moment – the Russian mafia. The '*Vorony*', as he called them.

The Crows.

But for how long? And who was the pretender to the throne?

9.00 p.m.

Anderson snapped his phone shut and made his way back to the table.

'Good news?' asked Moffat, coming back with the drinks.

'We think we might have a lead on an ID on the Bridge Boy. I'll be glad when he comes out of his coma and tells us who did that to him.'

Moffat nodded. 'Good. But what about Melinda Biggart? She was killed by blood eagle.'

Anderson sipped at his Coke, hoping that Moffat wouldn't dwell too much on the exact details of Mrs Biggart's demise; he was already feeling queasy at the memory.

But Moffat was well into his stride and not to be stopped. 'The blood eagle was something the Vikings used to do, only they did it from the back, disarticulating the ribs from the spine and flattening out the ribcage like wings.' He stretched out his hands in demonstration.

Anderson shut his eyes and swallowed hard.

'The Russians do it from the front, so the victim looks like the double-headed Romanov eagle. More like a spatchcocked chicken, actually.

'For each killing, by any method they like, the Russians get a black crow tattoo. Then once they have three black tattoos, they get to do the whole blood eagle thing. Not many men can cut the heart out while it's still beating, which is what the Vikings did.'

'Probably against health and safety regs now,' muttered Anderson. Considerable strength as well as manual dexterity, O'Hare had said.

'They do it to prove their allegiance, to show they have nerves of steel, that they're true soldiers. Then they get a red eagle tattoo. And that identifies them as a life member of the *Vorony*, I think they're called. Means crow, eagle, something like that.'

'*Vorony*?' Anderson was thinking of what Dr Redman had said, and the notes he had made – the words 'brawny', 'Trelawney'.

'These guys do not mess about. Are you OK?' Moffat was peering at him with some concern.

Just thankful that he hadn't actually thrown up or passed out, Anderson managed, 'Probably just a bit dehydrated, out in this sun . . .'

'You have to keep your fluids up, mate. Another drink?'

'No, thanks, I'm fine.'

Moffat looked at his watch. 'Nine o'clock. I'd better go.

Call me if you want to chat some more.' And with that, he slapped Anderson on the back and was gone.

Anderson drained the last of his Coke, then waited a few minutes for his stomach to settle.

'Hey, look what the cat drags in when you're not there to kick its arse!' Lambie shook the other man by the hand. 'Dr Batten, as I live and breathe.'

Mick Batten's eyes darted round the room. 'Have you lot been credit-crunched or downsized or something? Well, they do say small is beautiful.'

'Is this a social call?' asked Mulholland, after the initial round of hellos.

'No, I was called in by ACC Howlett,' Batten said, putting Mulholland firmly in his place. 'Where's Colin?'

Something in his voice made Lambie turn round from the CCTV film he had been analysing. 'That's just what ACC Howlett asked, but he's not back. Were you expecting him?'

'He said he'd be here by now. Do we know where he is?'

'He was heading out to meet DCI Moffat.'

'Did he say where?'

'It's on the chart – we can't even go for a pee without telling teacher. He's up at the lochside. Why – you expecting trouble?' asked Lambie.

'Like I'm expecting the rain. It's only a matter of time.' He put his satchel on the table beside Lambie and pulled a seat in so close that Lambie retreated at the smell of tobacco. 'What are you doing?'

'Tracing the CCTV from the bottom of Bruce Court. That's the flats where —'

'Thomas Carruthers lived and died. You trying to track down who threw him out the window?' Batten unwrapped some chewing gum, oblivious to Lambie subtly edging their seats apart. 'You looking at the main door?'

'I've just seen Mary going out at 10.04 a.m., so I think the killer will have been watching and will appear soon.' He leaned forward, concentrating on the four images on the screen in front of him.

'There are two doors?'

'Two plus another two you need a key for. These doors are just an entry pad.'

They watched in silence as people came and went, carrying shopping, standing chatting, walking quickly, walking slowly. A small dog kept running up to the door, hoping to get in, only to be thwarted.

'How much footage do you have to go?'

'A lot!'

'Well, you get on with it; I'm not going to interrupt. I'll just get myself up to speed.' Batten walked over to the board and stood, arms folded, with his back to them.

Lambie kept watching the CCTV footage. Every time the clock ticked over, he knew he must be closer to finding Mr Aspel. He had stopped the film a few times, noting down the time and a description of anybody who looked as if they might be of interest. Then the recognizable figure of Rene appeared, on the camera for the east door. She entered with a key, rather than using the keypad. For the next ten minutes nobody came or went. It didn't make sense.

He sighed loudly. 'He should be here somewhere.'

'Start before Mary leaves and run the film backwards,' suggested Batten. 'He might have accurately judged your thinking and been inside all the time, waiting for Mary to leave the flat. They might have known each other, remember – easy to say, "Oh, come round Monday morning, Mary's going out at whatever time." There might have been trust there.' Batten slid back into the seat beside Lambie. The time on the cloak was 8.55 a.m. A man appeared, coming out of the flat backwards, having held the door open for a woman reversing her shopping trolley out. He was walking quickly backwards, wearing dark glasses.

Batten tapped the screen. 'Take it back three minutes, then play it forwards.'

Lambie did so. The figure appeared, his head turned away from the camera. And it stayed that way. He was tall, male, slim, blond or grey-haired. He timed his approach perfectly to help an elderly resident come through the door with her shopping trolley. He looked respectable, and he entered unchallenged. Once in, he paused a little, looking up.

'He's looking for the camera,' remarked Batten. 'Do you know who he is?'

'Tall and grey-haired, tanned? Looks a bit like Michael Aspel? I think that's Eric Moffat.'

'I thought you said Anderson was out with Eric Moffat right now,' said Batten to nobody as both Mulholland and Lambie were already on their phones.

Anderson sat in his car for a few minutes with the window open, trying to clear his mind a little. He really felt like going to sleep, but he had to get home. It was just after half past nine, the sun was setting, and the light would soon be fading. He pulled out on to the dual carriageway and headed back into Glasgow. He had only gone a few miles when he began to notice that his vision was blurring, that the white lines in the middle of the road were drifting. He was starting to feel sick, his head thick and woozy. He wondered if the sun had given him a migraine.

He pulled into a lay-by and parked, got out and walked to the trees at the side of the road, thinking he was going to be sick. He heard a car pull in behind him but didn't turn round to look; he was trying to get his phone out of his pocket, and he had already dropped his car keys. He couldn't even think about picking them up. He was just going to sit here with his back against a tree and try to calm the turbulence in his stomach.

'Are you OK, mate?' It was Moffat.

'I think I'm having a stroke. God, I feel awful.'

'I saw you pull up.' Moffat hauled him to his feet. 'Come on out the sun, Colin, away from the road.'

Anderson was trying to say that there was no sun, and why should they move away from the road, but nothing was coming out of his mouth. All he could hear was the cawing of the crows that circled overhead. He suddenly thought of MacFadyean, dead among the trees, alone with the crows.

Moffat was talking, his voice sounding muffled in Anderson's ears. 'You know you'd never have got this far without help from us. But you were coming to that conclusion, weren't you? Slowly. Your problem, Colin, is that you're too bright.'

He was being pushed deeper into the wood, and tried to pull away, but his limbs refused to obey him. Whichever way Moffat moved him, his body agreed. Moffat pressed him up against a tree, pulling his arms behind him, and he felt plastic clips being put on his wrists.

The restraints were drawn tight, then tighter still. Any tighter and his wrists would start to bleed, and he'd get blood on his shirt, clean on that morning. He had ironed it himself.

Another man appeared out of the forest from behind them. He said something, but in such a heavy accent that Anderson couldn't understand. He tried to turn his head, to look Moffat right in the eyes. But Moffat's returning stare was that of somebody who was doing a job and doing it right. He stood back and rolled one sleeve up, then the other, so as not to get them dirty. Then Anderson saw the three black tattoos on the upper part of Moffat's arm.

Moffat clocked that he had seen them, and gave him a swift smirk. 'Oh, yes,' he taunted. 'I'm going for the red.'

Anderson felt his head being pulled back by his hair. He could see flecks of grey on Moffat's chin. By the time Moffat shaved that off, Anderson thought vaguely, he would be dead. In fact, by the time Moffat walked back to the lay-by he would be dead, and one of them would drive his car away. He had even left them his car keys, somewhere . . .

He saw the knife that seemed to appear from nowhere, a keen hunting blade with a curved edge like a bowie knife. He knew what was coming next. 'Oh, Bren, Bren,' he whispered silently, trying to picture his wife's face. But all he could see was Helena McAlpine's affectionately mocking smile. He tried to think of Peter and Claire, but could only remember them as babies. They were only wee, he thought, too young to go to Australia.

Then a moment of cruel clarity stabbed into his befogged brain, bringing images of splintered bones and blood. *Oh God, Oh God*, he prayed. *Please* . . .

He closed his eyes and waited. But he only heard a dull thud, and felt a very gentle punch in the stomach. He dropped his head, his brain telling him that he was feeling no pain. He knew he should be glad.

He opened his eyes. His stomach was bloodied, and grey matter was splattered across his shirt.

Moffat's head had exploded.

10.00 p.m.

Alone in the dark, Rosie had no idea how much time had passed or even what day it was. She was dry inside and soaking outside, and something had happened to Wullie. Or had Wullie come back and she had been asleep? Where had he been all this time? Maybe lying unconscious in a ditch somewhere, and then unconscious in hospital – where they would surely have seen his diabetic tag, and he would be brought round sooner or later. And now he had made his way home. She called out to him but there was no answer.

It was such a simple thing – before he went out she had asked him to pull the table that slid over the bed, holding the telephone and the laptop, to the side, over against the wall. Where she could not reach it. How could she have been that stupid? Before, she had always thought of it as being out of her way, not out of her reach. She knew she had finished the water in the jug, she knew she had eaten all her chocolate. She had fallen asleep with her throat dry and her lips flaking.

Until now she had been drowsy, almost unable to keep her eyes open, but now she was wide awake, staring at the full glass of water. A piece of cheesecake wrapped in a dirty paper napkin sat beside it on the bedside table. Wullie must have brought it back from the funeral for her. But why hadn't he wakened her?

She heard a noise, a thunk-thunk. Two feet landing. She couldn't turn on to her back to see without the handle that hung over her head, just out of reach. It wasn't Wullie, was it? Wullie had gone.

She thought about calling again, then she smelled that smell – a brief scent in the air of stale sweat and cigarette smoke. They were there again, the memory of them was clear now. They had been before. They had not harmed her. They had just observed her and made their way to the front of the cottage.

It wasn't Wullie, but somebody was looking after her. They had come last night. They were here again tonight.

She wished she knew who.

*

Anderson couldn't lift his head; even if he wanted to, he couldn't move a single muscle. He had seen the second man jerk once, then hit the ground. Now he waited numbly for the third bullet, and oblivion. But there was nothing.

Then he heard something – someone? – move in behind him, felt something pulling at his hands, and heard a snip. He closed his eyes, thinking that now was the time he was going to die. He breathed out, feeling strangely peaceful. His arms fell to his sides and a pain snapped across his chest as he heard himself breathing deeply in and out. Waiting.

But nothing.

There was silence. He opened his eyes; his vision was blurred but he thought he saw somebody. A shadow, moving quickly away through the trees? He couldn't be sure of his own name at that moment. He took a step forward, stumbled and fell, thinking that he was alive, and alone. He had no idea how long he lay there, waiting for his head to clear, his limbs to wake up. He could hear the muffled roar of the traffic, and some crows calling overhead, and it seemed to grow cold. He picked himself up and walked forward very deliberately, taking care to pick his feet up over the long grass rather than trying to walk through it. He vomited up the beer and the Coke, and staggered against a tree, but he kept going down towards the road; it seemed a lot further, going back, than it had on the way up. He shuffled out on to the lay-by. His car was there, but he had locked it and he'd lost the keys. And somewhere, somehow, they had taken his phone.

He wiped the sweat and vomit from his face, rubbed the unthinkable from his shirt, and began to walk home.

He was still walking when the police car drew up behind him.

Friday
2 July 2010

'I think you're supposed to stay here,' said Batten. 'Right here in this hospital room. If you go anywhere else, and Brenda finds out, you'll be wishing they'd left you up against that tree. And Howlett is threatening to put you under armed guard.'

'Bit late for that.' Anderson scowled at the peg in the back of his hand. 'Does Brenda know?'

'I think she got a watered-down version but she knows you are OK. I told her they are keeping you in so they can run bloods off you every ten minutes. O'Hare was telling me that you have R2 on the streets here – so, you're moving medical science forward just by lying there.' He handed Anderson a lemon-coloured drink. 'This contains all sorts of sugars and electrolytes. You could run a marathon on it. Though you'd fail the drug test.'

Anderson looked up, feeling as though he might smile if he could remember how. 'What happened, Mick?'

'The moment Lambie identified Moffat from the CCTV footage, a squad car went out to the Lodge on the Loch; they got there not long after you left. A nice young couple said you walked past them to answer your mobile, just as Moffat went up to the bar. They watched you because they thought you were leaving and were going to nick the table. And they noticed that Moffat went up to the bar even though the tables outside have waitress service. That's how the drug got in your drink. Then he must have waited in the car park and followed you out. He knew you wouldn't get far. What we don't know is who shot him, or the other guy. And why did they miss you? Good job you're not overweight; maybe they didn't see you hidden behind the tree.'

'I think you missed out a big chunk there.'

'OK, Moffat's head was blown off with a high-velocity bullet, by a crack shot with a very professional piece of kit. They're looking for a match on the bullet.'

'It was a kill shot. So, why did he let me walk away? Walk – I was bloody staggering! He could have got me any time. All he needed was a couple of seconds to reload and he could have blown my head away as well.'

'Go back a bit. Moffat – what did he do?'

'He tied my hands behind the tree, and pulled tightly, then another guy appeared. He said something, but I couldn't understand it. Moffat had my head pulled back, and he had a knife. I saw it. I knew I was going to die. Then his head . . . disappeared. The other guy just sort of jerked slightly, and fell down.'

'One bullet in the heart. Where did the shots come from?'

'From the side somewhere.'

'Silenced?'

Anderson struggled to remember. 'I don't know. Must have been. Not as loud as you'd expect.'

'So, how did you get out?'

'I don't know,' he said again, thinking of the ghostly

figure flitting through the trees. 'They cut me free. *Somebody* cut me free.'

'Guardian angel, eh? Interesting.' Batten didn't seem surprised. 'The point is, you walked – staggered – out of there relatively unharmed. Which might be exactly what was supposed to happen.'

3.00 a.m.

Anderson banged on the brass dolphin doorknocker that adorned Howlett's front door. Batten had tried to talk him out of going, but he had eventually persuaded the psychologist to drive him out to Howlett's house, threatening that he was going anyway, even if it was three in the morning, and it was up to Batten whether he went by car or taxi.

Anderson waited, his arm raised, ready to knock again, when he heard a slow shuffling and the door opened a fraction, caught by a chain.

'Who's there?'

'DCI Anderson. Can I have a word, please?'

There was silence. Then, 'Of course, Colin.'

Anderson heard a deep rasping breath, as though Howlett was having trouble breathing. Then the chain loosened and the door opened.

'I guess I owe you.

'I think you bloody do. An explanation, if nothing else. I was nearly killed out there.'

'Come in, you are still shaky on your feet.'

'I have Dr Batten in the car.'

Howlett shrugged a little, and his dressing gown slipped down his shoulders, as though it was too big for him. He peered out into the dark street, looking like a little old man. 'Well, I did get him up here because I thought he would be of some use to you on this case, but not as a driver. Just leave him there, what I have to say will not take long.' He retreated into his hall, then turned into a study. He switched on a side light and leaned on his desk, tired and weary.

Anderson's anger abated.

'You got him in on what case?' asked Anderson, sitting in a side chair. His ribs still hurt and there was a squeezing sensation behind his eyeballs. 'Because this is not a case where we need him to figure out a motive. We need to find out who is behind all this. And I think they know more about what we are doing than we do.'

Howlett looked at him, defeated. 'And what else is on your mind?'

'A young boy tortured and dropped off a bridge, a bar-becued drug dealer, a young girl chained to a ladder and left to drown. Not to mention my ribcage staying as God intended.'

'You're still in shock. You shouldn't be drinking but, if you'll forgive me, I shall have a wee dram.' Howlett poured himself a tumbler of whisky and water with laborious care and shuffled over to the armchair by the fireplace. He sat down opposite Anderson. He took a sip and leaned his head back, gazing up almost medita-tively at Anderson. 'What can I say? What drives men to have sex with a ten-year-old girl? Beat her? Brutalize her? Take pleasure in it?' he asked thoughtfully. 'Such men are extreme sexual sadists. And you are tracking down the kingpin of the organization, the man – or woman – who is happy to give these guys what they want. *Kukolnyik*. The Puppeteer. And you're right, I don't really have any real idea who he is. But you are doing the same job you have always done. The end result is the same. And our goal is the same. Anderson, you have kids. I have grandkids. I struggle to get my head round such behaviour, and, to be perfectly honest, I don't *want* to get my head round it. That's what Batten should be doing, not driving you around in the small hours. I don't just want this bastard arrested and charged. I want him dead.'

'But you just said that you don't even know who he is.'

'We know *what* he is. Have you noticed how organized everything is about the cases you are working on – how slick and well planned? How little evidence is left? This bastard has been pulling our strings since day one. Or a few bastards.' He shook his head. 'No, it is just one. It's too tightly controlled to be more than one person. They seem to know how cops think. I thought Moffat might help get us there.'

'He was a dirty cop and –'

'Yes, I know, he's been filthy for years. We let him run, hoping he'd lead us somewhere – and I used you as the lead chase dog.'

'Without telling me?'

'I didn't want to prejudice your thinking. I just don't know how to get ahead of the game any more.' Howlett looked old and defeated, so defeated Anderson almost felt sorry for him. 'I'm sorry about what happened tonight,

Colin,' he said. It sounded genuine, but he did not seem to be surprised by it.

Anderson leaned forward, and asked softly. 'What I want to know is why LOCUST is not doing all this. Is this not what the bloody thing was set up for? They would have the resources, access to the intelligence.'

Howlett's thin blue fingers seemed to grip the crystal tumbler a little harder, and his lips pursed a little tighter. 'I'd appreciate it if this conversation went no further.'

'Go on.'

'Your old DCI, Alan McAlpine, and I were not so different. We were old school. You are too. I knew you'd bend the rules; I knew you'd go out and talk to Moffat on your own. I owe you an apology, Colin. You were placed in danger this evening. Please believe that I did everything humanly possible to minimize any personal risk to you.' Howlett paused to take another sip of whisky.

'*You* set that up? I could have crashed my car, had my head blown off, had my throat cut. And for what?'

'For every other girl who gets tied to a ladder and left for the tide to come in. I owe you a safe passage through this investigation, DCI Anderson, which is why I insisted that you and your team left precise details of your whereabouts on that board at all times. It is important – do you understand that?' Howlett's tone allowed no argument; only a slight creasing of the fine skin between his eyebrows betrayed any hint of discomfiture. 'And as for LOCUST,' he continued, 'it doesn't exist. It never has, and it never will.'

Anderson took a deep breath and sat back. 'OK . . .'

But Howlett remained silent. That was all he was going to say.

'So, what happened?' Anderson demanded. 'Did you run out of money or something?'

'It was *never* supposed to exist. It was a smokescreen. We are at war, DCI Anderson, and in times of war you use intelligence, in every sense of the word, to combat intelligence. We have allowed the concept of LOCUST – an all-singing, all-dancing investigative team, multi-disciplinary, across all specialities, with everything at their disposal – to become known. And our target, the *Vorony*, have no doubt been watching our every move, noting where LOCUST is being set up, who is being recruited, and working out who they can lean on, or eliminate. It's the way they've always worked. Glasgow gangsters still live in their council estates, not in gated communities. They do not want to sit in Parliament or become part of society. They operate at their own level, as they always have. But the Russian mafia is entirely different: flash, totally unscrupulous and – worse – unpredictable. So, while their attention is diverted by LOCUST, we might have a chance to get ahead of the game.'

'Positive misinformation.'

There was the hint of a smile. 'Sometimes the old ways are the best. I don't think for a moment they suspect a two-bit operation in a spare room in a lecture hall. Five of you – five – taking on all that, and reporting back to me and only me? I've been monitoring you and a few others, over the years, watching your careers. You are totally clean. You've never played golf with Eric Moffat or his kids. Niven MacKellar does. Do you see my dilemma? I've had my eye on a few DIs, and DCIs, over the years only to see them . . . compromise themselves. I can think of five DCIs who have come under the scrutiny of the Russian mafia. The one good DCI I had who I was sure they had not looked at was Colin Anderson. You were lucky enough to slip under their radar. That's why I had to let Moffat get close to you. And I'm sorry I had to do it, but I would do the same thing again.' Howlett gestured an apology with the flat of his hand.

'What I want to know is how you knew Moffat was bent.'

'But it doesn't end with Moffat. We've learned that he is small fry.'

'Answer the question, please,' Anderson insisted.

Howlett sighed. 'I was always a cop, but Moffat had been a soldier first. We had different ideas on policing. We never saw eye to eye, and differences of opinion hardened into animosity. But it meant I always noticed him. When you run your eye down a list of names, your friends jump out at you, but your enemies even more so. MacFadyean also joined the force from the army, and I always thought he and Moffat were a bit too buddy-buddy. Nothing specific, but it didn't taste right. Back in the seventies there was a series of armed robberies in the city and there was apparently a report that one of the gunmen was holed up and living rough out on the Campsie Fells. Moffat was in charge of the search. A young officer called Jason Purcie was put right out on the flank, and he was shot through the head with a high-velocity rifle. It was given out at the time that the wanted criminal had killed him, but no trace of a gunman or any weapon was ever found. It was MacFadyean's day off.' Howlett's tired old eyes gazed levelly at Anderson. 'In this country, the police do not act as judge, jury and executioner.'

'Is that what you think happened? Why?'

'I have various thoughts on the matter, and on other incidents in Moffat's career, but I'm hoping your current investigations will uncover the truth about many things. At first I assumed Moffat was empire-building on his own account. Then it became apparent that, in fact, he was merely a puppet – a pawn, a provider of tasty morsels of information. Recently, he's had a chat with all five DCIs we had lined up for LOCUST, as if he was sounding them out . . . but for whom? About ten years ago, he went to Australia. But, even so, I could still discern his presence lurking in the shadows cast by events, as though the useful information was still being transmitted. Moffat has two sons in the force, you know, and he was always an efficient cop. He might live on the other side of the world but he would have grilled those two boys of his for all sorts of information, and they wouldn't even realize. All they would think was that they were having a casual chat with their dad about work.'

'They're only at DS level. What could they know that would be of any use?'

'Are you telling me your DS doesn't know things she shouldn't? If there's one like that in each station, and someone can get all the chit-chat, all they need do is put it all together and examine the bigger picture. It's not rocket science. But, like I said, I've come to understand that Moffat is rather further down the food chain than I had supposed. Never mind being a puppet master, he's not even a puppet – well, maybe in the sense that he's always had somebody's hand jammed up his arse. But whose? I do not know – and that's what we need to find out.'

Anderson thought for a few minutes. Then he said, 'As I see it, you had a suspicion amounting to knowing that Moffat was transmitting information, but you had no proof that he was, because you didn't know how he was doing it. Or exactly where it was going.'

'Imagine him Down Under, gathering all kinds of info over the phone from his boys. But we know he was back here every three months, taking cops out for lunch, having a boys' night out. He was the experienced one – they might have thought he was being helpful, giving advice, whereas in fact he was gaining info all the time. Then he put it into some kind of pattern and passed it on. Imagine, there could be a whole team of Moffats out there, getting information just from simple, casual one-to-one chats in a pub. We don't know. But the conduit from there to the organization is what we need. We cannot find it, so we cannot break it. Saying, "Take out Melinda Biggart," is one thing. The intelligence behind the speed and the execution of it is another. Moffat was only a link to the conduit, which is somebody in this city – the Puppeteer.'

'Mick Batten would probably say it was somebody unassuming, somebody we'd just walk past on the street,' said Anderson, frowning in thought. 'Moffat was far too flashy, drew too much attention to himself.'

Howlett declined to respond. Instead, he said, 'Colin, get your team, including DS Costello, to your room at ten thirty this morning. You ran her out to Glen Fruin, didn't you?'

'Last night, yes. Well, Wednesday night,' he clarified. 'She can't drive at the moment, with her head injury.'

'I know that. And you found the body of MacFadyean?'

'We didn't actually witness anything. We just stopped and found the body.'

'And how did you know the body was there?'

'We didn't. We saw the crows.'

Their eyes met.

Howlett smiled sadly. 'Crows, the most intelligent, most predatory of birds. Never forget that. And now, DCI Anderson, you had better go home and get some sleep.'

A few minutes later, Howlett stood at the window and watched the red tail lights of Batten's car turn out of his gateway.

Then he lifted the phone.

'Thanks for that,' he said, without introducing himself. 'And Anderson is well. Dr Batten is driving him home now. But there was so much that could have gone wrong. Too much. We can't take such risks again. Call on other people if you need them. But I want you and the team to keep close to DCI Anderson at all times. Keep him safe.' He wiped the sweat from his forehead as he listened. 'Yes, I know, I know. Not long now. Less than forty-eight hours. This is the start of the end of days, the new beginning. Just remember that, Pettigrew. Just remember that.'

Howlett put the phone down, and it clicked on to the handset. He looked at his own hand, nothing but paper-thin skin and old bones.

The end of days.

'I thought you'd given up the evil weed,' Anderson said, as Batten opened a packet of Marlboro Lights with the trembling fingers of the confirmed addict. Then he thought about his two hours' sleep and reflected that his own might not be any steadier.

'I stopped drinking a month back, and the number of fags doubled. So, I'm back on the booze as well. We're OK to have a puff here, aren't we?' Batten perched himself on the wall and looked around furtively, as if the nicotine police were lying in wait for him.

'Puff away all you like. The respiratory unit is just across the car park if you collapse.' Anderson pulled loose the knot of his tie, and joined Batten on the wall. He opened the small brown paper bag he was carrying, and took out two black coffees and two bacon rolls.

'Cheers, mate,' Batten said, helping himself. 'I spent what was left of the night with a few members of the Russian mafia and a paedophile called Cameron Fairbairn.'

'Night on the files, was it?' quipped Anderson, glad that somebody else was feeling the strain.

'How are you feeling?'

Anderson knew that the shock was going to hit him sometime, but at the moment he felt much better just not thinking about it. His brief sleep had been disturbed by repeated images of the second man jerking as the bullet struck him – something he had barely registered at the time – and the flashback was still haunting him.

'Why didn't Howlett call this meeting a bit earlier?' Batten asked.

'He wanted time to bring Costello back from her country estate.' Anderson sipped at his coffee, watching a couple of women weave their way through the parked cars.

Batten swung both feet up on to the wall, and blew the smoke of his cigarette directly up at the sun. 'Unlike Liverpool, you don't have a real problem here with gun crime, do you?'

'Not until recently. Up here, used to be that anybody who had a gun put in their hand was far too stupid to know how to use it properly. So, it always tended to be up close and personal, with a blade.'

'Like being split up the middle, eh?'

'You trying to put me off my bacon roll, Mick? No, that's something we haven't seen till now either.'

'And what gangs do you have up here?'

'You've read *No Mean City*? Well, that was ages ago. Those days are gone. And it wasn't in this area. It was in the north and east – Protestant McGregors in the north, Catholic O'Donnells over to the east. Roughly,' Anderson qualified the statement. 'But they're all dead now. Or safely locked up. One of them's still in the Bar-L, for taking somebody's head off with a machete.'

Batten raised an interrogatory eyebrow.

'Wee Archie O'Donnell. Son of Auld Archie,' Anderson explained. 'The guy he decapitated was a junior lieutenant in his own gang; it was assumed to be retribution, because he'd stabbed a pregnant woman. One of the other lot. Killed her. Costello was on the scene and so was Moffat. God, I bet he was dirty even then. That's why he sent Costello away – she was new to the force, and an unknown quantity to him.'

'Was that some kind of jungle justice?' Batten lay down along the wall, face up to the sun, his eyes closed.

'And in case you're going to go into your "the Krays loved their mother" routine, just remember it has always been believed that it was either the O'Donnells or the McGregors that took the wee Marchetti boy.' Anderson pointed to The Works bookshop across the road. 'There's the book there, right in the front window. She thinks she came up with that theory, but she didn't.'

'That was never proved, though, was it?' Batten said.

'It's what all the intelligence said at the time.'

'Intelligence implicated both families – but not one or the other, definitively. You can't have the same jam on two cakes, can you?'

Anderson sighed deeply. It was hot already, and he was very tired. Whatever they had drugged him with, the R2 was making his eyeballs hurt.

Batten sat up to light another cigarette, then lay back down again. 'There is one thing that will stop a gang in its tracks,' he said eventually.

'AK-47? Sherman tank?'

'Their own society. Gangs – well, Glasgow and Liverpool gangs – live by a code that is agreed, if you like. And dictated by the society they live in. Consent is given to a degree of lawbreaking, because it works for the good of that society. And consent is given to the hierarchical structure.'

'Forced consent?'

'Maybe. So, do you know anything about game theory?'

'The only game theory we have is that in any draw Rangers get a penalty.'

'Well, consider that. Consider Rangers and Celtic. They win everything, don't they?'

'More or less.'

'So, if you owned, say . . . a rubbish team.'

'Partick Thistle.'

'OK, Partick Thistle. You would be daft to take them on. Your best bet to win anything is to set those two against each other in such a way that they weaken each other, allowing you to take on the winner. The winner will inevitably be inferior to the original, giving you a good chance of success.'

'Where does this come into anything?'

'Substitute the MacGregors and the O'Donnells. Families that had ruled Glasgow for a hundred years or so with extreme familial, geographical and religious loyalty.'

'Loyalties run as deep as the Molendinar in this city.'

'The what?' asked Batten.

'The river that runs underneath Glasgow, right underneath.'

'And such loyalty, running deep, means a lot in a city like this. That's why the Marchetti kidnap caused so much mayhem. Drugs, porn, counterfeiting – that's all allowed. The senseless killing of a six-year-old is certainly not. The Marchetti thing was a can of worms that exploded. They were informing all over the place, on their own people as well as each other. More grasses than B&Q's seed catalogue. Previous loyalties were shattered. It was the end for them.'

Anderson just grunted, and shifted his rapidly numbing backside on the wall.

'The question is how much Howlett knows about it. You've seen him – the whites of his eyes are yellow, his jacket's swimming on him, and his belt's in a new hole. The man is not well. He wants this situation closed before he retires – if he lasts that long. I'm as sure as I can be that this is the last stand of a dying man with nothing to lose. As for this Puppeteer?' Batten stubbed his cigarette out. 'It might take one to know one.'

10.30 a.m.

Deliberately or not, Wyngate had arranged the seating in the lecture hall so that no one sat at the head of the long table, and the ACC – who was out of uniform – was simply one person sitting among his peers. Anderson, Batten, O'Hare, Lambie and Mulholland were already present, and there were two empty seats. The room was seething with tension but Anderson couldn't tell where it was coming from. He hoped Howlett had something up his sleeve to pull the team together.

The door opened and Costello walked in, holding the door open for another woman, diminutive and slightly built, who looked like a typical student in jeans and T-shirt, her jacket tied round her waist and a knitted handbag slung across her shoulder. It was obvious from the banality of the conversation that they had just met. Costello looked pale and tired, but behind her eyes Anderson saw the old familiar spark, and thought she looked more alive than he had seen her in ages. His thoughts were confirmed by the way she banged the chair back before sitting down. Keen to get on with it, then. He was glad she was back. She wouldn't let Howlett get away with anything.

The smaller woman pulled out the other seat. 'Hello,' she said brightly. 'I'm Matilda McQueen.' She opened her bag and took out a file, pulled the cap off her pen with her teeth and sat down, ready, totally confident, totally at ease.

'She is our forensic science expert, and the Prof here is our forensic medical expert. They are both very much part of this team,' said Howlett.

'Whether they like it or not,' said Anderson, which raised a smile and broke the tension.

Wyngate closed the door, then checked it was securely locked before taking his own seat.

'I'm not going to talk.' ACC Howlett stood up. 'I just want you to sit and watch something. It was bought in a pub toilet for three hundred pounds and handed to us. I'll show you the edited highlights only.' His eyes darted from Costello to McQueen, obviously slightly uncomfortable with the thought that women were present. He pressed Play on the remote control for the laptop that was linked to the PowerPoint projector. The screen went dark, and a few coded numbers and letters flashed across. The sound preceded the visuals by a few seconds, a primal scream of sheer terror, and Costello recoiled nervously. Then a girl's face came into view, her eyes screwed shut, her mouth open, screaming. Two rough hairy hands were holding her down. The screaming stopped, and words spilled out among the girl's sobs.

'What's she saying? That's not English, is it?' Wyngate asked.

'She's screaming for her mother, in Russian,' said Vik, without taking his eyes off the screen.

Anderson leapt to his feet, and his chair crashed over backwards. 'Christ, I'm not watching this!' he snarled. 'No way! Open that fucking door!'

Howlett nodded briefly to Wyngate, who jumped up faster than anybody had ever seen him move, key at the ready. Anderson stormed out, banging the door behind him.

No one uttered a word, or looked at anyone else. Wyngate righted the fallen chair on his way back to his place at the table.

On screen, a pillow came down on the girl's face and stayed there.

Howlett picked up the remote and the screen returned to royal blue. Matilda was in tears, and Costello sat with her arms folded, looking furious.

'That was by way of showing you why we are here,' Howlett said. 'I thought I would spare us the previous twenty-seven minutes. And what came after. The girl wasn't dead, just unconscious. She was revived from that, to go through it again and again. There are two men involved.

Matilda shuddered.

'This man with the bracelet tattoo, and a second with a "Rangers No Surrender" tattoo.'

'Well, that cuts it down to half the blokes in Glasgow,' said Mulholland with thin sarcasm.

'Tattoos may be of the same pattern, but they are all

unique. You know that,' Howlett answered. 'That is a start, and we need every –'

He was interrupted by Matilda blowing her nose loudly. Batten put his hand out and patted hers automatically, then went back to scribbling away in his notebook.

'Do we know who she is?' asked Costello.

'No. But we call her Rusalka,' explained Mulholland. 'It's the name of the water sprite in Dvořák's opera.'

'Dies in the end, does she?' Costello grunted. 'What age was she, do we think?'

O'Hare replied, 'I reckon about ten. There are two other girls. One found in Argyll and one up near Tain.'

'Their full PM results showed similar injuries to Rusalka's, so we conclude, tentatively, that they suffered the same fate,' said O'Hare.

Matilda stood up unsteadily, her face white. 'Sorry, I think I'm going to be sick,' she said, and fled.

'Do you want to go and make sure she's OK?' Howlett asked Costello.

'Not particularly,' said Costello.

Howlett took off his glasses and polished them, before putting them back on, and coughing gently to retrieve everybody's attention. 'I have something very important to tell you. But first I should say that I don't want any of this to leave this room. I know, and have known for a long time, that you are a close-knit unit. I doubt that there is any possibility of this unit being compromised.'

'No leaks, you mean?' Costello snapped.

'Indeed, that's why I took you all out of Partick – I needed to isolate you, to get you out on your own.'

'And what exactly are we working on?' Costello asked. 'I'm presuming we are all working on the same thing?'

'You are,' Howlett said. He picked up a file from the floor beside him, and pulled out a piece of white card, Wyngate's scale drawing of the floor plan of flats G1 and G2 at the Apollo. 'This is the unoccupied flat next to the one that burned. Now, Miss McQueen's report shows that the marks pointed out to us by DCI Anderson on the ceiling and the walls were bore holes that match where the lights had to be in relation to the object being filmed. The camera was hand held, as you saw, but the lights were steady. So, between Anderson and Matilda, we have independent, corroborative evidence.' Howlett took a deep breath. 'The samples from the towels Anderson sent to the lab mean we can now place Rusalka in that room. Matilda got enough DNA to get a positive match. Analysis of the child's hair indicates that she had been drugged regularly, over time. But the important thing for now is that Biggart has been stopped.'

'By the Bridge Boy?' It was Mulholland who asked. 'An arsonist as a hit man? That's novel!'

'But it would be nice to know why he was subsequently tortured, and by whom.'

'But we don't know who he is,' remarked Costello, with slight sarcasm.

Lambie said. 'I think we might get the answer to that later today. We have some information from –'

'Good,' said Howlett, not letting Lambie say any more. 'DS Wyngate, you can go and find DCI Anderson, and tell him he can come back in now.' Howlett turned to O'Hare. 'Jack? Have you anything else for us?'

'I have indeed.' O'Hare placed a post mortem photograph on the table. It showed the total disintegration of a head struck by a high-velocity bullet. He put down another photograph, of the skin crease of an elbow with three wavy lines tattooed on the skin above and a delicate band of barbed wire round the wrist. The prints were so fresh they still smelled of developing fluids.

Anderson and Wyngate came back into the room and sat down. Anderson reached for both prints and studied them wordlessly.

'That tattoo on the wrist matches, exactly, the one on the passenger in the white van,' said Howlett. 'And also the tattoo on the wrist of the man whose arms we saw in the film just now. Among the fingerprints lifted from the flat are some that match a set on file under the name Alexei Grusov, among many other aliases. A further distinguishing feature is white scarring on the iris of his right eye, the result of an old stab wound.'

Anderson looked up. 'Somebody mentioned that.'

'Janet did,' said Mulholland. 'So this man Grusov – the man in the van – was the man shot with Moffat. And he was a visitor to Biggart's flat.'

'It certainly seems so,' Howlett agreed. None of this seemed to be news to him. 'He was known on the street as Perky. I don't imagine his death will be regretted by many.'

'Perky? Why?'

'Because they work in pairs. The other Russian has the street name Pinky, due to the loss of the small digit on his left hand. But these are no cute wee piglet puppets. Both are trained pilots, ex-military. And they are well versed in torture, and survival techniques. Russian survival techniques usually involve killing the other bloke. Pinky is the more violent of the two.'

'Do we have any idea where Pinky is?' asked Anderson.
'Gone to ground.'

'And do we know who shot Moffat and Perky?'

Howlett appeared not to have heard Anderson's question.

'Whoever he was, he was a crack shot,' said Batten soothingly. 'What about the Bridge Boy's ID?'

Anderson noticed how Batten had steered the conversation away from his question, replacing it with another for which there was an immediate answer.

Howlett said, 'DCI Anderson, I'd like you to go and talk to a Dr Gaynor Spence, and confirm that she's the Bridge Boy's mother. Her neighbour saw the mock-up photo and called her. She was abroad at some conference and is flying back this morning. She didn't know he was missing. Go as soon as we're through here.'

'Is there anything I'm actually allowed to tell her?' Anderson asked.

'Just be circumspect,' Howlett warned. 'However, we're pretty certain one of the men who tried to kill her son is dead. You can tell her that, at least.'

Anderson nodded. 'But even though Biggart's gone, and Grusov has gone, the Puppeteer is still alive and kicking, right?'

'And not known to us. But he controls everything, and we need to identify him. Looking at any terrorism intelligence, the one fact that arouses suspicion is a lack of mobile phone communication. It's so easy to trace – anybody involved in serious activity avoids them. Hence the reason why we have looked at areas with no mobile phone signal.'

'Such as the glen?' said Costello.

'And when there, Wullie MacFadyean just falls into our laps,' Anderson said. 'Has Christmas come early?'

'And he was at Carruthers' funeral, and so was Moffat. You are the watching brief in the glen, Costello.' Howlett paused and looked round at them all. Even shrunken and ill, he dominated the gathering. 'There is no chatter on the ether, no texting, no emailing for the intelligence boys to trace, nothing to track. So, how does this gang communicate? Because they do – this is a well-tuned organization. But how are they doing it? Until we know that, we can't stop it. We need to ID the Puppeteer and take him out the picture. That is our job.'

As Howlett dismissed them, he gently put his arm out to stop Costello and said in a low tone, 'I repeat, you are the watching brief in the glen. Are you OK with that?'

She nodded.

'Well, I want you to know you can always trust Pettigrew.' Howlett looked at his feet. 'Good man, Pettigrew. Keep in touch with him.' He gave her a tight little smile and walked out of the room as Wyngate held the door open for him.

Costello looked round. 'Excuse me, Mick, can I have a word with you? About a boy called Andrew Elphinstone? I think he might be dangerous.'

'Just give me a minute. I need a fag after that.' Batten pushed his chair back.

Costello noticed his hand shaking. 'If not something stronger.' She smiled and watched him go, then turned to Anderson. 'Do you trust Howlett?' she asked, whispering in Anderson's ear once Batten was out of the door. 'Because I'm bloody sure that he knows exactly who the Bridge Boy is.'

'Why does that not surprise me?' Anderson raised an eyebrow at Costello. 'I overheard that wee conversation. So, Pettigrew is one of us?'

'Depends what you mean by "us",' Costello replied.

12.30 p.m.

Matilda slid into the seat beside DCI Anderson, giving him a concerned little smile. 'How did it go?'

'The moment Gaynor saw the boy lying there, she collapsed against the glass and sobbed her eyes out. So, we'll take that as a positive ID, and we'll request some DNA samples for you.'

'So, she didn't know her son was missing?'

'No, she was in Geneva and flew back first thing in the morning.' Anderson showed her the photograph of a handsome young man, with dark eyes and a smile that could melt an iceberg. 'Mum is a GP in Milngavie. She has a son – Richard, known as Richie – now nineteen years old. He was doing the gap year thing; working at a care home while Mum paid for his flat in the West End.'

'And only went to see Mum when he had run out of clean clothes.' Matilda wrinkled her small nose. 'He's a good-looking lad. But I need you to look at this.' She put an old photo of a room in the Marchettis' house in front of him. 'Do you see that, there?' She pointed to the blood

272

spatter on the floor. 'Somebody was bleeding as they were dragged towards the front door. The blood didn't belong to any of the family, so the police presumed it was Tito Piacini's. It was mixed with saliva, as if he'd been punched in the face. They thought he was injured defending himself.'

'Logical thought. But why take him?' asked Anderson, fingers drumming on the table. 'Why not just leave him?'

'So they could kill him elsewhere?'

'Why not kill him there and then and save the bother of transporting him?'

'Panic?'

'If they'd panicked, they'd have been more likely to kill him immediately.'

'Maybe they did, and took the body because it had something on it that could ID them.'

'Like what?'

'Can't think of anything right now, but there must be a reason. Anyway, the blood was only tested to determine blood type, for exclusion purposes. There was no DNA profile done; in those days it was so expensive they only did it when there was something to compare it to.' She pulled out a lab report on a single A5 sheet. 'See, the blood was AB. That proved it wasn't any of the Marchettis – the family are all O, the universal donor.'

'OK, so why are we spending money on doing a DNA profile now?'

'Because you have no other leads to follow.' When she smiled, she looked about twelve. 'And it's so much cheaper nowadays.'

'And what do you think that's going to tell us? He's

been listed as a missing person since the evening of the 8th of October 1996.'

Anderson saw the twinkle in her eye. 'But Eric Moffat was in charge, and maybe that DNA would have taken him somewhere he didn't want to go,' she said.

'Or didn't want anyone else to go, more like. OK, McQueen, permission to get started.'

Matilda beamed. Her enthusiasm was irrepressible.

As she slipped out of the door, Anderson muttered, 'And for an encore you can get me God's phone number. I could do with his help right now.'

1.30 p.m.

Costello had spent most of the journey in the taxi feeling guilty. A ten-minute conversation with Batten had provoked in her emotions of sadness and annoyance at her own prejudice. Drew Elphinstone was not well. He was a young man growing up without any parental help in a world he saw as persecuting him. Just imagine, Batten had said, when the thing that scares you most is inside your own head. You never get away from it. Costello could not think how frightening that must be. His parents provided for him well, but how could they not admit there was a problem? Rhona had said that the school had told them often enough. He was ill.

Based on Costello's short observation, Batten had thought it sounded like the onset of schizophrenia. Drew was ill, and he was alone in his illness. Batten explained that the boy had an inability to distinguish between what

274

was real and unreal. He would stop relating to others, and he would become increasingly paranoid and act in bizarre ways. He asked Costello to find evidence of Drew's paranoia, such as signs that he was preparing to defend himself from attack. Armed with that evidence, he would convince Drew's parents to get him the help he needed. If they refused, at least Batten had evidence to take it further.

Costello had thought about talking to the boy's classmates, Rhona, his teachers and Mr Ellis. She remembered hearing Libby shout what might have been Drew's name, when she was in the forest. She had injured herself in the trap and had called somebody 'fucking maddie'.

So, Libby Hamilton was a good place to start.

Costello was now watching her. The girl was sitting on the wooden bridge, feet dangling over the water, her cigarette smoke curling into the still, warm air. She was totally in a world of her own. She didn't move or look up, yet she was obviously aware of Costello's approach. The long echoing corridors of the school had given this lot a sixth sense about approaching authority.

'Fascinating, are they, your toes? They're the only thing you've been looking at for the last ten minutes.'

Libby wriggled her toes; her black flip-flops were lying on the wooden decking of the bridge. 'I think they're a work of art, feet.' She looked up at Costello through her dark heavy fringe, her eyes squinting into the sun.

'How is the injury?'

'Oh, it's fine. Stuck some antiseptic on it, didn't go near Matron – she's a sociopath. Have a seat, have a look at the view for yourself.'

275

Costello sat down beside her, and dangled her feet above the water. Suddenly she felt hot and sweaty, and wanted to pull her shoes off and dunk her feet in the cold stream. 'I love this view,' Libby said. 'It's the only good thing about the whole bloody place. Look, from here you can see right down the glen, and the trees cover all that military stuff. It's perfect, the way it's supposed to be. And it's beautiful in every season. You should see it in the middle of winter, when the river's frozen and the grass is white. The deer come down for the grazing, and all those trees –' she waved her arm '– change into white cobwebs that merge together to make a sort of enchanted forest. It's spectacular.'

Despite herself, Costello shivered. Libby had a way with words that was just a little too descriptive for her just yet. She had had enough icy water and snow to last her a lifetime. 'Do you know who was doing it? Making those traps?'

'I can guess.'

'Want to tell me?'

'Drew, probably. He's always doing things like that. He was damming up the river with his bare hands last week because it was circling the school and going to make us all invisible. But don't say anything – he's a loony, but he's harmless,' she said, watching a cloud of midges rolling their way up the burn.

'Has anybody tried to help him? He does need help, Libby.'

'He needs a dad who actually cares. He needs a mum who doesn't have such a busy schedule. I know from Pettigrew that Ellis has tried. Good that you are here.

Wouldn't want him being arrested for being ill.' Libby suddenly changed the subject. 'It's an unusual thing up here, a forest like that, full of oak and elm. The Forestry Commission chopped them all down before the days of biodiversity enlightenment, and replaced them with pine – pine planted in rows with military precision. All the same height, all the same width, depriving anything underneath of light and nutrition. In these enlightened days, they allow the land to lie after felling. They encourage the black and red grouse to nest, and catch the crows to feed to the eagles. The native Scottish birds are falling in numbers, they need their habitat back.' She nodded to herself, pleased, and drew hard on her cigarette.

Costello and Libby sat in silence for a while, listening to the chattering and bubbling of the burn. The water level was low, and the water seemed to tickle the small stones on the bed of the burn. An azure flutter appeared for an instant, a streak of brilliant silk, and then was gone.

'That was a kingfisher,' Libby whispered. 'You were lucky to see it.'

It was hypnotic, Costello thought, watching the busy little life of pebbles, midges, dragonflies and kingfishers. The racket in the great hall of Glen Fruin at feeding time, the busyness of Byres Road . . . all seemed like something from another planet. I could die happy here, was the thought running through her head. 'I can see why you like it here,' was what she said. 'Peaceful, isn't it?'

'Very.'

'Kind of disconnected from real life. Don't think that does the Drews of this world much good. I don't imagine the three supermodels on the lawn this morning hang about here when they have free time.'

'No, they get out. Saskia has a brand-new Mini convertible. Eighteenth birthday present a few weeks ago, from Daddy. Every Friday and Saturday night they're out on the town. Bunch of slappers,' she said dismissively. 'There they go now – you can tell by the inane giggling.'

Costello turned her head to watch the Three Graces getting into a soft-top Mini. Their laughter drifted across the car park, music blared up, and the car pulled away.

'Why do they even bother getting up in the morning?' asked Libby, 'I mean, they don't eat, they don't think. They just . . . are.'

'You know them well?'

'Don't want to know them at all. There're loads of rumours about where bloody Saskia's family fortune comes from. Probably produced by hundreds of poor buggers stuck down a salt mine in Siberia somewhere.'

Costello turned a little to watch Saskia, the one who had waved at her the first day she had arrived. A little hunch had told her then that Saskia knew exactly what Costello was, and she tended to believe her hunches. She shuddered as some crows briefly set up a raucous squawking somewhere downstream. She noticed Libby gazing intently at her before looking away again.

'Bloody crows, do you know they follow pregnant ewes just to rip out the innards of newborn lambs?'

'Nice,' said Costello. 'Don't think I'll bother with my tea, then.'

Anderson was standing in front of the wall, with a marker pen. He had written the word 'Puppeteer' at the top of the board, and then 'Glen Fruin' down the side, with 'MacFadyean' spanning the gap. They still had no idea where he lived but the insect activity on the body, lying as it was on the forest floor, strongly suggested that MacFadyean had been killed only hours after being seen with Moffat at the funeral. Anderson didn't ask for the precise details. The words 'insect activity' were enough for him. He was trying to avoid looking at the black-and-white close-up photographs of maggots that Matilda was studying so carefully. It was too soon after lunch.

Batten handed him a coffee he hadn't asked for. 'Get it down you, it'll do you good – help keep you awake.'

'Are we chasing the Russian mafia here? Honestly?'

Batten nodded, patting Anderson's shoulder. 'Hard people. They are tough, and the *Vorony* – Ekaterinburg's finest – are the toughest. That's who you have here.'

'It's pronounced "Voron-neigh". Well, that's as close as a Glasgow accent can get. *Vorony*, with the emphasis at the front, means "ravens". *Vorony*, emphasis at the end, means "crows". Voron-neigh plural,' Mulholland said authoritatively. 'A murder of crows, if you prefer.'

'Voron-neigh,' repeated Batten, rolling the word on his tounge. '*Corvus corone*, the carrion crow, is among the most intelligent of birds, highly aggressive, and with excellent communication skills. Good name for a gang of thugs, you must admit.'

'And back home, they are admired. The Shirokorechen-skoe is a cemetery dedicated to gangsters, with all these lavish memorials and portraits. It's practically a shrine – the hologram pictures of dead gangsters stand up and watch you as you drive past in the tour bus. And now they are here in the flesh.'

'Very nice of them to visit. So, if you two are so bloody well informed, tell me . . . how do they communicate with each other?' Anderson pulled the files out of the cabinet behind him, fishing out the photographs of Biggart's flat immediately after the fire and then the ones taken by the forensic team. 'Think – if I wanted to get in touch with you and keep it secret and untraceable, what would I do?'

'Use a code?' Lambie offered, stretching back in his seat and yawning.

Batten shook his head. 'Nothing so complicated. Do you remember that gang of diamond smugglers who sent millions of pounds' worth of diamonds through the post in those yellow boxes that slides are stored in? If I was communicating regularly, I'd make it look ordinary, something to be expected, not noticed. I mean, how often do we look closely at a cardboard package with the word "Amazon" on it? We don't.'

'OK, is there anything – anything at all – in these shots that could be used as a means of communication? Howlett has already said, no mobile, no computer. Snail mail?'

They sat in silence for a few minutes, peering minutely at every inch of the photographs.

'Can you pass me that close-up?' Anderson asked. He looked at it intently, then made a noise a bit like a low growl. 'There you go. What do you see on the floor, on the carpet by the side of the chair?'

'Nothing,' said Wyngate.

'Well, no table, which is what you'd expect to be there. But through the soot and the stains of water, you can see four distinct round indents in the carpet where the table legs were. And in this one, there's a table of the right size out in the hall. It's been moved. Someone carefully put it where the fire wouldn't damage it, but where the fire investigator would find it.'

'And look what's on it.' Batten tapped the photograph with the corner of another. On top of the table was a mobile phone, and neatly under the phone were two DVD holders shaped like pillar boxes. In the black-and-white photograph they looked grey, with darker grey tops. 'PillarBoxFlix.com? Haven't they been mentioned before? If they're communicating using DVDs, there'd be a legitimate rental company by way of a front. And PillarBoxFlix are legit, aren't they?'

Wyngate was tapping away at his computer. 'Here's the address of PillarBoxFlix, at the Phoenix in Paisley. Factory unit is owned by Red Eagle Properties.' Another rattle of fingertips on keyboard and the screen changed. 'Which is, in turn, owned by PSM.' He swung round in his chair, circling his finger at the wall. 'Red Eagle also own the flats at the Apollo.'

'OK, Vik, you go out to the warehouse at Paisley tomorrow and have a look around. Wyngate, can you find the actual DVDs taken from Biggart's flat, and check that they're what they say they are?'

'And that mobile phone has been put neatly on top of

the DVDs,' Batten said. 'That was left for us to find as well. I'd put my bottom dollar on it.'

'Why?'

'The arsonist didn't make any other mistakes, did they?'

'The other mobile phones found in the room were burned to cinders,' said Matilda, placing the photographs neatly in a pile. 'But I already have a printout of the activity on that phone. It's normal procedure now.' She shuffled through her folder. 'Here . . . look at this.' She handed it to Anderson. 'That's the SIM on that phone. Only two people were on it. Biggart and A. N. Unknown, who declined to identify himself when he answered. But it's a pay-as-you-go, one of three purchased in Glasgow by credit card on an expense account belonging to Biggart's lawyer, Faulkner, the week before Fairbairn got out. Faulkner says he gave the phones to a Robert McGee, a Gavin McCready and to one fine gentleman of the parish called Cameron Fairbairn, known to his friends as Skelpie.'

'God, that was quick,' said Anderson, really impressed.

'Not really – it's a card number we all know by heart. Most criminal lawyers deal in phones and phone cards now that fags are banned. And even criminal lawyers need forensic friends sometimes, so I called in a favour.' She shrugged.

'Good work, Matilda.' Then Anderson asked Lambie, 'What's the update on Gaynor Spence?'

Lambie said, 'She's OK. She's a single mother and the boy has no idea who his father is. And she wants to keep it that way. However, she has a nice house in Milngavie. She drives a big Mercedes. Holiday villa in

Spain. I don't see a single mum managing that on a GP's salary.'

'So, you think the dad has been helping out? Somebody rich but married? Is that why she's so secretive?'

'I'm wondering if the dad knows about the state Richard is in,' Lambie said.

'That's not really our business.'

'It might be, if the boy needs a bit of a liver from somewhere. In his case a live donation is preferable, so the first stop is the parents – them being the best probable match. She's being tissue typed at the moment, to see if she's a suitable donor. A better question is, where did Richie go to school?'

'Don't tell me.'

'Glen Fruin. He was head boy last year. Probably got really good marks in the chemistry of combustion.'

2.00 p.m.

'So, where is home, then?'

'Where's yours?' Libby didn't wait for a reply. 'I'm with Paul Young on that one. Home is wherever I lay my hat.'

Costello had an image of Libby sitting on her bridge like a garden gnome with a fishing rod, dangling information in front of her. But she was not going to bite, not yet.

'And where do you go to escape?'

'Some friends. Some family.'

'Family?' It was Costello who was fishing this time.

'Not close, but family is family. I think myself lucky. Look at Drew. And there's a girl in Third Year – her mum's in Edinburgh with a boob job and a drink problem, and her dad's in New York with the nanny. The poor kid gets passed around all over the place in the school holidays, and the rumour is she hasn't seen either parent for over a year, and I don't think she's noticed. This school is a dumping ground for career parents who saw kids as a must-have accessory and got bored with them. It's the way of the world. Even in the state system, they have breakfast clubs, after-school clubs, weekend clubs. Parents fuck you up.'

Costello pondered the truth of the statement.

'And they're a clever lot, our school board. They saw that the gap in the market is the holidays. This school takes being in loco parentis very seriously, so it never closes.'

'Does that bother you?' Costello didn't need to ask where Libby spent her holidays.

'Don't give a shit one way or the other. I'm not a stupid sixteen-year-old whose only chance of getting a flat is a quick shag to get pregnant. What's with all the questions?'

'Just trying to get my head round it. What are you going to do now that school has finished?'

'I have to hang around here until after the party on Sunday. After that, we'll see.'

'But where will you go?'

'Oh, I have a flat in Glasgow, in Maryhill – the posh part of Maryhill. It's been rented out, but it'll be all mine when I turn eighteen.'

'You're very young to have your own flat. It's a lot of responsibility.'

'Alexander III, the last Gaelic king of Scotland, was

king at eight, head of the military at sixteen, totally in charge by twenty-one. Revolution is the domain of the young. He reigned for thirty-seven years. I'll set my sights a bit lower; I'm thinking about university.'

'To study what?'

'English Lit, or Law, I think. Haven't really made up my mind. I'm only seventeen.' She sighed. 'So, no hurry. I could even go to Tulliallan, become a cop. But I wonder if I'm not too clever for that.'

So, she knew.

Costello couldn't look at her. Instead, she focused on the middle distance, trying to catch sight of the kingfisher again. 'How did you know?' she asked after a few minutes.

'I know everything that goes on in this school. And I recognized that look you have.'

'What look? And I thought I was blending in so well. Bought myself a good grey suit and everything.'

'It's the look in your eyes, the same look as an alkie sobering up, or a druggie in rehab. Wary. As if reality just might be a wee bit too much to cope with.'

'You ever thought of studying psychology?'

Libby grinned, the first time Costello had ever seen her smile. 'I do, here, every day,' she said. 'Place is full of bloody nutters.'

3.00 p.m.

Mulholland had decided to give Anderson his chance on the Fairbairn issue. He himself had set his sights on getting his promotion back, and he wasn't going to let

Anderson stand in his way. As soon as they were out in the car park, Mulholland took the DCI to one side.

'Skelpie Fairbairn,' he began.

'What about him?'

'I've been looking at his connections with Biggart. They had been in touch – the phone shows chatter between the two of them, and only the two of them. Don't forget, Biggart was paying his legal fees.'

'And . . . ?'

'I need my stripes back, so I want you to hear me out. Say Skelpie wasn't involved in the Osbourne case –'

'He was.'

'But let's assume for a minute that he really wasn't, as the law has it at this present time. That means that Lynda Osbourne was assaulted by somebody else. I bet that somebody was Billy Biggart, that Skelpie took the fall for him.'

'But Biggart wasn't a paedophile. He was a vile human being, but not that.'

'You think that's too much of a stretch for a man who will film it? Make the cake but not taste it? No way. And, if not, then why has Biggart covered his legal fees until now? It could account for the phone chatter between them.'

'Vik, we are not opening all that up again.'

Mulholland punched the wall gently. 'But it *is* all opened up again. And you need to be proactive to circumvent –'

'Circumvent what? The case went in front of a jury, fifteen men and women. I didn't say Fairbairn was guilty, they did.'

'You made sure they didn't hear all the evidence.'

'That's bullshit, Vik!'

'Look, I'm just trying to make this right,' Mulholland argued. 'Why was that mobile left in plain sight like that, away from the fire? Most people would stamp on the phone, destroy the SIM, flush it down the loo. Everything else in the flat was destroyed, but that was kept safe – almost like some kind of gift you were meant to find. Whoever left it knew how much information we could get from it.' He turned from Anderson to shout, 'They knew what she would get from it,' at Matilda, who was scurrying across the car park from her own lab. The way she turned and trotted over reminded Anderson of Nesbitt.

'What?'

'Can I have a word, DCI Anderson? I mean, not here . . .' Matilda's pinched face was pale, her brow furrowed.

Mulholland, who had been standing there, smiling, said with exaggerated politeness, 'Do you want me to make myself scarce?'

'Yes, please.'

Anderson and Matilda walked into the main hall. 'So, what can I do for you?'

'I wasn't sure about this at first,' she said. 'So, I ran it twice to make sure.' She pushed the file over to Anderson, who opened it.

He spent a minute or two comparing two sheets of paper, looking from one to the other in disbelief. Anderson didn't know what he was looking at, but as far as he could tell the bottom graph matched the top one. He knew that was important, but couldn't figure out why. 'So? They both look exactly the same.'

'That's because they are. They're a direct match, a perfect DNA match,' she said, slightly exasperated. 'I took a sample from the cuts of carpet from the Marchettis' flat – there was enough there to get a reasonable profile using a low-platform technique –'

'Good for you,' said Anderson, feeling rather threatened by her youth and determination. 'And we've a match? Piacini is still alive?'

'Oh, he's alive all right.' She pointed to the name on the bottom graph. 'Alive and living under the name of Cameron Fairbairn.'

4.00 p.m.

Colin Anderson had a sore ear. He would never again suggest, even politely, that Matilda McQueen might have contaminated a sample. She had been furious. And loud. Now he had one photograph of Tito Piacini in front of him and one of Cameron Fairbairn. The eyes were the same.

She was right.

For the first time, Anderson thought he might be getting ahead of the game.

Fairbairn had been in on the kidnap. Eric Moffat was the man in charge. It had been planned to damage the families, to allow the present state of criminality. And a member of the O'Donnell family had struck back hard.

But where was Howlett in all this? He could see a cop of Howlett's age knowing the families of organized crime personally. It was how things worked in those days. And if it kept scum like Fairbairn off the street, who could say they were wrong?

Anderson looked around the deserted room. The computers were all hibernating – even their geometric gymnastics had ceased. He flicked through his notes, Batten's untidy handwriting in green pen giving him a few tasty details about Carruthers' medical history. Batten had concluded that Thomas Carruthers was not the same man after 1977. Something had happened that had stopped him drinking – maybe something that had occurred while he was drunk.

Anderson looked at the Post-it note that had been left on the telephone, not dated, time-stamped or signed. The handwriting suggested it was also from Batten, who probably didn't know any better. Mary Carruthers had phoned in to say she had found the missing diary from 1977.

A wee job for Lambie, thought Anderson.

4.45 p.m.

'Am I disturbing you two?' Anderson said to O'Hare and Matilda, who were leaning over a table in the lab, heads down, looking at something of great interest, so absorbed that they didn't appear to have heard him enter.

'You can disturb us any time you want, because I was just about to phone you,' O'Hare said. 'Just wait to hear what else Matilda has discovered.'

'Well, you found it,' she said, beaming up at the pathologist.

O'Hare had the good grace to look slightly embarrassed. 'It's your story. You tell it.'

'Well, after looking at that film Howlett showed us, we tried a Quasar machine on Rusalka to try to photograph a fingerprint from the skin of her neck, but it was too late. She'd been in the water too long. But we did try. Then we did a much deeper search into the body cavities. Want to have a look down that microscope?'

Anderson leaned forward and looked. There was a single hair root, its bulb cut to a sharp end to harvest the DNA for analysis. Anderson withdrew from the scope and looked from Matilda to O'Hare and back again.

'Is that the DNA of Tito Piacini? Cameron Fairbairn, or whatever he's calling himself? Oh, please tell me it is.'

'It is,' said Matilda. 'And we can do even better. High up in her nasal cavity were some cotton fibres. As you know, on the microscope they match fibres from the towel you brought from the flat next door to Biggart's. So, we can put her and Fairbairn together at the scene. I don't think he's going to walk away from this one.'

Anderson straightened up, feeling both revulsion and relief run through him. 'OK, I think it's time to pick him up. But I'll tell Howlett. He needs to take on the media on this one,' he said.

'And tell him I can make all this evidence stand up so that Mother Teresa would be convicted on it,' said Matilda with a wide grin.

The door opened and a nervous-looking Wyngate appeared.

'Don't worry, there are no dead bodies here,' said O'Hare. 'Well, not in one piece, anyway.'

'Can you help me with this, Prof? Maybe you too, Matilda? I'm trying to trace what happened to a cop called Graham Hunter. Does that mean anything to you? He went missing up Seana Bhraigh in 1977.'

Anderson looked up. 'Really? Go on.'

'Hunter? Hunter? A cop? Was there a delay in finding that body?' asked O'Hare. 'Before my time, and not my jurisdiction but yes – I've heard about it. The body had been lying in a lochan for a good few months and was only visible once the water level dropped. He fell from an outcrop of rocks, something like that.' He stretched his spine, both palms kneading the muscles in the small of his back, then said, 'I can't now remember what the enquiry said at the end of the day, but it was winter, and a hill-walking trip with some colleagues went wrong. It happens all the time. It took his colleagues days to walk out safely and then, once the body was found, there was a disputed cause of death. It was ruled death by misadventure. But did the head injury cause him to topple off the summit, or did he fall and hit his head on the way down? No definitive answer.'

'But you do remember it?' asked Anderson, intrigued.

'It's the sort of thing we talk about down the pub, we sad gits. I'll track it down for you, if you want. It wasn't one of mine; I'm not that old. I take it from your enquiry that something about that case might be relevant now.'

'Maybe. And while you're at it, Prof, can we go for Jason Purcie, killed by a gunshot wound to the head on the Campsie Fells later the same year? Both friends or colleagues of Carruthers, both died in 1977 – the year that something stopped him drinking.'

'Well, I was directly involved in a review of the Purcie case. Why are you not going through normal channels? No, don't answer that. But even seasoned old pathologists like me are not totally insensitive to violent death. A young, intelligent police officer gets shot in the head on duty while out on a team search. Can't recall who they were looking for, but it was somebody armed and dangerous. It was a high-velocity shot, and you don't forget them. As far as I remember, the bullet was never matched to any weapon in the database, though the database was still fairly rudimentary back then. In fact, the whole investigation simply ran into a dead end at every turn. Anyway, we delivered our report, the enquiry was carried out, and the verdict was "killed by person or persons unknown". It'll all be on record.'

'Both connected to Carruthers? Get on to it, Wyngate.'

Anderson was halfway to the door when O'Hare shouted him back. 'Do you also wish to know that Mr MacFadyean was an insulin-dependent diabetic? He picked up his insulin script regularly at the McCrory medical practice in Balloch. I tried to trace the home address – the GP has an address for him, but he doesn't live there. And he had an appointment every three months, which he always kept, so they never needed to write to him. He did once tell the nurse that his home life was complicated, so if they needed to write to him to use the post office in Luss, as they knew him. She said there are a few homes high in the glen where the people come down for the mail to save the postie a long drive.'

'So, if Luss is his post office –' Anderson walked over to the Ordnance Survey map on the wall, and put one finger on the village of Luss on the west shore of Loch Lomond, and another on Balloch to the south '– and his chemist is at Balloch, he must live up the glen somewhere. He was walking back from a funeral, let's say with a drink in him, when he was killed. So, he must have been close to home.'

'Our Mr MacFadyean certainly went to great lengths to be public when he was public, and to disappear when he wanted to disappear.'

'Septic tank,' said O'Hare, suddenly. 'He could have wood-burning stoves, a generator, and a natural water supply. And the council tax list might give you an address but not a location. But the company that deals with the septic tank will have a map.'

5.00 p.m.

Leaving O'Hare and Matilda, Anderson phoned Lambie, to tell him to go and get the diary from Mrs Carruthers. 'I'm sure what we want is in there,' he said. 'There's a connection with Moffat, MacFadyean and Carruthers which might spread to two other dead cops – a Jason Purcie and a Graham Hunter.' In his mind's eye he could see Lambie scribbling it down.

'Well, Jennifer's cooking something special tonight, so can I pick it up on the way home, bring it in tomorrow? I know what you and Batten are looking for, so I'll have a quick read tonight with a nice glass of wine and present you with the edited highlights.'

'Of course. I'm going to go home too and have an early night. I think last night is starting to catch up with me.

And tomorrow we're going out to the post office in Luss, so that will be a nice wee day trip for us.'

'I'll be sure to wear my kilt – if I can get into it.' Lambie rang off and Anderson made his way towards his car. It was leaving five o'clock and he was dog-tired. He was going to sit in the garden with a pint of cold beer.

And if Mr Lomax got out his bloody lawn mower, he was going to shoot him.

Rosie could hear crows cawing out in the woods. She had no food left, and no water. Her throat was parched, and the skin round her mouth had cracked open and was bleeding. She was trapped in her bed, and the skin of her hip and thigh had been damp for days now. The urine was burning into her, and she could feel painful blisters forming, yet she couldn't stop her body weight from crushing them. Her hands were scaly, and her fingers were turning blue, her nails black. It felt as if a thousand ants were biting at her feet, burrowing in between her toes and working their way up. The flies laid their eggs in her flesh, uninterrupted. There was a clapping of black feathers at the window, and she could make out the crows on the ledge outside. They could smell the sweet stench of rotting meat.

She was dying from the outside in.

She wondered where the boy had gone, and then she heard the familiar thunk-thunk as he came in through the window and dropped down on to the worktop. She had been thinking about him – she was sure now it was a 'him'.

Singular. He must be slim to get in that wee window, but tall to be able to reach it from outside. One thing she did know about him – he was young.

And here he was now; she could sense that he had come into her room. She closed her eyes. It was a routine now. As long as she let him do what he wanted, she would stay alive. He cleaned her, he gave her water, he brought her a banana, an apple, some cake wrapped in a paper napkin that looked as though it had been carried about in his jacket pocket. But it was food – and with water and food, she was thinking again. Survival depended on her establishing a relationship with him. And all the time, subtly, she was gaining information. It afforded her some pride that she was starting to see herself in the role of a black widow spider. Once he was expendable he would be terminated, but for now she needed him in order to stay alive.

He was standing here, in her room, not speaking, hardly breathing. He smoked, she knew that. He was light on his feet, he never spoke, he wore leather even in this weather. And he was starting to smell.

She had tried to speak to him, but got nothing. This time she tried again. 'Hello.' She said it as a greeting, not a question. Something that didn't need an answer.

She heard him come up behind her, felt the cover on her face. It was an old tea towel this time, one he had used before – she recognized the shamrock pattern. But he then walked back out to the little hall. She heard him start to go through drawers and cupboards, carefully. He wasn't ransacking the place. Rather, he seemed to be looking for something. She had been stuck on her left side for years now, only able to move when Wullie was there to lift her flesh, so she had no idea what Wullie kept in the rest of the house – all she knew was what she could see from her bed. Everything else was a mystery.

She called out. 'Is it money you want?' She knew where Wullie kept the money.

He ignored her. He was definitely looking for something.

She stared into the little field of shamrocks that was her whole world at the moment and listened carefully. Some cop's instinct told her that the boy knew exactly what he was looking for.

8.00 p.m.

'Oh my God. Is that a skirt?' asked Costello. She walked up to Pettigrew who was standing, whistling, paying a lot of attention to the three young ladies in question.

'No, it's a pelmet. If she bends over in that, you can see her back teeth, you know.'

'It's a shame your job forces you to stand here and watch these beautiful young women with hardly any clothes on strut about like they own the planet. When do they go home?'

'I don't move in those circles, so don't ask me. The older pupils' parents tend to fly in so they can play happy families before they all go off to Antigua, or Largs, or wherever.'

Costello screwed her eyes up. 'Don't knock it – the chips in Largs are fine at this time of year. So, what happens on the last day? Do we have a fanfare or something?'

'They all get together, big party on the lawn, parents come along to take their children away. It usually rains.'

The brunette's very short dress rucked up under her shoulder bag and up over her bottom. She turned to tug it down and stumbled on her high heels, falling into the arms of the tall blonde. They giggled, their carefree happiness echoing across the glen.

'Do you think they're on something?' Costello asked. 'Something chemical and illegal? Is that why I am here? Or am I here to be an independent witness to the deterioration of Drew Elphinstone's personality?'

'Either, but as to the drugs, I do think they are on something. I think it's coke, but I've never caught them on it, never found any proof.'

'And you can't go round just making accusations, can you?'

'Well, I have tried, but my hands are tied somewhat,' said Pettigrew easily. 'They're off somewhere, those three.'

Costello noted the change of tack, and went along with it. 'I wonder where. Let's find out. Where's your car?'

'Parked behind the school, as it is normally. Why?'

'I think we should follow them. Would they know your car?'

'What do you have in mind, DS Costello?'

'A little bit of undercover work, Mr Pettigrew.'

'Fine with me.' He started to walk slowly back behind the school. 'I presume you have carte blanche to do as you wish here?'

'I was sent to do a job, and I intend to do it.'

'Come on, then. Get in my car, and hide low in the seat. It'll look like I'm going home. The minute we get to the gatehouse, we'll change to the wife's. We need to stay well back from them until we get to the main road. The high road here is far too straight; they'll see if we follow too close.'

'Tell you what, I'll call the local nick, see if they can sit a car on the slip road and let us know when they come out and if they go north or south. Then we can follow them at a distance.'

'If you want to phone, you'll have to wait till we get up to the gatehouse. There's no mobile phone signal down here.'

'So, why are we waiting?'

8.10 p.m.

'Gaynor? My name is Mick Batten. I'm a criminal psychologist. I'd like to talk to you about your son.'

'Oh,' was all she said.

'How is he doing? Richard?'

'He's holding his own but the drugs are causing more problems with the little bit of functioning liver he still has. They say he's definitely going to need a transplant.' She bit her lip, trying to hold back tears.

'He's comfortable for the moment. But you need something to eat, and some fresh air.' He held up a brown paper bag from the deli and wafted it under her nose. 'I got some salad sandwiches, and we can pick up some coffee on the way out.'

She was nearly swayed but her eyes darted back along the corridor. 'I don't think I should . . .'

'They have your mobile number. You'll be two minutes away – less, if we just go out and sit on the wall. You could be here for hours yet and you need to keep your strength up. Think what you would say to one of your own patients. You're going to have to be the strong one to help him get better.'

They walked down the stairs and queued for their coffee in silence, as though whatever they were going to talk about could wait until they were settled. Then they went out to the car park.

'You're not from these parts,' she said, jumping up like a child to sit on the wall. 'Liverpool? Somewhere down there?'

'Yes, I don't think it's an accent you ever lose.' He handed her a sandwich, still cold from the cooler in the deli, wrapped in a beige paper napkin stained to dark brown by the virgin olive oil.

She took a huge bite immediately. 'Thank you for this. I must give you some money. I never realized how hungry I was.'

'Munch away.' Batten lifted the plastic lid off his coffee cup and blew on the white froth.

'You said you're a criminal psychologist. I don't quite see how that fits in.'

Batten related roughly what he knew about Richard. 'Is that right?'

'Yes. He wants to go to university and study Law, I think. I was hoping he would do Medicine. Law depends so much on them getting a traineeship, and those are very scarce on the ground these days. I just don't want him to waste five years of his life.'

'And what about the last few months? Do you know what he's been doing?'

She pulled a little shred of lettuce from the corner of her mouth, gaining some time to think, and Batten knew he had her. She was definitely hiding something.

'I don't know what he was doing, but it must have been something really important for them to do that to him.' She started to cry, and he handed her a clean paper napkin.

'Well, he'll get a liver transplant, the rest will heal in time, and he'll go back to a relatively normal life,' Batten said, and started on his sandwich while carefully watching her reaction.

The tears started in earnest. 'I thought I'd be able to give him part of my liver. But I can't, it seems. I had rheumatic fever as a kid, had to have two heart valves replaced.'

'Does that exclude you?'

She nodded, and half laughed bitterly. 'But I didn't think for a minute that it would. And me a doctor!'

'Well, I'm a psychologist and the machinations of the human brain never cease to amaze me. People believe what they want to believe. So, what about Richard's father?' he asked, then softened the question. 'He'd be the next port of call.'

She lifted her coffee to her mouth but did not answer.

Batten pressed on gently. 'I am eternally interested in why people do things. For instance, I am interested why your son took a year out to work in an old folks' home. Just a wee piece of mental gymnastics, but where there is a trail I will follow.' He watched her become more uncomfortable. 'He worked in the home where Archie O'Donnell senior is resident. Gangster. He was friendly with Billy Biggart. Gangster. He knew Melinda. Gangster's wife. One move on from Auld Archie took me to his son.'

At that point, Gaynor looked up. 'Please, don't.'

'And sure enough, Richard has been visiting Archie O'Donnell junior in Barlinnie, every fortnight. He's there in the visitor's log. Richard Spence, law student.'

Gaynor looked as though she had been punched in the stomach. 'Oh my God. So, he found out. He knew.'

'Knew what, Gaynor?' asked Batten gently. 'You see how important it is now. Is Archie O'Donnell the father of your son?'

8.20 p.m.

Lambie pulled into the car park of the block of flats where Mary Carruthers lived, and had a good look around. There were no free spaces in the car park itself, so he did a three-point turn back out on to the street. Then he parked and checked his mobile phone. Jennifer had called.

More wedding stuff, no doubt.

His answering call went straight to voicemail. He said, 'Whatever it is, don't spend any money on it yet!' Then his voice grew serious. 'Look, honey, I'm going to be late, I got held up. Just got a wee job to do, and I'll be home –' he glanced at the dashboard clock '– about eleven or so.

Don't wait up, but I've not eaten yet. Can you leave the dinner out? Bye, see you soon.'

He snapped the phone shut and got out of the car. The air was still warm but the night would soon be darkening. He put on his jacket and locked the car. With a professional eye he looked around the concourse as he pressed the security entry pad. He clocked the area at the far side of the garages, noting a couple of teenagers hanging about and another three making their way across the car park, hands to ears, all talking on their mobiles. Some old guy with a stick was painfully shuffling across the grass round the concourse. And a younger bloke was standing beside a Honda Civic, his hand in his pocket, one toe tapping the front tyre. Rene's crackly voice came through. She had already pressed the entry button without waiting for Lambie to say who he was. He would have to have a word with her about that.

He opened the door and went in, watching the flashing numbers as the nearest lift came down to ground level. Just as the lift doors closed, he glanced back quickly through the glass front door. The five teenagers had met up and set off together, mobiles still in hand. The old guy seemed hardly to have moved at all. And the guy with the Honda Civic had obviously lost interest in the tyre and had lit a cigarette. He was looking around as though he was waiting for something.

9.05 p.m.

Saskia had obviously been a rally driver in a former life. It took her about nine minutes to get out of the glen and only twenty-seven to get to the Glasgow city boundary on Great Western Road before being caught in traffic, which slowed her down a bit. By that time, Costello was thinking about applying for a sick bag.

'Well, well, well,' she said, as they slowed down outside the Highland Glen Hotel. The Mini convertible was parked in the car park. 'This was the place Janet Appleby was sent when Biggart's flat went on fire, I'm sure of it. Just keep driving; we can double back.'

'You should be a cop; you could make a career of it,' Pettigrew muttered, not used to having a back-seat driver. He did a U-turn and parked the Rover neatly on the opposite side of the road with a full view of the front doors and the foyer of the hotel.

'Strange place to come,' Costello observed. 'Looks more like the kind of place that has bridge evenings, register office weddings and funerals of people who weren't that popular. What attraction does it have for these girls?'

'It's small and controllable. I bet they can drink and get a bedroom and nobody really cares. Just some lassies from outside the city having –'

'Sex? Drugs?' offered Costello.

'Whatever. Uh oh, what's going on now?'

They both instinctively ducked down in their seats a little as the revolving door began to spin, and the three girls came out again. The brunette, Keren, was on her mobile, the other two chatting nineteen to the dozen. A taxi appeared from nowhere, they got in and it pulled away.

'Oh, so they leave the car here, phone a taxi and now

they're on their way to Glasgow to get pissed or smacked or fucked.'

Pettigrew nodded, fired the engine, then pulled sharp left into the car park ready to pull out again and follow the taxi.

But Costello's hand stopped him mid-reverse. 'Hold on. How many coincidences can we have in one day?' She nodded ahead. 'A Russian and a white Transit van in the same place at the same time?'

9.06 p.m.

'Come in, Mr Lambie.'

'Is that the lad from the Co-op bakery?'

Mary met his eyes. 'She's not had her medication yet,' she said wearily. She held the door open, and stood back to let him in.

'How are you, Rene?' he said to the small figure standing at the end of the hall. She seemed slightly uneasy on her feet, so he offered her an arm, in an exaggeratedly gallant gesture.

She grasped his elbow. 'Oh, getting by, son, getting by. Now, you know you said something about the diary – well, we found it. Me and Mary, we found it. The missing one. Was that the one you wanted?'

Lambie's heart started to beat a bit faster in anticipation. '1977. Yes, that was the one.'

'1977?' she said vaguely. 'Cannae remember. Do you want a scone?'

'Well, my fiancée has my dinner in the oven. I've not

been home yet, and it's awful late.' His eyes were drifting to the neatly stacked red and blue diaries on the sideboard. 'So, you found the missing diary?' he asked brightly, before the onslaught of scones began.

'Yes, under the bed,' said Mary quietly. She didn't look at Lambie, keeping her eyes down. 'Why would he keep that one under the bed, and not the others?'

Lambie asked, 'Mary, had he been looking at the diary before he died? Did he seem protective of it?'

Mary shook her head. 'I said before, he was being perfectly normal . . .' She was going to add something, then stopped herself.

'Are you sure you're not wanting a scone?' piped in Rene.

'No, thanks.' Lambie turned to Mary. 'What is it?' he probed gently.

'I was thinking about that writer, Simone Sangster. He stopped writing the diary the day she came here. It ends on the 3rd of October 2008. Not a word since then. That was not normal.' The words were being drawn from her.

'Sticking your diary under your mattress is not normal, Mary!' Rene shuffled down the corridor and stopped at the toilet door. 'Did he think it was for the tooth fairy to read?'

'Between the mattress and the base, you mean?' Lambie asked. A quiet nod from Mary confirmed it. 'Like he was hiding it from somebody? Did he ever say anything to you about it?'

Again, there was a nervous shake of the head.

However, Rene wasn't so tactful. 'But he *had* been reading the diary. I saw him. He might have hidden it, maybe

– hidden it from that man in the lift, the man who was here. Was he the man from the Co-op?'

Lambie smiled reassuringly. 'I'll just take it away and have a look at it, shall I? I'll make sure it's all OK, and then I'll bring it back to you.'

'It's 1977,' said Rene, handing it over. 'That was the year of the Jubilee, all those bloody flags.'

But Lambie had noticed Mary's hand tighten slightly. She didn't quite look up, but she clearly did not want to give that diary away.

'Are you sure you're OK with me looking at this, Mary? It'll stay confidential.'

She nodded, not trusting herself to speak.

Rene was wittering on about the Queen Mother and her teeth. As she was speaking, Lambie let the diary fall open between his thumb and forefinger. The pages were full of dense handwriting – neat, tidy, all in blue or black biro. Mary was staring blankly at the wall. He could feel her just wishing he would go. He sat tight and tilted the diary so that it opened at the beginning of the year. It fell open easily, too easily. The handwriting at the start of January was slightly shaky, as if unsure of itself. Then he realized that there were pages missing – most of January, from the look of it – pulled out right at the bindings. He flicked forward, catching a few words – *God knows . . . God help us . . .* His eyes scanned down. *I know he's dead . . . and I'm sure we killed him . . .*

Mary seemed entranced by the wallpaper, but she was aware the minute Lambie raised his eyes from the page, as if she had been waiting for his question.

'Is this all there is? No loose pages anywhere else?'

She shook her head. 'It was like that when I found it.'

'Have you read it, Mary?'

'Why? Whit is it? A good story?' chirped Rene.

Mary shook her head again, imperceptibly. 'It was a private thing, for him.'

'And it really is OK for me to take it?'

She nodded, ignoring Rene's wittering. 'In fact, I'll be glad if you can get all the diaries picked up. I want them out this house. I just want you to find the man who killed Tommy.'

9.35 p.m.

Lambie thought about taking the diary back to the station, but the boss had said he could take it home – and he didn't think ACC Howlett was going to start accusing him of ripping out the missing pages. Better to go home, have something nice to eat with Jen, then sit and read the diary at his leisure.

Why did Carruthers hide a diary that had been written twenty years earlier? There was probably enough still in there to fill in the back story.

In the lift, he had another look. On the title page the handwriting was good, a perfect hand. It simply said the Gaelic name Seana Bhraigh – the mountain, Lambie supposed – then the date, the 1st of January 1977, and two words: *Bloody cold*. Then that gap, until the end of January. The names Hunter and Purcie jumped out at him. Faddy was MacFadyean, obviously. Hunter was the one who had fallen off a mountain – or had he? – and Purcie had died later from a bullet in the head. Both reports were being tracked down.

He tucked the diary under his arm, and walked towards his car. Despite having told her to go to bed, he hoped that Jennifer would still be waiting up for him. After looking after her sister Emily for so many years, Jennifer relished the simple domesticity of sitting down with a meal on a tray and a glass of wine, feet up in front of the television. So did he.

He fished the car keys out from his trouser pocket, turning slightly on hearing a noise behind him, expecting somebody to ask him for a light or for some spare change. The first thing he felt was a punch in the back, then a quick blow to the front. He looked the man in the face, but felt no recognition. He saw a hand reach for the diary, vaguely registered the tiny stub where the little finger should have been. Then he felt himself being lowered into the gutter between the car and the kerb, and felt the toe of a shoe nudge him, tipping his outflung arm into the shadow of the car.

As if he was a piece of dog dirt, he thought.

9.40 p.m.

'Batten called,' Anderson said.

'Hang on, I can't hear you.' Costello gazed around at the plague of Black Watch tartan that darkened the walls and floor of the lobby of the Highland Glen Hotel. A mangy stag's head glared down at her glassily. She pushed through the revolving door again and out into the car park, where Pettigrew was apparently enjoying a contemplative smoke, leaning against the bonnet of his car. 'Go on.'

'Mick managed to persuade Gaynor Spence to come clean about Richard's father,' Anderson told her. 'One Archibald O'Donnell. Wee Archie.'

'No wonder she wasn't so keen to tell you.'

'But the boy needs a new bit of liver. Blood runs thicker than water. And there's more. Mick played a hunch, and suggested I phone the Bar-L and pull rank to get some urgent information from the visitors' log. And he was right. Richard Spence, law student, has been visiting Archie every two weeks for a while now.'

Costello thought for a minute. 'Someone must have found out he burned Biggart. Do you think the O'Donnells are fighting back?'

'But all that was years ago.'

'But it kind of fits. Apart from the fact that old O'Donnell is gaga in a care home and his son is serving life for decapitation.'

'It was always rumoured he decapitated the guy who killed that woman in the car park; I'd buy him a drink if I ever met him.'

'And Moffat was there too, wasn't he? That's another bit of the jigsaw.'

Anderson yawned. 'I'm off home to catch up on some of the sleep I haven't been having recently,' he said.

Costello thought about telling him about the Transit, but reconsidered – better to wait until they had a positive ID.

'Look after yourself out there,' he said.

'I will.' She closed the phone but kept it to her ear. Anybody watching would think she was still having a conversation. She looked at the Transit, noting that it had a sliding side door.

Costello shut her eyes, trying to remember the photograph of the MacFadyean scene, the image of the tyre print. A 'cross-shaped insult', Matilda had called it. She couldn't recall which tyre. She was just wondering if she dared approach it and look herself when she saw Pettigrew stroll from his car over to the van, cigarette between thumb and forefinger, just a bloke having a fag in the car park on a warm summer night while his pint was lying inside in the bar. She saw him very casually looking at the Transit van, looking at the tyres, looking specifically at the front off side. Costello watched him closely as he then sauntered around, seemingly not looking anywhere in particular, but she knew he was scanning the back of the hotel, the doors, the windows, the fire exits. His eyes were wary and his face unreadable, but his right forefinger was tapping nervously at the cigarette. And he had put on a jacket. Costello noticed the slight bulge where the gun was.

Costello dropped her phone down by her side, suddenly feeling out of her depth. Her mind chased some thoughts about James Pettigrew – where his expertise came from, and what kind of 'security' work he actually did.

He glanced up as he walked back to his car and signalled, a slight thumbs-up so subtle that she doubted anyone else had seen it. Then a casual flick of the head towards the side wall.

Costello saw a tap, with a coiled hose attached. Handy.

He knew exactly what he was doing and what he was looking for.

Had he been a soldier at one time? He was in that age range where men who came out of the army often joined the police force or the fire brigade.

And he had a gun.

She jumped as her phone went; it was Pettigrew.

'It's a match. Get your forensics team down here. You might want to find out who exactly owns this hotel.' He rang off and continued his walk.

This time, Costello walked round the back of the van, appearing to check her texts in the light from the hotel bar window, then sauntered to the front again. She photographed the cut on the front right-hand tyre with her mobile, without appearing to do so, and sent it to Matilda. And she realized she could smell blood – not fresh blood, but the sickening sweetness of old blood. So, she texted Matilda and told her to get a move on. She then phoned the lecture room. Wyngate answered, and two minutes later she had her answer to her question. The hotel was owned by Red Eagle Properties.

'The company that owns the flats where Biggart was found,' Wyngate explained when she went silent. 'All the flats on the ground floor except Janet Appleby's. In turn, Red Eagle is owned by PSM, a bigger property company. And PSM rents the industrial unit from which PillarBox-Flix operates.'

'And what does PSM stand for? Pimp Somebody's Mother?'

She heard the click of a keyboard.

'Pavel Sergeievich Moro—'

'Morosova,' Costello said.

'No, Morosov.'

'Same friggin' difference,' said Costello and slammed the phone shut. She was calling up Anderson's number when Pettigrew marched over to her and grabbed her elbow.

'Get in the car. Howlett just called,' he said out of the side of his mouth. 'Something's happened.'

11.30 p.m.

Anderson felt completely helpless. There was nothing he could do or say. Words meant nothing. He sat with his arm round Jennifer Corbett, who was sobbing, tears pouring down her face.

He wished Costello was here, to make the tea and do practical things, and he tried not to look at the Congratulations On Your Engagement cards on the mantelpiece.

Jennifer straightened up slightly. 'He was on the phone to me just a few minutes before. Maybe, if I'd answered, it wouldn't have happened.'

'It would have made no difference,' Anderson assured her. 'Some boys in the car park called 999 straight away. The paramedics say that he was dead before he hit the ground. He didn't suffer, Jennifer. It was quick, very quick, and painless.' He knew he wasn't helping but it was all he could say.

'Does Dad know?'

'Yes, I already called him. He's on his way. I'll stay till he gets here.'

Jennifer wiped her tears with the cuff of her jumper. 'That's kind of you. But I'd rather you went back to being a police officer. I'll be all right on my own. After all, I have a lot of things to see to. I have a wedding to cancel. And I have a funeral to arrange.'

'Is there anyone who can help you with all that?' Anderson felt bloody hopeless. He had no idea what to say. Costello would have known.

Jennifer smiled crookedly through her tears. 'Just Dad, who'll take over and try to make it all go away, as he always does. When Emily was alive, there was no time for friends, there was always just David. We'd been friends since we were kids, you know. Childhood sweethearts. He made me a Valentine's card when he was in Year Seven. He wanted to take me to the school dance and Dad wouldn't let me go with him because his mum cleaned for us.' She blew her nose loudly. 'Do you know, I can't remember the last thing I said to him.' She looked blankly into space.

'It'll come back to you.'

She leapt up, panicky. 'I've left his dinner in the oven!'

'I'll get it.' He stood up, his hand on her shoulder.

She looked up at Anderson. 'Why was he killed? I mean, why him? What was he doing?'

'He was just walking down the street, Jennifer. That's all I know. I am so, so sorry.'

At that point, she collapsed into his arms and started to sob her heart out.

Saturday
3 July 2010

1.30 a.m.

Anderson stood in the shadow of the great beech hedge outside the Corbett family home, breathing in the warm night air and the scent of wild garlic. The street was quiet; everybody else was getting a good night's sleep, unaware that yet another tragedy had struck the family in the big house at the end of the drive. A car pulled up violently, and Jennifer's father, Donald Corbett, got out and rushed into the house – either ignoring Anderson or, in his haste, failing to see him.

His phone went, and he cursed. Could they never give him a break? He looked at the number, registering that he knew it and that it wasn't work. Not many people would call him at this hour from a 334 phone number – a West End number. It had to be something to do with Lambie.

He opened the phone, and a voice said, 'Hello? Colin?'

It took a moment for him to work out who it was. He was glad it wasn't Brenda. If it had been, this would be the 'sorry about your friend' phone call – the 'that's why you have to leave the job' speech would come later.

This was somebody who was concerned. Concerned for him.

'I'm so sorry, Colin. I've just heard; Donald just called me. How are you?'

'Oh, hello, Helena. It's all . . . it's . . . very difficult.' He felt his voice break. Another car pulled up, and he turned to face the hedge, aware that tears were now running down his face.

'I didn't want to phone Jennifer, but when the time is right, tell me and I'll call her.' She didn't need to add, 'I know what it's like; I've been there.'

'Her dad's just arrived.' He rubbed the fatigue from his eyes. 'Helena?'

'Yes?'

He couldn't say it.

But she did. 'You're only two streets away. Why don't you come round?'

He closed the call. A text had appeared. It was from Brenda. *When will you be home? How are you feeling?* Not her fault; nobody had told her. But he didn't want to.

Not now.

1.45 a.m.

How had he got here? He didn't recall getting in his car, or driving the short distance to Helena's house.

He parked at the bottom of the terrace and took his time over the long walk up. His brain knew that this thing had happened, but the rest of him – heart, mind, body – was deciding to be numb to the idea that Lambie was gone, gone for good, one small blade between the ribs all it took to end his life. Jennifer would not be his wife, his children would not be born, and he would never grow into the good detective he was planning to be. Such a waste. Such a waste, by such *scum*! And nobody yet knew why.

Anderson couldn't really come to terms with any of it. That night when they had tried to save the wee girl on the ladder in the river, Lambie hadn't hesitated to jump straight into the filthy freezing Clyde. He'd been there for his boss. But who had been there for him? He couldn't even bear to think what Brenda would say. If Lambie could get stabbed and killed, any of them could. He looked round behind him, checking whether somebody was following him. Too tired to think, he walked on, the heavy warmth of the night air making his breathing labour a little on the upward slope.

Maybe Brenda was right. Maybe they should get away from all this to pastures new. Life was a fragile gift that could be taken away in a second, with no warning. He remembered the horror of the previous night – was it only the previous night? – and Moffat's head exploding right in front of him. No matter how vehemently Howlett insisted, he himself had certainly been in danger. But somebody – capable of two kills with two bullets, with a high-powered weapon – had come to his rescue. Somebody who had run away through the trees. MacFadyean was hit by a car, Carruthers thrown from a high window. A slim blade had ended Lambie's life. Howlett had been very deliberate in the lecture room in ensuring Costello knew she could count on Pettigrew. Did that mean he thought Costello was in some danger? Then there was Howlett's insistence that the whiteboard should show where they were every time they left the station.

His pace quickened as he walked up the pavement of the high terrace. At Helena McAlpine's house, he knew, there would be a big sofa, hot coffee and fresh toast; it was that kind of house. He thought about the dead, about Billy and Melinda Biggart, about Tommy Carruthers and Wullie MacFadyean. He thought about Rusalka. And he thought – how could he not? – about David Lambie. His sergeant. His friend. How close had he himself been to joining them all in death?

He jumped as a crow swooped down from a tree on to the fence ahead of him and perched there, glaring evilly at him. Then a second came down, hopping sideways along the fence to join its mate.

The first wee craw was greetin' fer its maw.

The children's song came into his head and wouldn't leave. The first wee craw? That was poor little Rusalka, whose last frightened whisper had been '*Mamochka*'.

The second wee craw fell and broke its jaw.

Tommy Carruthers?

The third wee craw couldn't flee awa'.

A nightmare vision composed of Melinda Biggart, a woman who had been butchered, her arms pulled out like wings, but no chance of flight.

And the *fourth wee craw* – the one who *wisnae there at a'*?

That was Wullie MacFadyean – a shadow of a man who everybody knew, but nobody knew anything about for sure. Or was it the Puppeteer, *Kukolnyik*, the evil controlling bastard at the very heart of his web of cruelty and corruption?

Woozy with fatigue and grief, Anderson almost fell over his own feet, and stopped walking. Christ, he was no good to anybody like this! He looked up and realized he was at Helena's house. He heard the doorbell resonate all through the house, and the sound of feet coming to answer it, soft slippers on a tiled floor. Then the door opened, and there she was.

She didn't smile. She didn't say anything. She just held her arms out to him.

And he started to cry.

5.30 a.m.

It was five thirty in the morning, and the early sun was glinting diamonds off the tarmac. Anderson could tell from the number of cars round the front door of their little lecture theatre that the room was already busy.

He felt he had no idea what he was doing. He had no idea what he was doing here, with the case, with his life.

He had been unfaithful to Brenda. Full stop. There had always been that unspoken desire between him and Helena, but it should never have happened. It certainly should not have happened the way it had.

But last night he had been so alone, so bereft – at the lowest point in his life that he could remember – and Helena had opened her arms to him. It had seemed the most natural thing in the world. And he couldn't bring himself to regret a moment of it.

He had slid out of her bed and had a shower in the big bathroom on the half landing. Helena was still asleep when he laid the handwritten note on the pillow beside the auburn curls of her hair. She had not stirred when he let himself out of the front door. What he had said in the note was true. He loved her. And he thought he should say it, as if she hadn't known for the last ten years. He could fool himself that the rest of the world knew nothing about it and never would. But he was not a good enough liar to keep something like this a secret.

Brenda would find out, sooner or later.

And then there was Costello – she would know the moment she laid eyes on him.

He thought about going to Australia. The idea was becoming appealing. But first he had to go to work and face whatever was coming his way. It wasn't going to be good.

His phone went.

'Are you sitting in your car?' O'Hare asked. 'And don't lie, I can see you from here. I'm going across in a minute – do you want some coffee brought down?'

Five minutes later, the Prof opened the car door. 'I'll go away, if you want time alone.' He handed in a coffee on a cardboard tray; beside it was a paper bag, folded to a triangle, the toast inside still warm.

For a moment, Anderson thought about falling in love with the good professor instead. 'I've done enough thinking, thanks. Have a seat. You're up early.'

'I've not been to bed yet. Neither have you, from the look of you.' O'Hare swung his long legs into the car, carefully balancing a coffee of his own. 'Sad business, David Lambie.'

'The paramedics said he didn't suffer. Is that true?'

'He would have felt a small nudge in the back, that's all. And before you start feeling guilty again, you have nothing to blame yourself for, Colin; it's one of those things that happen when you do the job you do. No point in feeling that it should have been you. It wasn't you, so get on with finding who did it.'

Anderson nodded. He'd heard better pep talks but, coming from the Prof, this one worked. 'Pretty much what Jennifer said,' he agreed. 'I'm just gathering my strength to go in there.'

'Well, they all feel the way you do, so in there might be the best place to be.' O'Hare moved in his seat. 'Young Richard Spence took a turn for the worse last night, went into complete liver failure. Time for the daddy to step up.'

'Will he be allowed, do you think?'

'I damn well hope so. He's that boy's only chance.'

6.00 a.m.

ACC Howlett was looking more shrunken than ever in his ill-fitting uniform, but the tired old eyes were sharp and watchful.

'At the press conference, the official story will simply be that DS David Lambie was attacked with a knife and suffered a fatal wound,' he told the assembled company. 'We will take care neither to confirm nor deny any connection between the attack and any case he was working on, or even if he was on duty at the time.'

The rest of what he said was rather more what they had expected. They had all lost a valued colleague and a dear friend. It was a great tragedy. But while they mourned his passing, they must realize that he died doing a job he was committed to. They must show a similar commitment, and the guilty parties must be called to account. Only towards the end of his address did the ACC show the edge of his temper.

'I understand that DS Lambie was asked to fetch the diary, and was then given permission to take it home and bring it here in the morning. But there was no mention of that on the noticeboard.' He gazed around at the team, like a tired old owl. 'I'm not seeking to apportion blame for his death – I doubt if any details would have helped. But when I said "at all times", I meant it – for a very good reason.' He turned away, trying to compose himself.

'Are we being followed, sir? I mean, how did they know?' Wyngate voiced the question in everybody's mind.

'I can only presume, with hindsight, that they have been watching the flats at Bruce Court. They wanted that diary for something, and they had tried every which way to get it. They killed Carruthers but he wouldn't tell. His wife does not know. Tommy Carruthers might have hidden it so well that he took the secrets to his grave.'

'But what is the significance of the diary? Somebody killed Lambie to get it, but why?' asked Mulholland.

'That is something we do not yet know for certain. According to his wife, the diary was the 1977 journal, but David had pointed out to her that most of January was missing. Had he taken that section out and put it elsewhere? She also said that David had been asking about Simone Sangster's visit in October 2008. Carruthers had no involvement in the case that Sangster was writing about. But there must be a connection.'

'So, do we ask Sangster?' said Anderson.

'No,' said Howlett strongly. 'She's a media whore; we are not going there.' He dropped his head into his hands, as if the effort of thinking was physically painful. 'We have had the rest of the diaries brought down here. We might find something that makes sense of it all –'

'Please,' Wyngate interrupted, raising his hand tentatively like a nervous schoolkid. 'January 1977 was the date of the hill walk that Graham Hunter never returned from. I'm sorry to harp on about it, but it is important.'

'Go on, Gordon, everything is important,' said Anderson.

'It's just that David asked me to scout about for reports, so I Googled the police recreational magazine. I looked up the archive online. Who ran the police hill-walking club? Eric Moffat. So, he was nominally in charge of that walk. The Prof remembers the case, don't you?'

'I do,' replied O'Hare. 'And I'm tracking down both sets of records – Hunter's and Purcie's – just in case my memory misleads me. But I know they were both on that walk.'

'As were Carruthers and MacFadyean.'

It was O'Hare who broke the ensuing silence. 'Which means there's no one left to ask,' he said. 'They were "gey few and they're a' deid". I'll do my best with what's in the records, but those diary pages may provide the only real truth.'

'We have the diary from 1976 in which Carruthers is writing about the planned trip that proved fatal to Hunter. That may yield something.' Howlett coughed slightly. 'However, the diary from 1996 is also missing. That was the year Alessandro Marchetti was abducted. And, as you say, Simone Sangster had been sniffing around, researching her book.'

'And Moffat was in charge of that investigation. Wyngate will look further into the hill-walking incident in

1977. Dr Batten, maybe you could cast your profiler's eye over the journals?'

The psychologist nodded. 'Something in 1977 – something on that walk – changed that man's mindset for the rest of his life.' He sighed. 'The death of his companion is a pretty good bet.'

'Vik, I would like you to look into the events of 1996, and what Mr Carruthers was doing then. Especially what he was doing when the kidnap was going on. A kidnap, I will remind you, that may have ended up in Glen Fruin. I believe Mary Carruthers is going to see her solicitor this morning with regard to the money that was placed in a bank account in that same year. See if we can get any lead on that.'

'Do you think we're on the track of the ransom money, sir?' asked Wyngate eagerly.

'There was no ransom paid,' said Anderson.

Wyngate looked abashed.

'It wasn't a win on the horses, that's for certain, no matter what the paperwork said.'

Howlett then changed the subject. 'Yesterday evening, at the Highland Glen Hotel, DS Costello found the white Transit van that was used to run over Wullie MacFadyean in Glen Fruin. The paint seems to be a match for specks of paint found on his clothing. Matilda will go back to the deposition site, out near the Corbie Wood, today and review the evidence at the scene.' He coughed again. 'There is a great deal of blood – old, and more recent – in the floor pans. And the interior walls and floor show signs of having been rather inadequately hosed out.'

'The mobile torture site?' asked Mulholland.

'It seems that way. Costello reports they were using the van for the hotel laundry, and to go to the Cash and Carry. So, it could be out and about at all times of the day and night, keys left lying around.'

'We need to keep that hotel under surveillance,' said Anderson, scribbling something in his notebook.

Howlett shook his head. 'Well, whoever they are, they now know that we are on to them. But yes, subtle surveillance. Meanwhile, Matilda has all the blood under analysis but we do know that there is more than one type. Some of it has already been matched to Richard Spence, and at least four other blood types also appear to be involved. It is going to take a while.' Howlett bowed his head a little, as though suddenly tired. 'I think that's everything. Now, while we are all shocked by the events of the last twenty-four hours, we still want to nail whoever did this. And we want no leaks from this room – no more mistakes. From now on, you play by my rules. Whereabouts on the notice-board at all times. And we go in pairs.'

'What about Costello? She's a bit out on her own,' said Anderson.

'I'm sure DS Costello can look after herself.'

'She didn't do so well the last time she tried,' muttered O'Hare.

'Sorry, that wasn't all. DS Costello –' Howlett pointed at the board '– has made a connection that could be very significant. Saskia Morosova is at the school in Glen Fruin. Her father owns PSM properties. It could all be legitimate, but Costello and Pettigrew are keeping their own watching brief up there.'

'A Russian businessman who lives in Moscow and has

his daughter at school here?' asked Batten. 'Sounds good to me.'

8.00 a.m.

Auld Archie was having one of his difficult days, Agnes reported. Her actual words were, 'He's being a right royal fucking pain in the butt this morning.' She held her hand over the toaster, waiting for the bread to pop up. 'Over breakfast he started pointing at Alice because she was doing that moaning thing she does. Then it was Billy's turn to be pointed at because he was making slurping noises with his egg.'

'He always makes slurping noises with his egg,' Ella said.

'Then, when I tried to wheel him out the breakfast room, he just went apeshit, damn near bit me. Wanted to listen to the TV, he said. Ah, he's as deaf as a post, that one,' she scorned. 'Though maybe he's so gaga he doesn't know he's deaf yet.'

Marion started buttering her toast with care. 'He was sitting beside the TV last night, guarding the remote. I thought that was odd, because normally he hates the thing and goes out the minute it gets turned on. But all the rest were asleep, so I didn't think it worth winding him up.'

'He looked like he was waiting for the news at breakfast,' said Agnes. 'And then I caught him looking at the *Daily Record*. So, I took it off the old bugger and brought it down here,' she giggled.

'So, what was he so interested in?'

'The Lockerbie Bomber? Andy Murray? Christ knows.

Told you he was gaga.' Agnes turned over the page, not noticing the black and white image of the Bridge Boy. The sidebar read: *Mystery man still critical after expressway plunge.*

10.00 *a.m.*

'What do you have, DC Wyngate?' asked O'Hare, watching as Wyngate flicked the pages on his shorthand pad back and forth, each page covered with lists and dates in blue biro.

'Well, it turns out that Carruthers was off duty the night of the 8th of October 1996, whereas MacFadyean requested the night off.'

'In 1996? The day of the kidnapping?'

Wyngate nodded. 'And the senior investigating officer in the Marchetti/Piacini kidnapping was one DCI Eric Moffat.'

O'Hare felt relieved that Eric Moffat was in a cold drawer in the mortuary and had ceased to be a problem. He thought – not for the first time – how much less complicated the dead were than the living.

'I've got the post mortem reports on Graham Hunter,' he said. 'And I've requested the actual photographs of the skull. Maybe, if we have another look at those, we might be able to work out better now than we could have in 1977 what actually caused the injury.'

'And the weather reports at the time,' Wyngate said, with more flicking of pages, 'show that the weather was due to close in, but they still went. It was a full-blown

329

blizzard. I think the trip was supposed to be up and back, three days max, but they were away for nearly five.'

'Five days? In that weather? Madness. Makes you wonder why they set off.'

'Unless there was another agenda all along.' Wyngate shrugged. 'I suppose they argued that they were heading for a bothy, so they would hole up there and come back down once the weather was better.'

A thought struck O'Hare. 'At the enquiry, did they actually say how Hunter got separated from the rest?'

Wyngate flicked over his notes, 'No – well, yes. They all made it to the bothy, and then Hunter went out into the blizzard. They all said they tried to stop him, tried to restrain him, but Hunter was adamant. Four against one?' He handed two faded photographs to O'Hare.

'Sounds totally irrational to me,' said the pathologist. 'Something must have happened to cause that. Drugs? Or a slow bleed to the brain? I wonder if there's any mention in the diary that he fell earlier in the day and hurt his head. Wyngate, go over those statements very carefully, and compare them to the account in the journal,' said O'Hare absentmindedly, looking at the pictures.

Wyngate opened his mouth to point out that the account in the journal was missing, then shut it again as the pathologist went on, 'Ah, yes. These would have been taken in spring, when the body was found. Seana Bhraigh is a bastard of a hill, a great stack of jagged rock, with a brutal drop to the water below. Very dangerous to go near the edge in poor visibility. Hunter's judgement *must* have been compromised in some way. He wasn't an idiot; he was a good cop with a good career in front of him.' He peered at Wyngate over his glasses. 'Let's think about distances. They must have got to the second bothy for Hunter to get near the stack of rock that we presume he fell from. So, even if we say he got to the top of the stack of rock, fell off, and his head was damaged in an impact on the way down, that still does not account for the strange behaviour that got him there in the first place. They can't have it both ways.'

'Well, they all said the same thing. They got to the second bothy about nine at night, had something to eat, just as the weather was closing in, and Hunter went out against their advice. Purcie, his pal, went out to try and stop him first, and the rest followed, in the snow, the high wind, the dark. They failed to get Hunter back in, and they never saw him again. All the official statements were absolutely consistent.'

O'Hare raised a quizzical eyebrow. 'Absolutely consistent? In that weather and confusion? Don't you think that makes it all the more suspicious?'

10.45 a.m.

Costello was rather enjoying herself, and thinking that, in some small way, she was helping to avenge the death of David Lambie. She was sure bloody Saskia was the key to all this – she just could not yet see how. She recalled the way the girl had turned and waved at her on her first day, as if she knew who Costello was. However, at the moment she was having the time of her life going through Saskia's things, rootling through her wardrobe and doing a thorough search. The Russian girl had an awful lot of designer clothes, and very few books – though the ones she had were in Russian and Dutch, as well as English. There were shoes everywhere and, hanging on the back of the door, not good enough to go into the wardrobe, two sets of school uniform.

But she was Russian, and thin – and that was enough for Costello. It wasn't only Saskia's property – a search warrant was a mute point – but if she had anything to do with Lambie's death, she forfeited any right to privacy.

Pettigrew was outside, keeping watch for the return of the Three Graces in the slappermobile. Costello had faith in Pettigrew – he was ex-job, whatever his background, and he was a solid man in a crisis. She didn't really want to think about the way the jacket had hung on him last night, and the gun it was concealing. Important people sent their children to Glen Fruin. So, why would there not be special security measures. Government-funded security measures? Security measures that involved carrying a gun?

But James Pettigrew, she was sure, was no ordinary security man. Just as she was sure Saskia Morosova was no ordinary school pupil. Howlett knew that; he had known it all along. A pity she and Pettigrew couldn't have stayed around into the early hours to watch the girls come back to the hotel, and see who they came back with. But Lambie had died, and they had all rather lost heart. Matilda had got the van taken in for analysis, and Costello had left Mulholland with the paperwork and gone back to the school with Pettigrew.

He had been uncommunicative on the drive back, whistling to himself as he drove. Twice up the glen road she had caught the flash of headlights in the wing mirror, and told Pettigrew they were being followed. He had patted her hand and told her it was OK. He hadn't even looked to check; he knew there was somebody there, keeping their distance.

Once home, she had got out without a word, shot all the deadbolts and tried to sleep.

But sleep had refused to be her companion. The room felt smaller, and the ceiling of the mezzanine that held the bed seemed lower, darker. She had raised her hand to her cheek and felt along the skin for the little piece of mesh. It was still there.

She had put on the bedside light and picked up *Little Boy Lost*. On the back cover was a dark-haired little boy, with an impish smile to melt your heart, and a little gold St Christopher medal round his neck.

Then she began to read.

That precluded sleep for her completely. She had read on until morning, when Pettigrew had come knocking to say that Saskia and her friends were not back yet, and now might be a good time to have a look round her room.

So, here she was, in the Wallace Room of the school's accommodation block. Looking at Saskia's single bed, with its slightly chipped wooden headboard, and the marked wallpaper, she could understand why the girls went to the Highland Glen Hotel for their romantic trysts.

The bedlinen would be changed by a member of staff, so there would be no point in hiding anything there. A quick look through the wardrobe had revealed nothing except that Saskia was a size six and wore extra-long trousers. Costello was convinced this combination would lead to very early osteoporosis and dearly wished it would prove so. She bounced one foot a little on the expensive wooden slatted floor. None of the boards looked as though it was pulled up on a regular basis.

She looked under the bed – nothing. A pink laptop sat on the desk, but Costello didn't want to turn it on. Anything she would be interested in looking at would be secure and password-protected, anyway. Saskia might be a skinny osteoporotic slapper, but she would not be stupid. A couple of leads were plugged into the laptop: one looked like an iPod lead, and one might be for a camera. Beside it a pen, pencil and memory stick were lined up, ready. A *tidy* skinny osteoporotic slapper. Costello was hating Saskia more with every passing minute.

There was a safe in the wall, which Costello presumed was a remnant of older times when physical things could be stolen – not like identities, the tradable commodity of the twenty-first century. The door didn't actually close, and probably hadn't done so for years. Inside stood a female figure with eight arms, bearing loads of costume jewellery. Good stuff, probably, but not really valuable. There was a box of rings, one of bracelets, and a whole tray of earrings. Costello poked about a bit, more out of feminine curiosity than anything else, but found nothing of interest.

She looked round to see the shoe rack, and put her hand on the first pair of Jimmy Choos she had ever seen in real life. All the shoes were strappy except for the pair of trail boots at the door, a pair of school courts and a pair of Nike Pegasus running shoes. Then she saw a pair of winter boots paired neatly, kept upright with boot supports. She went over to them and looked at them, then picked them up. Something was wrong with their weight . . . they were lighter at the heel. Costello turned them upside down and had a good look. Oh yes. The thick sole on the heel? The tiny pin? She swung the sole to the side, revealing a narrow hollow in the heel. She stuck her finger in it, pulling out a memory stick with padding wrapped round it. She unwrapped it to reveal a printed label. Just letters, in Russian.

Costello put it back, carefully lining the boot up with its neighbour, before slipping quietly out of the room to join Pettigrew in the corridor.

'Oh, hello!' The voice sounded as though its owner had just had a fright. It was Rhona, the woman with the mad hair.

'Hello,' replied Costello, wondering what the chances were of a secret panel opening in the wall behind her so she could disappear through it.

'Are you doing detective things? Were you going to search Drew Elphinstone's room?'

It was a natural question, since Costello was in the accommodation wing. 'I was actually going to . . .' She pointed vaguely in the direction of Pettigrew, who was steadfastly refusing to look at her. Batten's words came back to her. There would be signs of paranoia, signs of persecution. The boy needed help.

'He's just gone out, you know, for one of his walks. He won't be back for a long time. But I have a master key, so you can go in and see what he's got in there.'

'And what do you expect me to find?'

'*Evidence!*' Rhona said, excitedly. 'What else?'

'What of?'

'Do you not think they should have stopped Columbine before it started?' Rhona asked, her hands stretched out as if she was pleading to Costello. 'Please.'

'Come on, then,' and Costello found herself being led through a huge wooden dividing door to a different accommodation block. The boys' block, she presumed. The tartan carpet here was a runner of well-worn Stewart. Rhona stopped and rattled a key in a door, which swung open. She turned her head from right to left, checking the corridors the way they did in films.

Costello stepped in, leaving Rhona to stand guard outside. The curtains were pulled tightly closed, so she put the light on. The wardrobe in here didn't hang open like Saskia's; it was locked shut. The room smelled of stale sweat and lack of ventilation. The bed had been made with almost military precision, yet hanging all the way round the walls at shoulder height were handwritten letters, each hanging by one corner from a drawing pin. All had been written to Drew – and all the handwriting was the same. Costello pulled out a jotter from under a pile of books. The writing was the same as that on the letters.

Drew Elphinstone was writing letters to himself.

She looked closely at the letters, noting the appearance of strange symbols now and again, then she looked at the dates. The more recent letters displayed more writing, more urgency in the style, and more symbols. She didn't recognize any of them.

She leaned over the bed to look at the letters hanging above it. They looked fingered, as if they had been read again and again. She would ask Rhona about the mail Drew received. How much of this arrived for him in the post and landed on that big table in the hall? Or did he just sit and write in his room on his own?

'Have you found anything?' Rhona called through the slightly open door.

'Nothing,' Costello called back, turning her attention to the bookcase.

Drew's choice of reading matter was all about survival. Costello pulled a couple out: an SAS survival handbook – the ultimate guide to surviving anywhere – and its neighbour, a book about animal traps and trapping. She knelt down to read the spines of the rest. Her foot kicked against something, and she crouched down, ignoring the dust on the parquet floor. Under the bed was a big old-fashioned leather suitcase with leather handles and metal buckles. There was no dust in front of the suitcase, so it had been moved, and recently. Costello kept an eye on the door as she pulled the suitcase out slowly and quietly. She undid the buckles, had a quick look inside, then looked again to confirm what she was seeing.

She pulled out a small brochure with illustrations on how to trap people without having to be there. She recognized the large-scale version of what she had seen beside the river – the pit that had hurt Libby. She flicked through the rest, stopping at a picture, obviously torn from a book, of a naked and brutalized body, with terrible cuts and slashes. Somebody had written over it the names of the arteries, whether each cut would kill, and how deep the knife had to go. Somebody was doing their homework.

She suddenly understood Rhona's concern – if the school merely thought they had a problem before, they certainly had one now.

Anderson was back at Glen Fruin, back at the site where they had discovered MacFadyean's body, waiting for Matilda to turn up. Mulholland was strolling around in the undergrowth, having a good look around for any sign of discarded evidence as to where MacFadyean might have lived.

Anderson pulled his sweat-sticky shirt away from his back and gazed up at Ben Lomond, feeling the confusion of his life seep away a little in the stillness of the warm air. The ben had stood there for millions of years, and it would still be there in another million years. Lambie's life by comparison was less than a blink of an eye.

Anderson felt himself hold back the tears – too much had been happening too soon. Costello had phoned him from a landline at the school and had reported that Saskia was up to something secretive. He had passed that on to Howlett, whose advice had been to wait.

In the early morning they had visited the post office at Luss to speak to the two sisters who ran it. Two cups of tea, two scones and a close encounter with an Alsatian later, they had some decent information. Wullie, as he was known, had been in and out of the post office nearly every day for years. They only knew he lived 'up there somewhere'. This was accompanied by a vague gesture westwards in the direction of the hills surrounding Glen Fruin. He had been seen many a time, walking along the Low Road. There were no houses up the High Road, explained one of the sisters.

Anderson looked around and mentally got his bearings. At the top of the glen, the new road went over to the naval base at the Gare Loch. The old road, a wee single track, went along the bottom of the glen. So, Wullie must have lived along here somewhere. It was still a decent walk northwards on a busy road to get to Luss, but there could be any number of old tracks and trails up there.

The sisters had been sure there was no Mrs MacFadyean, but he did eat a lot of Quality Street. And he was 'a fillum buff'. Gina explained he got them from a rental company. 'The one that uses those little red envelopes shaped like pillar boxes.'

There was one still waiting for him – it was now locked in the boot of Anderson's car, wrapped in a tartan paper bag.

So, they had a chatty, sociable recluse, a chocoholic diabetic, a married man with no wife and no known address, who had the same interest in films as a dead drug dealer.

Anderson was still thinking all that through when Matilda's Ford pulled up behind the Jazz.

She got out and announced, 'I don't like this place.' She gazed around at the trees. 'It gives me the creeps.'

'Are you scared?' teased Mulholland.

'Yes,' said Matilda, quite unabashed. At that minute, the crows were disturbed and started up with their racket. Matilda jumped at the sudden noise.

'And why are we here again?' asked Mulholland.

'I need to see if there are any more paint samples in the road, anything to ascertain where exactly MacFadyean was when the van hit him. And I'll be looking for evidence of how he got down there, off the road, to end up in the position he did,' Matilda said briskly. 'I have photographs of the body in situ, so between us we should be able to work it out.'

'Well, you two find what you need to find,' said Anderson. 'I'm going in search of the house.'

Mulholland protested. 'But I need to get back to Glasgow. I have to track down that DVD rental company. Maybe they can give us an address for MacFadyean's place.'

'I think you'll find it was always care of the post office. He wasn't daft, this guy, was he? But I'm sure if you speak nicely to Matilda she'll run you back when she's finished, seeing as you're both going back to the same place. I am going to drive up and down this lane endlessly until I find where MacFadyean lived, and then we are going to search the place. The glen isn't that long – nine miles or so – it must be somewhere along here, and within walking distance of the road. You've got all the details you need, so I'm taking the DVD with me.'

'Can I not come with you?'

'No, you can't, Vik, so bugger off.'

Anderson climbed back into his car, glad to be alone. He looked around the wooded hills, scanning the tops, knowing that there was somebody up there, watching out for him. He checked his mobile phone, wondering whether to text Helena. Phone her? Wait for her to phone him? He had no bloody idea what he was supposed to do now. How did men who balanced more than one woman ever manage? One was enough, but two? Add in Costello back on full form, and his life was over.

He glanced out of the side window and saw Matilda and Mulholland looking apprehensive, like Hansel and Gretel about to be abandoned in the forest by their father.

But Matilda had her car. And although they *were* in the middle of nowhere, Lambie had been killed in the city, in a quiet suburban street. Anderson wound down the window. 'One hour max, and stay together!' It would do them good, he told himself; every challenge was character building.

He waved at them in the rear-view mirror as he drove away, then decided to put both hands on the steering wheel as the road narrowed dangerously, the edges crumbling away, often to a drop with jagged rocks and deep ravines. But the sheep looked happy, standing at all kinds of odd angles and pulling at the short grass with little twists of their heads. As the road turned down the glen, closer to the river, the mountains receded to a glorious backdrop of lush greenery. There were no hidden houses here, just the odd farm dotted along the patchwork of fields that carpeted the floor of the glen. He stopped at a few of them along the route, knocking on doors. He chatted with a wifie hanging out the washing, with somebody standing in a mucky yard texting on his mobile, and with a man taking a tractor to bits.

The uniform branch of the local nick had been there before him. No, no one actually knew anything about Wullie MacFadyean. They recognized his description as somebody they had seen around, somebody they had stood next to at the post office – a farmer had even given him a run into Glasgow once.

But nobody had ever given him a run home. Nobody knew where home was. It was always 'somewhere up the glen'.

This man was steadily going up in Anderson's estimation. He spent the next hour driving up and down the glen, looking for houses on the high road and the low road, but he could see nothing. He scanned the dense, deep green blanket of trees on the north side before driving to the top of the glen. Here he got out and looked again, with binoculars. He turned at the sound of a car behind him.

It was the military police, wanting to know exactly what he thought he was doing.

'I think this might be it.'

'Big place, innit?'

'Site of the old Linwood car plant. Nearly eight thousand people worked here once. Then it was reborn as an industrial estate. Hence the name Phoenix.'

Wyngate looked around. 'Look at all that security.'

He was in one of his dumb moods. Mulholland wished, momentarily, that he was still in the car with the walking intellect that was Matilda McQueen. At least with her he learned something; with Wyngate he got the feeling he was babysitting.

He pulled his Audi to a halt at the security gate and they both showed their ID to the man in the booth. Even in the stifling heat he had a good uniform on, and his booth was full of all kinds of cameras and high-end security kit. He waved them through, and the barrier rose, but only to let the car through into an area enclosed by high railings, spiked at the top. On each corner were security cameras that swung to focus on the car. A second gate opened, and the security man signalled that they should pull through and park.

'What the hell is this place? Fort Knox?' asked Wyngate in wonder.

'Not far from it,' said Mulholland. 'Who knows what's in these warehouses? And there's PillarBoxFlix, right over there.'

The big security man gestured that they should get out, and they followed him one at a time through a turnstile. 'I'll see your warrant cards, please,' he said. He had the kind of face it was better not to argue with. They handed them over, and he nodded as he examined them carefully. 'Do you mind if I phone, while you wait here?'

Yes, I do mind actually, now get out the way, you monkey in a gorilla suit, were the words forming in Mulholland's mind. He said, 'Of course not.'

The man walked away.

'So, why is a DVD rental company in a place like this?' Wyngate asked.

'It'll all be computerized, with one huge bloody website and a small staff, but a massive amount of stock.'

'I wonder how much stock they hold and how much it's worth?'

'That's not why we're here. We know Biggart and MacFadyean got DVDs from here. PSM own it. Whoever torched Biggart left some for us to see and make a connection. I'd put money on it. So, we'll be careful what we say in here.'

1.10 p.m.

'I thought they were going to shoot me there and then.' Anderson sat down on the sandstone wall bordering the front lawn at the school and ran his fingers through his hair. It was oppressively hot, but at least he was out of the lecture room.

'No wonder, standing on top of a hill looking at a top-secret naval base through binoculars. What did you think they were going to do? Blow you a kiss?'

Anderson smiled. Costello the sharp mouth was on her way back. 'It took some smart talking to get out of it.'

'Oh, so who did the smart talking for you?' asked Costello. 'I bet one of the MPs walked away while the other one spoke to you.'

'Well, yes. He was on the phone to Howlett, I think. Probably making sure I was legit.'

'And then Howlett phoned here and authorized you to have free run of the place. If you want to practise the art of subtle observation –' Costello looked over his shoulder '– look at those two down on the lawn. What do you think the relationship is between them?'

'Who am I spying on?'

'The girl down there. Short black hair. Talking to Pettigrew. She's had some experience of cops; she could tell I was one just by looking.'

'Interesting,' said Anderson. 'But some people can. Mostly those who want to avoid us right enough. What's her name?'

The security man was standing and talking, as if he was explaining something. The girl was sitting, head in her hands, as if she didn't want to hear.

'Elizabeth Hamilton.'

'It doesn't mean anything to me.'

'I don't think that's troublesome pupil and security man, is it?' Costello suggested.

'They certainly look as if they have a bit of history, those two.' He watched as Jim Pettigrew shook his head and walked away, clearly with nothing resolved. Libby turned away, her chin on her hand, definitely not watching him go. Whatever it was he was offering had been soundly rejected. 'Have you asked him if there's an issue between them?'

'I think he has enough to worry about. See that boy there? The one in the vegetable garden? That's the one I was taking to Batten about. He's not well.'

'And hot, with that leather coat on. He's standing there swinging a stick in mid-air.'

'Fighting his invisible demons. But he is obsessed with survival and self-defence. That includes killing people. He draws pictures of people and describes how to defend yourself, what to shoot them with – and what happens to them when you do. He practises digging traps for people the way the SAS do. He knows how to do a blood eagle sacrifice – the Viking kind, not the back-to-front one we're dealing with.'

Anderson noted the 'we'.

'In fact, I'd say he's made a bit of a study of it.'

Anderson frowned slightly. 'Is he dangerous?'

'I bet they asked that at Columbine! I'm not joking, Colin.'

'That bad?' One look at her face told him that she was deadly serious.

'Rhona – that teacher, councillor or whatever – thinks he's the reason why I'm here, and I can see why. I can see the school's dilemma. The boy's parents are separated, and in different parts of the world. The words "washed their hands of him" come to mind. But if the school try to get him removed, or referred to a psychiatrist, they could be in trouble. They can only do so much without parental consent, unless he does something appalling. And *then* they'll be in trouble, up to their necks. Meanwhile, Daddy's lawyer just sends Mummy's lawyer a letter, and with each day that passes another sandwich leaves the picnic. It's fine to say "please come and remove your son" but how do you force somebody to do it? Physically, I mean? It takes time.'

'I don't have the answer to that one. We'll ask Howlett – he has enough shiny badges to pull strings, I'm sure.' Anderson contemplated for a minute. 'But you know why you were sent here, don't you?'

'Saskia. Do you think that memory stick is important.'

'The fact she's Russian, with the surname Morosova, is important. The memory stick is important enough for her to hide. But it might just be her bank account details, for all we know. Has it dawned on you that Pettigrew might have been watching her as well? Do you think he knew exactly where they were going last night?'

'I got the feeling it was no surprise to him. I think we are witnesses to it all. The Highland Glen is starting to look more and more like a Russian mafia base. Janet Appleby probably was sent to stay there by her insurance company because whoever insured the Apollo building had some sort of link – maybe perfectly above board – with Red Eagle Properties, which we know is ultimately owned by Morosov. It would have been useful for them to keep her under their noses. Thank God she flew out the country. And the van is registered there. Matilda will prove by the blood samples on the floor that Richard was in the back. No amount of hosing down removes blood from a floor pan. On paper, the van was being used quite legitimately to take laundry back and forth, or go to the Cash and Carry. They could hardly say on the expense accounts that they used it as a mobile slaughterhouse, could they? I suppose Howlett's theory is not to go in mob-handed, because that would just send the Russians and their entire network underground. We want to catch the Puppeteer guy, remember.'

'Softly, softly, I think. And keep them in plain sight.' Anderson watched as the boy leaned his head back, his mouth wide open as if he was baying at some secret moon. 'You do need to do something about that boy, by the way.'

'I need proof. I've asked Jim to come out with me tonight and follow the little bugger on his midnight wanderings.'

'Are you up to that?'

'I was sent here to do a job, and I will do it.'

'I hope Jim said no, you're off your head.'

'He didn't. In fact, he said yes.'

'Why do I bother?'

'I've often wondered.'

They sat in silence for a minute, watching the boy, who was still swinging the stick around, fighting some unseen enemy. There was a detachment and ferocity about his movements that spoke of true violence.

Costello shuddered.

'How are you sleeping?' Anderson asked.

'Actually I'm not really sleeping at all. I spent most of last night reading *Little Boy Lost*, that book about the Marchetti child. I've got to the bit where she is discussing the getaway and the alleged police incompetence regarding that part of the investigation. Simone Sangster says there were reports of a white Volvo being seen parked underneath the Erskine Bridge, and later a white car was seen coming up this glen – up the old road.'

'And?' Anderson was intrigued.

'She says a blue car was found burned out in the rough ground near the lay-by, down on the dual carriageway. One of Sangster's theories is that they switched cars there. The blue car took the boy from the flat to the lay-by under the bridge, where they swapped to the Volvo and torched the blue car. Then they drove through Glen Fruin in the Volvo to get to the west coast and the open water.'

'Theory, you say? Was the car driving up the glen identified as a Volvo, or just as a white car?'

'The latter. And she says that the white Volvo was never correctly identified, so I think you should have another go at tracing that car – in case it was another piece of Moffat's particular brand of policing. Go back to the original statements, check that all attempts were made to trace the plate. If the plate wasn't found, check the most likely mistaken numbers. Did any of them belong to a white Volvo? And go back to the DVLA – this was 1996, before automatic plate recognition, so you'll have to do it the hard way. Don't just take what it says on file as gospel, double-check. The only thing *we* know is that the babysitter was in on it all along.'

'But we don't know that for absolute certain,' Anderson reminded her gently.

'Why doesn't Howlett just bloody find Fairbairn, arrest him and get it out of him?'

'Because the wee shite has disappeared, that's why. He's nowhere to be found. And Howlett can't go public with it, as he wants it all to be kept very low key. Nothing's been released to the press. Nobody even knows yet that Moffat is dead. Or his sidekick, Perky. Apart from the guy who shot them. And anyway –'

Anderson's phone rang.

'You have to walk further up the hill for a good signal. The terrace here is too much in the cradle of the mountains.' Costello just caught sight of a figure in the trees, pulling back into cover, as she pointed the way to Anderson.

He started to walk, telling his caller to hang on, he was waiting for a better signal.

The figure in the trees set off in the same direction as Anderson. Costello kept her eyes on the treeline, her glance flicking from the retreating figure of her colleague to the trees where the figure had been.

Nothing.

1.15 p.m.

'How can I help you?'

The air in the warehouse was deliciously cool, the air con was on full blast. So was the smile of Sally, as she introduced herself. She smiled at everything – even if you told her she had halitosis, Mulholland thought, she would simply stand there and smile. She was smiling now at him and Wyngate, apparently not at all fazed by two detectives standing in her office.

'Just some background, Sally. How long have you worked here?'

'About ten years.' She brushed aside the long blonde hair that fell like snakes across her black dress.

The office was ultra-modern, with a thin blue carpet and two desks. Beyond a glass screen they could see a huge library of the same red sleeves as they had found at Biggart's flat.

'I run the place.'

'All on your own?' Mulholland smiled back.

'I've another two girls who come in during the week, and there's a guy part time. But they're all on their lunch break at the moment – or they've nipped out the back for a fag,' Sally admitted.

'Can you tell us about an address in Apollo Court?'

'Up the West End, the old cinema? I know we send stuff there. Any address in particular?'

'Just tell us about the whole building. And do you do any stuff that might be a bit under the radar? A bit on the rude side?'

'Only legit X-certificate.' She folded her arms, pushing up her bosom – an intentional distraction? 'All our stuff's legit. Customers pay a monthly fee and we let them have four films out at any time. As long as they send them back, we don't care how many they take over the year. They're all originals, no dodgy copies or anything. You can come and take a look, if you want.'

'Can we have a printout of all the films ordered to number G2 Apollo Court in the last year? Surname doesn't matter, just that address.'

'I'm not sure if I can do that.' Did the smile slide just a fraction? 'Do you not need a search warrant or something?'

'We could go and get one, but as the tenant of the flat is dead, it might be less hassle if you just print it out for us. Now.' Mulholland leaned across, his seductive smile more than a match for hers.

Wyngate wondered how he did it.

'No harm, then. Do you want to watch me do it?'

'Oh, I'm sure we can trust you,' said Mulholland, not taking his eyes off her as she called up a screen and scrolled down, her false nails clicking in a way that made his fillings hurt.

'For the last year?' she confirmed.

Mulholland nodded, carefully watching what her fingers were actually doing.

Wyngate sauntered over casually to the storage bins, keeping up an audible monologue for Sally's benefit. 'Right, so these are the films that are sent back, waiting to be put back on the shelves. So, an order comes through online. The DVD is stored according to a code, it gets taken off the shelf, checked off and sent out – is that right? Just three people to handle all these DVDs?' Wyngate was playing the village idiot.

'Hardly nuclear physics, is it?' Sally said loftily. 'The brains are in the system.'

The printer jumped into life, and a single sheet was fired out. Sally handed it to Mulholland.

'Funny how you can tell so much about people by what

351

they order,' she observed. 'Whoever lived at that address liked mindless violence and kiddies' cartoons. I bet that's a weekend father keeping his child amused.'

Mulholland looked down the list of films as Sally accompanied him back to the warehouse entrance. Wyngate trailed close behind him. *Goodfellas*, all three *Saw* titles, *Scarface*. Some vile-sounding things he'd never heard of – and didn't want to. Then *Shrek*. *Toy Story*. He had to agree with her. At the bottom of the headed paper he found the VAT number and the company registration. PillarBoxFlix was owned by PSM Ltd.

Sally tapped out the exit code and escorted them out. The security man was outside, waiting for them.

'Don't hesitate, will you, if you need to know anything else,' Sally said, the smile still firmly in place. 'I've never been involved in a murder investigation before.'

Wyngate waited until they were in the car, door closed, before asking, 'Did we mention the word murder? We didn't, did we?'

2.00 p.m.

The moment Mulholland walked into the lecture theatre, he went up to the board and read the notice about Pavel Sergeievich Morosov. The background check had borne little fruit, just a long list of business interests and two addresses – one in Moscow city centre, one outside the city. He was a wealthy, well-respected businessman who travelled a lot.

'Is that all we have on him?'

'So far,' said Anderson, who was trying to concentrate on tracking down Mary Carruthers. 'He appears legit. One hundred per cent.'

'Of course he does. You looked at those DVDs yet?'

'I was waiting for you.' Anderson indicated the brand-new DVD player on the table, its flex still wrapped. Mulholland plugged it in while Anderson scowled at his telephone and punched Redial yet again. 'Mrs Carruthers has been at the solicitor's for bloody ages,' he complained. 'We really do need to talk to her – softly, softly or otherwise.'

'Probably gone into town to spend all her dosh.' Mulholland switched the machine on, and a digital HELLO appeared.

'That's what my wife would have done.' Anderson winced as he remembered that he still had to face Brenda; he couldn't put that one off for ever. He went to the end of the table where Lambie had sat, and flicked through his odd bits of paper. His heart dropped at the sight of the doodle in his colleague's notebook – a small heart with the letters 'J' and 'D' coloured in. He tore the page out and slipped it into his pocket.

He'd make sure Jennifer got it.

'Howlett did say it was this morning Mary was going to the solicitor, didn't he? You'd think she'd have been home for her lunch long since.' He flicked through more notes, found a phone number, dialled it and sat listening until the ringing went to answerphone. 'No answer from the solicitor either.' He put the phone down, and picked up a few typed sheets clipped together. 'What's this?'

'Oh, I've summarized that for you,' said Wyngate. 'It's

the HR record of Rosita Maria Harmon, who became the second Mrs Wullie MacFadyean.'

'I thought I told you to do that, Mulholland.'

'Well, I'm doing this.' Mulholland opened the red DVD cover, read the label. 'It's a kiddies' film, looks original. Don't tell me MacFadyean had kids too.' He slid it in and pressed Play. The machine growled quietly, showing an error signal. He shrugged, ejected it and tried the other. The label was the same. *Error*. He looked helplessly at Anderson.

'Give it here,' said Wyngate. He looked closely at it. 'This is a CD, I think.' He slipped the first disk into his computer, which whirred obligingly. 'Password-protected,' he reported.

Anderson leaned over his shoulder. 'Can you hack in?'

'You watch too many films, boss.' Wyngate tapped a few keys. 'But from the size, it's just a document, nothing complicated.'

'OK,' Anderson said slowly, sitting down. He pointed at the computer, a hunch forming in his head. 'So, could this be their method of communication? As simple as that? Just that – through the post?'

'Difficult for us to trace. Will I take it down to the IT guys?'

'No, get them up here. Good work, you two.' Anderson's mind was working overtime. 'So, to the lovely Rosita, who became Mrs Wullie MacFadyean. How did you get that information?'

Wyngate smiled cherubically. 'A friend in the Police Federation.'

Anderson flicked through the sheets. 'This is a *summary*?'

'It's a long story.'

Anderson glared at him. 'Just tell me, Wyngate.'

'Well, she was one clever cookie – she was a tactical chief.'

Anderson looked blank.

'In charge of tactical firearms teams and an adviser to the Public Order Incident Team.'

Anderson breathed out slowly. 'OK, so not somebody to be crept up on in the canteen.' The little hunch was starting to play a tune in the back of his mind.

'Despite her office job, she still had to do her officer safety training. She kept dodging it due to health issues that were unspecified. But, reading between the lines, she has dietary issues.'

'Too fat or too thin?'

'The former. She injured her knee on the training day and took the police force all the way. She never returned to her not very active duty, but the force refused to pay out and punted her off the job.'

Anderson sighed. 'OK, longer summary than that.'

'She had a little alcohol in her bloodstream, and they argued that it contributed to her fall, and therefore her injury – and therefore she was liable. She shouldn't have been at work having consumed alcohol, so she was booted out with no compensation. My friend said that Rosita was hell-bent on screwing the force for every penny they had, but got nowhere.'

'And . . . ?'

'Well, she was brilliant but her career was already on a shaky peg – she'd had two formal warnings. One for having an affair with another officer. He was married.'

'Wullie MacFadyean.' Anderson scanned the rest of the papers.

Wyngate lowered his voice. 'The other warning got her bumped off the ITU, the equivalent of the Intelligence Cell Team in those days, for misuse of intelligence – looking up things on databases she'd no right to look up. She was already bitter when the legal battle over the knee injury started. It went on for three years, which is why my pal remembers it so well.'

'Embittered ex-cop. Ripe pickings for somebody on the lookout for a police informer. Well, more than an informer. She knows how we work. She could . . . God, she could apply that know-how to any organization.'

'Such as organized crime?'

'But once she was off the force, she'd have no contacts.' Anderson drummed the desk with his pen. 'So, what do we think? What was she looking up on those databases? She was turned, wasn't she? It might have happened before she left. She knows how to hide, as she knows how we track people.'

'She'd know not to use a mobile phone or the Internet. So, where the fuck is she?'

'And where was Wullie? He was still on the force. We could be looking at a team, operating like that for years. She's still out there somewhere. So, let's find her before somebody else does. Do we have a picture? If not, get one.'

'Here's her last picture from her ID, but that was years ago.' Wyngate pinned the printout on the wall. A cheery, pretty face, short dark hair, chubby-cheeked but pretty.

Mulholland was standing, looking at Anderson and waiting for Wyngate to finish. 'Until Mrs Carruthers comes to light, can I talk to you about this?' He put down a pile of notes, indicating that Anderson should follow him to the corner of the room. 'Skelpie Fairbairn didn't do it.'

'Didn't do what?'

'Whatever else Skelpie Fairbairn, Tito Piacini, did, I don't think he had anything to do with the Lynda Osbourne case.'

'I'm not really in the mood for this, Vik. I have rather a lot on my plate at the moment, in case you hadn't noticed.'

'Have they brought him in yet?' Mulholland demanded.

'You know that he's gone. He's not returned to his digs, and the lawyer's claiming ignorance of his whereabouts. We're all getting a bit uneasy about it.'

Mulholland threw Anderson a look that could have turned the tide. 'I've noticed in McAlpine's notes that there was a taped interview with Fairbairn at the time. I think I'd like to get hold of that and hear it.'

'Your wish is my command, fill your boots,' Anderson said acidly.

'And I think there's somebody else I should talk to. Lynda's father.'

Anderson stood back and looked at Mulholland. His voice was quiet but staccato with anger. 'Vik, Fairbairn's DNA identifies him as Tito Piacini, the babysitter in the Alessandro Marchetti case. We also have him raping that girl on the DVD. If you remember, Lambie and I found her chained at the bottom of a ladder in the bloody Clyde. She *died* there, Vik. And you want me to go on some sort of campaign to prove that scumbag's innocence? Sorry, but am I missing something here?'

'Yes, you're missing the fact that we still need to catch the guy who sexually assaulted Lynda Osbourne, if Fairbairn did not do it — which is the state of the law as it stands.'

'But he did.'

'He did not, Anderson. And your personal conviction that Fairbairn was guilty is exactly what got you into the mess that you're in now.'

'I'm not in any mess.' Anderson raised his voice.

Wyngate looked over, then looked away quickly.

Mulholland raised an 'if you say so' eyebrow. 'Well, I'm going to go and have a word with Lynda Osbourne's father.'

'Why?' asked Anderson quietly.

'Because I want to.'

'That would make it official.'

'Well, so be it.' And Mulholland walked off.

Anderson covered his face with the palms of his hands and sighed.

11.20 p.m.

Looking in the mirror, Costello felt like the man in the old Milk Tray advert. She was dressed in black jogging trousers, dark trainers and a black jumper. She glanced around the room, looking for anything else to take with her. All she really needed was her phone. She had Pettigrew for protection.

She glanced at her watch — eleven twenty. Outside there was still a vestige of light around the fringes of the sky.

She closed the door quietly behind her, and crept round the gravel of the big car park without being seen from the school.

They had agreed to meet down at the wooden bridge.

'We've to move quickly. He's already on his way,' Pettigrew said.

'He's early.'

'This way.' He moved into a strange low run that easily ate up the ground. Costello tried to emulate it but each footfall ricocheted up her body, jarring every bone until it reached her left cheekbone, where it hurt like hell. She wondered who had taught Pettigrew to run like that. She trotted along instead, more noisily than she had intended, but at least she was keeping up.

A few minutes later, Pettigrew stepped behind an oak tree. It was very dark here under the canopy of the trees. There was a loud cawing of disturbed crows, then they settled back to silence. 'You keeping up OK?'

'I'm fine.' Costello caught her breath, wiping the sweat from her eyes. 'How do you know he's on his way?'

'He's over there, moving in that direction.'

'I can't see anybody. But then he's probably read some SAS book about how not to be seen,' she said sarcastically.

'I was scouting about a bit today. I found the track he uses, parallel to this, just over there. So, we'll go this way.'

'He put some traps on the path down there –' she pointed down to the river '– so maybe we should go there. He might be trying to protect something that is important to him, to his psyche . . .'

'No, I think we should go this way,' Pettigrew said, allowing no further comment.

Costello hesitated, then followed him, keeping her eyes down, watching where she put her feet, aware that deep in her police brain a little voice was telling her something was wrong.

After five minutes or so, she tapped Pettigrew on the shoulder. 'Aren't we going too far south?'

'No, we're going slightly north.' He pointed. 'Where we want to be is right over there. He's still moving, and moving fast. He's in a hurry to go somewhere.'

'I can't hear him.'

It was really dark now, and nothing could be seen through the trees.

'He's there all right, and he's getting ahead.' Pettigrew moved off, darting confidently between the trees.

Costello hesitated. What was the big hurry? Maybe Pettigrew had seen something she hadn't. She set off again, trying to catch up, but he was gone. She stopped in her tracks, and looked around, listening hard. Nothing. Pettigrew had disappeared. Could she find her way back? Of course – if she went north, sooner or later she would come to the road. Or she could call out. Drew must be way ahead, and Pettigrew couldn't have got that far. She walked on quickly, listening hard but still hearing nothing. She jumped as a crow cawed loudly above her and swooped low over her head. Another three flew off after it, black shape-shifters gliding through the night.

She was out in the forest on her own.

Suddenly, two hands grabbed her shoulders, and she felt herself being dragged. She tried to struggle, to kick herself free, but her arms were pulled back and held tightly. She cried out as something soft went over her head.

The darkness really was total now.

'Batten?'

'Dr Batten to you.' Mick offered ACC Howlett a cigarette. The late night was still warm, but the slight breath of wind coming up University Avenue promised a change on the way.

'I shouldn't, you know,' the older man said, taking it gratefully.

Batten flicked the top of his battered lighter. He lit Howlett's cigarette and then his own before perching on the wall. 'How are you keeping?'

'You have no idea how good that feels.' Howlett leaned against the wall, looking out at the closing-time crowds spilling out of the pub, all laughing with the ease of the slightly drunk. He contemplated the end of his cigarette, then looked at Batten with weary eyes. 'How did you know?'

'You've lost a lot of weight, too quickly for your clothes to keep up. Your eyes are yellow. There's a tremor in your right hand. And you're not like the ACC Howlett I expected from your file. For a man who has a reputation for being cautious, you're suddenly moving very fast. And for a man who's a stickler for the rules, you're breaking them right, left and centre. So, what are you trying to achieve before you shuffle off your mortal coil?'

'Trying to put something right. I want to rid this city of a great evil.' The words were breathed like some kind of personal mantra, and Howlett sounded as though he didn't care if Batten believed him or not.

'I see. Something you've tried to achieve all through your career is suddenly going to come right for you.' His voice was calm, contemplative.

'Sometimes the only thing you need do to succeed is to give up hope.'

'And is that worth endangering the lives of good men? My friends?' Batten's voice was interested, non-confrontational. They could have been discussing the merits of the canteen coffee.

'Something is going to happen in this city. And we shall see a new heaven and a new earth.'

Batten glanced quickly to see if ACC Howlett had started to foam at the mouth, but he was merely speaking with a quiet certainty.

'It will be the end of days. And we are, like it or not, moving towards it with every hour that passes.'

'Are we getting a new Christ or something?'

Howlett drew on his cigarette imperturbably. 'Not far from it. A new beginning. The good will rise up, and the evil will be driven out. I've just been trying to stack the odds in favour of the good. That's all.'

'Is that what you think?'

'OK, more like the lesser of two evils. Always better the devil you know.'

Batten nodded. 'I am glad it's only me you're talking to. Anyone else, they'd wonder what else you've been smoking.'

Oh no, you bloody don't! Costello tried to think clearly. She let her body go limp, allowing herself to fall to her knees, and pitched sideways, pulling her knees up and trying to roll, head tucked in. But somebody grabbed her arms through the blanket that covered her, tighter this time. She cried out involuntarily, and heard a voice say, 'Don't hurt her.' Then she felt a warm hand over her face, and fingers forced her mouth open, a cold liquid crept along her tongue, and her mouth was closed over it. She felt her nostrils being pinched, and tried not to swallow, but the tasteless liquid was going to make her choke otherwise.

She had to. She had no choice.

She lay there, heart pounding, feeling a vague rush through her head, a dulling of her thought processes, and then felt herself being lifted up. Her legs took her weight, and she was moving again. Hands on her shoulders stopped her stumbling but pushed with just enough force to steer her onwards. Her brain was confused; it was telling her legs to stop, but they kept going. Why was she not screaming? Not terrified? Her brain was panicking, her body was not. Under her feet she felt the path give way to grass, then clumps of longer grass and, finally, a smooth carpet of turf. She felt the hands pressing on her shoulders, and another hand on her ankle. Then hands were all over her, under her arms, behind her knees. She was being lifted, carried, and she felt herself acquiescing meekly.

She couldn't resist.

She heard a gate creaking open, then the metallic grating

of ancient hinges. She felt herself being bundled, down, down, somewhere damp and musty. And dark. She knew it was dark. And cold.

Her feet were guided down metal rungs – how many? Then she was shifted sideways, and she sat down. Correction – someone had sat her down. On something very cold and hard. She felt something – a chain? – being put round her waist, and heard the click of a lock close by. Then her perch vibrated and lurched as someone transferred their weight from it, and their feet clanged on the rungs as they climbed up again.

Then there was that grating noise again. Some sort of trapdoor being closed over her head. Then silence.

She waited.

And waited, shivering with cold, but not fear.

She was underground. This place had seen none of the recent sun.

A strange calmness fell over her. *Don't hurt her.*

She could sit here; she could wait. She still had her senses, she told herself; the drug would wear off.

She rubbed her cheek against the shoulder of her jumper, trying to wake herself up, though she knew she had not been asleep. Then she realized her hands were free. She slipped the cover from her face, and opened her eyes to the blackness. Cold damp air wafted against her skin.

She felt about with her fingers. She was sitting with her back against a wall of smooth brick, yet under her was cold metal mesh that bit into her thighs. She was numb, with that damp cold that eats into the bones. And she could smell water, hear it trickling far below. Yes, she was underground, yet high up. It made no sense. She stretched out her legs, quickly folding them again when she became aware that there was nothing in front of her, and a drop beneath her. She was on a ledge. For a minute she thought she would fall, and held herself totally still. Then she inched back to the wall behind her, the chain clinking in the dark. It was looped round a metal stanchion. Through a fog of not knowing what to do, she became aware of something hanging from her neck. A noose? One move too far, and it would tighten, and that would be the last thing she knew.

Yet she still wasn't panicking. She should have been half dead with terror. Instead, she was starting to think a bit more clearly.

She felt for the noose. Not a rope, a tape. Weighted. She fumbled for the weight, and recognized it for what it was – a small stainless-steel torch. She switched it on and shone it slowly around her.

She was in a rectangular vertical shaft, lined with brick. In front of her, the wall glistened with water. To one side, a dark gaping chasm – a sewer? Some kind of underground communication tunnel left over from the war? Whatever it was, it disappeared into fathomless blackness. Fragments of stuff she'd had to read at school chased around inside her brain: *Great God! This is an awful place . . . caverns measureless to man . . .*

Close beside her, to her left, the beam caught a metal ladder. She followed it up all the way to the top. Twenty feet, then a grating – her way to reach the outside world. If she could get up there and get it open . . .

She moved forward carefully, then froze as she heard

the rattle of a chain echo around the tunnel. She traced the chain with her torch beam. It was new, shining. But it was a chain clipped to the metal grid, easily unclipped with the pressure of her thumb. She ran it through her hands. Just enough slack to let her move, to tighten before she went too far. Were they keeping her safe? She unclipped herself, shining the beam around. There was only silence, except for the gentle gurgle of the underground stream.

To her right, the metal platform extended a few feet to the corner of the shaft. There was something on it, she could just see it, a few feet away. She edged along it, a strange confidence rising in her now that her limbs were once more under her own control, and shone the torch to see what it was. An animal, she thought at first. A rat? But it was just a small pile of . . . her heart began to race.

Don't hurt her.

Bones.

Small human bones.

She sat and gazed at them, totally mesmerized, for a few minutes. Then she carefully lay down on her side and reached out towards the hint of gold gleaming in the torchlight.

She knew she had been drugged. And that some drugs can wipe the short-term memory. She had to remember this, had to obtain proof that she had been here, proof of what she had found. Just as she brought the little medal within reach, the torch beam picked out something else that made the blood almost stop in her veins. Hooked round the farther metal stanchion was something that looked all too familiar – a pair of handcuffs.

Stretching her arm out as far as she could get it to go, she managed to slide the very end of the torch under the fine gold chain, and with infinite care tugged it towards her, trying not to dislodge the little bones. Yes, she was disturbing a crime scene, and she'd get into trouble for it.

On the other hand, she might never get out of here at all. And in a hundred years' time her own bones would be found, her skeletal hand still clutching Alessandro Marchetti's gold St Christopher medal.

11.55 p.m.

Anderson watched the minute hand move on to twelve, joining its mate at the bewitching hour. He closed his eyes, letting his head fall back against the sofa cushions, enjoying the tick of the clock and the gentle snoring of Nesbitt in the corner. He wondered if he could train the dog to bite Mulholland on demand. He always knew that his constable was a career cop. If he saw a way to make his name, why should it matter to him that it would be at the cost of his boss's career? They had worked together for six years or more. Six years. It meant nothing. Loyalty meant nothing. No loyalty as deep as the Molendinar for cops – there was more honour among thieves.

His thoughts were broken by the sound of Brenda coming downstairs, her gentle footfall on the carpet. He heard Nesbitt's tail tap on the floor as she opened the door.

She perched on the arm of the sofa, wrapping her dressing gown round her, pulling her knees up to her chest. 'You awake?'

'No,' he said, patting her on the knee.

'How are you feeling now?'

'Kind of numb, I suppose.'

'Are you thinking about David Lambie?'

'Mostly,' he answered, with partial honesty.

'Because you should be.' She paused. 'When all this is over, do you think we could plan a holiday? Not to go now, but plan it, for Christmas. I feel we have hardly seen you this summer.'

'I know, I'm sorry. It's all been a bit horrid.'

'And it is not over, is it?'

'No.'

'We don't have to live like this. We can have a new start.'

'I know.' He opened his eyes, staring at the ceiling. 'Yes, I know.'

She reached for his hand and wrapped her fingers round his. 'And another thing – all these Russian gangsters. Do you ever stop to think that one day they might come after you? After all, they came for David. I wasn't going to say it, but it could have been you out there. And then where would the kids and I be? I know it's your job, but is it worth it?'

'How do you know about Russian gangsters?'

'You think just because you walk about half blind, half asleep, everybody else in this family does. We watch the news, we read the newspapers. You need to leave the job.'

He sighed. 'Yes, I know,' he said again.

'So, are you coming to bed?'

'I'll come up soon.'

'Promise?'

'Promise.'

He rested his head against the back of the sofa, closed his eyes, and thought very seriously about ignoring his mobile as it rang.

Sunday
4 July 2010

Sunday
July 2010

'Stay still, will you?'

'I don't like people sticking needles in me. What are you doing?'

'I need to get bloods off you, one sample every ten minutes.' O'Hare held up a syringe and bent down to find the vein. 'Matilda needs these samples, so be quiet.'

Costello was lying on her bed, seething. 'Why am I stuck here?' Downstairs, the door was wide open, and she could hear the crackle of a radio – somebody was standing guard at her front door. She was being kept in her room, under supervision, while out in the early dawn forest there was a hive of activity. O'Hare kept insisting that she needed to rest. But she didn't. She had got herself up out of the drain, she had staggered high enough up the hill to get a signal on her phone, and she had made it through the forest and back to the road. Then she had waited in the dark, marking the spot where she had left the treeline.

After twenty minutes, Pettigrew's car had pulled up. He had a map of the old drainage pipes and tunnels, and all the shafts – gated shafts, lidded shafts, open shafts, closed shafts – were marked and numbered with an army of little ticks and crosses advancing across the map, showing how far the recommissioning work had progressed. Before driving her back to the school, he laid the map out on the bonnet of the car and talked her through how she had got out. From her description, he seemed to know whereabouts she had been. Shaft 36A was the one Pettigrew put his finger on first, then he circled 37 and 38. But she couldn't pinpoint exactly where she had been.

O'Hare made her jump by sticking another needle in her elbow.

'You do realize you were drugged, don't you? That stuff they put in your mouth? You're lucky to be alive. Do you think you'll ever learn to do your job and keep out of trouble?' O'Hare was speaking while filling up phial after phial of blood, peering through his reading glasses and then writing labels.

'Bollocks,' Costello growled. 'And I'm not sure I really was in trouble.'

'No, Costello, you were drugged, blindfolded and put down a hole. The same shaft that . . . You were put down that hole and left there. It was very dangerous – one wrong move and you would have been off that ledge.'

'No, I wouldn't.' She folded her arms defiantly. 'There was a wee chain. And I was left a torch, so I could see. That was Alessandro Marchetti, wasn't it?'

O'Hare unpeeled a small sticking plaster and put it on her arm. 'I can't answer that yet. It's getting light, so I'll go out there as soon as I know you're OK.'

'Wait – I've just remembered something.' She shifted her hip and dug into the front pocket of her trousers. 'I thought maybe the drug would wipe my memory, so I took this. As proof.'

She held out her closed fist, and O'Hare opened his

hand. She dropped the gold chain and medal into it. Then she picked up the book from her bedside table and held it out to him.

He looked from the medal to the photograph of Alessandro and back again. Then he smiled sadly. 'Yes, this probably is proof. I'd be surprised if my examination finds anything to contradict it.'

'And there were handcuffs.'

'Handcuffs? Where?'

She pulled herself up on her elbows. 'The platform they left me on was bracketed to two metal poles up against the wall. The handcuffs were on the one opposite. And –' she shut her eyes, straining to remember '– they were hooked round a long bone. It was too big to be an arm bone. It must have been a shin bone –'

'Because his hands would have been too small,' O'Hare finished for her. He pushed her back down on to the pillow. 'Don't think about it.'

'But you know what that means? It wasn't just where they put the body. He was alive when they put him down there! And they just left him to die in the dark, where nobody would hear him. I was down there, and it was a horrible place. Prof, he was six years old!' She sat up, then tried to stand up but had to sit back down again. Her head thought it was a good idea while her legs had made a decision to stay where they were. 'One thing I'm sure of,' she said. 'The people who did that to Alessandro are not the people who put me down there. Somebody led me to that . . . place . . . to find him.'

O'Hare sat down on the bed beside her. 'And why would they do that?'

Costello screwed her face up, thinking hard. She rubbed her forehead with her wrist, making her fringe stand on end. 'Look, they never meant me any harm. Someone said, "Don't hurt her." It was –' she searched for the right word '– gentle. I don't know . . . it was kind of . . . I mean, I wasn't hurt. I wasn't pushed or manhandled; I was just moved along. They guided me down the ladder carefully . . . the torch, the chain . . . They were intended to help me get out. The cover wasn't locked.' She repeated. 'Oh, yes, I was taken right to the place where the body was. I was meant to find it.'

'And why would they do that?' asked O'Hare again. 'Apart from the malicious pleasure of proving that bloody Sangster woman wrong.'

Costello's grey eyes opened wide. 'Because the drain was about to be recommissioned. It would have been filled with water, flushed through. Those small bones would have been washed away like twigs. He would have been lost. The truth would have been lost.'

8.00 a.m.

The lecture room was quiet, with a cool stillness in the air. No students, no cops, no computers, no phones, just the gentle drone of the traffic outside. Mulholland was sitting with his feet up on the desk, skimming through the reports about Lynda Osbourne. He had intended to go home the night before, but there had always been another page, another statement to read. His mind abhorred disorder, so in the end he had pulled out a clipboard, fixed a sheet of paper to it, and started to write and cross-reference.

The 22nd of July 2005. Midsummer, he told himself, a hot day. The park around the Botanics would have been sweating with people. There'd have been ice cream vans, a puppet show, hot dogs, a man making hats by tying balloons together.

Lynda's parents had taken their wee girl to see the fun. The whole family had seen the bus driver and waved hello to him. Then they had met some friends, who wanted to talk about arranging a birthday surprise. So the friends' two boys were given some money and told to take Lynda and buy ice creams. But the boys had met some pals from school and had left Lynda to join the queue on her own. They'd seen her go to the front to join a man she seemed to know. Their description of him matched Fairbairn. But a short while later, they'd lost sight of her and run back to their parents.

Ten minutes later, wee Lynda was found wandering out from the trees.

Mulholland looked at a plan of the park. The little girl had gone away from the crowd, and a tall man – Mulholland checked a few eyewitness statements, and they all said tall – was seen following her. But few people would describe Skelpie Fairbairn as tall. In fact, the man was marvellously average. Yes, Fairbairn admitted, he was there, saw Lynda in the queue, and bought her an ice cream. He said he'd watched as she went back to join the two boys. Then he'd returned to the pub on Great Western Road. Two dubious characters, Wood and McAdam, had each given a statement to back him up. And a statement was a statement. The timing was a little inconvenient, out by about ten minutes, but nobody really believed the two guys. Most important, none of the investigating officers believed them. Or maybe they did, and realized it was too convincing to put in front of a jury, so they buried it. And that could well cost Anderson his career.

Mulholland drew a big question mark, and read on.

Lynda was very quiet after they found her, her mum and dad said, but she knew she'd done wrong to wander off – and anyway, it had been a long day. So, they took her home, tired and drowsy. Her mum took her upstairs and popped her into her bath. It was only when she was putting Lynda's things into the laundry basket that she found the blood on her knickers, by which time a whole load of evidence had been washed away.

Lynda's clothes were examined. Fairbairn's DNA was found on her dress, but he claimed he'd licked his finger and scooped up a spilled drop of raspberry topping. The defence argued that she knew the bus driver and, at six years old, was more likely to describe somebody she knew than say it was a stranger.

Mulholland looked again for any indication that the two statements from the guys in the pub, McAdam and Wood, were ever put through to the defence by the fiscal. He didn't find anything. Deliberately and thoughtfully, he wrote the words 'cover-up, evidence disregarded', and saw his own promotion. Though some, he thought, would say there were a few wee girls out there now who might be six feet under if Fairbairn had been out for the last four years.

He shrugged to himself and flicked through more statements, loads of photographs. He soon realized that, for all the stuff in the file, what wasn't there was much more significant. There'd been no timed walk of the route

Fairbairn said he'd taken to go back to the pub. And there should have been. He came across some page-filler photographs taken throughout the day by the photographer from the *West End News*, and pored over them, studying faces in the crowd, particularly the queue for the ice cream van. And there, near the trees, eyeing the queue, was the figure – the *tall* figure – of Billy Biggart.

Mulholland picked up the phone and called ACC Howlett.

9.30 a.m.

When Anderson arrived at the lecture room, he had a brief word with O'Hare, who reported that the compliance effect of the R2 might be working off and that Costello was getting stroppy again.

Batten and Wyngate were already there. In the car park he had phoned Helena, but the call went straight to her voicemail. He didn't know what to say. He stuttered out a few words, and rang off.

Wyngate looked up as he came in. 'Still no sign of Mrs Carruthers, sir. Do you want us to go out to the solicitor's office and have a look? A uniform went round yesterday and said it was all locked up. Do you want us to track down a keyholder?'

'What does the sister say – Rene?'

Wyngate shrugged. 'She's not making much sense, just knocking on her sister's door every two minutes. But the neighbour has been phoning us. She's worried because Mary rarely leaves Rene alone, for obvious reasons.'

'Just try to find her as soon as you can. We need to know more about that missing diary.' He sat down heavily. 'Anybody heard how Jennifer's doing?'

'I think she's gone into hiding, courtesy of her father.'

'I wonder if he'd take me into hiding. Wyngate, do you have your car out there?'

'Yes, sir.'

'Call up Central Records, and go and collect the Marchetti files in person. Get a uniform from Partick to go with you, and tell them Howlett said. Come straight back here, do not pass Go, do not collect two hundred pounds. Understand?'

Wyngate nodded.

'So, why are you still standing there?'

'I hear Costello found the boy's remains,' Mick Batten said, once Wyngate had gone. 'Do we gather she was blindfolded and led there, but not hurt?'

'That's right.'

'Typical gangland behaviour. It avoids untidy tip-offs. And they score Brownie points with you guys, while being seen to flex their muscles.'

Anderson scrolled through his emails, trying to ignore the psychologist.

Batten pulled his chair very close to Anderson, and the smell of cigarettes came with him. 'Do you really know what we're getting into? You seem to think you guys are handling this. You are not, Colin. All you're doing is allowing yourself to be pulled along by them, every step of the way. You have to be careful.'

'Look, what would you have me do, Mick? What do *you* want me to do? I'm trying to get ahead of the game, that's all. You might be able to sit about all day and ponder the nature of the criminal mind, but I, sitting here at this desk, have the rather more stressful job of dealing with what the criminal mind comes up with.' He pointed at the whiteboard for emphasis. 'Do you think I don't know that I'm being played like a fish? But –' he rammed his forefinger into his own chest '– it was *me* who was drugged, tied up and shot at, it was my colleague who was put down a hole, and my friend who was killed. And I take grave exception to all of it. I will get the people who did it. Do you see that?'

'But you weren't shot at in the same way that David was stabbed, or you wouldn't be here,' Batten said reasonably.

Anderson had to control a sudden rush of temper.

'You were shot at in the same way that Costello was kidnapped last night. One was fatal, the other benign. I'd say you're being helped along the way here. After all, that bullet found its mark, and it wasn't you.'

10.30 a.m.

By ten thirty the bearded man swigging the Red Bull had been sitting at the computer for an hour, alternating hitting the keyboard and flicking his unruly ringlets back from his face. His eyes had never left the keyboard.

'Who's that? asked Anderson, getting absolutely no response from his cheery hello.

'IT guy, can't you tell?' said Mulholland.

'Has he cracked the code on the CD yet? Has he found anything?'

'Only a lifelong friend in Wyngate, so far. He ran a Brute Force program; don't ask, but it worked. He called an old colleague of Rosie's, who was a bit of help – he knew what Rosie had been trained in. The document is coded but it looks simple. And it might be in Russian, so he says he will crack it and then we can decode it and read it.'

'What have you been doing?'

'This!' said Mulholland, putting something down on Anderson's desk. 'It's the tape of the Fairbairn interview. I've been going through it.'

'Why, are you bored?' Anderson was flicking through a set of A4 sheets, looking up all the places they had searched for Fairbairn. 'Look, he's gone to ground. Is that the action of an innocent man? What the fuck are we meant to do?'

Mulholland took the papers off him. 'Colin – sir. This situation is not going to go away. Whether you like it or not, questions are going to be asked. And you need to have answers to them before it goes to an enquiry, or before we get him to court for Rusalka.'

Anderson tried to ignore him.

But Mulholland opened up McAlpine's notes and stuck them under Anderson's nose. 'Here – there's a break of twenty minutes when the tape isn't running. There's the time, recorded. McAlpine went out to speak to Lynda Osbourne and her dad, leaving you and the accused, Cameron Fairbairn, alone. An officer of your experience, alone with the accused? The same accused whose evidence you neglected to safeguard? Up to that precise minute Lynda Osbourne's account was none too clear, to her mum, her dad, or to the nice police lady.

The bus driver bought her an ice cream. A big man took her into the trees and hurt her. Was the big man the bus driver? You can't tell. Then suddenly, after talking to McAlpine, she's absolutely sure. Yes, it was the bus driver. But during those twenty minutes Lynda only had her dad with her – no independent observer, no child protection officer. The interview was in a room with no observation window. There was no one to see that her dad was not coaching her or guiding her answers. Or that the cop was, for God's sake! That was an unsupervised, uncorroborated interview with a minor. A six-year-old minor. That's against the law.'

'I don't take kindly to suggestions of witness tampering, DC Mulholland.'

'Nothing to what you're going to be accused of at the appeal, when those two statements are produced, with your signature on them. And the buck will stop with you. McAlpine won't be around to help you out – or say it was his idea to have you in one room, him in the other. Both those infractions . . . God, you'll be out on your ear!'

Anderson ignored him and went back to his papers, a list of Fairbairn's known recent haunts. There weren't many; Skelpie had been living a quiet life since he'd got out of jail. Too quiet. Was he waiting for something?

Mulholland tried a different tack. 'OK, look at it like this. You all knew he was a paedophile. The dad knew his daughter had been assaulted. McAlpine suggests to him – just suggests – that it was Fairbairn. He was at the scene, the girl had been seen with him, and the ice cream man identified him. Mr Osbourne gets Lynda to tell her story, just helping out with the bits he says Lynda had

383

told him before. The kid is traumatized and compliant, and probably just wants to be given some chocolate and go home; she goes to role-play and does exactly what you'd expect, given the injuries she'd sustained. But that does not point conclusively to Fairbairn. It could have been anybody. It was probably Biggart.'

'You saw that film. We know Fairbairn was involved. So, get out my way!'

Anderson's phone rang. He stood up and swung his jacket back round his shoulders. No matter who was on the phone, he was using it as an excuse to get out.

'OK, go and talk to David Osbourne before you go any further. Then get back to me, if you still think you have to.'

11.00 a.m.

Matilda had been up all night, processing the root of a tooth so they could get a DNA sample and maybe a definite ID. But she had also been busy on the handcuffs. Standard police issue thirty years ago, they had a serial number showing that they had been issued to Strathclyde force. But in those days they had no designation to any particular officer. O'Hare was still trying to grapple with the idea that a Strathclyde officer had been involved.

Matilda came scuttling in efficiently, waving a white envelope. 'Trace DNA from inside the clip of the handcuffs,' she announced. 'Guess who?'

'Apart from Alessandro Marchetti? Tell me.'

'It matches Wullie MacFadyean's. I'll do a chain reaction on it, and make sure, but the markers are there.'

O'Hare said carefully, 'It means he touched them – so what?'

'He was a working cop,' Matilda persisted. 'So, everybody and his dog's DNA should have been on them.'

'And you're saying it wasn't? You're saying they were cleaned beforehand?'

Matilda shrugged. 'Of the five who went hill-walking, five are dead. One of them was handling handcuffs found near the remains of the Marchetti boy. And he lived in hiding out near Glen Fruin Academy.'

11.30 a.m.

All the cops had gone. The last of them had left the car park of the Highland Glen Hotel at half seven that morning. The word was the hotel's laundry van had been involved in some road traffic incident, but Skelpie knew different. The housekeeper and her staff had been interviewed. And now they were talking to anybody who had driven the van recently. It had been a tense few hours. But, technically, Skelpie's room at the Highland Glen Hotel was unoccupied – the booking system had it marked as vacant – so as long as he stayed in here, they would not come looking.

He had no idea who was looking after him – Wee Archie O'Donnell had been vague in the Bar-L, talking almost in riddles, like a spy. Skelpie'd thought it strange that a player like O'Donnell would lower himself to speak to him, but maybe he himself was now a player too. Maybe Archie O'Donnell, with his life sentence, had chosen him, Cameron Fairbairn, to be the Daddy –

as a just reward for his loyalty in the Marchetti kidnap, and his loyalty to Biggart.

Outside, the heat was relentless, and the patchworked repairs on the tarmac car park were melting. Skelpie thought about going out for a fag but decided against it – too easy to run into a cop. He still had a red patch on his arm where his tattoo was gradually being erased. Another five treatments and it would just look like a burn. But an eagle-eyed cop with not enough to do might spot it for what it was, and wonder why he was getting rid of it – not worth it.

Lynda Osbourne. Lynda with a Y. Funny how you never forgot those things. She'd be ten or eleven now. Twice, he'd walked right past her. Fairbairn closed the Black Watch tartan curtains and the room fell instantly dark.

And Wee Archie'd promised him the chance to settle a score with DI Anderson. He wasn't going to let that pass.

He jumped as the phone went. It was a female voice, husky, sexy-sounding. She called him Mr Fairbairn, as if she respected him. She knew his codeword, which meant she was legit. She said she had a list of instructions for him. He was to get the train to Helensburgh, and they would send a car to pick him up. The driver would be expecting Mr Fairbairn.

Mr Biggart had always been very grateful for his loyalty, the woman added – it wouldn't go unrewarded.

12.00 p.m.

The offices of Napier Grey were on the second floor of five in an old building just off Otago Street. Outside, a few black bin bags had spilled over. Their contents had been further decorated by kebab-ridden vomit and urine from the drunks coming out of the comedy club at the bottom of the street, and the heavy air hung on to the stench. Now the street, at midday on a Sunday, was deserted, devoid of traffic or parked cars apart from the police vehicles pulled up around Number 4.

As Anderson got out of his car, he subtly checked his phone. There was a text from Helena. Five words. *Call me when you can.*

No *Love*, no *X*. Just *Call me when you can*. He deleted it.

Mulholland was on the door of the building, having taken refuge within range of the fresh pine disinfectant.

'So, what do we have?' asked Anderson.

Mulholland indicated that Anderson should go up the stairs first. 'Cleaners got here before we did. The place was locked up as usual, except that the alarm hadn't been set properly. They found Mr Grey with a head injury from the usual unidentified blunt instrument. He's already been taken away in the ambulance.'

Anderson paused on the first flight and took a deep breath. Just what I need, he thought. 'Any sign of Mrs Carruthers yet?'

'No, just the solicitor.'

They went through the reception area, which was cluttered with SOCOs' equipment. A SOCO handed them a couple of shoe covers each and said, 'We haven't collected any samples yet, so –'

'I know. Touch nothing.'

As Anderson walked into the office, the tart chemical tang of adhesive hung in the air. A SOCO was videoing the scene, panning slowly all the way round the room from a central point. Filing and paperwork lay everywhere. Grey was a successful family solicitor, and he had looked after the Carruthers since they were married.

'I don't think they wanted to get any info out of him – otherwise, he would look like the Bridge Boy.'

'Richard,' corrected Anderson.

'Well, they just whacked this guy over the head.'

Anderson nodded and retreated. 'Well, whoever killed Lambie did it for the diary. If he didn't get what he was after then, he is still going to be looking for it. Sorry for stating the bloody obvious.'

'Something on the missing pages? Sorry for also stating the obvious.'

'Must be. The solicitor wouldn't know anything – but what about Mary? Has anybody found a desk diary here, an appointment book? Do we know who was supposed to be here yesterday?' Anderson squeezed past the SOCO and went back out to the reception area, where another SOCO was sitting at the desk. He pointed to the computer. 'Can you get that thing up and running?'

'No,' the SOCO said. 'We've tried but it's not booting up, not doing anything at all.'

'No wonder.' Mulholland leaned over the computer and sniffed. 'Smell that? Probably some sort of insulation foam – polyurethane. Like the stuff they use to take out speed cameras. I bet they've sprayed it in the guts of every machine here. Go round and have a sniff at them all.'

'I've also looked for a desk diary, but there isn't one.'

'OK, but we know that Mary Carruthers had an appointment here yesterday. And we know it was about a will, about that twenty grand. Thomas Carruthers will be the file name. Have you seen anything lying about?'

The SOCO shook his head. 'Nothing.'

Mulholland spoke up. 'I've phoned Grey's secretary and she said it wasn't like him to work on a Saturday morning. But he'd made an exception "due to the sensitive nature of the meeting". Her words.'

'And it was the cleaners who discovered him?'

'Yes. I had them taken up to Partick Central.'

Anderson looked at a photo on the wall, of Grey and a fellow solicitor, taken possibly twenty years earlier. 'Business partner?'

'Napier. He's on holiday. Haven't contacted him yet.'

'So, no sign that Mary actually made it here?'

Mulholland shook his head. 'Do you think this was the same person who killed David?'

'Well, I don't think we have a homicidal pensioner running around in the shape of Mary Carruthers. The Russians? Well, we know one of them – Perky – is dead. I saw him shot right in front of me. It's Mr Pinky we'd like to get our hands on.' He patted his constable on the arm on his way past. 'We *will* catch them, Mulholland. We won't rest until we do. No sign of Mary at home?'

'No.'

'*Sir!*' The shout came from the back room. 'Can you come in here, please?' The voice was full of panic.

Then it was joined by another voice – not quite a squeal but a noise of shock. A young uniformed constable ran out, hand over his mouth, and gestured behind him. The back room was another office, with two desks, four chairs, two computers, a massive printer and a photocopier. The bitter chemical smell of the spray foam was very strong. In the far corner, a heavy metal door stood ajar, opening away from them. The SOCO opened it further, and it swung as if well oiled. It was a walk-in safe. Inside was a chaos of files, papers, Manila folders, storage files, CDs and box files, all tossed off the shelves, their contents allowed to spill out.

On the far wall, the beige paint was marked by a long smear of red that widened downwards like a comet tail. Sticking out from a pile of handwritten papers, half covered by a box file, was a shoe – the sort of black patent-leather shoe an older lady might wear if she suffered from corns.

'Jesus. Mary?' He put his finger on her neck, pushing papers to the side. 'Get an ambulance, Vik, she's alive. Then could you do me a favour? Go out and see her sister, Rene?' Anderson sighed, trying to remember the next bit. 'And take some discreet protection with you. If in doubt, don't go in. However, I think they probably have what they wanted, so you should be OK. But take no risks, even so. I presume Grey gave them the combination for the safe. And they ransacked it, either for the missing pages or another diary – or was it something to do with the money?'

'And if so, the question is, did they find it?' asked Mulholland.

'It would help if we knew exactly what they were after. But what do we think happened here? They cosh Grey, bring Mary in here, ask her to look around, identify the . . . the diary, you think? Then they found it, closed the safe and left her to die like a dog. This safe is little more than a hermetically sealed room, and there was a great weight of paper piled on top of her. I bet there's no trace of that diary, or the money, or the bank account. That's why they trashed the computers. We can't follow the money now, there's nothing left,' argued Anderson.

'I still think it's the diary. But whatever it is, it can't be worth killing for.'

Batten's voice came from the door. 'If life is cheap, then many things are worth killing for.'

'You might be right,' said Anderson, heading towards the door.

Mulholland nodded. 'Where are you going?'

'I'm going to do exactly what Howlett has been doing all along. I'm going to flush the bastards out. I'm off to a garden party. Right into the eye of the storm.'

2.00 p.m.

'So, how are you?'

'I think I'm OK,' Costello answered, paying attention as she walked down the stone steps to the walled garden. Her feet still didn't seem all that keen on doing what she wanted them to do. 'So, what happened to you last night?'

Pettigrew shrugged, annoyed. 'One minute you were there, and the next you were gone. The Elphinstone boy has gone AWOL.'

He sat down at one of the small tables that were being placed in a precise pattern on the lawn. Catering staff in black and white were working like a well-oiled machine, joining up tables, spreading big white tablecloths, and refreshing flower arrangements with sprayed water. The air was heavy with an oppressive sweltering heat. Costello looked up, expecting to see clouds rolling in, but the skies were clear. The hills were keeping their own counsel and simply looked green and splendid in the afternoon sun.

'And what are you doing about him?'

'We're looking for him. It's under control. Nothing for you to worry about.'

'But you sound worried.'

'The one thing we are good at is security. But the school wants us to be good at PR as well.'

It obviously was not a matter for discussion. 'What's going on here, all this?' Costello asked.

'Oh, it's a sort of cheese-and-schmooze that the Warden puts on for the rich folk coming to take their little kiddies away. They look at an exhibition they have done in art, listen to a few poems. Wine and chit-chat, lots of tiny things on plates. I get a doggy bag. I have to wear black and walk the perimeter of the garden, looking like I can kill with my bare hands.'

'And make sure no riff-raff crawl out from under a stone?' She looked down towards the river. 'Is that a helicopter landing pad?'

'Yes, indeed. The military police have a fit each time something flies in and out, but it's a ten-minute shuttle from the airport. And to these people, time is money.'

A refrigerated van drew up in the car park, ready to open its back doors. A woman with a clipboard shouted to the driver to reverse it up to the kitchen, where the fridges were.

Pettigrew got up and came back with a jug of cold

orange juice and two glasses. 'So – last night. I know you can't tell me what is going on but was it the Marchetti boy you found?'

'You're right, I can't tell you.'

He raised his eyebrows, as if to say he'd noticed that she didn't deny it. 'Looks like the rumours at the time were right – they did try to get away across the glen.'

'The rumour was they planned to take the kid to the coast. The fact is, he was brought here and left to die.' Costello's voice was bitter. 'Makes you wonder just how much the police covered up their own incompetence.'

'If it was incompetence,' said Pettigrew.

'Stop talking in fucking riddles.'

'Imagine that it was all planned. Get the boy here and dispose of him. Imagine the irritation when the car was spotted driving through the glen. That was a mistake. This place may be isolated but a strange car sticks out like a nun in a brothel. Would have been better to stick him on the M8 in a traffic jam with mud-covered number plates.'

'You've given that some thought.'

'Let's go back a bit and think of it as a military exercise that needs tactical expertise. If you were planning a bank raid, you'd never leave yourself just one escape route, would you? That white Volvo was waiting at the bridge for two reasons. As a decoy if plan A went ahead, and as a backup if plan A failed. A good decoy plan to muddy the waters of any CCTV sightings along the route. And it was that theory which, God bless her, Sangster has picked up and perpetuated.'

Costello picked pieces of fruit pulp out of her drink with her thumb. It was the proper stuff, made from real fresh oranges. 'So, where does MacFadyean live? Marchetti was brought up here. MacFadyean died here.'

'He's dead, so he doesn't matter.' Pettigrew took a sip from his glass. 'You know Eric Moffat was in charge of the Marchetti investigation? MacFadyean worked with him a lot.'

'You are so well informed, Mr Pettigrew.'

'Just trying to be helpful.'

The conversation ceased. She never knew with him if she was being questioned or informed. But then, he used to be a cop as well. He was a bit younger than Carruthers and his friends, but still of an age where they might have known each other. Pettigrew was avoiding her eye. Instead, he was gazing out across the glen, watchful. The forest was as green and as dense as ever, and there was no way of knowing what activity was going on in there.

Costello sighed. She had done her bit last night. It was up to them now. 'Did you follow Drew?' she asked.

'For a bit. He was definitely a man with a mission. Then I got a bit concerned that you might have fallen over or knocked yourself out on a branch or something. So, I went back, but you'd gone.' He shrugged. 'Actually, I thought you'd got scared, given up and come back to the school.'

'Really?' She bristled at the insult.

'Then I found you up on the road, but Drew is still AWOL. He has missed breakfast and lunch. I know he's out there, holed up munching roots in a lair, thinking he's in the SAS, the last sane man on the planet, hiding from zombies. He won't break cover until after dark. I'm going out then to get him. I'll take him to hospital, where he belongs, and send his fucking parents the bill. Sod the school's reputation – I'm fed up with it.'

'Good luck with that! He's a young lad, he's strong. He's prepared for an attack of some kind, he could be armed to the teeth.'

'Well, come with me and give me a hand – before you go back to the day job?'

Costello felt an unsettling twinge. 'OK. But you'll forgive me for wanting a bit of backup with me this time – just in case I end up down another drain.'

'Bring Anderson. Tell him he can join us now in the buffet.'

3.30 p.m.

Rene tottered around her cluttered living room, her fingers in a fist round her damp handkerchief. Her thoughts drifted from trying to make them tea, to talking about Mary as if she was still next door. She had lost her brother-in-law, her sister wasn't here and she was still asking for 'that nice red-haired policeman' who had visited before. Batten just said he was otherwise engaged at the moment. And then he stretched a point by telling her that he was a doctor, here to help.

The female police officer Mulholland had left with Rene, who was perched on the edge of a messy sofa, knew nothing, so couldn't answer any of Rene's questions. Just as well, Batten thought. Another uniform, an older man called Bob, was out in the Aladdin's cave of a hall. He was going through Rene's address book, looking for the number of her son.

Batten hadn't received a precise answer to his question. 'Was the nice red-haired policeman ever in your flat, Rene?'

Rene's flat was on the same landing as the Carruthers', but across the way. He went out of the open door, noting Bob's slight shake of the head – no luck yet.

Even before he pushed the door of the Carruthers' flat open, he knew the place had been expertly searched. He pulled on a pair of plastic gloves, and ran his hands over the inside of the lock. A very professional job – just a light jemmy to the door, pop the lock, and pull it over when you leave, letting it jam slightly as it closes. It would take a hearty shove to open it again. He went in, noting the microscopic disturbance of everything. Oh yes, this place had been illegally searched, he could tell. The search had been recent, so maybe they hadn't got what they wanted from the solicitor's safe, after all. He went to the window and spent five minutes just watching the street below, checking that nobody was waiting for them out there. He would make a point of making sure that they all left together – safety in numbers. He would tell the uniform at Rene's flat to use her radio if there were any signs of trouble. The street was hot; from up here, he could almost see the heat shimmering in the air. It was too close, too warm. It had to break soon.

He went out into the hallway, where Bob was pacing, on his phone. He shook his head again – still no luck.

Batten got out his own phone, considering. He wasn't a cop, so he couldn't really make any decisions without consulting Anderson.

He went back into Rene's flat to get some privacy for his call. It might prove fatal to go and stand in the middle of the car park. In Rene's hallway, he knocked a John

Menzies carrier bag off the cluttered top of a bookcase. It slithered to the ground, taking copies of the free newspaper and *The People's Friend* with it. He bent down to pick it up, noting the bag contained a slim volume, A5 size. He closed his phone and looked closely. It was a journal, like the others, dated 1996. He opened it. A few pages had been hastily jammed in halfway through, older pages from another diary, from another time.

Had Thomas Carruthers had some presentiment of danger, torn out the pages and put them in this diary, then moved it to a safe place? With the batty sister-in-law, who everybody ignored? Or had the batty sister-in-law picked up the bag, as she picked up everything else that caught her fancy in her dementia?

Batten had a terrible image of Carruthers, near the window, being threatened, being asked to hand over the diary . . . and it not being there. It was a chilling thought. He *had* to get this back to Anderson.

Batten thought of himself as unflappable. But his heart was thumping as he decided not to take the lift, instead going out through the fire door and down the concrete stairwell, listening for any other footfall above or below him. There was nothing. He knew he did not look like a cop. Taking either of the two uniformed cops with him would just attract attention. His best camouflage would be plain sight.

He walked across the foyer, opened the door and looked out. His hired car was less than fifty yards away. He looked left and right, carefully scanning the garages and the area around the incident tape – all that was left to show Lambie had been this way. No cop was standing by to protect the scene. It looked quite deserted, absolutely clear. He tucked the diary in its plastic bag firmly under his arm, and got out the car keys, ready to press Open. The blue Focus was parked along here in a line of cars. It bleeped and flashed at him in greeting. Batten walked towards it smartly, not rushing, not drawing attention to himself, listening intently for any footsteps behind him or any movement between any of the cars.

A bus passed. A man with a collie was asking it to sit before setting off across the road. A carrier bag wedged against the paving stone rustled slightly in the gentle wind. Batten glanced at it as he walked towards the Focus. Only a few more steps to go. Then, in the wing mirror of the car in front, he saw a movement – someone closing in behind him – and his heart skipped a beat. In broad daylight? There would be a wee shove, a knife, nothing to see or hear.

But he was not a cop, he did not look like a cop, he must not act like a cop.

He could be anybody.

He kept walking past his car, towards the bus stop. He started whistling, not a care in the world.

3.40 p.m.

O'Hare liked skulls. He liked the way the bony plates fitted together, like an intricate jigsaw, so much more precise and exact than long bones that just articulated top and bottom. Flat bones – they either fitted or they didn't. And like a missing piece in a jigsaw, a pathologist might not know what he was looking for, but he knew what shape it was. And there was always a pattern to any damage.

Moffat and his friend were simple, their bodies shattered by the impact of a bullet at high speed and the accompanying pressure wave.

He was looking across at Alessandro Marchetti's skull now, on its stainless-steel platter. It was largely complete, as was the jaw – apart from a few baby teeth. He took a sip of his coffee, feeling his age, trying not to think about the bigger picture. He was unhappy – no, uncomfortable – with the case the team was working on. Anderson had nearly been killed . . . or had he? The first bullet would have sliced through Moffat's brain long before the sound could register, and the second man would have been dead before he heard it. Anderson had been tied to a tree, unable to move. The sniper could easily have taken him out with a clean shot.

But he hadn't.

And whoever put Costello down the shaft wanted her to find the remains of the boy. But they also wanted her to get out, so she could report what she had found.

O'Hare had no intention of taking the bodies of Graham Hunter and Jason Purcie from their final resting places, but Wyngate had tracked down Hunter's post mortem file and had got the photographs from a storage facility in Inverness. O'Hare himself had obtained the photographs of Purcie, shot on duty up on the Campsie Fells, within his present jurisdiction. Jason Purcie had been shot with a .303 bullet, probably from a Lee–Enfield rifle. There was a good selection of not-so-glossy black-and-white photographs, and the striations on the bullet were clear. He texted Matilda, who no doubt would have her eye glued to a microscope in the university building across the street.

How Hunter came to meet his fate on the hill was less clear. His body had not been found until four months after he was reported missing. O'Hare looked at the map, at where the body had been found, and the site of the higher bothy. O'Hare pondered Hunter's erratic behaviour. Had he stumbled and fallen earlier on the way up to the bothy, maybe hit his head? The resulting slow bleed in the brain might have made him act so irrationally. Would Carruthers have recorded that in his journal? But that was nobody's fault. If the diary was deemed so important, it must threaten to reveal something someone wanted hidden – something about the way Hunter died.

And O'Hare only had one conclusion to come to. Hunter had been murdered.

He put down his coffee and fiddled with the photographs of the remnants of Hunter's skull, looking for evidence of foul play. Weeks under water, depredations by wildlife, then an old-fashioned scrub by a mortuary assistant, had left the bone fragments clean, shiny and difficult to fit. He tried moving the pictures about, using different focal lengths, different positions, but achieved nothing.

He heard Matilda come in, and looked up to see her smiling at him quizzically.

'Why not come into my parlour?' she asked. 'And bring those pictures with you.'

3.45 p.m.

A few Bentleys had made it along the old road and up the drive without totally wrecking their suspension, and the noise of a helicopter overhead heralded the arrival of somebody else important. Anderson looked around in amazement. He'd never been at a gathering like this before. Lots of the male guests were in kilts, and the women were struggling in unsuitably high heels.

An eldritch wailing sounded from the terrace where a piper was tuning up to serenade the assembled guests, and a bodhrán player was carefully letting the skin of his drum stretch in the sun, adjusting to the warmth.

Batten had phoned, telling him in a low voice that he had the all-important diary for 1996. 'And the missing pages from 1977,' he added jubilantly.

Anderson's immediate response had been one of panic. 'Now you've got all that, you'll be a target. Say nothing to anyone,' he warned.

But Batten knew the danger he was in. 'I'm going back right now, on a crowded bus. I'll read it when I get there,' he answered, his voice quivering.

'OK, but let me know when you get there safely.'

'Good news?' asked Costello, as he finished the call.

'I think so. Mick has the missing diary.' He looked up at the blazing blue sky, shutting his eyes against the sun. 'I wish the weather would break. Then the case will break, and all will be well.'

'I'd stay off the champers, if I was you.'

'Who are we keeping an eye on?'

'The glorious Saskia over there. She and her dad are the reason we are here, we just need to pin it together. What we really need is some reason to allow us to search her room, and take a look at that memory stick.'

'Will we get a reason?'

'Oh, I'll get a reason all right!'

'Aren't you just a little worried that we're out here on our own? Aren't we being a wee bit foolhardy?' But Anderson's questions were almost playful. The weather was glorious, the champagne was cold, the salmon was fresh and he had his old sparring partner back. Just for that minute, Australia could take a running jump.

'We're not on our own. Howlett said he would send a few reinforcements. I'd say anybody not getting pissed on the Pimm's and champers is one of ours.' Costello frowned dourly at her orange juice. 'So, that'll be me, then,' she muttered.

Another helicopter flew over the head of the glen, making people look up. It flew down over the river then started to lose height, ready to land.

'Your friends are on the move,' Anderson said. The Three Graces, all looking rather wonderful, were strolling arm in arm down towards the helipad.

'They're going to get their Louboutins dirty. It'll take more than a few days' worth of sunshine to dry out the bottom of that mire,' Costello said, with a sour hint of Schadenfreude.

'Has anybody tracked down Drew?'

'Not yet. Jim Pettigrew's been keeping an eye out for him all day.'

'He's obviously not well. Why can't the bloody school get a specialist to look at him?'

'Rhona says it's complicated. Schools are worse than us for bureaucracy. Seems the Warden can't take action without informing the parents. In this case, his parents don't want to believe there's anything wrong. Meanwhile,

Drew's slowly going off his head. The school can't just chuck him out; he has to be collected,' said Costello, stealing a chocolate strawberry from a passing waitress.

'I don't think "slowly going off his head" quite describes it. He's obviously very sick.'

'Well, we can't touch him. I think Pettigrew is waiting until he does something wrong before we can intervene.'

'Do you think that's why Howlett sent you here initially?'

'No. That was Rhona's misinterpretation. We're here to look at Saskia and to see her father. End of term's the only time her dad would be here, good time to catch him. I choose my words carefully.'

Anderson rolled his eyes. 'So, apart from champagne and strawberries, do we have a game plan?'

'Well, I don't think Drew was one of the people who grabbed me last night. But he's out there on his own, planning something. Who knows?'

'Oh well, we're in for a good night, then.' Anderson cast his eyes around, looking for the extra security Howlett had promised.

He couldn't see any.

3.50 p.m.

'Now what we do is scan in the pictures of the bone fragments one by one, and press some buttons,' said Matilda. 'Good of them to be all together like this, after being in the water for so long.'

'If someone smashed your skull with a blunt instrument,

Matilda, the *galea aponeurotica*, the tissues of your scalp, would hold the fragments together – apart from at the site of impact, where there would be a depression. And that depression would have a precise and recognizable pattern. They might not have been too hot on that in 1977.'

O'Hare looked around him, feeling a bit like a dinosaur. He had to admit, he was impressed by the set-up, and by the standard of contamination control, if nothing else. He and Matilda were both gowned, while more caps and gloves hung on hooks on the wall. And he could see a second row of hooks through the glass panel of the airlocked door. He wondered what was through there. One of the best DNA labs in the world, he guessed. The microscopic traces of Alessandro's DNA would be in there, being 'bred' and duplicated until there was enough to get a profile.

'And then we play at jigsaws.' Matilda was using a mouse to move each skull fragment to the centre of the screen. A curtain of pixels fell and then rose. The bones were outlined in bright blue now. She went through them all – sphenoid, parietal, occipital, frontal, then the smaller fragments. 'So, we now have a 3D image of each. And look what else we can do.' She clicked on each piece, picking it up and dropping it into position on a skull facing to the left. Then she highlighted it and turned the image round.

'Now we just slot in the right parietal,' she said to herself. 'Or what's left of it.'

'Forced trauma, weighted, slightly pointed,' said O'Hare. 'Definitely not self-inflicted. Hunter was hit with something.'

'Or impaled on it as he fell.' Matilda shrugged. 'But now I'm going to show you the really big trick.'

Another few buttons, another few clicks, and the right parietal filled the whole screen, the broken edges of the bones jagged, like the outline of a blue glacier. The pixel curtain worked its way down again. Another few taps, and an image appeared.

'The computer is giving you its best guess at what shape made that injury – something long, slim, pointed. The white band at the top is definite, the yellow band is predictive. Ring any bells? Recognize it?'

O'Hare peered more closely, recognizing a shape he had seen many times. 'I think I do. Google a few ice axes for me, then let's see what your wee machine will do.'

4.45 p.m.

Mulholland parked the Audi and went into the Blind Pig. He ordered a Coke and took it to the window seat, where huge open panels let in the fresh air. He could have done with a double vodka. But if he was caught driving with that inside him, not getting his stripes back would be the least of his problems.

He sat and thought about Lynda Osbourne, and the conversation he'd just had with her father. He could see where the problems lay. Adult rape victims found it hard to give the police enough to build a case. But a tearful child – with a father determined that someone should be nailed for what he'd done, and a cop with a paedophile in his sights – was going to say what she thought they wanted to hear. Lynda's dad had handed Mulholland a photocopy, a little girl's drawing of a wee stick figure in a dress, and a huge dark figure looming over it. The drawing was shockingly graphic. Mulholland shut his eyes. If that was what had happened, would she even have wanted to remember clearly?

As their conversation went on, Osbourne had sounded less certain. He was nervous that Fairbairn had got out, but also seemed less sure of himself. Eventually, the reason emerged. 'Lynda saw an old photo in the paper a week or so ago. The man who died in the fire at the old Apollo – she said it was the man who molested her.'

Billy Biggart. Who had been at the fair. Who had been a 'big man'. Who was now dead.

And Fairbairn had now disappeared.

Mulholland tried not to think of Osbourne's parting words. 'DCI McAlpine and me, we did the right thing. Justice is justice. Does it matter who it's for?'

They'd stitched up Skelpie Fairbairn.

And Anderson had been complicit. He had broken the law, betrayed his duty as a police officer to collect corroborated evidence and report it, not to pick and choose whatever was needed to make a case. Mulholland downed his drink. He would betray his own duty as a police officer if he picked and chose who to report for breaking the law.

And Anderson had.

The icing on the cake was that this would get him his promotion back.

6.00 p.m.

Batten sneaked into the bottom end of the lecture room and pulled out a seat. He had the diary, covered with a copy of the *Sun*, and he had a bottle of Coke and a sausage roll. This was going to take a long time. When he returned, he had started with the pages torn from the now-missing 1977 diary, and had lost himself in the story.

The five men had gone out on Thursday the 6th of January, allowing two days to get up to the hill and two days to walk back out again. There was a lot of predictable stuff in the first few pages: they had been heading up to somewhere Batten couldn't pronounce, and the weather was bad and was going to get worse. Carruthers was the voice of caution, constantly doubting if they should be going at all. The narrative implied Moffat was keen to press on, insisting there would be nothing they couldn't cope with.

He flicked over a few pages of anecdotes about meals eaten and distances covered. On Friday the 7th Carruthers was writing light-heartedly about Purcie trying to light the Primus stove, and there was a slight undertone of Moffat needling Hunter. Then there was a gap of a few lines, and the handwriting changed, the tone changed: *Don't really know what to write. Don't really know what happened. Hunter has gone missing. He just upped and offed. It's five a.m. and none of us are asleep, we are listening to the wind, knowing that he's out there.*

Batten turned back to the earlier part of the day before: *Moffat's winding up Hunter.* He read the early pages again with more care, making notes and calculations as he went. The weather was bad, Moffat was the one who was keen to go higher – closer to the stack Hunter had fallen from. During the hike MacFadyean was striding out, Purcie and Hunter together at the back. Batten noticed the pattern in the writing: Moffat alone, MacFadyean and

Carruthers as a pair, Hunter and Purcie as a pair. Carruthers noticed more than once than Purcie and Hunter were close: *Made their beds next to each other. I'd never noticed the relationship before.*

Batten read on, wondering about the relationship between the two young men. Homosexuality wasn't illegal in 1977, but what would it have meant for two cops in Glasgow back then? If they were a couple, the bond between the two men was very close. Purcie would not have walked off that hill reflecting on the loss of a colleague, but in mourning for a lover.

He flicked forward to the morning of the 8th, where Carruthers was trying to make sense of what he had witnessed the night before. There were no notes at all around the time that Hunter left. Purcie was crying, Moffat was nervous, but MacFadyean was quiet: *Lying on his sleeping bag, watching the flames and occasionally tending the fire.*

Batten read the next bit carefully. Carruthers' memory was dulled by drink and fatigue but he had put all his thoughts down in words, as if trying to make sense of it himself. Hunter left the bothy in the middle of the night: *Het up and angry. Purcie followed him.* Carruthers recalled hearing raised voices, distorted in the wind. Carruthers had joined them, struggled with them and ended up waking up back in the bothy with a bloody face: *The next thing I remember, Moffat was wiping blood off my anorak with water from the flask. I had sore knuckles and a sore face, and all I wanted to do was sleep. Purcie was lying in the corner of the bothy with blood pouring from his nose. God, I'm tired.*

Hunter never came back off the hill.

And Tommy Carruthers had not touched a drop since

that night. Batten didn't need his PhD to work that one out.

Purcie had only survived till September 1977, killed by a single shot out on a night search. Batten thought that if Purcie had been asking questions about the death of his lover, then his own death was very convenient for somebody. He rooted around in the evidence boxes that had been brought over from Mary's flat, searching for the diary for 1978. Carruthers might have reflected on Purcie's death in 1977 at the start of another year. He did – but not until mid-January, when he started complaining about nightmares and lack of sleep. Batten, reading between the lines, thought about post-traumatic stress, and wondered what Carruthers' subconscious might have been trying to tell him. He wrote about how the 'army boys', Faddy and Moffat, had reassured him that Purcie had not suffered: *It was a clean shot – and Faddy would know, being the expert.*

Batten marked the line with a Post-it note.

But Carruthers appeared to reflect no further on why his colleague had been shot on duty. He just accepted it: *Good mates. Sad to think there's only three of us left.*

6.15 p.m.

'Oh, look. Here they come.'

Saskia's father was a tall, solidly built man who looked like someone you wouldn't want to mess with. When they climbed up to the garden, she was almost hanging round his neck. To Costello's eyes, it was an over-the-top display – more like a rich older lover and his trophy girlfriend

409

than father and daughter. But how would she know how fathers and daughters behaved? She turned away.

Three times Anderson had asked her what she was expecting to happen. But her eyes mostly were on Pettigrew, who was walking round the opposite perimeter of the garden, gauging the lie of the land.

She caught sight of Libby, who was dressed in a long black skirt, white make-up slathered on her pudgy face, huge black rings round her eyes. Rhona was talking to her, obviously telling her to get off the wall and 'join in' with things, but Libby was resolute. She wasn't for joining in.

'She is one scary girl,' Anderson said.

'Misunderstood,' corrected Costello. 'She makes a damn sight more sense than those three over there.'

'I think that's your own prejudice talking.'

'Of course it is. But it's my prejudice – and I reserve the right to abuse people, if I feel like it.' She eyed up the buffet, watching the flamingo-like ladies peck at the table. 'How's Helena?' she asked carelessly.

Anderson opened his mouth, but said nothing.

'Oh dear. There was a big pause there. There's normally a little pause, then you say, "Oh, she's OK." But that was the daddy of all pauses.'

Anderson still said nothing. And Costello, for once, thought it best that she also said nothing.

6.20 p.m.

'You busy?' asked Mulholland, slipping into the seat next to Batten. The lecture room was deserted again.

'Yes.' Batten leaned back to look at the younger man, seeing the burning light of ambition in his eyes. He could remember feeling like that. Once. Long ago. 'Been reading these diaries. It's shocking, what they did. Shocking on a humane level. But just as shocking on a psychological level was the power Moffat seems to have exerted over Carruthers. And I think he was still exerting it, all these years later. Moffat was definitely in for the long game.'

'Carruthers and MacFadyean,' said Mulholland, picking at the fringe of Post-it notes sticking out of the pages, ignoring Batten's raised eyebrows. He opened the journal and began to read Batten's chosen highlights. 'So, there were still three of them left by the time Alessandro was taken, nearly twenty years later. And you only have Carruthers' word for what happened – or for what he thought happened – up on the hill, don't you? Interesting to see if it matches the forensic evidence. Interesting to find out what really happened. What does the subtext tell you? Who was the psychopath? I'd have thought you'd have it all worked out by now.'

Batten ignored the taunts. 'Moffat was a blowhard army bully. MacFadyean was an inconspicuous, manipulating little shite. I think he was already manipulating Moffat, but Moffat had no idea. I can see exactly how this little group worked. The diary is all Moffat this and Moffat that. Faddy hardly features – he keeps well below the radar. The 1996 diary makes very interesting reading. No wonder Carruthers kept it hidden all these years.'

'Then he suddenly tells Moffat that he recorded it all for posterity? I don't think so,' said Mulholland scornfully.

'But I bet Simone Sangster mentioned it. And remember,

Carruthers didn't realize at the time what he was actually witness to, or complicit in. Look here, Carruthers says Moffat told him his son had been threatened. So, he had to see that various cars were at various places at the right time – or else. I don't think that was true. I think Moffat was lying. But I also think MacFadyean had dripped the idea into Moffat's mind, subtly enough to let him think the story was his idea all along. All Moffat actually asked Carruthers to do was drive a car, on the evening of the 8th of October, to the north end of the Erskine Bridge and wait. The next day he writes: "What was all that about? Waited for two hours, nothing happened, so drove home."'

'Decoy,' said Mulholland immediately.

'Hogmanay is the first time he mentions Glen Fruin, as he ruminates on the year. And I think he might have gone back and had a look at it just recently, after Simone Sangster's visit, in light of her questions. For the first time, Carruthers might have been able to see the bigger picture.'

'I could find out if he owned a white Volvo at that time,' offered Mulholland.

'He certainly refers to it as "the Volvo".' Batten tapped his fingers on the diary.

'But later, when he realized that was the night the boy was taken, surely he would have come forward? He was a cop, after all.'

'Yes, but a cop who never made it past constable. He was a cautious man, a good man, Carruthers. Good men have the habit of seeing the best in others. I bet he thought of Moffat as a good mate until Moffat turfed him out the window. Think of the magnitude of the can of worms he'd be opening if he said anything. As it was, he could just tell himself he had done nothing wrong, but had helped to save Moffat's son from some unspecified grisly fate. Somebody else's son suffered the grisly fate instead. Look, Vik, say Colin Anderson asked you a similar favour, for the sake of young Peter? You'd do it.'

'Would I hell!'

'Oh, I think you would. But then imagine Costello telling you that you shouldn't. You'd argue with her, and end up talking yourself into it, just as she intended all along. Which I'd bet is how MacFadyean manipulated Moffat and Carruthers into doing what he wanted. A very clever man.'

'So, you're saying MacFadyean was really in charge, not Moffat? That Wullie manipulated Moffat and Carruthers into kidnap and murder?' Mulholland frowned disbelievingly.

'Not directly. I'd bet he worked gradually on Moffat, manipulated him into doing it by suggesting it would break the Glasgow families. We're talking about 1996, remember. The Russians were moving in. Moffat would want to be their main man, the big cop. And it would suit Wullie to let him think he was. Carruthers, the more moral man, was merely used as a decoy. Who knows what else Wullie had planned? Carruthers knew nothing. And bear in mind that he had reason to be grateful to Moffat, who looked after his men after the incident on the hill. And after twenty years that gratitude would have simmered down into firm friendship. A cautious man, a moral man – there was quite a hold over him. Look at the length of time it lasted.'

'But why would a guy like Moffat be scared of Carruthers, after so many years?'

'Scared of the diary, more like. And having killed Carruthers and been unable to find the incriminating diary in the time he had, I think he sent our Soviet friends Pinky and Perky after it – and after anybody who might have read it.'

'You mean, they killed David Lambie for nothing? What was the point, once Moffat was dead?'

'Pinky didn't know Moffat and Perky had been shot, did he? There was a media blackout.' Batten leaned back and put his feet up on the table. 'Killing the captain doesn't mean the army won't fight on.' He picked up the picture of Alessandro. 'He's a tribute to the success of game theory, the poor kid. He was a sacrifice. He was killed to start a war.'

8.00 p.m.

By eight in the evening the change in the air was perceptible. It was still cloyingly hot, but clouds were gathering in the far distance, the birds had fallen silent, and the midges were moving up from the river. It was going to start pouring before the end of the evening, and it didn't look as though the heat was going to let up first. People began to wander indoors.

Costello was standing on her own, scanning the crowd from the balustrade, voraciously munching tiny salad sandwiches. She was looking along the treeline, looking as deep into the forest as she could. Drew was out there somewhere, and she was getting worried about him – at the end of the day, he was just a troubled kid. Every so often she would catch Pettigrew's eye, and a sideways shake of the head indicated he hadn't seen the boy either.

Every time she saw Rhona, she was biting Libby's ears about something. Costello had tried to have a word with the girl, just a casual hello in passing, but all she got was a look that suggested Costello had gone over to the dark side and was no longer to be trusted. Costello could understand that. Libby was out of her depth here, and she was doing exactly what Costello would do – retreat to the sidelines and think catty thoughts about people.

Costello didn't know what Anderson was thinking, and she normally did. Lambie's passing, and the manner of it, had remained largely undiscussed. There was a tacit agreement that to talk about it would mean taking their eyes off the ball. There would be time for that later, in the pub, once this case had been closed and the man known as the Puppeteer was caught.

She looked around again with her binoculars, as though she was checking out some security. She found Saskia, her sunglasses now pushed up on to her white headband. Her dad was talking to the man who had got out of the helicopter with him. They were looking, not back at the school or up to the hills – to which everybody's eyes were drawn when not looking up at the encroaching clouds – but up at the forest, as if searching for a way in.

Something prickled at the back of Costello's neck. Saskia laughed, throwing her head back, and said something to her father, who was dismissive in his answer. He smacked at his own arm, smacked it again, then rolled up the sleeve of his shirt to examine the damage. The midges were getting to him. Costello smiled, enjoying the Russian's discomfort. She had smeared her wrists and neck with citronella to keep the critters at bay, and she'd bet Libby had disappeared somewhere to have a sneaky fag for the same purpose.

Morosov peered closely at his forearm, as if it might be bleeding. Costello looked through her binoculars as he pulled the cuff up further. Three black lines came into view, then one red, and another . . . another . . . another . . . Costello took a step back, and lowered the binoculars.

For an instant, she felt her heart stop. Then she took a deep breath and regained control. 'By their deeds, ye shall know them,' she muttered. She tried to turn up the resolution on the binoculars but lost focus instead. By the time she had the correct adjustment, Morosov had gone.

She looked around to find Anderson, only to see him walking hurriedly away up to the higher ground to take a phone call. She almost went after him. Then she looked over at Pettigrew, but he was already looking enquiringly at her, alerted by the way she had moved. She tilted her head towards the Russian. Pettigrew shrugged, and set off down the garden. She started down the steps, the word 'puppeteer' going round and round in her head. She tried not to draw attention to herself as she zig-zagged over to Pettigrew.

Morosov and his associate were deep in conversation, striding purposefully towards the edge of the trees.

Pettigrew was moving off in pursuit. Out of the corner of his mouth he asked, 'What's eating you, apart from the midges?'

Almost running to keep up with him, she said breathlessly, 'Morosov. He has loads of those tattoos, the Russian ones.'

'Assorted bird life?' Pettigrew pulled back some low

branches as they went into the wood. 'Of course he would; he's a Russian, from Ekaterinberg.'

'But so many? Black crows, red eagles – the full set?' panted Costello, indicating the size of them on her own arm even though Pettigrew had his back to her.

Pettigrew stopped against a tree. 'Houston, we have a problem,' he said, and his fingers crept down to his waistband. 'He and his mate came through here, looking like they knew where they were going – which they shouldn't, if they're who they say they are. OK, army rules from here on in. I'm in charge, DS Costello. You speak only when spoken to, you do as you are told, you stay close to me, you do not argue and you don't get fucking kidnapped.' All the time his eyes were focused deep in the trees. 'Where did Anderson go?'

'He's away . . . phoning somebody.' Costello paused, suspecting it was Helena he was phoning.

'They're over there, moving away from us at speed. Two o'clock.'

'How do you know?' asked Costello, who could hear nothing but the noise of the garden party behind them, and see nothing but the shadows of the trees.

'What did I say about not talking?' As he went ahead of her, she couldn't help but notice the precise cut of his jacket, which looked smart without being close-fitting. She knew he had a gun.

They moved through the trees, crossing a path every now and again. Occasionally she caught the chit-chat of voices ahead, and Pettigrew would slow, put one finger up, stopping her, then they would move off again. He signalled, tapping his eye, holding up two fingers. But all

Costello wanted to know was where they were going, and who he thought the Russians were going to meet.

Suddenly, he stopped and signalled to her to be quiet. The Russians seemed to be discussing something, and one of them was not happy. Moving slowly, almost imperceptibly, Pettigrew pulled himself back into the trees, his hand on his right hip. The Russians continued to argue for a minute, then took off again almost at a run along a gap in the trees, before cutting sideways off the path. Pettigrew waited until they were well out of sight and walked up to where they had disappeared down a narrow disused path that seemed to go deep into the forest.

'This is recent.' He pointed at the broken end of a twig. 'And these have been broken, these ones bent, over the last few days.' He spoke in a low voice, avoiding the harsh sibilants of a whisper. 'Somebody has been coming along here a lot recently.'

'Who?'

'Did I tell you you could speak?'

8.30 p.m.

Anderson felt a tap on the shoulder. It was Howlett, looking more shrunken than ever inside a good linen suit he obviously hadn't worn since he became ill.

The ACC gazed over the assembled company, then up at the sky, as if willing it to rain. 'I was just wondering where DS Costello had got to.'

'She was here a minute ago.' Anderson looked around. 'But I don't see her, and I don't see Pettigrew, so I presume they're together somewhere. Why are you here, if you don't mind me asking?'

Howlett almost growled. 'I want to look that bastard in the eye. That's all. One look and I'll know if it's him.'

'I'm not sure if I want it to be Morosóv or not.' Anderson glanced at his phone. 'But I'd be a lot happier if there was a decent phone signal here.'

'Grand place, isn't it? A bit run-down now, but still a fine building.' He glanced down at the phone in the palm of his hand, with a subtle movement. 'Have you been down to the river at all, Colin?'

'Are you joking? Not with these midges!'

But there was more than the spoken question there. 'It would be nice to go for a walk, though, don't you think?' There was more than a mere suggestion of a stroll.

'I think the weather's going to break,' Anderson observed.

'And I think you're right. But there are much worse things in this world than getting wet.' Yet Howlett didn't seem keen to move. He was looking at the sky, watching the rain clouds roll over the hills from the north. It was going to get nasty.

The crowd was mostly indoors or under the cover of the gazebos which had been erected. But guests were still chatting, and the champagne was still flowing.

'We'll go for that walk in a little while,' said Howlett. 'Humour me, I am not a well man.'

'I kind of gathered that.' There was no point in polite denials.

'I'm about to retire soon,' the ACC sighed. 'I don't know which I shall retire from first – life or the job – but

I will soon be elsewhere.' He looked down at his phone again.

Anderson noticed a slight nod; something had pleased him.

'I thought I'd better leave a mark, achieve something before I go.'

8.40 p.m.

The air was heavy, like warm water. Costello was covered in sweat, and dead midges were stuck to her skin. They had been walking for thirty minutes, making slow progress through dense trees, and her face was smarting where twigs had scratched her.

And she was nervous.

Pettigrew had changed. He was wary, almost apprehensive. He had no idea where they were, she thought – the path seemed to go in circles. They were moving forward silently now, their feet making no sound on the carpet of pine needles. She really wanted to know where she was; she wanted to know a lot of things. She knew they must be skirting round the far edge of the Forestry Commission land, and she tried to visualize the map, trying to judge how far they had actually come. The old forest must start again soon.

Pettigrew stopped, checking more broken ends of twigs at shoulder height, and the pine needles that had been freshly disturbed. Then they moved on, tracking the way the Russians had gone, into the old forest. The cover was less dense here but it was shadowy, so she couldn't see where she was putting her feet. Twice she stumbled, and Pettigrew signalled to her to be quiet. Ten minutes into the old forest, she was starting to be scared – scared of the thought of the Russian mafia up ahead, and of the idea that whoever had covered her with a blanket and bundled her down a hole was still out there, was watching her now.

But if she looked around, all she could see were the ever-present crows.

Pettigrew stopped behind a big elm tree, and she pulled herself in behind him. He poked his head out cautiously for a few seconds, then indicated that she too should look but say nothing.

She wiped the sweat from her eyes and looked, letting her vision adjust to the twilight. Down the slope a little grey fairy-tale cottage lay in a bowl-shaped hollow, totally encircled by trees. She could see no road in or out, and certainly the track that they had just come along was not in long-term use.

There was the noise of birds screeching. A door slammed, then Morosov and the other man came running out of the house, and hurried away through the trees at the far side.

Pettigrew swore. 'They're heading up to the high road.' He looked up along the line of the hills, trying to get his bearings. 'I confess I'm a bit lost. Should have brought a compass.'

'How can you be lost?' Costello argued.

'Happens to the best of us.'

Now Costello was convinced he was lying. He really knew exactly where he was – he was just unsure about what to do next.

Then Pettigrew pulled out a small gun. 'Just insurance. Three safety catches, all of them on.'

She nodded, and followed him down the slope towards the cottage, noticing that the darkness was nothing to do with the time of night.

There were black clouds rolling in.

9.00 p.m.

Ella looked out of the window, listening to the thunder crash above the garden of the nursing home, waiting for the lightning. 'So, how's the old bugger tonight?'

'Grumpy as ever.' Agnes walked over to the window to join her, a mug of Horlicks clasped in her hands. 'He had a visitor today. I'm not sure it cheered him up at all.'

'Who was it? Do you know?'

'No idea. A Mr Pettigrew he called himself. Not a relation, probably a lawyer. Though he didn't look like a lawyer. He was a fit wee man, whistled a lot. Might be an old gangster pal of his.' Ella sat down and turned over a couple of pages of the *Daily Record*. 'As long as the auld bugger doesn't take a contract out on us. He's enough of an evil-tempered old scrote to do that.' She continued scanning the paper, taking crisps from a packet one by one and using her fingers like tweezers. 'Phew – you just can't get your breath in this heat, can you?'

Agnes sipped her Horlicks. 'It'll break soon, then it'll be peeing down. And then you'll be moaning.' The night sky was grey and louring, and there was thunder in the air – she could sense it. She heard a distant roll, far away.

She walked out of the staff room, taking her Horlicks with her, and went along to the reception area. On the patio, outside the French windows, she stood and looked to the north of the city. Something that may or may not have been a flash was there and gone before she could register it. More thunder came growling across the sky. The storm was moving this way. She closed her eyes and felt the first kiss of rain on her face, then bigger drops coming down – spit, spit, spit. The weather had broken, at last! Lightning flashed, electrifying the whole garden in a blaze of silver, and she counted. Then another grumble, rolling down from the hills above Loch Lomond, clapped deafeningly, and the heavens opened with a vengeance.

'My God,' she said out loud. 'Just listen to that!'

'That,' said a voice behind her, growling along with the thunder, 'is the sound of the end of days.'

9.20 p.m.

As the door swung open, Costello recognized the smell. She had encountered it often enough. Somewhere in here was a body, a dead body in a state of rank decomposition.

Suddenly a squawking black demon shot out of the dark, and she yelped and ducked. Then she straightened up, her heart hammering, to see the crow glide into the trees. Was it her imagination, or was – *something* – dangling from its beak? She stood in the doorway, her face turned to the open air, and took a few deep breaths, waiting for the panic to die down. Whatever she would find in there, it was going to be bad.

In the dim front room, she could see a bed, with something covered with a sheet.

Pettigrew was still outside, checking round the back. Costello let her eyes adjust to the gloom, and saw a small computer desk on wheels, a laptop with an extension cable, and several stacks of boxes. Carefully, she flipped a lid open with the point of a pen; the box was full of computer disks, new, unused. Another box with a commercial printer's label was full of cards.

She turned back towards the bed, holding her breath, feeling for the sheet, and pulled gently. A cloud of flies swarmed up out of the dark into her face, and she screamed.

Pettigrew slammed in through the door, gun in hand. 'What the fuck . . . ?'

Hands clamped over her mouth, unable to breathe or speak, Costello nodded at the bed. Lying on it was the huge mass of a dead woman, crawling with maggots. The bed was stained with faeces, and the stench in the small room was unbearable. For a long moment, all Costello could hear over her own pounding heart was the flies dashing themselves frantically against the closed windows.

Pettigrew put his gun away, and pulled at her elbow. 'Out,' he said. 'You need to breathe.'

But she shook her head mutely. She risked moving one hand from her mouth and nose to reach over to a pile of red envelopes shaped like pillar boxes. She held one up for Pettigrew to see. It was a sleeve for a DVD, addressed to PillarBoxFlix.

Pettigrew just said, 'Oh, right.' He sounded almost relieved. But he didn't seem surprised. 'You, out,' he said again.

Costello hovered in the doorway, within reach of some fresher air, and watched as Pettigrew switched on the laptop, slightly shifting the trolley it stood on, and looked at the neat cables to see if they would stretch to the bed.

'What are you doing?' she asked.

'My job,' he said, tapping away at the keys.

Intrigued, Costello put a handkerchief over her mouth and came closer to look over his shoulder. The screen was a mass of unintelligible words. 'What is it?'

Pettigrew was following the text with a fingertip. 'It's in code. But I bet it's the plan to take out Richie Spence.'

Her stomach lurched. She was going to be sick. 'How do you know that?' she forced herself to ask.

'It's dated the 26th, two days before he was taken.'

It wasn't only the smell and the shock that was making Costello feel ill. Pettigrew had no way of knowing when Richie had been taken. She muttered an excuse and bolted out into the cool, refreshing rain. And then was violently sick. Once she straightened up, she realized Pettigrew had followed her out.

'I'd better go back to the school.'

'I don't think so.' And then he pointed the gun at her.

9.30 p.m.

Anderson was beginning to wonder where Costello and Pettigrew had got to. He knew that Howlett was taking him somewhere, but had no idea where. And there was no sign of the backup the ACC had supposedly organized for them. As they trekked through the Forestry

425

Commission planting, the strangely warm refreshing rain began to bucket down. Big drops came pattering like tears through the pine needles, and the little sky that could be seen was rapidly darkening.

'What's that?' Anderson asked, halting. Through the trees he could hear a strange high-pitched mewling, the sound of a human being in distress. Disturbingly, it reminded him of the sound Rusalka had made as he held her on the ladder. He had no idea where the noise was coming from, but it didn't seem to be close by.

'We'll walk on a bit,' was all Howlett said.

But Anderson was reluctant to move. 'I think that noise is coming from over there, so we need to go through here.'

'Humour me. We have better things to do.' Howlett stepped aside as if exhausted, letting Anderson move ahead of him into a clearing, where a group of people were waiting for them.

'Hello, DCI Anderson,' Cameron Fairbairn said, grinning like a jackal. 'Nice to meet you again. I don't know your colleague, but I'm sure we'll become acquainted. Briefly,' he added. He looked at his watch, twisting the gun he was holding slightly. 'You came the quick way through the trees – unlike your friend here, who went the long way round.'

He flicked the gun casually to the side where Costello was standing rooted to the spot, pale and terrified, blood streaks across her face. Pettigrew stood behind her, preventing her from retreating. On a pile of logs, casually smoking, sat the fat girl from the school. Her heavy mascara had run in the rain and was drizzling down her cheeks. She wiped at it impatiently.

Anderson noticed too late that Howlett, his soaked linen suit clinging to every bone, had moved in behind him. He and Costello were trapped, totally. The ground was rusty with fallen pine needles, the smell of it warm and earthy in the long-awaited rain. The sky rumbled and for a moment the scene lit up, making Libby Hamilton look like a Hammer Horror zombie. And all the while that ghostly keening emanated from somewhere. But where?

As water poured down the drought-baked ground, a small stream was forming, determinedly making its way to a huge grated drain cover in the centre of the clearing. Anderson shivered, despite the warmth of the evening air, his ears straining to track the sound. At some distance, deep in the bowels of the earth, it sounded as if somebody was screaming.

No one spoke. No one had moved. Apart from the smoke streaming from Libby's scarlet mouth, it could have been a tableau from a cinema still. Anderson sized up Fairbairn. Despite the new haircut, he decided, Skelpie was still an evil, nasty little man.

It was Libby who broke the silence. 'You should ask them to stand with their hands out from their sides, Tito. That way they can't pull a knife or a gun, or phone for help,' she advised, as if talking to a slightly backward child. She rose slightly, pulling her skirt straight before sitting down again, like an efficient secretary. 'The thing is, Tito, they don't really respect you.' The *they* was punctuated by a flick of the cigarette in Anderson's direction.

'Don't call me that!'

'Sorry – *Cameron*. All I meant was that I don't really

think they have the measure of you, of how good you are at what you do.' She lit up another cigarette, holding it in an elegantly gloved hand like a femme fatale in a black-and-white movie. 'Actually, I take that back; DCI Anderson had to fit you up to get you behind bars four years ago, so maybe he does know how good you are.'

Fairbairn said, 'Well, you did that once, DCI Anderson, but you'll never do it to me again. You see, Archie O'Donnell and I were in the same unit for a while, and he told me what was going to happen to Biggart. He said if I behaved myself, I would get out – maybe take over his empire. And here I am.'

Anderson shot a look of disbelief at Costello, but having a gun levelled at his stomach indicated that sarcasm was not the best response.

Costello glanced at Libby, who just shrugged – as if to say, 'Well, you heard him.'

Anderson was too busy trying to quell the panic that roiled inside him. He thought of Lambie. Of Moffat. It was too much to hope that someone would come along a second time and blow Skelpie Fairbairn's head off.

'He doesn't believe me,' Skelpie sneered, still with that weird grin.

'Told you they wouldn't,' said Libby, backhanding rain from her forehead. 'They think you're just a noncy wee child molester, but really you're a clever bastard. Look at the way you nearly killed that wee Russian lassie.'

Costello stared at Libby, confused. This was not the girl she thought she knew. She was in charge. She was taunting Skelpie Fairbairn.

But Skelpie took it as a compliment. 'I could have killed

her any time, you know. I was *that* close,' he boasted, and held up his gun inches from his other finger. 'That close. I decided if she lived or died.'

'And that makes you a big man, does it?' asked Costello, her voice dull with mock tedium.

'Not now, Costello,' Anderson warned her out of the corner of his mouth.

'And don't forget the wee Marchetti boy; you killed him too,' added Libby. 'You got away with that one. Well done.' Her voice was warm with congratulation.

'Aye, I did.' The gun waved back towards Anderson's stomach. 'But do you know the good thing, the really good thing? It's not the killing.'

'No?' asked Anderson, soothingly. 'So, tell me what is. I really don't understand any of this.'

Costello recognized that Anderson, standing there soaking wet in the pissing rain, with a thunderstorm raging overhead and a gun at his stomach, was following procedure. Be nice, empathize, engage at all times, then smack the bastard on the back of the head once his guard was down. Trouble was, it tended not to work with psychopaths. Especially when you were outnumbered by more psychopaths.

'It's the power,' Skelpie gloated. 'The power to let live or let die. And I still have the pleasure of the kill to come. What I like is the feeling that I can. At any time.' He walked up to Anderson then to Costello.

Costello sensed Pettigrew move slightly behind her, blocking any possible escape route. Fairbairn raised the gun, placed it against her cheekbone, and slowly moved it back and forth. She could feel the mesh in the bone tingle under the cold metal. She could see spits of saliva in the corner of his mouth, small red veins running across the whites of his eyes. He could blow her head off with one squeeze of his forefinger.

'The big deal, you see, is the power. It's my choice whether you live or die, DS Costello. My decision. And it's my decision who I shoot first. And where.'

'Well, if you can chain up a child down a drain, and rape a ten-year-old girl, putting a bullet through the head of a stupid cop should be easy.' Libby sniffed and stubbed out her cigarette as if bored. 'Did she cry for her mother, the Russian girl? Did it make it easier or harder, the wee lassie crying like that?'

The muzzle of the gun pushed into the flesh under Costello's jaw. 'I like it when they cry,' Fairbairn grinned. 'She might have lasted another week, but there were other plans for her.' The gun pushed in a little harder. 'The next one I was going to kill myself. And earn my new tattoo.'

'So, I guess killing two cops is easy-peasy lemon squeezy,' said Libby, a challenge in her voice rather than a question.

'Oh, it'll be easy.'

'Well, take your time,' said Libby conversationally. 'And after those two, who have you got lined up?'

'Lynda Osbourne. Lying little cow.' Skelpie swung round to jam the gun into Anderson's stomach. 'And then there's this girl,' he said nastily. 'I think she's called Claire.'

Costello was sure she heard Anderson stop breathing.

'He's not joking,' said Libby.

'I didn't say he was,' answered Anderson, his voice trembling, recalling Helena asking how long he thought it

430

would take Fairbairn to figure out that the girl who came to the gallery was his daughter.

'Show him your phone,' said Libby. 'You may as well – they can't run away and tell anybody.'

Fairbairn opened his phone with one hand, tapped a few times on the touch pad and turned it to show Anderson.

Even from a few feet away Anderson could tell it was a covert picture of Claire. She was standing outside the gallery, the sun shining off her dark hair.

There was silence, just the steady patter of rain on the carpet of pine needles.

Costello watched Libby get to her feet and fling the cigarette butt down before walking over to Fairbairn and taking the gun off him, like a mother removing a dangerous toy from a child. For a moment, she stood in front of him, the gun levelled at Anderson. Costello held her breath . . . and then slowly, very slowly, the penny dropped. This young woman, with anger behind her eyes, was intelligent and determined. This young woman with her dark hair wet against her face, her prominent cheekbones, was the same face she had held in her hands in that car park all those years ago. Then Libby smiled and the moment was gone.

'There you are, DCI Anderson; you have your confession.'

'What the fuck?' bellowed Fairbairn.

'Don't make so much noise, you horrible little shite, you're disturbing the crows.' Libby spun the gun, and Anderson instinctively took a step backwards.

Then he realized she was handing it to him. He took it automatically, and it fell heavily into his hand. 'You didn't think I'd let a thick bastard like that loose with a gun, did you?' she said, her voice heavy with irony. 'I've taken the safety off now, DCI Anderson; you can shoot him. And I would, if I was you – because you're never going to get him behind bars now, not with your previous failed attempt at banging him up. So, you might as well go ahead.'

Costello watched as Anderson's hand tightened on the gun. 'Colin?' she whispered. She looked round at Howlett and Pettigrew who were statues, blocking their exit, their faces unreadable.

Libby lifted herself up on tiptoe to whisper in Anderson's ear. 'You saw the film,' she said. 'Remember, that wee girl died in your arms. Think of the other girls who died. Think of your own daughter. One shot, one bullet.' She walked round behind him and spoke in his other ear. 'And no reprisals. You and him, end of.'

Without realizing it, Anderson had raised the gun, and was pointing it at Fairbairn. It was warmer than he had expected, heavier. He usually only held a gun when it was wrapped up safe in an evidence bag. The power felt dangerously good.

'Of course, you could try to send him back to jail,' Libby went on dispassionately. 'Until he gets out through another legal loophole, so you have to wait until he kills another child. But even if that child is yours, it won't matter, because you'll have done the right thing.'

'This isn't justice,' said Anderson, his voice trembling. What frightened him was how good the power felt, how comforting it was to have that weight in his hand, how reassuring. Then he realized he was squeezing the trigger gently and relaxed his hand. 'This is not right.'

'So, put the gun down. But do you think he'd hesitate

for a second to take you out? Apart from the fact that he couldn't hit a cow's arse with a banjo.' Suddenly Libby spun like a dancer and kicked Fairbairn in the back of his knees. He collapsed to the ground. 'It's easier to shoot people if they're on their knees,' she observed dryly.

The water was running down Fairbairn's face just as it had run down Rusalka's. Anderson remembered the tape of her rape, how she had screamed in agony and fought for breath. And he remembered that last pleading whisper – *Mamochka* – and his finger tightened. He found he couldn't force it to relax. Then, with a real effort of will, he lowered his arm.

Impatiently Libby took the gun off him, clicked the safety catch off, and shot Skelpie once through the head. The crows rose squawking from the trees, the body jerked slightly, swayed on its knees for a moment, then crumpled like a paper bag.

'I had the second safety on for you, DCI Anderson, but I had to get your prints on the gun. My insurance.' She smiled almost impishly and shook him by the hand; her grip was tight, firm. 'That was justice, my justice, a concept you'll have to get used to.' She looked down at Fairbairn's body. 'The problem with such people is that they're so stupid they believe their own publicity.' She straightened up briskly, put the gun into a deep pocket, and said, 'Come on, we'll see how the big fish is doing. Hopefully he'll be drowning and not waving.' She started along the path out of the clearing, confident that she knew where she was going.

Anderson put his arm round Costello's shoulder, and squeezed her tight. She was shaking.

Libby turned back briefly. 'Come on,' she said, as if chiding dawdling children. 'You won't come to any harm. This way.'

Anderson noticed how easily Pettigrew and Howlett moved into position behind them, without talking, without communicating. They knew each other well, these two, and they knew each other as a functioning unit. He also had the feeling somebody else was out there, tracking them.

Libby went striding ahead, scarcely visible in the twilight. Then, without warning, she turned off the path to a wide clearing between the trees. The path was hardly even a track, only there because somebody had walked this way recently. Anderson held up his arm, trying to keep the branches from whipping Costello in the face.

'Are you OK?' he asked her quietly.

'She'll be fine,' answered Libby from in front. 'She's Tony Costello's daughter – it's in her blood, remember?' She turned to look at Costello, challenging her to argue.

In answer, Costello's face twisted with the flicker of a smile. All her questions about who this girl actually was were starting to answer themselves.

Libby marched on into the trees again, then out into another clear space. If she was trying to disorientate them, she had succeeded. Anderson could hear the mewling sound again, quieter now. Then somebody – a man – began shouting, screaming almost, in a language that Anderson could not understand. But it sounded like Russian. He almost tripped over an open drain cover, and stopped. Libby was standing on the far side of it, gazing down at a metal grating about a foot below ground level.

Between the bars, Anderson could see writhing fingers, and the face of the man beneath. Water was rising round the man's shoulders as the rain ran straight off the hard-baked ground into the drain.

'*Pomogite! Luidy!*' The man wasn't screaming now; he was furiously demanding to be let out.

'What's he saying?' Libby asked Pettigrew, who was gazing impassively through the grating at the upturned face.

'Rough translation – I'm a celebrity, get me out of here. Fuck him!'

She turned to Anderson, while pulling something from the belt of her jacket. 'You know the meaning of the tattoos?'

'Yes,' he answered.

'Then you know who he is. You know what he is.'

'We both do,' said Costello, her voice stronger. She walked over to stand beside Libby, catching sight of the bone-handled knife in the girl's hand. She had seen that before – on the floor of the car park, lying in a pool of blood and oil.

'Good. He'll never stand trial in a British court, will he, DCI Anderson? Him or his bloody daughter? I'm going to cut his fingers off.'

'Don't do that, Libby,' Anderson said. 'Let him out. That grating's padlocked, and water's rushing in there. He'll drown.'

'Aye, I know. Removing his fingers would be kinder, make it quicker. So maybe I won't. And that is the death of the Puppeteer.'

At that moment, Howlett fell to the ground.

Pettigrew grabbed Costello, pulled her behind a tree and crushed her against the trunk.

Instinctively, Anderson flung himself sideways. He had registered a quiet thud. They were being shot at. After a little while, he cautiously raised his head.

Libby had gone.

Howlett was lying still. The only sound, apart from the pounding rain, was the sound of their own breathing.

'If you move, DS Costello, I will fucking shoot you myself,' said Pettigrew kindly. 'Stay here, and don't even fucking breathe!'

There was a ping in the ground close by, then another, and the pine needles seemed to explode. Costello was gazing at Pettigrew with a strange kind of respect, but he was peering uphill into the trees, his eyes scanning right to left and back again.

'What is it?' asked Costello, her stomach churning.

'Single sniper, rifle, up on the hill,' he said tersely.

Howlett's body jerked again, and Costello retched up bile – all that was left in her stomach.

'If you're going to throw up again, learn to vomit upright so you stay hidden behind the tree,' Pettigrew scolded her.

When she had finished, Pettigrew had gone.

Anderson took a breath and darted over to Costello's tree. There was another thud into the ground. He took his phone from his pocket and shook his head at her – no signal. 'OK, Sundance, what do you think?' he whispered.

'They didn't make it, did they, Butch and Sundance? Colin, do you have any idea what's going on?'

'Not a clue.'

'I'll just stay here. I don't think my legs will take me anywhere.'

'OK, we'll just stay here, then.' He looked at his watch, remembering the way Moffat's head had exploded. 'For as long as it takes.'

Monday
5 July 2010

'So, who lived here, apart from her?' asked Matilda. 'Him, presumably?' She tapped at Wullie on the wedding picture.

'I think that's what DCI Anderson wants you to find out.'

'How is DCI Anderson? Is he OK?'

'As well as can be expected after being shot at. He and Costello hid behind a tree for about twenty minutes after the shots, then they ran for it. Brave – but they had to move sometime.'

'And what has this got to do with it?' She held a dark green oiled rag to her nose.

'I think that might have everything to do with it,' said O'Hare.

'I should know that smell.' Matilda sniffed the rag again.

O'Hare lifted the mask from his face and pulled the gloves from his hands. 'Indeed you should. It's gun oil,' he said. 'I'd say that was wrapped round a rifle until very recently, a well-kept rifle – in the well-looked-after sense, not the under-lock-and-key sense. And two of our detectives have just been shot at, so get somebody to take that rag back to the lab. Anderson's around somewhere; phone him and tell him we think there was a firearm stolen from here. What with the broken window, the disruption of the furniture, and the deceased . . .' O'Hare paused, struggling to find the words.

'Good plan,' said Matilda, 'except there is no signal, is there?'

2.20 a.m.

Anderson was still wearing his good suit, which was sodden and filthy, and his eyes were sunken with tiredness.

'Good Lord, Colin!' O'Hare was shocked. 'You look like the wrath of God.'

'I've had better times,' he grunted. He stood and looked at the body of Rosie MacFadyean. Parts of her body were black, parts purple, and her eyes were missing. Something had been eating at her.

'The door was left open, and the window was broken,' O'Hare said. 'The crows got in and had a nibble.'

Anderson nodded. Just another horror to add to the day.

'Sir, we want to do a search on the laptop,' Matilda said. Even at this ungodly hour, and in this stinking place, her chirpy energy was relentless. 'OK to remove it? And all these disks? You might want to have a look at those notebooks before we take them.'

'No, you take them.' Anderson rubbed his eyes, feeling the grit behind his lids. 'Take them back to the lecture room, though, not to the station. We have an IT guy there at the moment.'

'Too late – we have him here now. One of these computers must have coded those documents, so his job just got easier. Look at all these blank disks. Was Rosie the Puppeteer everybody's been looking for? A morbidly obese woman just sending out stuff through the post?' asked Matilda.

'Could be,' said O'Hare. 'She lived all these years under the radar, so why not? The thing is – I can see how she would send information out, but how did she get it in?'

Matilda started enthusiastically, 'It's probably very simple, as all the best systems are. Morosov picks up the intel, gives or sends it to his daughter on a memory stick, and she goes out for a walk and leaves it somewhere for Mac-Fadyean, who brings it back to Rosie. Rosie plans the next move, puts it all on disk and Wullie puts it in the post looking like a rental DVD. Easy.'

Anderson, feeling shattered, had ceased listening, and instead was watching with idle interest as Matilda and her bearded sidekick undid wires, coiled them, bagged and labelled them, then took the monitor and bagged it, sliding it into a box.

O'Hare said, 'I don't know about you, Colin, but I need to get away from the stench in here.' They walked out into the clearing at the back of the house. The damp night air was filled with the scent of pine cones. Four crows were perched on the roof, watching the two men with beady eyes. Anderson watched them back. He found himself feeling a grudging respect for them, even if they were evil opportunists waiting to pick off the weak. He shrugged mentally. Maybe that was the way of the world.

'They found the body of Jim Howlett, in the clearing, right where you said,' O'Hare told him. 'He'd been shot. Twice, just as you thought.'

'Who would want to take him out?' Anderson shook his head. 'But it was pissing with rain, visibility was bad. Everything was shades of grey.' He ran out of explanations. 'It's all a bit of a nightmare. And there was a man locked in a drain full of water. Did they get him out?'

'The water level had dropped, and they recovered a body at the bottom. An initial look at the tattoos suggests it's Morosov. Interpol have quite a file on him, so you can take a step back now, Colin. Take a leaf out of Costello's book, and go home and get some sleep. There's a team coming up to search the house, though it's already been searched recently. I think somebody was looking for a rifle.' He pointed at the stained oily rag. 'And we need to know who found it.'

3.30 a.m.

A PC from Helensburgh was sitting on the sofa, thumbing through a magazine. The door was open, so Anderson walked in, his shoes silent on the wet flagstones, making the woman jump to her feet and reach for her radio.

'DCI Colin Anderson,' he identified himself.

The PC took her time looking him up and down. He knew he must look like a scarecrow. 'You got your warrant card?'

He patted his pocket as sarcastically as he could. 'No, not on me.'

'Let him in,' called a familiar voice from high on the mezzanine.

'OK. Up you go.'

Costello was lying on the bed, hands behind her head, staring at the ceiling. Her hair was swept off her forehead, and the scar was clearly visible. Her face looked tired.

Anderson sat down on the edge of the bed. 'You OK?'

'No. You?'

'I was taken to the Warden's office and made to write a report for a man in a suit. He didn't identify himself.'

'I guess there was nobody else to report to.'

She turned on her side, clasping her hands underneath her cheek. For a moment she looked like Claire – just a child, a frightened child.

'Colin, why do we do it?'

'Because we believe in it.'

'Do you, still? When Libby put a bullet through Fairbairn's head, I really did think she'd made a change. I was willing her on. And don't say you weren't.'

'The only change was from Fairbairn being alive to Fairbairn being dead.'

'At least he won't be out there on the street. She has made a difference.'

'You sound impressed.'

'I think I was.'

'But how did she know about Fairbairn and me? And how did she know about your dad?'

Costello smiled. 'She is Pauline McGregor's daughter.'

Anderson took a moment to let that thought sink in. 'Pauline McGregor!'

Costello sighed. 'I presumed the baby died. Look what she grew into. Exactly what I always thought I would be – a righter of wrongs. But I'm not, am I? I get up in the morning, I come to work, I do my thing and I get paid. And I have to be careful, have to do the right thing. But the right thing isn't always the right thing, is it? It's all crap.' She didn't look at him as she added, 'You did the right thing, but you're probably going to pay with your career. But if they fire somebody like you for putting Fairbairn in the nick, then what's the good of even doing the job? It becomes pointless.'

'So, I'll go to Australia. These things have a way of working out for the best. I don't think Vik can let it go, though. He can't ignore it, he's too ambitious.'

Costello sighed. 'If you go, I'll go.'

'No need.' He put his hand on her knee.

'No point in staying. There'd be nobody to argue with. Is Howlett dead?'

'Yes. And Morosov is dead too.'

'Libby?'

'Not found her yet. They're searching the hill.'

'They'll be searching a long time. It's a wilderness up there.' Costello looked at the ceiling, her eyes wide and worried. 'She's survived up to now.'

'And she'll finish off what her mother started. Don't worry about her, worry about yourself – you don't look so good.'

'Neither do you, you shouldn't be driving home. I phoned Helena.'

'Why?'

'Why not?'

Anderson leaned forward and kissed her on the forehead. He had really missed Costello.

4.30 a.m.

As soon as they arrived at Glen Fruin Academy, Matilda and her IT sidekick spent half an hour on Saskia's computer checking documents. The bearded wonder had already discovered regular character groupings from the computer at the cottage – which suggested the codes being used – and this seemed to make him very happy. Examination of Rosie's notebooks had given them a brief key – simple notes made in pencil over a paragraph here and there, referring that operation back to its code. He muttered a lot about asymmetric key algorithms and cryptovariables; they needed a specialist in for that.

But Matilda had recognized an OS reference, followed by a GPS reference. Rosie had a folded map at her bed, which suggested she had been checking exactly where something was coming ashore. Matilda didn't know if it was drugs or human trafficking but she went up to the office of the school to commandeer the first private phone she saw. Saskia herself was in custody, under the pretext that her father was missing and that she herself might be in danger. The date-labelled memory stick had been checked. It contained the same coded text as the CD that had been delivered to Luss Post Office, and also the stuff in Rosie's office. Matilda was sure they would make sense of it all.

Costello was watching from the window of her cottage.

The car park of the school was alive with cars and lights, and the incident van had arrived. There was still no sign of Libby. She hoped she had made it out of there alive, but she had no way of knowing. The door knocked and opened, and Rhona showed in a very tense Helena McAlpine.

'Officer Costello will tell you all about it,' Rhona announced excitedly, showing every indication of wanting to stay. Helena sat down on the sofa and refused to encourage her. Finally, Rhona was left with no choice but to go.

'Is that woman quite unhinged?' Helena asked, as soon as the door had closed.

'Can't imagine why you'd think that.'

'Blethering on about "they've found him, they've found him".'

'Found who?'

There was still no news of Pettigrew or the other Russian.

'Some boy who was missing, up on the hill. Some odd-ball running around with a gun. What's being going on up here?'

'The place is heaving with nutters,' Costello said. '*Deliverance* has nothing on Glen Fruin.'

Silence hung heavy between them until Helena asked, 'Why did you phone me, Costello?'

'I think Colin needs somebody to talk to, that's all. He's had a bit of a tough time tonight. And losing David.'

'And I don't want to lose him. I don't want him to go away,' Helena burst out. 'I've realized that . . . well, I don't want him to go.'

'No, neither do I,' said Costello, suddenly remembering Libby saying 'my insurance'. She added, 'But he might not have a choice.'

12.00 p.m.

Anderson sat down in the lecture theatre, amazed that nothing was happening. If it was, it was happening else-where. He had turned his phone off for ten minutes; he had had enough. 'Howlett was dead when they found him,' he told Costello. 'Turns out he had pancreatic can-cer. He knew he didn't have long.'

Costello was flicking through a pile of messages and memos, none of which could have had anything to do with her. 'How's the boy?' she asked.

'Doing well, I think. You know they operated on Archie O'Donnell in the Western today? Richie got his transplant and apparently he's holding his own; the new liver is work-ing so far. The doctors sound happy.'

Costello looked up. 'Not that boy. I meant Drew. Did he finally morph into the Terminator? Do we know why?'

Anderson shrugged. 'Paranoid episode? I don't know. But it seems he'd been visiting Rosie MacFadyean, and found her husband's rifle. He was lying in wait at the top of the glen, trying to pick off anybody who entered that clearing. But he wasn't a very good shot. He'd read all about it, but had no idea how to do it.' He looked at his watch. 'They took him off the hill at six this morning, with soft-tissue wounds to the front of his neck.'

449

Costello looked confused.

'It's an army thing, seemingly – how to sneak up on somebody and disable them. Physically he'll be fine. But mentally? Who knows.'

'Mentally ill or not, he wasn't such a bad shot. He was bloody close. He hit Howlett twice.'

'But Pettigrew would have known it was an amateur at the end of that gun. He's an expert on shooting people at long range. It was a Lee–Enfield fitted with a Parker Hale sight, but Drew didn't know how to use it. So, he couldn't get us in range. If he'd had more time, he might have worked it out.'

'Which means Pettigrew knew what he was doing, running up that hill in the dark and tackling a screwed-up kid with a big gun.'

'You remember how, when I was tied to that tree, some-one came and cut me loose . . . ? Pettigrew – is he ex-army?'

'More than that. I suspect he was one of those people who have numbers rather than names.'

'At least Drew is in hospital now, nursing his neck injury. He'd been smoking skunk, and that can trigger the onset of some kind of acute sociopathic disorder, particularly if you're prone to it and have a first-degree relative with schizophrenia. His brother's in a long-term institution somewhere. The school should have acted sooner.' Anderson shrugged and switched his phone on.

'But I wasn't sent here because of Drew, was I? The school technically has still done nothing.'

'We'll view the fact that Drew is now getting the treatment he needs as a happy by-product. Howlett was a good people manager – he knew you were right for the job.'

'How?'

'Just that a woman with your slight prejudice against the rich and beautiful would naturally notice a woman like Saskia, and that is what Howlett wanted. You were ideal for the job.' Anderson pretended to read a text message. 'What did you say to Helena? You two were having a fair old natter when you came to get me.'

'Yes, we were.' Then Costello's mouth closed in a way that told him he'd get no more out of her.

His phone rang in his hand. 'DCI Anderson . . . Drew Elphinstone? Yeah, test it for DNA but I think you'll be right. Thanks.' He closed the phone. 'They are just confirming Drew's presence at the cottage.'

'So, we are just filling the blanks in now.'

'Once MacFadyean was killed, Rosie was on death row, anyway. Drew found the cottage, did his SAS scout-about, then broke in and found Rosie lying there helpless. And he found Wullie's rifle – he must have thought all his Christmases had come at once when he discovered that gun.'

Costello picked up a sheaf of paper, Mulholland's small block-capital handwriting all over it.

Anderson pretended not to see as she covertly folded it and put it in her jeans pocket.

'Did you understand all of what happened back there?' she asked.

'We'll find out more at the debriefing tonight.'

'We'll be told what it suits them to tell us. The "them" in grey suits, not the "them" with guns.'

451

They walked out and across the car park, the sun warming them after the chill of the lecture room. Costello was thinking of the cool and assured way Libby had shot Fairbairn in the head, and the way Pettigrew had deferred to her. Pettigrew was a man not impressed by much, but Libby had his respect. Her family had his respect. 'All this has been carefully planned for a long time. Libby and Pettigrew put me down that drain to find Marchetti. Pettigrew was guiding me all the way, telling me I was following Drew. Then pulling the gun on me when I threatened to go back to the school. He couldn't tell me. He needed me to witness it . . . they needed us to witness it,' she said thoughtfully. 'And there's no way Libby planned this all on her own. It's more like –'

'A professional strategist? Someone like Rosie?'

'More like Archie O'Donnell, father or son. They would have the connections to pull off something like this. And think of the army training behind it. God, I was following Libby when she went to meet Pettigrew. I thought she shouted "Drew" when she tripped over that pit. But she must have said "Pettigrew", and I just caught the end of it. It was him she was expecting to meet. Oh yes, there is a huge organization behind all of this. They have been planning it for ages. And as for Libby, I'd say it was in her blood. Colin, do you ever wonder where the grandchildren of all the old gangsters are now? I bet the answer is Glen Fruin Academy, Chamberlain's, any of the posh schools. Guys like Auld Archie were intelligent but uneducated. But the next generation – God knows what they might become.'

'I don't want to tarnish your shining vision of an army of clear-eyed young vigilantes taking to the streets and cleaning up the Russians. How much is organized crime worth in Glasgow? About five million pounds, maybe a bit more,' Anderson said. 'It's not altruism, it's business.'

'So, why did Rosie do it, then? Why did she start working with Morosov? She wasn't exactly living in the lap of luxury.'

'Batten hit the nail on the head with that one. She had severe psychological issues that the force never picked up. They should have offered her help, rather than trying to get rid of her. That just bred a deep resentment, and made her ripe for Morosov to corrupt. It wasn't money. It was power. Power to live as she liked, in isolation – without people looking at her, making fun of her. If you have no power to stop eating, I think you might like to make up for it by the power you can exert over others. Just a small thing like the power of life and death.' Anderson stopped and examined the back of his hand. 'I confess, I felt it myself when I picked up that gun. It's so easy, Costello. So easy.'

Costello took his hand. 'But you did the right thing. I would have blown his head off, like Libby did.'

'And can I just point out that Libby is nowhere to be found. She disappeared into the forest, and so did Pinky. For all we know, she could be down a drain by now.'

'Nae chance. She'll find us when she wants to.'

Costello eventually traced Mulholland to his flat at Port Dundas. It was a penthouse with lifts, underground parking, gym, swimming pool, the lot. Easy when you have a rich mum. But maybe she and Libby had a greater sense of loyalty, coming from the shittier side of the street.

And Vik was going to get a lesson on that one.

She knocked on the door loudly, even though he knew she was coming up – she'd said so on the entry phone. Even so, he kept her waiting. When he opened the door he was still doing up his tie, nuzzling the knot up to his neck, and the jacket of a good suit was lying across the back of a white leather chair.

'You going somewhere?' she asked, checking the huge TV for the DVD slot in the top.

'Yes. It's important. What do you want, Costello?'

She picked up the remote, and slipped the DVD into the slot. Then she pulled the paper from her pocket. 'Is it something to do with this?' She was glad to see Mulholland look rather scared.

'That's private.'

'It has to do with the case. What were you going to do, Vik? Go creeping to the new ACC with your evidence of Colin's alleged compliance in non-disclosure? Are you selflessly campaigning for justice for the late Mr Fairbairn? Or are you just stamping on Colin's career to get your stripes back?'

'Nothing *alleged* about it. He misfiled an inconvenient piece of evidence.'

Costello just glared at him and pressed the remote.

The DVD clicked into its slot, and the screen came to life.

'He's not exempt from the law, you know.' Vik smoothed his collar down. 'Anyway, he'll be going to Australia, so it's no skin off his nose.'

'And what if he stays?' Costello asked. 'His career is over, if you take this further.'

'I've no choice.' He went to pick up his jacket. 'And I am going to be late.'

'Your choice is to file your evidence where nobody will find it.'

'I can't do that.'

'Of course you can. You owe him some loyalty, Vik. He had loyalty to McAlpine. And there were times when they were both loyal to you.'

'He was guilty of non-disclosure. I have proof that he had sight of the statements from Wood and McAdam. He signed them, Costello. He's in it up to his neck.'

Costello pressed Play. The image of Rusalka's small terrified face filled the screen, her eyes screwed up in agony. 'He was in the bloody Clyde up to his neck, you arse, trying to save *her*!'

'Turn that off!' snapped Mulholland, grabbing for the remote.

Instead, she turned up the volume. The screams filled the room, and they could hear the child snatching for breath.

'Ten years old,' Costello insisted remorselessly. 'You'd have put that bastard back on the streets? You'd get Colin the sack for sticking *him* behind bars?'

'It wasn't his call!'

'Wrong answer.'

Mulholland didn't get the chance to reply. Costello's fist, fuelled by six months of being nice to people, rammed into his nose. The blood pulsed down to his chin and on to his nice silk tie.

'I've had enough of you little public school shites to last me a lifetime,' she snarled. As she opened the door she said, with sugared venom, 'Watch the time. You don't want to be late.'

2.20 p.m.

Costello walked across the car park, ignoring the impulse to skip. She was happy. She realized that punching Mulholland had made her feel alive again. She pulled the band from her head and ruffled her hair. Let them look at the scar if they wanted. She'd phone the hairdresser tomorrow and make an appointment to go blonde again. The pain in her face was gone, and she realized she wasn't feeling for the mesh in her cheek the whole time. It was part of her history now.

Earlier, O'Hare had phoned and asked her to pop into the mortuary at the hospital for a mug of tea.

But once there, her good mood deserted her. She was looking down at a zipped body bag, tagged and still unidentified.

'So, what happens to her, little Rusalka? It's not right, her lying cold in a drawer. Will you be able to send her home, one day?'

'We'll look after her until we can, don't worry. There'll

be further enquiries with the embassy, try to establish who the three dead girls are, where they are from.'

'Will there be an official enquiry about Tommy Carruthers' twenty grand? And where it came from?'

'I doubt it. I don't think Mary has any real idea – Tommy never told her, and Rene doesn't know whether it's Montrose or Monday. We'll know more once we can decode all Rosie's stuff – which is not only coded, but coded in Russian! She was a nasty piece of work, that woman, lying in her bed and sending out instructions to all and sundry to torture and kill. Clever, but very unpleasant.'

'How did she and Wullie stay hidden for so long, in this day and age?'

'Good geography. Hidden paths. God knows, our team got lost more than once. Only three and a half miles from the next house, but you could be wandering about for ever out there. Wullie and Rosie MacFadyean were well protected by the *Vorony*. The Russians considered them a golden couple. Her laying out strategies to get the drugs and the girls in, and the money laundered and out. Wullie her invisible scout. Anything to disrupt any chance of the O'Donnells and the McGregors getting together.'

'The five cops, were they –' Costello struggled for the right word '– bound together by what happened at Seana Bhraigh all those years ago? I still don't get that.'

'You don't have that mindset, Costello. Or maybe you do. What if your encounter with Fairbairn had gone differently, if Colin had pulled that trigger? You would have stood by him, lied through your teeth that he'd fired in self-defence. Mulholland, on the other hand, would have dropped him right in it.'

'I think you're right.'

'Both Batten and I think it was Moffat who put an ice axe through Hunter's head and tipped the body off the edge and down into the lochan. Moffat and MacFadyean could have largely engineered that situation. Purcie and Carruthers were fairly easily controlled. Hunter was probably too dominant a character, too career-orientated, to be seduced in the same way. He might have sealed his fate by asking too many awkward questions. Can't imagine what they must have thought in the morning; no sign of Hunter, Purcie guilt-ridden and covered in blood, and Carruthers much the same. And both so grateful to Moffat for keeping it all quiet. Moffat was too full of himself to notice that it was MacFadyean, moving like a shadow, who was manipulating them all. It was all planned to get those three good cops amenable to working outside the law. At least, that's what Moffat must have thought he was doing. It certainly came to fruition when they needed a clear run to get the Marchetti boy out.'

'Nearly twenty years later? There must have been more in the meantime.'

'And do you not feel bound to those who were with you last night? What you witnessed created a bond.'

'You might be right. But twenty years?'

'And I have no doubt at all there will be much more to uncover. How many times do you think a wee favour was called in, a blind eye turned?' O'Hare went quiet. 'I wouldn't call Colin Anderson a corruptible man, but even he stepped outside the law when he thought it was the right thing to do. It's all a question of values.'

Anderson pulled up outside his house, surprised to see a car parked across his driveway. He parked a little way down the street. As he got out of the car, a voice came from behind him.

'Hello,' it said, female, confident. 'I just want to thank you in advance for not arresting me.'

'Libby?'

She wound down the rear window, smiling at him quizzically. 'I'm thanking you in advance, for the future.'

'That might be a bit hasty. I know ACC Howlett was happy to help you put a bullet through a paedophile's brain, but you were still wrong to do it.'

'You should look the other way, if you don't like it.'

'You know I can't do that.'

'But you already have. If you hadn't, I'd be banged up in the Vale at Her Majesty's pleasure by now on a whole load of charges.'

'There's still a line that should never be crossed,' said Anderson, trying to maintain the high ground, and hearing the tone of voice he sometimes used to his daughter.

A large man he didn't know got out of the car and opened the door for him.

'I'd like you to come for a short drive.'

The presence of the large man, now standing behind

him, left him no choice. He got in beside Libby, and the large man got into the driving seat.

'You're quite safe,' she said. 'You'll only be twenty minutes late home.'

The car pulled out and headed slowly down the street, out to the wide road leading to the docks.

'If you're going to ask me to join up, you're barking up the wrong tree,' Anderson said.

She laughed, and for the first time he was aware that she had a real but steely charm, like a latter-day Cleopatra.

'Don't forget, I've got a gun with your prints on it – the gun that killed Skelpie Fairbairn. Anyway, you're much more valuable being what you are – a good cop. So, I'm going to help you cross the T's and dot the I's in your report without too much digging. I know you'll get hell from your bosses if you don't. But you have better things to do with your time.' She handed him an envelope. 'Don't worry, it's not a bribe. It's information that you would get no other way. It's about those three dead girls, so you can send them home.'

'How did you . . . ?'

'Don't ask. You'd only get nightmares. Let's just say, when you find him he'll have fewer than nine fingers.'

'Libby, you are a scary young woman. You are Pauline McGregor's daughter?'

'Indeed. My mum and Mo O'Donnell tried to stop the turf wars years back. When she was stabbed, Costello was there. She called the paramedics and they kept Mum going until she got to hospital and they got me out. She was then allowed to die. That's how the story was told to me. And I wanted Costello to be there, at the start of it all. It was good Howlett found her.'

'So, you knew she was a cop all along?'

'Of course I did.' Libby turned to look out of the window. 'Do you know that Robert the Bruce was born by caesarean after his mother was killed? She broke her neck falling off her horse. I like that story.' She smiled. 'He went on to great things. And so shall I.'

Then Anderson asked, 'And Richard Spence is Archie O'Donnell's son?'

'Yes. His dad chopped the head off the man who ordered the hit on my mother – he never got the hitman, though, contrary to popluar belief. It's a bond of sorts. Not traditional – but it's something, I suppose. Richie and I were at Glen Fruin Academy together since we were twelve years old. He had no father, and I had no parents at all. Like I say, it's the sort of thing that creates a bond when you're that age.'

There was a pause while Libby took out a packet of cigarettes, lit one, opened the window and blew a plume of smoke away from Anderson.

'Modern Romeo and Juliet, eh? We have the "civil blood", only we're not for dying young.'

'But what the hell was Richie doing, getting that close to the Russians?'

'Know your enemy, DCI Anderson, know your enemy.'

'Richie nearly died. You do know that?'

'Yes, I do. But he'll mend. He will,' she insisted, almost fiercely. 'We worked out that the only way to destroy the Russians was from the inside. We had our own name for it – the end of days.' She looked out of the window, her eyes scanning the river. 'That was where you found the wee girl, wasn't it, down there?' For a moment her gaze was grave

461

and sympathetic. Then she took up her narrative briskly. 'So, one of us would have to work our way into the organization, like a Trojan horse. We realized it would involve sex, whether we liked it or not, and we probably wouldn't. I was prepared to do it, to take the risk. But look at me – I'm just a fat girl with bad skin. I wouldn't have lasted five minutes – not worth keeping alive. But Richie – well, you know how beautiful he was, before they . . .'

Anderson was touched by the tenderness in her voice. 'He'll mend. You said it.'

'But he'll never be that beautiful again. Anyway, Richie started running errands, obeying orders, that sort of thing. Then Melinda Biggart moved in on him. The woman was grotesque, but it was a huge opportunity. Actually,' Libby corrected herself, 'he quite liked her. She was pissed off with her perv of a husband, and all alone in her grand house. You've seen that place, haven't you?'

Anderson nodded, and Libby took a deep draw on her cigarette.

'Yeah, if it hadn't been for the sex, Richie said, she could be good fun. Liked a laugh. But then Biggart made a move on him too. And that was no fun. But he did it, for weeks, until he found out that Biggart was making those films at the Apollo Building, that two wee girls had already died and that there was a third one and it was her turn. He couldn't let that happen, so he torched Biggart's place, and made damn sure Biggart got torched too. Grusov guessed it was Richie who'd done it, and they . . . they . . .' She took a deep shuddering breath, fighting to keep her tears under control. 'They tortured him. He never said a thing, though – otherwise I wouldn't be alive to have this conversation.'

'I know,' Anderson said, and patted her hand before realizing what he'd done.

She smiled at him, the steely glint gone for a moment. 'He went through all that for me.' Libby threw the end of her cigarette out of the window, and turned to look earnestly at Anderson. 'But the wee girl died anyway. So, I'm more determined than ever, for Richie and for her, that it won't happen again.'

'How can you stop it?' wondered Anderson.

'We have stopped it. Didn't you notice? Three generations of O'Donnells have put a stop to Morosov's trafficking in underage girls, and to his little snuff movie sideline.'

'Did you get Fairbairn out of jail just so you could kill him? Was the lawyer involved from the start?'

'Of course.' She said it dismissively, as though Anderson had asked a silly question. 'Wee Archie sorted it from the inside, Auld Archie on the outside. We did it so you could kill him, if you chose to.' She continued to look out of the window. 'We are gradually cutting off the supply of red heroin, chasing the dealers out. Shoot a few more in the head, they soon learn it's too dangerous to touch.'

'The Balfron three?'

Libby nodded. 'Rosie MacFadyean isn't the only one with a good strategic brain. Try five minutes with Auld Archie O'Donnell! If you ever want to hide, go and live in an old folks' home – you become bloody invisible. Oh, don't look at me like that. You guys couldn't have done what we did. The police have to fight by the rules, which means they'll never win the war. But we don't. Violence needs to be fought with violence.'

463

'What if another Morosov appears?'

'We'll deal with that as well. Think of us as a public service, we keep the city clean.'

'Why not just go to university, Libby? You're a clever girl. Why do this?'

'What could university teach me? The only way to save this city is our way. It's in my blood. It's my birthright, and it needs to be done.'

'Libby, you'll be dead within a year, you know that.'

'The only hope we have is no hope. It makes us invincible.'

Anderson thought about that for a moment.

'We're both after justice, you and I,' Libby went on. 'We'd both like to keep the peace. The difference is that no one's going to mess with me.'

'Even so, I'd rather do it my way.'

'Of course you would. You do your paperwork and get to the Rusalkas of the world too late to save them. We'll get on with killing the bastards who do it. '

Anderson almost laughed. 'And you think you can hold both factions together? With their history?'

'Just watch us. We tried it before and only failed because bent cops took the Marchetti kid. That was the start of the civil war, just the way they wanted it to happen. And that's another case we've closed for you. Took us months of searching down holes and drains at the top end of the glen to find where he'd been all these years. Though we had help,' she said enigmatically.

The car drew to a halt and Anderson realized with a shock that he was outside his own house.

'Here you are, safe and sound, as promised,' said Libby. 'Thank you for your time, DCI Anderson.'

The large man got out and opened the rear door, and Anderson got out too. He leaned down to talk through the open window.

'Thanks for the information about the girls, Libby. But promise me you'll be careful. There'll always be someone who thinks they can mess with you and get away with it.'

'Well, they'll learn better, won't they?'

Anderson started up his own driveway, and heard Nesbitt barking behind the door.

Libby was right – anyone who messed with her would come off worse. 'Even you, you daft wee bugger,' he said to the dog.

Tuesday
6 July 2010

Anderson drove to the very top of the glen, pulled the car over and killed the engine. He got out and leaned against the door, gazing out over the beauty of Glen Fruin lying at his feet, and thought about those closest to him. Lambie was gone. Costello was ready to take on the world – although Pettigrew had proved that all you need do to make her do as she was told was point a gun at her. Helena had texted to say she had broken up with Gilfillan and was going to buy out his share of her gallery. And Brenda wanted to take his kids to the other side of the world.

He just wanted some peace and quiet.

He was way above the highest treeline here, where the grass was short and boulders and rocks littered the landscape. He could hear the munching of sheep somewhere below him, and a slight wind was whistling in his ears and through his sweatshirt. Despite the sun, he was chilled. They were back to normal Scottish weather, that chill in the air that was always there.

There had been a meeting, of course – a complete debrief, supposedly. Question after question. Then Anderson had been taken into a smaller room with some thick-necked men, men in dark suits with bland faces, who did not introduce themselves. Special Branch, he presumed. He had seen the pile of files and computer disks, all tracing the police career of Eric Moffat. They had placed in front of him photograph EC 2218. Twelve men playing a round of golf at a charity tournament in Turnberry, in 1993. Moffat and Howlett were there for the police. Morosov was standing smiling at the back, the respectable businessman. It was being mooted as their first contact. Anderson had been questioned about Moffat's colleagues, and about his cases, especially those with 'lost' evidence or unsafe convictions. They were leaving no stone unturned. He had signed some very important-looking papers and had been glad to walk away.

He had been given a few days off. He was going to use those days to think about his future. And he was going to use the important-looking papers to justify his decision. No matter how good a shot Pettigrew was, and no matter how confident they were that they could keep their colleagues safe, it was Anderson himself who had been at the business end of Moffat's knife. The way he saw it, he had been nearly killed by his boss's inability to trust him with the bigger picture. All he'd had to work with was smoke and mirrors. He was a cop, not a bloody spy.

The only bright spot in the last few hours had been the highlight of the early part of the meeting – Mulholland turning up holding a small ice pack wrapped in a hanky over his nose, armed with a picture of Biggart at the fair. Fairbairn was only the pick-up, he postulated. He had taken the kid to the edge of the trees and passed her to Biggart before walking back to the pub. It fitted the time-line, and it explained why Biggart and his lawyer were so helpful to Fairbairn, keeping him sweet. Until the lawyer had been called in for a wee chat with Wee Archie O'Donnell.

Mulholland had been very polite to Anderson, and very careful to avoid Costello. That was a story he was going to get to the bottom of.

The biggest Russian gang operating in Scotland had been broken. Pulling apart the white Transit van had uncovered a veritable archive of some of the biggest hits in the last five years – a mobile killing ground for Pinky and Perky. Pavel Sergeievich Morosov was dead, and Saskia had been sent back to her mother. Strathclyde police were now in possession of intelligence concerning the flow of red heroin and the new form of Rohypnol, R2, into the country. Mulholland had proved very useful in helping to translate the decoded text, and plans were no doubt being made to intercept and control the situation.

At that point, Matilda McQueen nearly opened her mouth but Batten had nudged her to be quiet. In simple terms, they told her over a pizza later, Special Branch now had the DVDs and knew the route they'd travelled. So, once they'd cracked the code, they would pick up where Morosov and Rosie had left off, and see how far up the chain of command they could get. The two sites for making the films – the flats and the hotel – were being watched. Morosov's company, PSM, was trading as usual, but being monitored every minute of the day.

There was now a vacuum at the top of the tree, and Special Branch knew it wouldn't be long until somebody tried to fill it. And came up against the O'Donnells and the McGregors on their home turf. Rosie, the cog it all rotated round, had died because MacFadyean had died – and he had died because some journalist had decided to write a book and had set the whole house of cards slowly tumbling. Carruthers had become edgy, flicking back through his diaries, thinking about how Graham Hunter had died, about the night little Alessandro had been taken and his own possible part in events. It had been the money Carruthers was concerned about. Moffat had sweetened him, and maybe others too, with a payout once it was obvious the wee boy wasn't coming back. Anderson could imagine that preying on Carruthers' conscience, and MacFadyean smiling at the irony of it.

Then along came Simone Sangster to stir the hornets' nest.

It was the why Anderson couldn't understand. Was it seeing his control slip, after all those years of silence, that had prompted Moffat to murder his erstwhile colleagues? Anderson still couldn't imagine the hold the incident had on them. Were they bound by the horror of it? Or by the subconscious fear that what happened to Purcie might happen to them? Or was it simply the discovery that the waterways and shafts in the glen were to be recommissioned? Perhaps Batten was right. Once a psychopath, always a psychopath. Anderson remembered the way Moffat's old crew had greeted him. The man had had charm, had kept their loyalty. Any cop that popular must be a psycho, he decided.

His phone rang. It was O'Hare.

'Hello, Prof. How much sleep have you had?'

'About the same as you, I should imagine,' the pathologist said grumpily. 'But I knew you wouldn't have been home to bed yet. It's not the sort of thing you go home and sleep soundly after. Anyway, I thought you'd like to be told that the markings on the bullet that killed Howlett match those on the bullet that killed Purcie on the Campsie Fells thirty-five years ago. Matilda's comparison microscope proved that both bullets were fired from Wullie MacFadyean's Lee–Enfield.'

Anderson sighed thoughtfully. 'So, do we think Moffat put Purcie out on the far right flank of the search line, so he would walk straight into MacFadyean's sights?'

'It looks like it. We'll never know exactly why. But Moffat probably knew that Purcie had come to realize that Hunter's death hadn't happened the way Moffat said it had, and that keeping silent served no purpose.'

After the Prof's call, Anderson sat in the heather and cogitated for a while. Rosie and Wullie had been Morosov's right-hand men. Rosie's laptop, slowly being decoded, was revealing a horrific catalogue of crimes. Details of children targeted for trafficking. Details of flights for drug drops. Details of who was to die, and how. Yet it was apparent that Rosie had no idea who their real enemies were, and how close they were. Even when Richie burned Billy Biggart to death, she didn't understand that he was an infiltrator, with access to all the Russians' operations. Pinky and Perky had had some suspicion, and had attempted to beat information out of the boy, then dispose of him. Yet no matter how they tortured him, he had kept quiet about Libby.

Costello was right that Libby had played the moral card, and Anderson couldn't help letting it colour his thoughts about her. Libby had known she would have to solve the Marchetti mystery to allow the families' history to settle before the new generation could rebuild their empire. So, she and her mysterious 'help' had searched all those tunnels in a race against time before they were recommissioned. They had found the tiny skeleton, but had left the evidence untouched, so forensics would prove once and for all who was at the bottom of it. Then they had quite literally sat Costello down face to face with that evidence.

Anderson had been told there would be no public enquiry, that the security risk was too high. It wasn't his decision, so he wasn't going to think about it. He wasn't going to think about how much Howlett actually knew about Morosov right at the start, and yet had been content to let the team take all the risks in order to track down the nuts and bolts of the operation. Howlett had known about Moffat. Following Moffat's electronic footprint would have led him eventually to Morosov, and that might have sparked the memory of that game of golf. What happened then was open to conjecture.

Did Morosov, with his veneer of total respectability, send his daughter to this country in order to forge the link to the recently recruited MacFadyeans? It sounded a lot of trouble – until he recalled that five million pounds was at stake. It was a good investment. And the only day Howlett could guarantee that Morosov would be in the country was his daughter's leaving day. Anderson wondered what had forced Howlett's hand. Saskia's leaving day? The recommissioning of the shaft? Or his fatal prognosis?

On reflection, it might after all be better to leave it to somebody younger – someone like Libby. Let Special

Branch monitor the movement of small aircraft dropping suspicious-looking packages on the east coast. The Strathclyde police service would sit in their offices, only venturing out to arrest shoplifters.

And what was he going to do?

He had no idea.

His mind turned to happier things. Mary had moved to a rented flat in the city and from all accounts was slowly getting her life back together. She was visiting her sister daily at the hospital, where Rene was being assessed at the memory clinic. Without her, they might never have got Moffat – he simply never saw an old dear who was practically gaga as a threat.

He turned round at a hard clapping sound behind him. Two crows were joined on a rocky outcrop by a third. They all looked at him, tilting their heads slightly. Studying him.

Then a fourth cawed loudly and settled, regarding him, its beak open as if half smiling.

Four wee craws.

They all four seemed happy, coming home to roost.

12.10 p.m.

Anderson turned off the engine of the Jazz outside his house, and sat for a few minutes listening to it ticking as it cooled. The side gate was closed, which meant Nesbitt at least was in the garden. He opened the window to get some fresh air, scenting the heavy peaty smell of a rain-soaked garden.

It all signalled a new beginning. The horror of the last week was over. Everything, from here on in, would be a decision made by somebody else.

Except for that one decision he had to make himself. He lifted his mobile from its cradle and rang Helena.

She sounded tired, but pleased to hear from him. 'Sorry, I've had a bit of a sleepless night. How are you?'

'I'm OK, considering. There's a lot going on, and it's all a bit up in the air . . .'

He ran out of words. 'You've got lots of opera CDs, haven't you?' he asked, awkwardly.

'Loads,' she answered. 'Why – have you suddenly been seized with a passion for Wagner or Puccini?'

'There's something I really need to listen to,' he said. 'I thought you might know it.'

She didn't ask any searching questions. 'Tell me.'

'It's by Dvořák.' He pronounced it as he'd seen it written.

'Dvorzhak.' She yawned.

Somehow, he didn't mind being corrected – not by Helena.

'Which one?'

'Rusalka,' he said.

He heard a slight smile in her voice as she said sleepily, 'Yes, I've got it. Do you want to borrow it? Or would you like to come round and listen to it here?'

'Why don't we meet for a coffee, and you can tell me the plot.'

'It's not that complicated.'

'It's always complicated,' he said. And by the following silence, he knew she had got the subtle message.

'OK, let's meet for a coffee, then.' And she rang off.

Anderson closed the window and saw through the gate that Nesbitt was wagging his tail, watching. He picked up the 'Discover Australia' travel brochure that was lying on the passenger seat – a vague idea of the holiday budget had already formed in his mind.

He had never thought about surfing. But there was a first time for everything.

Epilogue

Epilogue

It was five past midnight as the young woman walked up the path. Her straight black skirt stopped at the knee, and the peplum of the tailored jacket swished from side to side as she moved. Her bare legs were salon tanned, and above her red stilettos a small silver anklet glistened as it caught the moonlight. She walked purposefully, with conviction. A small leather handbag bounced slightly on her hip, her jet-black hair was cropped smartly.

She could have been any successful young woman going about her business.

But she was Elizabeth McGregor, and she was in control.

She strode across the lawn, ignoring the Keep Off signs, up to the front door of the St Boswell's Care Home. She had told the driver to keep the car at the front entrance, engine running; she would only be a minute.

Auld Archie O'Donnell was in his wheelchair, his hand-made shoes resting on the footplate, cardigan folded and ready. He had been waiting. Her intense brown eyes met his, pale blue like a cornflower faded by the sun. She could see in them the respect due from an O'Donnell to a McGregor.

'How is he? My boy?' The old man's voice was a growl.

'He's going to be fine. They let his dad help him, your son. All will be well.'

'So, all is well? Like I said to Richie-boy, nothing wrong in sleeping with the enemy, as long as you stay wide awake.' The words were quietly spoken but had the strength of certainty about them. The old man's bottom lip quivered a little, and he gave a slight nod of the head, as if assuring himself that all he had hoped for had come to pass. 'Well done, hen. You're a credit to those McGregor bastards.'

She smiled at him while he pulled his collar closed a little, as if he wanted to look smart. She wondered just how handsome he had been in his day. Too handsome, no doubt. She could still see a young Richie in there somewhere, half a century ago. She pushed him out of the door and down the path to the waiting Jag. This was exactly what Richie had promised his grandfather, on the very first day he had come to work in the care home.

The driver got out of the car to open the door for him. The boot was open ready to take the chair.

'This is Mr Pettigrew, our chauffeur for the evening,' she said.

She looked away as the two men embraced slightly, the way old friends do, holding on to each other for a wee bit too long as Pettigrew assisted Auld Archie into the car.

'Don't take me home yet. Give me a wee drive around ma city.' Archie's voice was strong from the back.

'Our city,' corrected Libby.

Acknowledgements

A good book is always a team effort. I'd like to thank everybody on my 'team', especially all at Gregory and Co. and at Penguin for being so supportive throughout the process. The Stephanies deserve a special mention for their endless patience. Also big thanks to everybody at work – who allow me to skive out of clinics and get on with the writing. As usual, special mentions for Annette, Liz and Karen who take up the slack. Special thanks this time to my esteemed colleague Vadim Kolganov who has tried, with no success whatsoever, to teach me the basics of the Russian language. It all ended up sounding like a Monty Python sketch.

A wee thank you for 'Wee John' and his expertise on all military matters, which were discussed at length over a good curry. And a big thank you to 'Big John' and the other members of the mighty JWG for their weekly 'no holds barred' edits. Much gratitude to R. Kerr and J. Manson, the legal beagles, for keeping me right on all issues of disclosure and Scots law, and to Dr John Clark for his expertise on forensic pathology.

And of course, a big thanks to the home team: the parents, Emily and Pi, and to Alan for the endless supply of black coffee and Pringles.

Caro

He just wanted a decent book to read ...

Not too much to ask, is it? It was in 1935 when Allen Lane, Managing Director of Bodley Head Publishers, stood on a platform at Exeter railway station looking for something good to read on his journey back to London. His choice was limited to popular magazines and poor-quality paperbacks – the same choice faced every day by the vast majority of readers, few of whom could afford hardbacks. Lane's disappointment and subsequent anger at the range of books generally available led him to found a company – and change the world.

'We believed in the existence in this country of a vast reading public for intelligent books at a low price, and staked everything on it'
Sir Allen Lane, 1902–1970, founder of Penguin Books

The quality paperback had arrived – and not just in bookshops. Lane was adamant that his Penguins should appear in chain stores and tobacconists, and should cost no more than a packet of cigarettes.

Reading habits (and cigarette prices) have changed since 1935, but Penguin still believes in publishing the best books for everybody to enjoy. We still believe that good design costs no more than bad design, and we still believe that quality books published passionately and responsibly make the world a better place.

So wherever you see the little bird – whether it's on a piece of prize-winning literary fiction or a celebrity autobiography, political tour de force or historical masterpiece, a serial-killer thriller, reference book, world classic or a piece of pure escapism – you can bet that it represents the very best that the genre has to offer.

Whatever you like to read – trust Penguin.